Shattered Lands

PAINTING THE MISTS, BOOK 8

PATRICK G. LAPLANTE

Published by: Patrick G. Laplante
Editing and Interior Design by: Crystal Watanabe
Cover Illustration and Design by: Samuel Alves
First edition, 2020
ISBN: 978-1-989578-10-0

Other Painting the Mists Books:
Clear Sky
Blood Moon
Light in the Darkness
Pure Jade
Corrupted Crimson
Kindling
Shattered Lands
Edge of Oblivion (forthcoming)

Violet Fate Duology:
Violet Heart
Converging Fate (forthcoming)

Dedication

To those who are scared. We live in difficult times,
and I wish you all the strength you need to carry on.

Author's Note and Acknowledgments

The world feels much less safe than it used to a few months back. In January, we were celebrating the Chinese portion of our wedding. A few weeks later, full lockdown. As many of you may know, I live in Beijing, China, and when COVID-19 started getting out of hand, it was all hands on deck.

I won't preach on best practices, as many tend to do these days. No doubt, you've seen hundreds of articles by now on self protection and social distancing. I won't criticize either; propagating blame serves nothing; it causes chaos when stability is what the world needs now more than ever.

What I will do, however, is tell you that there's light at the end of the tunnel. Nearly two months ago we were afraid to go outside. In fact, we couldn't go outside, even with face masks on. When we returned to Beijing, from Shenyang, where we'd been visiting for Chinese New Year, we quarantined ourselves as everyone was required. We measured our temperature every day while reading ever-depressing news. People were dying, and many more were getting sick. Wuhan was sealed off, isolated from the rest of the world to give it what it needed most: time.

Let's fast-forward two months. Now, people walk on the streets. They still wear facemasks—you'll get scolded by the police if you don't—but more than grocery stores are open. You can go shopping, though every shop has a maximum occupancy. Restaurants now accept sit-down customers, but not many at once, especially not at the same table. But life is starting back up again. People who worked from home now go back to the office one day out of two, and some schools are even resuming classes. Everyone fought together to contain the spread, and the fruits of their labor are finally showing.

I suspect that such scenes will play themselves out globally as governments and individuals come to grips with the pandemic. For now, everyone is suffering, but that suffering is what will usher in a new normal. There's hope for the future and hope for a vaccine. This difficult stage in our lives is only temporary, and at the very least, those of us who make it through will have a few good stories to tell their children and grandchildren.

Now, enough about viruses. I wrote a book, and I'm sure you're eager to get on with it. I finished it a little later than I expected due to a combination of weddings and virus lockdown and a half dozen other reasons you don't care about. And at 152,000 words, it's my longest yet. I sincerely hope you enjoy Cha Ming's adventure in Southern lands.

I try to improve with every book, and this time is no different. New to this edition is a recap from the last book. Readers have been asking for me to include one for months now, so I thought it only fair to indulge them. If you like reading summaries, enjoy. And if you don't, feel free to skip it. It's all the same to me, as my only request from you as you read this book is that you enjoy it.

Before moving on, however, I'd like to start off with some words of thanks. Thank you to my wife, Xing Wen; two wedding receptions later, we've dotted all our i's and crossed all our t's. Thank you to my parents, my brothers, my sisters, and wedding guests for making it a great event—for make no mistake, my personal happiness is directly corelated with the quality of the books I write.

I'd like to thank this book's beta readers: Dave Yeung, Aljoscha Volk, Drew Kennedy, John Wilson, and Ardash. Your feedback was a great help in improving the story.

Many thanks to Crystal Watanabe for her excellent support while editing my novel. My writing continues to improve with her help, so I'm glad to have her on board. Thank you to Samuel Alves for the great cover, and for finally fulfilling a long-time wish of having all of Painting the Mist's covers match again.

Last, but not least, thank you to my readers. I write to tell stories to people, and a story is worth nothing if it isn't shared. I hope you enjoy reading this book as much as I enjoyed writing it.

Cheers,

Patrick G. Laplante

Previously in Painting the Mists

To fix his core, Cha Ming travels to Haijing City, the underwater capital of the Sea God Empire with Huxian and his four disciples. By joining Haijing Academy, he swiftly climbs up the ranks to the peak of mortal alchemy. He finances his journey by discovering Grandmist flames, a mysterious alchemical flame capable of creating Grandmist pill seals.

With the help of Sun Wukong, he attempts to forge a Nirvana Pill, a transcendent item that can heal his core. He succeeds in crafting the pill but fails to protect it from the plane's pill tribulation. Defeated, he is forced to pursue a new path through runic alchemy, leaving his fated opponent, Zhou Li, to plot and scheme freely with the upper echelons of the city.

Earlier in his journey to Haijing, Cha Ming had befriended the crown princess of the Sea God Empire, Gong Shuren. To spite Zhou Li, who'd gone out of his way to destroy the Water Source Marrow Huxian and friends had discovered, Cha Ming participates in the legendary Sea God Trials. Little does he know that this is a trap. Due to his two soul-bound treasures, the Clear Sky Brush and the Space-Time Camera, the trial's difficulty increases exponentially. Zhou Li and his favored candidate for emperor manage to squeeze out a narrow victory and claim the Sea God's Crown.

Cold and defeated, his core still broken, Cha Ming is ready to give up. Fortunately, Huxian discovers the secret of the Sea God Trials: the Sea God Clock Tower. With his help, Gong Shuren begins attuning the artifact, which is a step up above the Sea God's Crown.

Time waits for no one, however. While she is busy attuning the artifact, Zhou Li instigates a war between Haijing City and the Northern Alliance using a combination of clever manipulation, fiendish sharks, and an armada of battleships from the South. Desperate to defuse the situation, Cha Ming rallies the scholars in Haijing, allies of his disciples, remnants of the city guard, and friends of Huxian. They arrive too late to prevent conflict but just in time to stop a total rout. Gong Shuren arrives just in time, wielding the Sea God Clock Tower to execute the Southern Alliance's forces as well as the traitorous ministers of her brother, the emperor. Disaster is prevented, but much blood is shed.

In Gold Leaf City, Hong Xin stabilizes her power as the new Red Dust Mistress. In so doing, she discovers a terrible secret: The Red Dust Pavilion was involved in an illegal and despicable scheme to harvest souls for the Spirit Temple. A faction in the city uses evidence of this wrongdoing to blackmail her and her sisters into indentured servitude.

To make matters worse, Hong Xin and the Red Dust Pavilion are forced to kill and capture their former members, important agents of the Spirit Temple. Cornered, with angry Spectral Assassins breathing down her neck, Hong Xin goes to Wang Jun for help. Together, they are able to extract secrets from their captured members, facilitating a heist that they use to counter-blackmail their oppressors.

Wang Jun, riding on the coattails of his victory in the Song Kingdom, comes home to a less-than-pleasant reception. He is given the title of auditor general of the Wang family. Part and parcel with his role is a noncompete with his brother, whom he must outearn to win the family leadership. Desperate and willing to try anything, he starts an industrial revolution by endowing all non-cultivators in the North with qi-cultivation capabilities. By heavily leveraging his position in this growing market, he gains significant ground on his brother's assets.

Unfortunately, his duties as auditor general uncover a dark secret of the Wang family. His brother, Wang Ling, has been secretly enriching himself through illegal soul trade with the Spirit Temple. Frustrated by both the ethics of the situation and the potential legal ramifications if discovered, he reveals this to the family patriarch, Wang Wuling, but it turns out he's known all along. Angry and dejected, Wang Jun helps the Red Dust Mistress, the disguised Hong Xin, to deal a dreadful blow to the Spirit Temple. In their fight, he discovers her true identity, a silver lining to the otherwise depressing situation.

Cha Ming has left Haijing and is journeying southeast from Beihai to Gold Leaf City. Hong Xin, having finally freed her sisters, turns her attention to rebuilding the Red Dust Pavilion. Demoralized by the state of his family, Wang Jun decides he can no longer play an honest game with them. West of the Song Kingdom, a calamity awakens.

Prologue

All was quiet around a dark pit, carefully wedged beneath two demonic mountains far away from human eyes. There were no birds flying above, and no rustling of tree leaves in the gentle wind. For there was no wind here; the light breeze that normally blew through these mountains was stagnant. It lost all momentum the moment it reached the darkness and lingered around the pit, where something breathed. It was a continuous breath, always inhaling and never exhaling. The sides of the pit crumbled away little by little with each passing second.

A horn poked out from the pit as a creature—black and humanoid, yet walking on all fours—pulled itself out. It had been resting, for eating was hungry work. Days ago, he had successfully devoured the nearest mile of spirit woods. It had taken him until now to convert the vital demonic energy into something useful.

Now, he hungered. The ravenous pit inside him was empty and needed to be filled. He looked around, scanning east and west, looking for something, anything that moved. Not even the wind did. Everything he'd missed in his first pass had run away, forsaking their birth land rather than facing certain death.

Which way should he go? How fast should he travel? These basic instincts were in their infancy, nudging him slightly to the northwest. There, a mountain stood strong, its powerful beasts keeping watch on him, hiding among the deep-rooted trees reeking of demonic qi.

The creature walked, slowly but surely, his footsteps leaving only a dull thump behind. He breathed in as he walked, consuming the thin demonic qi that leaked off the demonic mountain. It powered his initial-purification fiend body just enough to bring it to a group of pines, whose inhabitants ignorantly chattered away as it placed its clawed hand on the sappy red bark. The color where it touched faded, and the tree cracked. The squirrels and birds, initially indignant at his presence, began dying. Only the smartest among them flew to another tree branch.

One tree, many lives. Two trees, many more. Two became three, and three became many. One by one, a carpet of darkness expanded around him, swallowing lesser spirit beasts in his wake. A boar charged toward it, cutting deep into his body before ultimately being swallowed by him. Birds followed suit, plunging at him as directed by the sovereign of the mountain. For they would never stoop so low as to challenge him, weak as he was. A mistake, he knew. Demons often made mistakes like these when dealing with his kind.

Wave after wave of demons swarmed toward him, and though the swarm didn't harm him, it slowed him greatly. Annoyed, he fought back. In response, the waves increased in intensity, and before long, he could take it no longer. He dissociated into nothingness, leaving behind only a black stain on the forest floor. All stood still.

A mountain lion, the sovereign of the mountain, let out a sigh of relief from her perch in a nearby tree. She had been watching the dark creature, praying to her ancestors that it didn't head her way. The creature felt ancient and terrible. And worse, she knew nothing about it. It was weak, so it wouldn't be honorable to face off against him. Yet that weakness conflicted with the sense of danger it gave her. It was a rare moral dilemma, a question of honor that couldn't be ignored.

Fortunately, all was well now. Her minions had destroyed it in roughly thirty seconds, and there would be peace once again. Or would there be? Her eyes narrowed as a cluster of black stains, remnants of the creature, merged together in a puddle of black ooze. It writhed violently, black horns poking out and stabbing creatures that had moved back into their homes. Endless moments passed as an arm poked out, then another, then two legs. A large horn sprouted on its forehead, and its eyes, blacker than the deepest shadows, opened.

The creature lashed out, horns shooting out from its back in every direction. Tiny tentacles of blackness touched the nearby forest dwellers, draining their life in an instant. The mountain lion called out orders, rallying her lords to the cause. They ran from their dwellings, and on her orders, slayed the foul beast once again. It only took thirty-one seconds to down their fierce opponent.

Only a single black stain remained, but the sovereign dared not trust it. Like clockwork, it wriggled and reformed, coalescing into the fearsome creature from before. The lords pounced again, and they defeated it easily. This time, it took thirty-two seconds.

Far in the Southern lands, a man lay dying. The infected wound on his side sent pain lancing through his entire body with every breath. It was a welcome pain, for it told him he hadn't yet passed. *Anything* was better than what awaited him, even the agonizing seconds before his demise.

It served him right, he supposed. He never should have left. Things might have been different then. At the very least, he wouldn't have been killed like a common criminal. Death would have come for him anyway, but through it, he might have gained something greater: immortality.

Only the Spirit Temple could grant immortality, and even then, only to the worthy. He was a true believer. Life was unfair, the temple taught, and as such, it was full of suffering. The only way to transcend it was to embrace the suffering, embrace the regret of a life wasted. Only then could one become an evil spirit, free from the fleshly woes and carnal desires of the living.

Unfortunately for him, it took strength to do that. Not of body, but of spirit. As an acolyte of the Spirit Temple, he'd been pitted against the others like gu in a jar, killing each other until only the most poisonous remained. He'd thought himself strong, but a few days in, he'd been relieved of that notion.

He'd left the Spirit Temple that same day. Out the front door, no questions asked. The Temple didn't punish deserters in the flesh but in the spirit. They simply waited till the parting, when shackled souls returned to their origins. There, they became fodder for *true* remnants, *true* believers with strong spirits and a *need* for vengeance. They were the core of the spectral community, the assassins that roamed the lands and the watchers that saw through all. They were the shepherds that consumed souls and saved the few members of the flock they could.

Spirits, what possessed me to steal that sword? he thought, the pain preventing his mind from wandering further. The wound on his side had festered, and black lines radiated outward from it, poisoning the rest of his body. Stealing the sword had seemed like a good idea; it had been right out in the open where anyone could take it. Unfortunately, someone had spotted him, and during the brief tussle with the merchant's guards, he'd suffered a shallow cut to his side. The merchant must have also been a believer, for who else would arm their guards with poisoned weapons? The wound had festered that same night.

The man sighed—a sigh of regret for a life poorly lived. It was the sigh of a man who'd sworn oaths that shouldn't have been. It was the sigh of a man who'd been dying, for life no longer remained in his body. All that remained was a spirit, its incorporeal form covered in crimson veins and tangled karma. One of them, a thinner string, led to the west, where his parents still lived. A slightly thicker string led back to the merchant who'd killed him. The thickest line, however, resembled more a chain than a thread. It was made of crimson links covered in blackened runes that reeked of hatred.

That same chain ran all the way back to the Spirit Temple. The moment the man's spirit completely left his body, the chain pulled him away at a speed no mortal could travel, leaving the reaper that had come for him empty-handed. He left the woods and entered infertile plains where serfs worked themselves to the bone. Their sweaty, dirty figures brought up painful memories of the things he'd done to leave such a life in the first place. He traveled quickly, so the plains soon gave way to rocky hills, which then became the foothills that led up to the capital of the Ji Kingdom, Bastion. It lay just south of a canyon that led deep into the mountains, the Shattered Lands filled with life-leaching death.

The distance between the spirit and the city shrank quickly. Though Bastion was covered in a thick shield of soul-repelling runes, the spirit passed through them without a hint of difficulty. He bore the mark of their temple, after all, and the temple welcomed its own. He zipped through the houses of rich and poor men alike, through markets, through bars, through gambling dens and inns, before finally arriving at his destination: the Bastion Spirit Temple. He was forcibly dragged in through the front door and brought across active traps, spying specters, and Spectral Assassins. Some new acolytes—those who weren't yet aware of their impending doom—looked up as they performed their menial duties. The more senior ones ignored him, as they were too focused on their brutal competition with their peers.

The spirit passed a few priests, some mediums, and even a high priest. Eventually, his soul settled in a small pond in the temple's deepest room. To his surprise, the Shepherd wasn't there to welcome him as he'd feared. Instead, the leader of the temple was seated behind the pool at an elevated table with eleven empty seats.

No, not empty, he thought. They would have seemed empty if he were alive, but as a spirit, he could see them clearly. They were spectral substitutes, a disposable ghostly body used to facilitate communication between leaders. After all, why waste spirit stones on valuable core-transmission jades when souls were freely available?

He was safe, for the time being, at least. *Maybe the Shepherd won't notice me,* he thought. *Maybe I'll get to roam the Pool of Souls until he needs a servant.*

It was a feeble hope, but he clung to it like a drowning man clung to a piece of flotsam in a stormy sea. He wandered over to a corner of the pool and tried to look as inconspicuous as possible, just in case. As he did so, the Shepherd spoke.

"Your failure in Gold Leaf City is inexcusable," the Shepherd said. "The forces in our temple are spread thinly enough as it is. And now you're expecting reinforcements?"

"It's truly not my fault," one of the spectral substitutes said. "We're a branch temple, not a main temple. Even so, we had mediums and spirits monitoring everything. We had all our servants bound by enforcement specters so as not to leak out our activities. Yet somehow, the fledgling Red Dust Mistress managed to pry information from their captured members, thwart a very important deal, and kill dozens of Spectral Assassins. The first and last of these things should have been impossible for her to accomplish."

The Shepherd sighed. "How did they even manage to locate their old members?"

"You know full well how they did," the figure huffed.

"It was the Greenwind Pavilion," another figure said. Unlike the other spirit, his soul body was almost tangible, a testament to the strength of his soul. Only another Shepherd could achieve such a thing. "I spoke to Elder Zhong. He admitted to selling the information."

"Likely as a reminder," a third Shepherd at the table said wryly. "They're always telling us we'll regret not buying confidentiality on our own information."

"The cost is too high," the Shepherd of the Bastion Temple said.

"And it continues to be too high." He sighed again. "Did you at least manage to wriggle out how they extracted the information from our contracted servants?"

"He didn't know," the second Shepherd said. "As an apology, he let us know how the Red Dust Mistress killed all those assassins. It was Wang Jun from the Wang family who helped her. He speculated she was able to pry information from their former members using that man's unique abilities."

The Shepherd of Bastion Temple cursed loudly. Then, he stood up, calming himself before speaking again. "You'll get your reinforcements, but not as many as you'd like. Your quota will remain the same."

"I'll... try to fill it," Gold Leaf City's spectral substitute said.

"Failure is not an option," the Shepherd of Bastion Temple said. "I also want the Red Dust Pavilion eliminated, and Wang Jun along with it. His family won't care, and very few people will miss him." He gestured to the pool, and the spirit, who'd just arrived, floated into his hand. The soul shivered as it lay there naked, unprotected by a fleshly shell. "If you let me down, you won't fare any better than this acolyte."

"Acolyte?" Gold Leaf City's spectral substitute asked.

"He thought he could escape my grasp by leaving the temple," the Shepherd of Bastion Temple said, "only to realize that his soul was mine. When he arrived at my spirit pool, he tried to hide in the hopes that I'd forget him. But I have a long memory, and I forget as often as I forgive."

The Shepherd clenched his fist, and the spirit writhed in pain as, slowly but surely, it was converted to pure soul energy. "I hope you understand my meaning."

"What about *that man*?" Gold Leaf City's specter said, his voice becoming softer and softer. The spirit, who was still listening, quickly realized that it wasn't the voice that was growing softer, but himself that was growing weaker.

"*That man* won't interfere," the Shepherd of Bastion Temple said. "Not even for his own disciple."

"But how do you know?" the specter muttered.

"He told me," a whisper said.

Then, the spirit heard nothing. His awareness, no, his existence, faded. For that was the horror of the Spirit Temple. There would be no rebirth for souls like his, nor would there be existence as a spirit body. Even a merciful existence full of pain and misery would be beyond him. What awaited him was unattached and unfettered oblivion: a fate much worse than death.

Just how do these things happen? Yama thought as he massaged the space between his brows. His flowing white hair, untied today, covered his immaculate desk like a flowing river. Finding no relief, he grabbed hold of a tiny sand rake, which he used to groom a tiny fengxue garden filled with sand and a few rocks. It helped, if only a little.

They'd committed a blunder, and a big one at that. The worst thing about it was that there was nothing they could have done to prevent it. Nothing, save perhaps not choosing Judah in the first place, to stop it. Yama glared at Judah, the hopeful mayoral candidate, who sat nervously before him. And nervous he should be. As the most powerful man in the universe, the only being who could forcefully reincarnate any spirit he desired, he inspired fear wherever he treaded.

His timeless black eyes staring daggers at Judah, Yama pressed a bony index finger on the daily paper's front page. There, on the crisp but cheap soul paper, was a moving picture of the mayoral candidate. He was running around waving his hands, making sounds that spirits didn't normally make. He also looked younger; it was difficult to say by how much, since time passed strangely in Diyu. His transparent white skin, the kind that came naturally to spirits, was covered in vein-like crimson streaks. He wore a transparent black cloak that also emanated a crimson glow. It was covered in runes, but they were obviously fake, as this was a cheap costume he'd bought at one of those pop-up stores that took over deserted locations once a year.

"Why did it have to be ghostface?" Yama finally said.

"In my defense," Judah said, raising his hands. "I didn't know what ghostface was where I went to school. Besides, it was for a school play. I wanted to look the part. You know, Ghost of Christmas Future and all."

"And this?" Yama asked, flipping the page. The ghostfaced Judah was running around scaring normal spirits and performing obscene acts. He was quite the barbarian, and everyone around him laughed. "It just so happens that ghostface is the most insulting thing evil spirits—or ghosts, as they are often called—have ever heard of. In fact, it wasn't so long ago that ghosts were nothing more than slaves and servants. Maybe a billion years. Back then, ghosts couldn't even act their own roles in plays, since pure spirits didn't want the ghosts tainting their performance. Instead, they'd have normal spirits dress up as an exaggerated caricature of their kind, taking every opportunity to insult and debase them and put them in their place. The resentment still hasn't died down."

"A billion years ago?" Judah said incredulously. "And they still remember? Lord Yama, that's a little extreme."

"Tell that to the media," Yama said wryly. "Now what are we going to do about this?"

"Apologize, I guess," Judah said, looking none too worried.

"Again?" Yama asked, surprised. The Lord of the Underworld didn't apologize, and though it wasn't him that would be doing it, he wasn't sure if he'd ever get used to the concept. Further, he wasn't sure he'd ever seen a politician apologize either.

"They bought it last time," Judah said. "They'll probably buy it again. They're not used to seeing us humble ourselves, and something about it comforts them. No, maybe it's *better* that this ghostface scandal happened. It'll make me look more like a *real* spirit while our competitors look like they're used to lording it over them from an ivory tower. My main competitor went to private school for Diyu's sake."

"His father was mayor, so he could afford it," Yama said. "But we're not getting into an argument about public school versus private school again. You go do your thing, and I'll stay here and do mine. I still have a lot of work to do today."

"Sure thing, boss," Judah said, giving a sloppy salute.

Once he'd gone, Yama pushed a button on his desk, calling for his trusty assistant, Lily. She appeared almost immediately, her ghostly figure cutting through time and space to get here.

"Reporting for duty, sir!" Lily said, giving him a sharp salute.

Yama nodded and waved her over. Judah had his advantages, like his relatability and likeableness, but he lacked the strict discipline Lily brought to the campaign.

"How did it go?" Yama asked, summoning a map of Diyu. The projection, which fit snugly on his desk, perfectly replicated the city's iconic skyscrapers. It was divided into prefectures, which were in turn divided into districts. Every district would elect a councilor, who would in turn nominate a mayor.

"It went well," Lily said. "Councilor Ruthar has promised his support, though he'll require funding for three orphanages in his district—random reincarnations due to the past few epidemics that have hit his district hardest. He'll also need someone conveniently removed."

Yama nodded. "We can take care of both of those things, but the removal will only happen if Judah wins. I want him to feel the pressure and motivate him to talk to the other councilors."

"That brings us up to one thousand and seventy," Lily said. "Still very short if we are to win the election."

"Hm…" Yama said, fondling his wispy beard. "Have we tried funding other candidates? Getting them to fight one another to split the vote?"

"We have, but it's a balancing act," Lily said. "Our campaign analysts are generating targeted ads on social media. We're spreading as much disinformation as possible, while making sure we can claim plausible deniability if this gets out."

"Plausible deniability is everything," Yama said. "No one will be willing to go all in and investigate us. Especially not considering they could be next on my random reincarnation list."

"A fact I've taken great care in reminding them about," Lily said. Yama nodded.

Elections were a tricky thing. Democracy was great in theory, but in practice, it led to huge polarization in the population. Taken to one extreme, facts became optional, and opinions became everything. Judah was somewhat naïve in thinking charm could win him the election, but he hadn't done anything to relieve the man of the notion. They would take care of all the hard work involved in winning votes, keeping him blissfully ignorant for as long as possible.

Yama didn't like meddling in the affairs of mortals, but something needed to be done. The fate of the city—no, the universe, depended on it. He'd been given a job, and by Pangu, he'd do it. He wouldn't have a second world-ending apocalypse as a black mark on his resume. One was already enough.

Chapter 1: The Perfect Number

A gentle wind brushed past Cha Ming as he walked across a fertile meadow. Grazing demons looked up at him, their curious eyes evaluating his threat level as he passed. The demons—redwood elk demons—had healthy coats of thick red fur and elaborate horns. You could find them everywhere around here in the Redwood Forest, conveniently located between Beihai and Gold Leaf City.

Cha Ming, curious to see how they would respond to a strange human, reached out to one of the demons with his bare hand. It inched back slightly but stopped once it noticed the pure and kindly aura coming from him. He scratched the rough fur atop its head, which was slightly sticky and stuck to his fingers.

It's like the sap that oozes out from behind the tree bark, he thought, looking to the red trees beyond the meadow. He wondered if the substance grew naturally, or if it was simply a byproduct of the creature rubbing up against them.

Life is so fragile, Cha Ming thought. *Even among demons.*

Though the herd wasn't well organized, there was a method to the way they moved. The young were evenly spread out across the group to protect them from the carnivorous birds that patrolled the skies above them. Feeding time was a gentle dance, and the slightest lapse in judgment as they ate the emerald-green spirit grass could mean the death of one of their younger members.

A short while later, Cha Ming walked into the woods. Unlike the meadows beneath the open sky, no grass grew here, as the redwood trees blocked out any sunshine that might have otherwise pierced through their massive branches. Instead, mushrooms grew beneath the wide canopies, providing shelter to the demons and beasts that lived there.

As he continued his journey, he looked around and noticed that the demons who typically lurked in places like these were unusually quiet.

"Jun Xiezi," Cha Ming said, sensing the source of the disturbance. "I'm glad you could make it."

"I couldn't pass up the opportunity finally travel again," Jun Xiezi said, walking over on a well-maintained path from the opposite direction. The silver-haired man bowed lightly, and Cha Ming reciprocated. Now that he was stronger, he could finally evaluate the man's cultivation realm: the peak of core formation. It was much higher than he'd expected. He was likely one of the strongest residents of the Quicksilver Empire.

"When I saw the Redwood Forest was on the way, I couldn't resist asking a local to show me around," Cha Ming said. "By the way, I finished a few pieces before you came. Catch."

Several talismans flew out from the Clear Sky World and stopped an arm's length away from the older man.

"Good lad," Jun Xiezi said, picking up three sheets of thin red paper. "That painting was one of the best investments I ever made."

The painting he'd created for Cha Ming, *Samsara*, had proven extremely useful. Its soul-replenishing properties had been especially useful to the weaker Cha Ming.

"I should have given them to your earlier," Cha Ming said. "Unfortunately, I had something on my mind back then. I call these three the 'kindling,' 'dousing,' and 'energy' talismans. They keep the same symmetry as my earlier poetic talismans. One day, I hope to complete one for the wood element."

"Living and dying," Jun Xiezi said. "That will be a challenge for someone so young."

"To be fair, I'm over a hundred and thirty now," Cha Ming muttered.

"Been to a place with compressed time, I see," Jun Xiezi said with a bemused expression. "Good thing I wasn't talking about your physical age but your mental one."

Cha Ming scowled, but the man ignored him.

"Let's get going. There are many good things to see here."

Jun Xiezi pushed off the ground and floated onto one of the thick rust-colored branches that loomed overhead. He twisted his body, expertly avoiding demonic cobwebs that lay in wait for lesser prey. Skeletal spiders scrambled away as Cha Ming followed. Demons were especially sensitive to strength and wouldn't be caught dead tangling with two superior cultivators like them.

Cha Ming was amazed at the sheer variety of beings in the treetop environment. Here, a whole new world appeared, complete with demonic versions of things like squirrels, birds, and even house cats. There were plenty of insects too. Colorful butterflies fluttered around them as they ascended; they took advantage of their presence by intimidating natural predators, creating a beautiful spectacle in exchange for safety. Fearful spiders with bladelike appendages glared at them with hateful eyes as they fluttered through their traps with uncharacteristic ease. Cha Ming, who'd never been fond of spiders, was only too happy to oblige, circle of life be damned.

"There aren't many butterflies flying around these days," Jun Xiezi said, catching a seven-colored specimen on his finger. "They're much livelier around hatching time. Their predecessors, a variety of demonic caterpillar, take nine years to grow. We're in the eighth year of their cycle now, so most of them have died off. Next year, the remaining butterflies will lay a batch of eggs that become the next wave of caterpillars."

"It's always nine, isn't it?" Cha Ming asked.

"Nine is the most perfect number," Jun Xiezi said. "Though many would argue seven is. There are seven virtues and seven vices, after all."

Eight, if you count hope and doubt, Cha Ming thought to himself.

He considered this as they flew through a horde of flying squirrels. The deceptively thin creatures flew from branch to branch despite their low cultivations. Like their mortal counterparts, they were always searching for food. The eight virtues and eight vices were lost to these creatures. They were intelligent, of course, even more so than the average human, but demons focused on survival rather than higher callings like morality. Barring their strange sense of honor and respect, they preferred to avoid the squabbles of men and discourses on religion. Unlike people, the right course of action was engraved into their very bones.

"We're here," Jun Xiezi said after they'd traveled for a half hour. Demons began to scatter up ahead, and soon there was not a demon in sight. They crossed a night-invisible threshold that Cha Ming recognized as a demon-repelling formation. It surrounded the nearby area like a bubble. The strange three-dimensional formation was the result of 1,080 smaller ones drawn on redwood bark. He could see the compact runes drawing power from the trees and their nigh-limitless vitality.

"Impressive," Cha Ming said. "This was the work of a grand-elder-level figure in formation arts."

"The first inhabitants of Redwood Forest were the servants of a mighty cultivator," Jun Xiezi said. "He eventually transcended, but the servants and their families remained. They loved the wilderness and hated cities. They preferred a simple life, free from war, politics, and other things that plague dense pockets of humanity."

"Why did you leave?" Cha Ming asked. The man was an enigma, and the sheer variety of paintings he'd created showed how well-traveled he was.

"To live," Jun Xiezi replied. Seeing Cha Ming's puzzled expression, he elaborated. "You can't live if you stay cooped up in the same place all the time. You need to experience life and its complexities and contradictions, its terrible choices and its bittersweet moments. You need to find a home. Then, when you've grown comfortable, you need to move on. If you keep doing that for a while, you'll find a feeling deep down that everywhere, in a sense, is your home."

"I can't say I relate," Cha Ming said. He'd only lived in a half dozen places now, but most of them seemed transient. Even Haijing City, where he'd spent most of his life, was nothing more than a stepping stone. Yet when he thought about home, he remembered a quiet clearing in Jade Moon Garden. He thought of Green Leaf Academy, his time in Quicksilver, and the people he'd befriended there. He thought of Li Yin, the mortal doctor.

"One day, you will," Jun Xiezi said. "Now follow me and don't say anything funny." He landed on a thick platform made of wooden boards and drew back his soul force. As he walked, his aura grew more and more reserved. His active cultivation receded until he appeared to be little more than a foundation-establishment cultivator. Cha Ming followed suit, suppressing his cultivation to early foundation establishment and early bone forging. They walked directly into the village without anyone stopping them.

"No guards?" Cha Ming asked.

Most cities, even those without cultivators, had guards. Only the smallest farming communities were unguarded, and even then, they posted a town watch.

"Do you have any idea how difficult it is to guard against intruders in three dimensions?" Jun Xiezi said, pointing up at the leafy canopy. "There are no walls, so people can come and go from any direction if they're skilled enough. Plus, demons can't come inside. People trust each other here, and the guards roaming around are merely respected members of society that are looking out for their neighbors. They'll help if someone gets hurt or someone's cat gets caught up in a tree. Assuming the cat isn't just being needy."

Oddly, Cha Ming thought of Mr. Mao Mao. He missed the cat, and he was sure Huxian did too.

Jun Xiezi led them from bridge to bridge, platform to platform. On one of the bridges, they saw a group of youngsters. They were around ten years old, and to Cha Ming's surprise, they were having fun by hopping off the bridge using crude ropes. They swung about, knocking into each other with little fear of falling. He soon saw what gave them the courage to do so: A thin net covered the area beneath the bridge. It wasn't large, but anyone unfortunate enough to fall off the bridge would be caught.

"Master Xiezi!" a voice called out.

"Master Xiezi!" another called out alongside it. A boy and a girl ran up to Jun Xiezi and hugged his loose robes.

The older man laughed as he kneeled and rubbed their heads. "No need to call me master or anything like that. Just calling me Teacher is fine."

"We'll remember, Master Xiezi," the girl said. "Are you opening up your shop again after so long?"

"What do you mean, so long?" Jun Xiezi said. "I only stepped out for a year this time."

"After only staying for a month," the girl grumbled.

"I was traveling," Jun Xiezi said. "I always travel. It's how I get ideas." The little girl crossed her arms in displeasure. "I'll tell you what, I have something here for you if you'll forgive me."

"Really?" the girl asked, her anger vanishing as quickly as it had appeared.

"Yes, really," Jun Xiezi said. A small one-foot-by-one-foot painting appeared in his hands. It showed a bird's-eye view of Quicksilver City in all its radiance. With his keen eyes, Cha Ming could spot an exquisite amount of detail in the painting. It even showed the workers building the rails that crisscrossed the city. "I made you a small painting. Remember how you said you always wanted to see a city?"

"Is that really a city?" the girl said, her voice filled with awe. "I don't see any bridges or bark. How can they live there?"

"They live in stones on the ground," Jun Xiezi whispered with a mischievous grin.

The girl's frown deepened. "That seems really unsafe. How do they stay away from the monsters down below?" She shuddered. "I like it better here."

Jun Xiezi chuckled. "That's fine too. Do whatever makes you happy." He then looked to the little boy standing beside her with an expectant look on his face. "I know you don't much like paintings, but I know you like games."

He waved his hand, and a deck of exquisitely painted cards appeared. He waved once more, and the cards collapsed into a deck, which the boy grabbed.

"I'll go play right now!" the boy exclaimed. He ran toward a row of houses that were built of redwood, either directly within a trunk or on a platform built along a larger tree branch. The girl hesitated before ultimately chasing her brother.

Both Cha Ming and Jun Xiezi laughed as they walked past the remaining children hanging off the bridge, completely oblivious to them in their games, and headed toward where the buildings grew larger and denser. There, they saw busy people going about their daily lives. Bakers baked, merchants sold, and smiths shaped metal. That last one surprised Cha Ming, who'd always seen metal as the antithesis of wood.

"What, you think people can survive without metal up here?" Jun Xiezi said when Cha Ming asked.

"No, I just thought the high heat required for spiritual blacksmithing might damage the trees," Cha Ming said. Though he wasn't a spiritual blacksmith, there were commonalities between smithing and alchemy. Even without training with a hammer, he could generate flames that would melt peak-core-formation treasures given enough time. These massive redwoods were much less sturdy in comparison.

"Hah," Jun Xiezi said. "These redwoods would survive an all-out war between the North and the South. There's nothing on this plane that could take them all out. And if one tree was damaged, the others would all support it. The trees are like a community, Cha Ming. If one of them is hurt, the others all pitch in to help it get better. It's been that way for thousands of years, and it'll continue being that way for a long while yet."

They continued down the busy streets, peeking into the various open-air shops they saw. Eventually, they came upon a small building with no sign. There, Jun Xiezi took out a dull iron key and unlocked it. He tapped his finger on the wall, and colors flowed from his hand onto the building's exterior, which now seemed more like a canvas than anything else.

Vivid yellow, orange, and red colors appeared along with the green and reddish brown of the redwood trees. The sky in the painting was obscured with smoke, and fire ravaged the lands. Cha Ming blinked when he realized that Jun Xiezi had painted exactly what he'd imagined—the redwood trees were burning, and the source of the fire was a spiritual smithy.

"Won't this upset people?" Cha Ming asked nervously.

Jun Xiezi shrugged. "If they're not used to my antics by now, they never will be." He flicked his hand as they walked in, and instead of turning on a light, the colors in the room grew brighter and more vivid. A tiny fireplace lit up, and dried up plants, which had been dead in their pots, came to life as though he'd never been gone in the first place. "Now make yourself at home. I'm about to get really busy."

Busy was an understatement. By the time the man was sitting down with a brush in hand and a blank canvas before him, four people had already entered the shop. Jun Xiezi, not wanting to be bothered before finishing his first painting, grunted and summoned hundreds of paintings that flew onto special stands on the walls. Each one was accompanied by a note explaining the scene in question. The paintings were all highlights of his travels, available for very modest sums.

There was an unofficial system in this shop. For the most part, the clients walked in and chatted with the elderly painter, who was only too happy to share stories of his travels as he painted. He answered any questions they asked, and after three or so questions, they chose something from the walls and put their payment inside a bowl at the front of the room on their way out.

Every person that left meant one of the many people lined up outside could enter. The older man painted as he talked. Occasionally, he asked his own questions. The customers found themselves pouring out their greatest joys and most terrible sorrows.

Whenever he heard something especially moving, Jun Xiezi

would pause and begin to paint what they described. He didn't paint exactly what had happened, but his interpretation of the events. He brought life to their weal and woe in a way only he, the painter, would ever understand. These paintings were gifts, and each one was at least a magic-grade treasure. Occasionally, however, he was able to create something more vivid and lifelike. These paintings were core treasures, but he still gave them out to mortals and cultivators alike, who had no knowledge of their true value.

Three days passed in this way. During that time, Cha Ming watched Jun Xiezi paint. Occasionally, he brewed tea or picked up something for them to eat from a local establishment. He saw life through many different viewpoints and considered many things. He tried to use these to supplement his understanding of life, but unfortunately, there was something missing. Their experiences were not his own; they were but a mere shadow of something real.

"What makes a painting good?" Cha Ming asked at the end of the third day. He, too, had taken out a canvas. He was painting a familiar scene with his Clear Sky Brush, depicting the warm reception he'd received from the Hong family in Green Leaf City. It was a decent painting, but compared to those he painted of Yu Wen or his experience in Crystal Falls, it lacked something. This one was just a mortal-grade painting, a far cry from the peak-magic-grade treasures he sometimes created.

"That's a difficult question to answer," Jun Xiezi said, putting the finishing touches on his own painting. Like many of his creations, it featured ponds, lilies, and people bathing. The man never seemed to tire of painting some rendition of this scene. It, like most of the others he painted, became a mid-grade-magic treasure. "You can achieve the peak of spiritual painting through technique and mimicry. Or, you can fumble around blindly until you get there. The former is more reliable, while the latter is ephemeral but allows one to paint something beyond one's technical skill. Only by combining the two can you make a true masterpiece.

"Where did you study?" Cha Ming asked.

Though Zhou Li had been a peak-grandmaster painter, he'd

never found any literature on the subject in Haijing's library.

"Painting is only taught through apprenticeship," Jun Xiezi said, "as books are considered too shallow a medium to pass along the exquisiteness of the art. At lower levels, class sizes can be quite large, but higher-level arts are only taught to a select few. Teachers lecture as they paint and teach techniques on a whim. They usually do it at the end of their lifespan, however, when they feel they can contribute nothing more to society."

"Strange," Cha Ming said. "No one teaches for money?"

"Painters make money," Jun Xiezi said with a smile. "But those who focus on money won't ever reach the peak of their craft. It cheapens the art, much like it does poetry and writing. Selling your work is fine, of course, though many would rather detach themselves from the process and hang their works up in an art gallery and be done with it.

"Most successful painters are surprised at the success of the works. The works they're most proud of get little attention, but works they casually painted, those filled with flaws and misconceptions, tend to attract the most buyers and collectors." He shook his head. "It's truly a strange thing, but I suppose it's like the rest of life and all its wonders."

"Can you teach me?" Cha Ming asked.

Jun Xiezi chuckled and shook his head. "No, I'm afraid I wouldn't be a suitable teacher. You're a strange man, you know. You're too powerful, too lofty for your young age. You've seen too little of the world and too much of it at the same time. Besides, I feel you'd resent the technical aspects of painting. You're the type of person who paints with your heart. And I want you to know that there's nothing wrong with that."

Cha Ming mulled over these words. It was true that he enjoyed the process, and the thought of imitating someone else's hand irked him. Still, specific tips would go a long way.

Just as he was about to ask, however, the door opened abruptly. A dozen men with angry looks on their faces walked in. Their leader was an arrogant-looking cultivator who'd reached the peak of core formation. Cha Ming frowned when he saw them. He looked to Jun Xiezi, who simply smiled and held up his hand, signaling that he'd take care of it. Ironically, to them, it probably seemed like a greeting.

"What can I help you gentlemen with?" Jun Xiezi said pleasantly.

"You know the drill," the leader replied, puffing out his chest in an unsubtle effort to look tough. "Just like the past eight years, you give me a third of your profits, and we don't mess up the place."

The men behind him nodded with crossed arms. Cha Ming couldn't help but chuckle inwardly at the situation. They could no more rob Jun Xiezi than a newborn child could scold him.

"I was wondering when to expect you," Jun Xiezi said, still smiling. Then, to Cha Ming's surprise, he summoned a pile of spirit stones from his spatial ring and placed it on a small table beside them. "I hope my results aren't too disappointing."

The leader grinned and picked out a few choice stones. "Look at what we have here," he said, inspecting a high-grade spirit stone in the pile. "We don't see a lot of these around here."

"I thought you'd like it," Jun Xiezi said. "I put it there because I wanted to ask you for a favor."

The man frowned at that. "A favor? What kind of favor?"

"Nothing much, nothing much," Jun Xiezi said. "You see, I've been working on a painting for the past nine years. I was hoping you could help me out with it. It's almost done."

"A painting, eh?" the man said, stroking his chin. "I've never considered myself much of painter, but I suppose I could try."

"Don't worry, I just need a model, not an assistant," Jun Xiezi said, motioning to a spot beside him. He then walked to the back of the room where Cha Ming noticed there were nine stands. The older man waved his hand, and nine canvases appeared, facing the men. "The first time I saw you here, you were just an innocent man trying to make ends meet for your new family."

Jun Xiezi's brush flowed along the canvas, and many colors seeped onto it. The painting took three seconds to materialize before Jun Xiezi walked up to the next one. "The year after, it seemed you had something on your mind. You came here with friends that year.

It looked like you were trying to impress them." Once again, his brush touched the canvas, and a painting appeared. He did the same for the third.

"It was the next few years where things really hit a groove," Jun Xiezi said, touching the fourth through sixth canvases. The mood in the paintings grew harder and darker. While the first three depicted a man who dabbled in thuggery, the next three highlighted a deep change in character. The man no longer doubted himself. He grew harder and more confident, and his posture seemed to reflect the violence he'd grown increasingly comfortable with committing. The seventh and the eighth highlighted these features even more. The man's appearance was growing ugly, almost devilish. Cha Ming could see a subtle turning point. The ninth painting would define the man's character for the rest of his life.

"Ling Yu," Jun Xiezi said. "What would you like me to paint on my next canvas? What type of man would you like to become this year? They say nine is the perfect number. Nine defines all facets of a person's character."

Ling Yu had been staring at the paintings all this time. His expression had grown dimmer and dimmer with each painting that so perfectly captured his history and his descent into darkness.

The eighth had been particularly hard on the man. His eyes twitched, and his hands shook. "I've never hurt anyone too bad," Ling Yu said. "Not too bad."

If Cha Ming wasn't looking the man straight in the face, he'd guess the man was crying.

"But you *have* hurt others," Jun Xiezi said. "I can feel it in each painting, the deepening darkness. You were driven by necessity at first, which was why I let you take some of my earnings those three times. But after the fourth time, it seemed like you wouldn't change your ways. You grew dependent on my money, dependent on the thuggery. And in the subsequent paintings, you can you see the result of your actions and the man you're becoming."

The ones accompanying Ling Yu were shifting around uncomfortably. They clearly wanted to leave, but Cha Ming saw that

Jun Xiezi had used his powerful soul to lock them in place.

"What is your choice? What do you want me to paint this time? You won't be taking stones from me again either way. I've been painting this for nine years, and today, I will finish it."

Ling Yu's throat trembled. His eyes watered, and he suddenly fell to his knees. Then, the man who'd hardened over the eight consecutive paintings did something no one would have thought possible. He wept. He wept tears of regret that poured onto the wooden floorboards beneath him. He cried out years of pent-up frustration and regret.

As he blinked away the tears, he saw that Jun Xiezi had already finished the ninth painting. He'd painted the weeping man and his plea for redemption, his willingness to change. This wasn't a man whose character would be locked in for the rest of his life, but one who was undergoing a metamorphosis, a transformation, like a caterpillar into a butterfly.

"Go," Jun Xiezi said. "And never come back to my shop. If you regret how you've treated others, make it up to them. Do you understand?"

The man wiped his eyes and nodded. Then, to Cha Ming's surprise, he kowtowed to Jun Xiezi. "Thank you," he said.

"No need to thank me," Jun Xiezi replied. "Now, are you going to scram, or do I have to kick you out?" He sent his resplendent force out at the men, who instantly fell over themselves as they scrambled to get out of the room. Ling Yu was no exception. After giving one last deep bow, he shut the door, leaving the bewildered Cha Ming and a scowling Jun Xiezi alone inside.

The scowl turned into a smile the moment the door was shut. "Well, that went well."

"That's an interesting way to make a painting," Cha Ming said. "Most people try to flesh out what they've experienced, not stage the experience in the first place."

"It's interesting to capture the lives of others as they are changing," Jun Xiezi said. "And some people need a bit of a push. Like writing a book, painting is a way to live a second life. Your own experience isn't the only valid one."

As Cha Ming stewed on this thought, Jun Xiezi made tea. They drank and chatted for the remainder of the evening. When they stopped, the sun was rising above the Redwood Forest. Soft streaks of yellow light peeked through the cluttered branches that loomed above them.

"I think it's about time I went," Cha Ming said. "I have an old friend to visit, and by my count, I haven't seen his face in over a hundred and twenty years."

"Go on ahead," Jun Xiezi said, nodding. "I'll stay here for a few more days and head back to Quicksilver. Heavens know when I'll finally be able to retire."

Cha Ming chuckled. The man was always talking about retiring, but it was obvious to everyone that he enjoyed his work. "Good luck with your paintings," Cha Ming said, clasping the man's hand.

"Good luck with life," Jun Xiezi replied. They shook hands, and Cha Ming left the treetop village by flying through the canopy above it. A multitude of birds flew out around him as he entered misty skies still red with the rising sun. He heard a yip in the distance. Huxian appeared along with a frog, a mouse, a bird, and a purple mist. The mist was bunched up like a tiny purple pyramid.

"It took you long enough," Huxian said. "Did you find what you were looking for?"

Huxian and his friends hadn't been able to cross the demon-repelling barrier—at least, not without destroying it. Therefore, they'd decided to play in the redwoods and bully the local wildlife.

Cha Ming shook his head. "The essence of living is difficult to capture. I doubt I'll find it by staying here."

"Then where to next?" Huxian asked.

"Next?" Cha Ming said. "Next, we live. Let's find Wang Jun. It's high time I pay back the favor I owe him."

At Huxian's signal, Silverwing transformed into a large, 330-foot falcon. They hopped onto his back and flew east toward the capital of the Golden Kingdom, Gold Leaf City.

Chapter 2: The Favor

The journey to Gold Leaf City proved uneventful. Cha Ming and Huxian walked through the city gates, where they were welcomed by the head of the city guard. To their surprise, the man was a peak-core-formation cultivator. The nervous man took great care in explaining the rules of the city.

After assuring the man that they wouldn't cause any trouble, they proceeded to the city's bustling streets. Gold Leaf City was the most prosperous place on the continent, as evidenced by both its architecture and the people inhabiting it. They saw very few non-cultivators as they walked through the compact yet large city. The vital underclass remained mostly hidden, relegated to slums kept far away from busier streets.

They really like ostentation, Huxian said as he admired a particularly dazzling storefront. *Delicious and decadent ostentation.*

The building resembled a local fruit-based dessert, and the runes on its walls could literally be smelled and tasted. There were many buildings like it competing for the precious attention of the masses. Every street-facing structure was covered in runes that both enhanced their beauty and drew uncertain eyes.

The entire spectacle was overwhelming even to them. They rushed past it all, making their way to Gold Leaf Square. Unlike other cities, the central square was designed more like a park than anything else. Families led their children through the carefully tended rows of gold-leafed trees while spirit arborists tended to the flowers that grew beside them. Only four buildings stood tall in the square: the Jade Bamboo Pavilion, the Greenwind Pavilion, the Red Dust Pavilion, and the Spirit Temple.

"What a peculiar square," Cha Ming thought out loud, stopping in front of a tree and admiring a beautiful golden leaf that was about to fall off. Most central squares would be hubs of commercial activity. Gold Leaf City, the commercial hub of the continent, had instead relegated it to a public attraction.

How so? Huxian asked. *Seems symmetrical. And the plants here are all very tasty. I'd eat them if it wasn't against the rules, and if that pesky cultivator wasn't hiding behind that tree over there.*

"It's peculiar because of who's in charge in the kingdom," Cha Ming explained. "The Golden Kingdom is officially ruled by the Jin royal family. It's a monarchy that draws its divine mandate from the Church of Justice. That they would allow a thorn like the Spirit Temple to exist here is curious. What's also curious is that they aren't located in Central Square with these other four powerhouses. If I were the Church, I'd want the cathedral on the continent in one of these four spaces, if not directly in the center.

"It's largely symbolic," a familiar voice said from behind them. "They keep their church to the north, and their reasoning is that faith should be kept separate from money. A doctrine the Spirit Temple obviously doesn't subscribe to." A figure they both knew all too well walked out of the shadows.

"Wang Jun," Cha Ming said, grinning. He gave his friend a tight hug. Huxian ran up to him and hopped onto his shoulder, licking his cheek. Wang Jun laughed and pet his small head. The man had changed substantially since last time they'd met. He looked harder, more practical than before—something Cha Ming hadn't considered possible. Moreover, his cultivation had increased by leaps and bounds. He was now a half-step transcendent, just a sliver away from carving his core. "I see your advancement is as quick as ever. If only I were so talented."

"Nonsense, my friend," Wang Jun said. "You're much stronger than I am as it is now. I wouldn't stand a chance fighting against you. If you could catch me, that is."

"I could catch you," Huxian said.

"I don't doubt you could," Wang Jun affirmed, chuckling. He scratched the back of the little fox's ears as he looked back to Cha Ming. "It seems my estimate on how long you'd be gone for was off. You're getting *old*, Cha Ming. I didn't give you nearly enough tea."

"Look who's talking," Cha Ming said, picking a lock of white hair from Wang Jun's long blond hair. There were many more than before. "You're right, I ran out of good tea decades ago. Fortunately, Jin Huang invented Strongman Coffee, so all is well in the world."

"Bah," Wang Jun said. "Coffee is just a passing trend, a trend I'm happy to ride out until it stops making me money. Tea is integral of the Ling Nan Plane's culture. And I insist we have tea after such a long time apart. Follow me. I know the perfect place."

Wang Jun began walking, not toward the Jade Bamboo Pavilion like Cha Ming had expected, but toward the red building in an adjacent corner of Gold Leaf Square.

"Wang Jun, I never took you for the type," Cha Ming said as they entered the red-and-gold establishment. They were greeted by two women in red, who bowed as they entered. Wang Jun thanked the "mistresses" on their way in.

"Young Master Jun," a voice said. "I didn't expect to see you today. With an important guest no less."

"Mistress Bai Ling," Wang Jun said, greeting the newcomer. The pretty lady in red had a competitive look about her. "Cha Ming, Bai Ling is the best *Angels and Devils* player I've ever met. You'd do well to learn from her."

"Nonsense," Bai Ling said, only giving a token protest to hide her pleasure at the mention. "You've never lost a game, though you've tried very hard. And you," she said, looking to Cha Ming, "must be the illustrious transcendent elder from Haijing City, Cha Ming."

"I'm surprised you've heard of me," Cha Ming said. "I just left Haijing a couple weeks ago."

"We're in the business of knowing," Bai Ling replied with a sweet smile. "What will you be needing today, Young Master Jun? I would offer entertainment in the form of a game, but I feel you're looking for a private place to catch up."

"The headmistress?" Wang Jun asked.

"Indisposed," Bai Ling said, pursing her lips slightly. "While she's more than happy to meet with you privately, she's not willing to meet strangers." There was an awkwardness to the exchange Cha Ming couldn't put his finger to.

"Unfortunate," Wang Jun said, the frown on his brow disappearing as quickly as it came. "I'd like a private room for the both of us. Many vegetable dishes, many large meat dishes for the fox, and your best tea. Do you have someone who could play the zither for entertainment? Someone trustworthy?"

"Mistress Huang happens to be available," Bai Ling said. "She is the most discreet of our members."

"Thank you," Wang Jun said.

They walked down a hallway with red carpets and gold runic gilding on the walls. There were also paintings, several of which Cha Ming recognized.

"It's impressive that the Red Dust Pavilion was able to commission so many of Brother Jun's works," Cha Ming said, admiring the set they had on display. "He's very selective with his customers."

"Ah, those," Bai Ling said. "He painted them for the Red Dust Mistress from two generations ago. He was a young budding artist back then. Hong Yinyue saw potential in him, so she did her best to secure a few paintings. Though they aren't his best works, the passion contained in these paintings doesn't miss out to his masterpieces. Not many people get to brag about being a fan of someone before they become famous."

They soon arrived at a door in the hallway. Bai Ling slipped her hand across a strip of runic symbols, and something within the door clicked. She slid it open and led them to a table that would normally seat eight. It stood right before a small stage.

"I assume that the demon accompanying you suffers from the usual demonic food lust," Bai Ling said.

"Doubly so," Cha Ming replied.

"Then we'll make sure he's adequately fed," Bai Ling said.

"Much obliged," Cha Ming replied as she excused herself. They took a seat, and by the time Wang Jun had brewed the first pot of tea, the first dishes arrived. Mistress Huang also arrived alongside them. She pulled out a gold-and-red zither and began playing a relaxing tune. The music had a calming effect on his soul despite its transcendent nature. "Good music."

"The musicians of the Red Dust Pavilion are the best in the city," Wang Jun said. "That's one of the reasons I brought you here."

"The other is to avoid your family," Cha Ming said.

"You guessed right," Wang Jun said. "Things have never been more tense between my family and me. You see, we're competing financially, and I'm winning. Unfortunately, it's going to take far more to convince them I'm the right man for the job." He motioned to the cooling cup in front of Cha Ming. "Please, drink. This tea is rather special. It's a very difficult tea to obtain here in the North. It's from a place called the Shattered Lands, located in one of the few wealthy kingdoms in the South, the Ji Kingdom."

Cha Ming took a sip. "Metallic," he said, letting the tea roll around on his tongue. "And earthy."

"Right," Wang Jun said. "The Shattered Lands contain the single most concentrated ore deposit on the continent, though it's very difficult to extract due to an ancient curse. Anything that grows near there and survives absorbs some of its metallic aura, giving it a unique flavor."

"It's good tea," Cha Ming said. He ate a few pieces of a strange green vegetable with a spiraling stalk and enjoyed its pungent flavor. "I take it your information network has kept you up to date on my activities?"

"Most of them," Wang Jun said. "Everything from when you came back to Quicksilver, your trip to Haijing, and the rest. I don't know anything about what happened on the Bridge of Stars. Care to talk about it? It must have been an exciting journey."

Cha Ming's eyes dimmed somewhat at the mention.

"Ah. Never mind Jade Moon Planet. It's not important."

"What's there to say?" Cha Ming said with a sigh. "I found a way to heal my core, but the price was too great. I met the love of my life there, Wang Jun. And I lost her." An awkward silence ensued, and they ate away at their dishes as memories flitted through Cha Ming's mind.

The rollercoaster of emotions he expected didn't come, however. Instead, every memory that came and went seemed to give him a sense of closure and resolution.

He soon realized the memories came to his mind at a certain rate and rhythm, and that rhythm was the same as the music they listened to. One section, one memory. Minutes passed, but to Cha Ming, they felt like a relaxing eternity. The music didn't stop until he'd gone through each key memory, and though they weren't any more distant, he felt more comfortable with them.

"Did you find her?" he asked, finally dragging himself out of the musical trance.

Wang Jun took a sip of tea. "No, I didn't. I did everything I could to find her, but as far as I can tell, Hong Xin no longer exists on this plane."

Cha Ming sighed. "A pity," he said. "She was such a fragile thing, with such a caring family. I don't think I can muster the courage to see them anymore, seeing as how I've failed them."

Wang Jun shook his head. "It's not your failing; it's mine."

"It's both our failings," Cha Ming said. "Now, tell me about your problems, Wang Jun. Tell me what I can finally do for you. I don't have long left here. Once this most recent war with the South is over, I'll transcend to a higher plane of existence. It's a long road to immortality, and I can't afford to wait too long."

"Sprinting when the race is a marathon, I see," Wang Jun said. He took another sip of his tea. "All right. Let me lay it out for you." He snapped his fingers inaudibly, and the shadows in the room moved as he willed and formed two figures. Though these weren't illuminated, the depth of the shadows allowed Cha Ming to see their details in the darkness. "The one on the left is my brother Wang Ling. Like I told you before, he killed my younger sister, Wang Hua. The one on the right is the patriarch of the Wang family, Wang Wuling."

He summoned a third shadow behind them. "The third figure is Grand Elder Wang. He's the family's transcendent, the core pillar of our family. He isn't very active in our affairs, and mostly lets his will be known through Wuling."

Cha Ming took in a deep breath. "And you still want me to kill your brother? Is that still necessary?"

Mistress Huang, who'd been calmly playing the zither, missed a beat in her song. Cha Ming raised an eyebrow to Wang Jun, who reassured him it was all right. Cha Ming shrugged. For the most part, he wasn't worried about a single transcendent trying to act out against him.

"If only that was all it took," Wang Jun said with a light laugh of exasperation. "My family's problems run much deeper than a single person. These three people, the heads of our family, are currently entangled in dark business with the South."

"How dark are we talking?" Cha Ming asked.

"Have you heard of the soul trade?" Wang Jun asked.

"I can't say I've heard of it," Cha Ming said. "Though I don't like where this is heading."

"The Spirit Temple doesn't usually do this kind of business in the North," Wang Jun explained. "So your ignorance is not surprising. In theory, they're even stricter in the Golden Kingdom. The process of extracting a soul is quite gruesome, so I'll skip those details. The end result, however, is that they capture tens of thousands of resentful souls. They do this by inflicting unspeakable horror on innocents then capturing their spirits before they enter the Yellow River. They use them to feed other evil spirits in the Spirit Temple, or they make them devour each other in competition, like gu in a jar. The winner becomes a proud member of the Spirit Temple, and the losers are wiped out from existence, never to reincarnate."

The chair in which Cha Ming had been sitting cracked as he

accidentally crushed the wooden armrest. He looked to Mistress Huang in apology but realized the wood was enchanted. It slowly began repairing itself without any outside intervention.

"That's atrocious," Cha Ming said hoarsely. "And the Church of Justice is fine with it?"

"Officially, they don't do it in the North and focus on their soul communion and assassination businesses," Wang Jun said. "Their contract business isn't very popular in the North since the Church of Justice officiates most documents here. The Spirit Temple does a damn good job of convincing the Church of Justice they don't trade in souls in the North, so they're left alone.

"Regardless, they've been culling souls in secret over the past ten years. Wang Ling has been facilitating shipments for tens of thousands of souls. I'd love to expose him, but my entire family would get caught up in an inquisition. I'm in a very delicate position, and the Church of Justice isn't exactly on good terms with me."

"Then what can I do for you?" Cha Ming said. "You'd be hard-pressed to find a better formation artist, talisman artist, or alchemist on the plane."

"If making money was all it took," Wang Jun said, "I'd have already solved the problem."

Cha Ming nodded. "Not only do you need to win this competition, but you need to disentangle your family and the Spirit Temple."

"And I'd prefer to do it without a mass slaughter," Wang Jun said. "I can definitely identify those responsible—and trust me, I'll be doing my best to give them an untimely ending—but that's not enough. I need the Spirit Temple to be *enemies* with my family. Only with open hostilities between our two organizations will the Church of Justice be convinced of our sincerity after this is all over."

"Can't I just destroy the Spirit Temple in Gold Leaf City?" Cha Ming asked. "I doubt their transcendents could do much about it. Besides, we're in the North."

"You make it sound so easy," Wang Jun said in bemusement. "You and Huxian wouldn't be at risk. Neither would I. You have a transcendent soul, so you'd be immune to most of their attacks, while Huxian is a Godbeast. I could hide indefinitely from them. But tell me, what about the people we know? Our roots? It wouldn't take much for them to find out where you've been, where you're from, and who you know. They're assassins, Cha Ming, and there's a good reason the Church of Justice hasn't uprooted them. More to the point, you'd have trouble *seeing* most of them. Your strong soul will help, but many would still escape your detection."

Cha Ming clicked his tongue. "That's quite the problem."

"Yes, and it's not one that can be solved in Gold Leaf City," Wang Jun said. "Which is why I want you to go south of the border."

"Wait, what?" Cha Ming said. He'd expected something in their area of influence. But in the South? How could he possibly do anything there undetected?

"We have an unofficial family branch in the Shattered Lands," Wang Jun explained. "It's run by my brother Wang Qian and makes him quite a bit of illicit money."

"So, instead of destroying your family's relationship in the North, you want to do it in the South," Cha Ming said slowly. "I'm not sure I'm the right man for the job."

"Oh, I think you're exactly the man I'm looking for," Wang Jun said. "My teacher spoke quite favorably of the technique you practice, the Seventy-Two Earthly Transformations. It seems a monkey used it to cause quite a bit of chaos in the Seven Heavens and the Seven Hells."

He's right, Sun Wukong sent from within the Clear Sky World. *If you want to hide, I can teach you. I'm the best at hiding.*

Except for your tail, Cha Ming muttered.

Wait, how did you know that? Sun Wukong said. He coughed in embarrassment. *I fixed that problem aeons ago. It won't be an issue.*

"I take it you have a plan?" Cha Ming asked Wang Jun.

"Yes, as a matter a fact, I do," Wang Jun said. "I don't know who exactly is working there, as many people are running interference, but I have it on good authority that our family is helping the South develop a special weapon in the Shattered Lands. I want you to pose as a spiritual blacksmith and somehow enter our Wang family. Then,

PATRICK G. LAPLANTE

I want you to use this identity to sow conflict and discord between our family and the various factions in Bastion, the capital city of the Ji Kingdom."

He summoned a black folder and placed it in front of Cha Ming. Cha Ming perused its contents, then summoned Grandmist flames to annihilate the papers after memorizing them.

"All right, I'll do it," Cha Ming said. Then he noticed something in the information he'd just read. "The most concentrated source of gold energy on the plane? High possibility of forming Gold Source Marrow?"

"You're welcome," Wang Jun said. "You can look for the Gold Source Marrow while sowing chaos in the South. Besides, I heard that whatever they're building, it's Zhou Li's pet project. He cares a lot about its success."

"Then I can't let it go as planned," Cha Ming said. He held up his cup of tea. "To our success."

"To our success," Wang Jun said. They clinked cups and drank. "Now, let's stop talking business. Let's talk about life, adventure, and the future."

They switched to wine, and the rest of the evening was a blur.

Chapter 3: Shadow Fate Redemption

"How much did I drink?" Wang Jun muttered, looking around blearily, his memories returning to him. He closed his eyes and circulated his qi, purging the alcohol from his system. Dozens of bottles littered the floor, some of them weaker immortal wine, others god-slaying whisky, a potent drink from Haijing City.

I let myself get carried away, he thought, shaking his head. He summoned a portal in the shadows. Then, on second thought, closed it. Instead of going back to the Jade Bamboo Pavilion, he slunk through the shadows of the Red Dust Pavilion, carefully skirting around the few customers that had trickled in and the mistresses entertaining them.

In one room, he saw dozens of sixteen-year-old girls. Each of them was a talent in one art or another and had above-average cultivation talent. They laughed and sang as they learned instruments and learned to kindle each other's emotions.

They all look happy, Wang Jun thought as he watched them practice. *They all want to be here.* Though many of them bore signs of past poverty, very little of it remained. This stood in stark contrast to the tale of horror and blood Hong Xin had told him about. Many of her sisters had died undergoing cruel training, freezing their hearts and emotions as quickly as humanly possible.

After spectating for a short while, Wang Jun walked through

several walls before arriving in the larder, where he grabbed a piece of sausage to eat. Then, he walked into the kitchen. The cooks were busy preparing dish after dish of spirit-infused food for the evening crowd. Spirit chefs worked in tandem with mortals to cook delicacies common people could only dream of. They didn't see him as he walked, sampling easy-to-nab goods. The ache in his stomach from all the drinking eased with every bite he took.

He shifted again, this time appearing in a shadow behind the curtains in Hong Xin's office. She was busy looking over ledgers. She looked up briefly as he entered, surprising Wang Jun. Could she spot him, despite being hidden from everyone else?

"You can come out now," Hong Xin said. She smiled as Wang Jun walked out from behind him, shaking his head in disappointment.

"How did you know I was there?" Wang Jun asked.

"Women's intuition," Hong Xin said. "That, and you walked out from your hiding place to confirm it. It turns out I'm right about half the time."

"A very useful trick," Wang Jun said. "I should try it one day."

She chuckled but continued looking over the document in her hands. She stamped it as reviewed and put it off to the side. "You try your best not to stand out. Sometimes that's just as telling as doing the opposite. The essence of blending in is drawing just enough attention to seem normal but too little to seem unimportant, is it not?"

"True," Wang Jun said from beside her. She jumped at his sudden teleportation but took it in stride.

"That's new," Hong Xin said, raising an eyebrow.

"I've been learning much from my master," Wang Jun admitted. "There are limits to mortality, but certain rules can be bent or ignored entirely if you know the secret."

Hong Xin sighed. She lifted her hand to Wang Jun's long white-blond hair and ran her fingers down it. As she did so, he stroked her cheek and pressed a soft kiss on her outstretched lips. "Why the spying?" Hong Xin asked.

"What, I'm not allowed to come watch you work?" Wang Jun said. "I'm wounded. Now tell me, what's bothering my fair lady?"

Hong Xin hesitated, then tapped a stack of papers. "We have a few dozen sisters from the old administration remaining in the city. They were each attached to various noble households, but recently, they founded their own organization—the Icy Heart Pavilion."

Wang Jun nodded.

"They offer services that calm the mind and soothe heart demons. They also gather information like we do here. In addition, they also train their members for combat. Many of them are versatile bodyguards. It's eating into our bottom line, and they aren't being even slightly unethical."

"Furthermore," she said, summoning a pile of jade slips, "from what I've gathered from the Greenwind Pavilion, though many have done a few ethically dubious things, they've never committed outright crimes. There are no cases of outright murder, nor any cases of fraud."

"Then what's the problem?" Wang Jun asked.

"The problem," Hong Xin said. "Is that they're cold-hearted psychopaths. And they're training others to be the same."

"It's a common problem," Wang Jun said. "At least a third of the high-ranking executives in Gold Leaf City have this trait. As do one in fifty normal people."

"Fair enough," Hong Xin said. "I'm just concerned. What if they do something terrible, like those sold to the Spirit Temple did? I know anyone could do it, but isn't it much more likely in their case?"

"Then we should preemptively arrest every cultivator in the world," Wang Jun said, sitting down on a chair beside her desk. "For I can hardly think of anyone better equipped to commit crimes."

Hong Xin shot him an irritated glare. "Perhaps I just don't approve of the way they're training their new recruits. They're helpless girls who don't know any better. They take them and break them just like they did to us. They have them sign contracts that effectively make them indentured servants until their training is over. I've been through what those girls are going through, Wang Jun, and it's not pretty. Many of us died back then. I'll not have any more helpless women subjected to brutal torture."

Wang Jun remained silent for a moment. "Is that a decision you can make for them? Can you deprive them of that choice?"

"I just don't know," Hong Xin moaned helplessly. "But heavens know I want to."

He nodded in understanding. "Morality can be gray sometimes. In most cases, there is no right or wrong answer. What matters is whether you're willing to do what it takes to get what you want."

Hong Xin frowned. "That's new. More teachings from your mysterious master?"

Wang Jun coughed lightly. "More something I heard in passing."

Hong Xin shook her head. "I'd love to entertain you, but I should get back to work. I have many things to look over before the evening rush."

The sky was dark, and it was just after dinnertime. There were still many hours left in the night.

"I'll come to visit soon," Wang Jun said into her ear. He moved to leave, then hesitated. "Why don't you want Cha Ming to know about you? He's worried sick, you know. He blames himself."

Hong Xin pursed her lips. "I don't think he needs to know what I've been through, or what I've become."

"A powerful, independent woman?" Wang Jun asked.

"A frightened but dangerous lady, who lives on lies and playing with the hearts of men," Hong Xin said. "He doesn't need to know that or the dangers I'm facing. He'll butt right into them and meddle in my affairs. Besides, you have no right to talk. You left out quite a few details yourself." She sighed. "I may have had Mistress Huang report to me after your meeting."

"He's always been an idealist," Wang Jun admitted. "Though, he'll hardly be pure after he does what I've asked him to do."

"Destroy a bunch of bad guys and upset them?" Hong Xin asked.

"Lie, hide, and instigate," Wang Jun said. "These three things go against his character, and I'm truly not sure if he'll follow through with them. If he can't, such is life. I can't do it myself, and none of my people are capable of accomplishing it."

"Lying and hiding seem easy enough," Hong Xin said. "But I have issues with instigation."

"It's not much different than blackmail," Wang Jun said, standing up and walking beside her. "Except with instigation, you pull the trigger instead of threatening to." He pulled her into an embrace and kissed her cherry-red lips. He didn't know how long the moment lasted, only that it wasn't long enough. She pulled away from him with a conflicted look in her eyes.

"Hiding is difficult too," Hong Xin whispered. "I have to hide, I know that, but I wish I didn't." She rested her hand on his chest and felt its soft heaving as he breathed.

"When I sort out things with my family, and the Spirit Temple is dealt with, you won't have to," Wang Jun said softly. "I'll marry you out in the open. I'll take you back to your family and apologize to them. We'll live a happy life together. I promise."

"I hope so," Hong Xin said. She looked at the clock on the wall, then winced. "I *really* need to get back to work. There's much to do, and so little time."

He planted a kiss on her cheek. Then, when her eyes were still closed, he walked into a shadow and vanished. Hong Xin continued trudging along until the sun disappeared behind the horizon.

In most cases, there is no right or wrong answer. What matters is whether you're willing to do what it takes to get what you want, Wang Jun thought as he flitted through shadow after shadow, killing time as the sun set on Gold Leaf City. The many shops closed one after another, carefully ushering out needy customers who refused to leave at the stated closing time. Most people returned home from work, and a minority wandered between restaurants and taverns or engaged in more secretive activities. There was little you couldn't buy in the capital of the Golden Kingdom.

"Oh, how the rich are careful," Wang Jun said, watching one such transaction between an older man and a woman far too young for him. His voice didn't carry far enough to reach anyone's ear. As he walked, his footsteps echoed strangely, the sounds shooting back at him and no one else.

He took a step, and his surroundings shifted to that of a cleaner place. It was a wealthy residential area with rows of gated mansions. Every gate had a couple of guards, and even more cultivators patrolled the streets to chase miscreants out, redirecting them to less affluent areas.

Unlike the poorer districts in town, no garbage littered the streets. Every paving stone was perfectly clean. Those who'd built the streets had covered the gray rocks in some sort of varnish or coating. They reflected light just enough to expose the cleanliness of the rock below but not enough to blind those who walked upon them.

"Here it is," Wang Jun said to no one in particular. "Don't mind me. I'll be fine on my own." The pair of guards he spoke to didn't hear him. One of them, however, shifted uncomfortably as Wang Jun made his way across the threshold. He took note of the man. Tomorrow, he'd have someone hire him for his own guard. After all, the man would be looking for a new job after tonight.

In the dimly lit house, a family feasted. They ate to their heart's content as cooks slaved away in the kitchen to make dish after dish for the family of six. Zhen Fa, his mark, stood at the head of the table. He and his two eldest sons drank strong cultivator's baiju. As was customary, they used small glasses to drink the frighteningly strong drink. It didn't take them long for red to flow to their cheeks.

The two daughters and their mother drank nothing as they ate away at the dishes. They would likely drink tea after the meal, as many people insisted that tea and food didn't mix. Instead, they chatted about everyday things, like gossip and the family business. Every member of the household, no matter whether they were weak or strong, young or old, was involved in running it.

Wang Jun didn't interrupt their merry supper. He didn't lace any of the incoming dishes with poison, nor did he intercept any of the servants as they took back partially eaten dishes to the servants' quarters, where the family's well-treated employees could partake in the luxurious fare. He simply watched and waited, peering into the shadows both past and present, looking for something. It was tiring work, and at one point, he suspected that he was attempting the impossible. But then he reminded himself that his master must know best. He continued to search.

"Three leads," Wang Jun said. "Three times where he flouted the law, only to eliminate all traces of wrongdoing."

There had been no need to ask the Greenwind Pavilion for this information. Everyone knew about the fraud, and Zhen Fa had even insinuated his guilt at the many banquets and gatherings he'd attended. Unfortunately for the authorities, no one had any concrete proof of wrongdoing, no smoking talisman or even a starting point for an investigation. Today, Wang Jun would fix that.

Peering into the shadows, he investigated the most recent misdemeanor. Events flashed before his eyes like an ultra-fast record, and each image was covered in countless shadowy strings. He searched for quite some time before confirming, unfortunately, that Zhen Fa wasn't guilty after all. Surprisingly, he wasn't responsible for the crime he'd practically admitted to doing.

Undeterred, Wang Jun continued his search. The second set of images, nonsensical to even him, was more jumbled than the first, likely due to the amount of time that had passed. In this case, a moderately wealthy family had accused Zhen Fa of forcefully appropriating assets by confiscating documents and having them retroactively changed. Once again, he found no evidence. The story was apparently a complete fabrication by a rival, one that the Zhen family hadn't even bothered trying to suppress.

Third time's the charm, Wang Jun thought. He dove into the final bundle of dark, shadowy strings he'd summoned. This time, he found what he was looking for. It was a simple letter, but the letter was particularly damning. It was a written request to the Spirit Temple for an assassination. Normally, this wouldn't have been a big deal, but in this case, the request was to assassinate the head of a clergyman's household. Apparently, the clergyman wasn't on good terms with Zhen Fa and had repeatedly rebuffed his attempts to obtain mining permits. After years of back and forth, Zhen Fa had paid for his death.

The Church of Justice had investigated the case. But even with their wonderful powers of investigation, they had failed to find any solid evidence of wrongdoing. According to their rules, that meant they couldn't prosecute. As such, Zhen Fa had gotten off easily. His success had propelled him to the head of the main Zhen family, which boasted twenty successful subsidiary households and substantial assets in Gold Leaf City.

Having found what he was looking for, Wang Jun tugged on the string connected to the shadowy letter, and the object appeared in his hands. It wasn't enough, so he reached deeper until he found a few more strings associated with other documents. They were financial documents that traced the specific transactions. He pulled again, and a dozen or so strings reached across space and time, as fate wasn't restricted by things like time or place. These things weren't part of the current timeline, and all that remained were memories, or shadows of them.

Wang Jun took those shadows. They floated in the air before him, perfect replicas of things that once had been. He breathed in, then blew out a cloud of thick black smoke. It poured into the objects, which solidified. Their emptiness filled in with color, substance, and karmic attachment. The items, which had been destroyed to cover up any evidence, were whole once again.

Task completed, Wang Jun took a step forward and walked into a shadowy room at the top of the mansion. There, he found Zhen Fa's wife fast asleep. The family leader was in his study, busily working away at a business plan for a new mine. Wang Jun cleared his throat, and this time, he allowed the man to hear it.

Zhen Fa looked up with a start. He frowned when he saw Wang Jun's shadowy figure, whose features were completely obscured. "Who are you?" he asked. "How did you get here?" He summoned a spirit sword. The silver blade was an initial-core treasure, a fine weapon for fighting off a typical nighttime invader.

"Relax," Wang Jun said. "Sit down." Then, seeing that the man wasn't going to play along, he pointed his finger downward. Shadowy tethers wrapped around the man and forced him back into his chair.

"Guards!" Zhen Fa shouted. "Guards!" He looked around worriedly, as neither his wife nor the guards showed any signs of responding.

"They can't hear us," Wang Jun said. "But don't worry, I won't be here long. I just wanted to have a nice chat with you in private. It wouldn't be good for either of us if this conversation leaked out."

Zhen Fa struggled for a few moments, unleashing his power as an initial-core-formation cultivator to struggle against his bonds. The shadows surrounding him held fast. "What do you want?"

"I came across some interesting things lately," Wang Jun said. "Exhibit A is a letter I'm sure you're familiar with." He tossed an envelope to the man, who opened it slowly and gasped as he saw the contents.

"How could you possibly have this?" Zhen Fa said hoarsely.

"Money can accomplish many things," Wang Jun said. "Here's another."

He tossed him a black ledger containing transaction records from the same time period. The man's eyes widened as he realized what the documents detailed.

"Oh, and I almost forgot." This time, he walked up to the man. Three glowing blue gems showed different records of a cloaked, semitransparent assassin entering his victim's household. They detailed his journey through each stage of the murder, ending with the assassin retrieving the gems. The same gems he'd given to Zhen Fa to prove the murder had been completed as requested.

The final item was a letter from the Spirit Temple confirming the deed had been done. "I burned this!" Zhen Fa exclaimed. "I crushed those! How can you possibly have them?" By now, all color had left his face, and his hands were trembling. He was livid, unable to calm himself. "Who *are* you?"

"Who I am doesn't matter," Wang Jun said, scooping up the

items. "What you need to know is that I have these and could easily restart the inquiry. The penalty for having a clergyman assassinated is quite steep. I'm sure you'd rather avoid it."

Zhen Fa's shoulders slumped. "What do you want me to do?" he asked.

"I want you to cancel your weapons-purchasing contract with the Wang family," Wang Jun said. "Then, I want you to engage in negotiations with the Brightmoon Trading Group and the Long family. Negotiate hard, but ultimately, award a sole-source contract to the Long family."

Zhen Fa frowned. "That's it?"

"That's it," Wang Jun said. "As the owner of one of the continent's largest mining companies, you spend a substantial amount of money arming both your guards and your miners. The profits involved are substantial."

"And you'll give me the evidence?" Zhen Fa asked.

"No," Wang Jun replied. "That, I'll be keeping safely. It's worth far more than a simple trade contract."

"That's ridiculous," Zhen Fa said. "How do I know you won't just come back and threaten me again?"

"You don't," Wang Jun said. "But you're hardly in a position to bargain." He bowed a deep, mocking bow before turning around and stepping into the shadows. "I look forward to hearing the good news, Zhen Fa," his voice called out as the shadows receded.

A few minutes later, Wang Jun sat inside his room, panting heavily. The ability he'd used, Shadow Fate Redemption, was a draining one. By using the powers of shadow and fate, he'd retrieved objects that had been lost to all but memory, regardless of whether they'd been destroyed. Space and time might have lost them, but shadows remembered. By tapping into the imprint these objects had left in the shadow plane, he'd created identical copies of them.

It wouldn't work for everything, of course. Living things were impossible to retrieve in this way, and anything stronger than a spirit treasure was too powerful to copy for him. But simple things like papers and low-level recording orbs? A piece of cake. Or at least it would be, once he'd completely mastered the ability.

"Was I right to threaten him like that?" Wang Jun said. "Even though he was a bad man?"

His master, Daoist Obscurus, appeared on a chair inside his room. He was reading a book with black pages and shadowy writing. He flipped a page, which let out an inaudible rustle. "It's not like he didn't do anything wrong," the dark man said. "Shadow Fate Redemption only works with real things. He did something, and it's come to bite him back."

"I'm hardly suited to dispensing justice," Wang Jun said.

"This has nothing to do with justice," Daoist Obscurus said, closing the book in a silent *paff*. "We're using information to get something done. You asked if you were wrong to threaten him, and the fact stands that he deserved to be punished. Therefore, why bother with silly things like whether he deserved to be punished by you or the clergy? Isn't it good enough that you did what you did, and he's hardly undeserving?"

"But—" Wang Jun started.

"Enough," Daoist Obscurus said. It was difficult to disobey such a direct command. "Do you want me to teach you or not? If yes, shut up and do what I tell you. If not, just say the word, and I'll leave with not another peep. Are we clear?"

Wang Jun took in a deep breath, then breathed out slowly. "Yes, we're clear."

"Excellent," the man said. "Now rest up. We'll have many busy days ahead of us. That man wasn't the only one in this city keeping a secret. We'll tackle them one by one, and soon, every corrupt man in the Golden Kingdom will be dancing in the palm of your hand."

Wang Jun closed his eyes. He thought about what he'd done, and though it didn't feel terrible, it was a dull ache that kept prodding his sensibilities.

You're just learning, he told himself. *You did nothing wrong. The man deserved it. You did nothing wrong.* He repeated these words like a mantra as his energy stores replenished.

Finally, once the last of his exhaustion left him, he realized how childish he had been. Who on this plane was perfect? Who didn't do morally questionable things? Sometimes there was no right or wrong answer. What mattered was whether you were willing to do what it took to get what you wanted.

Chapter 4: Initiation

Small drops of water formed on Cha Ming's skin as Silverwing descended through the clouds, revealing lush greenery with a large neighboring city. This expanse of wilderness, filled with both humans and demons, was the Evergreen Battlefield, one of the few areas along the North-South border with ongoing skirmishes.

Despite the area being mostly jungle, large mounds that resembled small mountains jutted up from the earth. They weren't rocky like proper mountains; instead, they were covered in greenery, lakes, and bogs. Human combatants roamed these lands, making careful use of the hazardous—and often poisonous—terrain to launch ambushes or fortify their positions. They largely avoided dense demon populations, who had no interest in petty squabbles between good and evil.

Silverwing landed just outside a military encampment located on the north edge of the jungle. "Looks like this is my stop," Cha Ming said to Huxian, hopping off the large bird's back.

And mine as well! Gua said, hopping off with him. Huxian, Lei Jiang, and the mist that was Mr. Mountain remained on the large falcon's back.

We'll be in the North in one demonic territory or another, Huxian said. *We'll need to find a place with dense natural energy for each of us if we want to reach the initiation realm.*

"Initiation?" Cha Ming asked. "Like a senior initiating a junior?"

Something like that, Huxian said. *Demons are of nature, so it is nature itself that must initiate. By occupying a location with dense demonic energy like this one, a demon can draw the power into himself and condense an initiation mark.*

"Take care out there," Cha Ming said, waving. He wasn't worried for the fox's safety, since there were few creatures on the plane that could cause him problems.

Will do, Huxian said,

"Let me know if you need anything," Cha Ming said. "I'll drop everything to come help you if you need it."

Same, Huxian said. He hesitated, then leaned in. *You should know something, Cha Ming. There's something happening out there, something wrong.*

"Like a world war?" Cha Ming asked, perplexed.

Worse, Huxian said grimly. He looked to Silverwing and the others, who nodded back. Even the joker Lei Jiang didn't offer a hint of a smile. *We've started losing dominion over some demons,* he continued. *Inexplicably, and uncontested. There's only one explanation for that: They were killed. Many tens of thousands over a short period of time.*

I've also lost influence over my demonic mountain west of the Song Kingdom, Silverwing squawked. *No one replaced me. It's like the demonic energy just vanished. Things like that don't just happen overnight.*

Cha Ming frowned. "Could it all be a coincidence?"

Maybe, Huxian said reluctantly. *But do you remember that time near Westvale Wall where Wang Jun warned us not to go further?*

Cha Ming nodded.

Well, I scouted further. I didn't like what I saw there. If I'm right... Well, let's just say it doesn't matter who wins the war.

"What was it?" Cha Ming asked.

It doesn't help if you know, Huxian said. *Its name is meaningless. Just know this: If you ever see a creature of darkness covered in horns, a creature that is unkillable and swallows all, don't fight it. You can't kill it, and it will never stop. Run like your life depends on it and hope someone stronger takes care of it. As mortals, we don't stand a chance.*

Dramatic message delivered, Silverwing flapped his massive wings, propelling him and the other two far into the sky.

Hopefully it's nothing, Cha Ming thought. He shook his head and looked to the south. Another wave of fighters was rushing into the battlefield. Cha Ming looked to Gua and summoned 720 sigils of various elements, which shifted into a concealment formation like the one he'd used on Jade Moon Planet. The man and the demon flew into the humid jungle, and Cha Ming ignored the foreboding feeling that gnawed at the back of his mind.

I'll be entering demon territory here, Gua said. They'd reached the center of the Evergreen Battlefield. Here, there were demons aplenty. A poisonous bog covered ten square miles to the west. *I'll be fine, but an ugly human like you would get attacked on sight.*

I think your sense of aesthetics needs work, Cha Ming said dryly, noticing a wart-covered serpent slithering in the brush beside them.

I think your face needs work, Gua said.

Cha Ming was about to retort, but then he noticed something on Gua he hadn't seen before: lipstick. Did the demon really care about his appearance?

Take care, and don't die, Gua continued. *Huxian would be sad if you did.*

Violet demonic energy oozed out of the ground. It turned brown and murky as it surrounded the toad, then melted back into the soggy earth below with Gua in tow.

I wonder how Huxian deals with that narcissist? Cha Ming wondered to himself. As he walked farther south, he took careful note of both the plants that surrounded him and the demons that lurked about. Now and again, he discovered shallow bodies of water covered in thick carpets of leaves and dirt. Anyone unfortunate enough to step there, whether demon or human, would sink into a poisonous trap where thousands of tiny demons waited.

You know, this concealment formation is good and all, Sun Wukong said from inside the Clear Sky World, *but you're missing out on some prime training time.* His spirit appeared beside Cha Ming. The red-bearded man, who now wore a red tail and a thin silver crown, walked through the jungle, expertly avoiding trees and branches as they zoomed past them.

You mean the Seventy-Two Transformations Technique? Cha Ming asked. *How in the heavens did Wang Jun find out about it?*

Sun Wukong shrugged. *No point in worrying about it. He said it was his master who told him, though I'm a bit skeptical but curious about that. I've only revealed my power two times on this plane. The first time was to help you with the lightning tribulation, and the second time was to forge the Nirvana Pill. Not many people were present for these events. Perhaps only the old Sea God Emperor would have understood the significance of my crown and tail. As for that Protector Song, he wouldn't have spotted the truth even if it smacked him in the face. Not that it matters, since he's dead now.*

Could someone have watched in secret? Cha Ming asked.

That's the only way, Sun Wukong said. *But that worries me. A mere transcendent shouldn't have been able to spy on me. Then again, an immortal shouldn't have been able to either.*

Why not? Cha Ming asked. Immortals, along with gods, were the strongest beings in existence. If they couldn't detect Sun Wukong, didn't that mean he surpassed them?

Because immortals are too powerful for a small plane like this, Sun Wukong explained. *If an immortal tried to enter the plane, the plane's will would reject his or her entry. If they tried to enter forcefully, the plane's will wouldn't sit still and would use all its power to force him out, even if that meant wiping out every living thing inside it. Even the slightest leak of immortal power would destabilize the plane. Not many people have the ability to completely hide themselves like that. I doubt even the Jade Emperor could do it.*

Then it's as you said—there's no use worrying about it, Cha Ming said, nodding. *We can't stop anyone that powerful from doing anything to us, so we might as well focus on things that we can affect. Like practicing.*

Like practicing, Sun Wukong agreed. *Now show me what you can do.*

Cha Ming hesitated, but he obliged. He contorted his facial features to match Wang Jun's. At the same time, he changed his height, the color of his skin, his hair, and his eyes. In mere seconds, he was the spitting image of the second young master of the Wang family.

You're still missing something, Sun Wukong said, carefully inspecting his disguise. *Aura.*

Aura? Cha Ming asked.

You've changed your body, Sun Wukong explained. *Now you need to change the aura you release from your cultivation and your soul.*

He tapped Cha Ming's forehead and transmitted a simple creation-qi technique. The technique was easy to understand, so Cha Ming immediately flooded his qi pathways with potent creation qi according to the technique and emulated the feel of Wang Jun's qi. The aura around him darkened, but something still seemed off.

You can't imitate the rest. He has a special constitution that obscures fate. If that could be imitated, everyone and his dog would be doing it.

Fair enough, Cha Ming said. Aura completed, he moved on to the next part: the soul. He merged his transcendent force with creation qi before picturing the feel of Wang Jun's mind and personality. Everyone's soul contained a unique quality that others could use to identify them. He calmed his mind, and the soul-infused creation qi became a blank slate. He wrote it over with everything he knew about Wang Jun: his calmness, his fervent devotion to his family and friends. His dreams for vengeance.

"How's that, my dear heavenly teacher?" Cha Ming asked with a flare. "I doubt anyone would be able to see through this wonderful disguise."

Unless you tried holding a conversation, Sun Wukong noted. *That's why you'll need to use the second technique I gave you—soul skimming.*

Cha Ming nodded. Soul skimming was a non-intrusive technique that picked through a nearby person's recent memories, his aura, and his personality. Not only would it provide him with the necessary tools to imitate a person on a superficial level, he could also use it while speaking to obtain tidbits of relevant information or impressions that would reinforce his disguise.

What about the plan? Cha Ming asked. *Ten years is too much time for me to commit. I know it's important to build up a reputation, and my debt to Wang Jun is as high as the heavens themselves, but the war could be over by then. We need to act faster than that.*

I have a way, Sun Wukong said hesitantly. *But I'd need to take an active hand and alter memories. Given enough time in one location, and sufficiently weak people, I could create a memory of you. That way, if anyone were to pry into your origins, there would be some substance to any false information you plant. As for the rest, you'd need to pay someone to create a fake historical record. Not an impossible thing to do in a big city if you have enough money.*

Tampering with other people's memories, Cha Ming thought. He was uncomfortable with the concept. What were people, if not the sum of their experiences and relationships? Still, he weighed the tampering with the alternative. If he didn't act fast, and the South moved on the North, the consequences would be dire. Countless innocents would die.

Let's do it, he decided. *I've done worse things to people. Since they're innocent, make sure to give them pleasant memories.*

Those take longer, Sun Wukong warned.

That's fine, Cha Ming said. *I'm only willing to go so far. Even in enemy territory.*

Decision made, they continued walking in the Evergreen Battlefield, and as they did, Cha Ming practiced his new techniques. He became the short, devilish Jin Huang. He became the calm, icy Luo Xuehua. He finished off his acquaintances with Jun Xiezi, the calm painter who had lived many lifetimes vicariously.

After perfecting his acquaintances, he began to imitate the many soldiers and mercenaries on the battlefield. One moment, he was a spear-wielding madman. The other, he was a competent tracker, a man of nature who made few mistakes. He used creation qi and creation essence to imitate their weapons, their clothing, and their armor. Anything weaker than a core weapon was easy, but core-formation items could take several minutes to imitate and wouldn't last very long. Time became a blur as Cha Ming lost himself in a sea of new thoughts and emotions.

A week later, Cha Ming sat by a fire under the guise of a soldier. Sun Wukong sat beside him, invisible to anyone else.

You've got humans down to a science, Sun Wukong said. *You've imitated thousands of Southern and Northern cultivators alike. You can imitate devilish auras and transformations, the baleful aura of blood masters, and the pure aura of inquisitors of the Church of Justice. The only people who are beyond you are those from the Spirit Temple.*

They're just too difficult, Cha Ming said, poking at their fire with his spear. *There's something intangible and ethereal to them I can't quite put my finger on.*

How can I complain about your progress when I couldn't hide my tail for aeons? Sun Wukong mused. *Now let's try something fun. Let's try demons.*

Demons? Cha Ming asked, startled. *Is that even possible?*

Why wouldn't it be? Sun Wukong asked, a puzzled expression on his otherwise impish face. *You can change your face and your height, and even your aura. You can see demonic energy currents. The Seventy-Two Transformations Technique, when cultivated to its fullest, will allow you to imitate anything in nature.*

But the internals, the bones, the size, Cha Ming protested.

Just try it! Sun Wukong said.

Cha Ming looked around for a demon, and the first one he spotted was a spirit wolf. It was only twenty feet long, not much bigger than he was. He scanned it with his transcendent soul and began to transform. Pain was the first thing he felt as his bones began creaking and shifting, realigning to fit the image in his mind. Hair grew out of his entire body, and his nose and mouth elongated. His eyes changed, and his teeth grew sharp. Before long, his balance was off. He fell forward, catching himself on two newly grown paws.

Then, he grew. His skeleton was like a blacksmith's puzzle, manipulating it freely until it couldn't move anymore, then somehow finding a way to break apart. His tendons shifted, and his muscles grew. Even his digestive tract grew. Long strands of sinew linked everything together, his vitality knowing just what to do to complete the image in his mind.

As the changes in Cha Ming's body finalized, he became aware of new sensations. His eyes were sharper, and his ears could pick up sounds from a mile away. He also felt a deep hunger for things that revolted the human Cha Ming. He quickly suppressed these feelings and reminded himself that he didn't need to sate them. His mind was still human, after all. Or was it?

It took a full minute to fully transform, after which time Cha Ming mirrored the wolf's behavior and changed his posture and thinking pattern. He was an honorable beast of the forest, a follower in his pack. He kept his head slightly low in a gesture of submission. As for the urge to rejoin his pack, Cha Ming suppressed it.

Good, good, Sun Wukong said. *Very good for a first transformation. Now you just need to learn how to do that about a hundred times faster.*

A hundred times? Isn't that a bit exaggerated? Cha Ming said. He blinked, however, and realized that he'd already transformed back into a human. It had only taken a fraction of a second. His fur had vanished, and his personality had reverted to normal in the blink of an eye. His qi pathways, which had contorted into their demonic equivalent, were back to normal, connected to his Dantian in its independent space. The entire process seemed law defying, but upon closer inspection, wasn't everything he did? Didn't he get his body half destroyed and grow it back again? Couldn't he lose his head and have it grow back? What was a body to him now that he'd reached the peak of marrow refining? He didn't need to eat, drink, or even breathe anymore.

Sun Wukong grinned. *Try it again.*

Cha Ming did so. The transformation only took twenty seconds this time. After a few dozen more attempts, the transformation took less than one second. According to the Monkey King, it would only get faster.

Just like your beast friends can grow and shrink in an instant, so can you, given enough practice. Your first few beast forms will take time to get used to, but soon they'll become second nature. We'll spend the next two weeks practicing on this mountain before leaving.

Cha Ming nodded. The ability to transform into whatever demon he liked would be useful, if only to cut down on travel time. *Let's get started,* he said, picking the next form he wanted to try out. It was a fifty-foot-long badger with bloodred eyes.

Baby steps, he told himself as long claws sprouted out from his hands. The accompanying rage almost overwhelmed him.

Chapter 5: Pai Xiao

Three thousand miles away, an eagle soared across the blue skies of the Ji Kingdom. The eagle was a large demon, a fledgling lord-level demon beast that was a long way from home. Wind ruffled its feathers as it circled down to the forest below, likely looking for a smaller demon to catch and devour. It was hungry, for it had flown for many days to get here.

Using its keen eyes, the eagle scanned its potential victims. It ignored anything larger than a few dozen feet long, as it would take too much time to consume before local predators forced it away.

That's the one, the eagle thought. It spotted a spirit elk measuring twenty feet long and fifteen feet tall. It was a male with smaller horns than most, meaning that it wasn't very important to the nearby spirit elk. Its fate was to wander about the woods and attract predators, sparing the other more important elk from an untimely fate.

The eagle pulled back its wings and lowered itself toward the forest. It increased in speed but nothing major. No need to alarm any beast. Then, when it was a mile away, it pulled its wings back even further, entering a free dive. It shrank as it accelerated, eventually passing the forest's tall trees, evading branches as it went in for the kill. It managed to dodge most of the larger branches, and those smaller ones it hit broke off as they smashed against its surprisingly solid wings.

The small breaking sounds were nothing in the grand scheme of the forest below, but they were enough for the watchful spirit elk. The herd bolted, but it was already too late. The eagle's prey froze in fear as death on wings advanced with unstoppable momentum, holding out its sharp claws and opening its massive beak, landing on the ground with soft feet, and... stopping? Where was the eagle? The creature blinked and realized that, standing before him was a human of all things. The elk blinked again and saw not a human, but an elk. And then a lizard. And then a wolf. The demon constantly transformed until it left the confused elk's line of sight.

When the demon finally reached the edge of the woods, it turned into Cha Ming, who stretched out his now-human limbs and walked to a nearby road that skirted the edge of the forest.

"It doesn't seem so different than the North," he said, casting out his transcendent soul and encompassing a nearby city and a large chunk of the spirit woods around him. There were a few groups of adventurers and bandits camping nearby. Outside the woods and closer to the city, farmers tended the lands. And within the city, all sorts of trade could be seen. He didn't spot the slightest baleful aura among its residents. The city's residents, and even the bandits in the woods, had a normal distribution of merit and sin.

As Cha Ming walked, he passed horses and beasts of burden traveling on a well-worn road. On occasion, a few foundation-establishment cultivators passed him on flying swords. Most of them were guards, but others were traveling adventurers who were here to harvest resources from the spirit woods. Overall, the place reminded Cha Ming of Green Leaf City.

There were some differences, of course. The spirit woods, for one, were far smaller than the large swaths of land near Green Leaf City. The lands were also less fertile. Normal people couldn't live off the activities of local cultivators and needed to tend fields and grow grain and raise cattle. The land here was divided into large plots that were farmed communally. The many families that tended it lived in central residences, a common practice all around the continent.

There's one big difference, though, Sun Wukong said, floating beside him but invisible to anyone but him.

Cha Ming nodded. Now that he was paying attention, he noticed the brands. Every person tending the fields had a dark brand on their forehead. The same applied to those living in the communal residences. The few guards patrolling the fields weren't branded, but they bore small marks on their right or left forearms that matched an insignia on the supervisor's mansion.

Curious, Cha Ming skimmed the thoughts of those he passed, whether they were guards or peasants. He caught glimpses of normal worries when he did. The peasants who tended the fields worried about this year's harvest, their children, and the weather.

The guards, whom Cha Ming had thought were only there to repel predators from the spirit woods, also had another, more important mission: They were there to prevent the peasants from escaping. The peasants weren't normal farmers but serfs. They were property, branded with the mark of their master. Cha Ming's expression darkened as memories of Crystal Falls resurfaced.

Serfdom isn't an uncommon practice in the vast universe, Sun Wukong said as Cha Ming watched them. *The universe is filled with millions of mortal planes. Even good-aligned planes can have a serf system for the lower class. The main issue is that of treatment.*

Slavery, in good-aligned planes? Cha Ming asked doubtfully.

Justice is not the only virtue, Sun Wukong replied. *And there are countless cultures in existence. In some places, serfdom is seen as a kindness to the weak, who would otherwise be unable to take care of themselves.*

Cha Ming looked around. Though the serfs didn't seem unhappy with their predicament, they didn't seem blissful about it either. Moreover, he spotted some lash marks and scars on their bodies. *Not here it isn't.*

Not here, Sun Wukong agreed. Knowing that whatever they did here wouldn't make much of a difference in the grand scheme of things, they continued their journey. The closer they came to the small city, the more cultivators they saw. The nature of the serfs changed as well. In addition to normal mortals, there were also cultivating serfs. All of them were lower than the third level of qi condensation. If there were any at the fourth level, Cha Ming didn't see them.

These cultivating farmers used their affinities to harvest more lucrative crops. Low-level spirit herbs and spirit grains were nurtured by wood and water cultivators. Fire and metal cultivators were busy making tools and construction materials, while earth cultivators either erected buildings or tilled the soil. It was all very orderly and efficient.

When they finally reached the one-mile boundary just outside the city, everything suddenly changed again. They no longer saw any serf marks, and every person in sight was free. Cha Ming passed the guards at the gate using his transcendent force to mask himself. Then, he ducked into a back alley, where he transformed his features to that of a burly man with short black hair. The man didn't need to enter the city, for he hardly ever left it. Pai Xiao, the man he'd just become, straightened out his dark-brown cultivator robes, for what self-respecting smith would ever wear bright colors? He walked back onto Main Street and took in the local environment.

Liaoning was a small city of a million people. It was known as an agricultural town with good access to the spirit woods. As such, not only did it have competent spirit arborists, but it was also home to a few supporting professions. Alchemists, blacksmiths, and spirit doctors were the most common professionals, though there were also a few geomancers. Here, runic artists were rare. Talisman artists were practically unheard of, while formation masters wouldn't deign to live in such a small city. Unlike the North, professionals here didn't associate with guilds. Instead, they learned their skills from families and companies. To advance, one needed to pass a board examination.

Pai Xiao, Cha Ming's new persona and the smith the inhabitants of the city would come to know quite well, had never concerned himself with these exams. The smith had grown up here. No one knew who'd initially taught him, but he advanced through trial and error and had gotten to where he was through sheer experience. His advancement was impressive, given that he'd never hired himself out to any of the bigger families or companies. In fact, he was less than a hundred years old, about middle age for a foundation-establishment cultivator.

First things first, a forge, Cha Ming thought as he reached the industrial area, where he found a small but otherwise well-stocked forge. He knocked on the door, which was quickly opened by a female attendant. "I need to speak to the owner of this forge," Cha Ming said gruffly.

"Do you have an appointment?" the attendant asked.

Cha Ming shook his head, then released a fraction of the cultivation he wanted to project—peak foundation establishment, peak bone forging. The woman yelped and ran to the back, where the pounding of a hammer could be heard. It continued for a few minutes before finally stopping. An older man walked out from the back, shielding the timid attendant that had fetched him.

"Can I help you?" the older man asked, wiping the sweat and soot off his face with a gray towel.

"You can," Cha Ming said. "Do you have a private room we could speak in?"

The man shrugged and led him upstairs.

"Have a seat," the man said as they entered his office. He walked over to a corner, where a kettle and a couple of cups sat. The man ran his fingers along the side of a kettle, which instantly came to a boil. He then poured Cha Ming a cup of tea. "What business does a strong cultivator like you have with a lowly smith like me? There's no way you'd want me to build a weapon for you. It'd break the moment you swung it."

"That's right," Cha Ming said, taking a sip of the hot tea. He grimaced but choked down the bitter concoction. "My name is Pai Xiao, and I'm a spiritual blacksmith. I'd like to buy your workshop."

"Not for sale," the man said, an air of finality to his words. "You can leave now."

Cha Ming nodded, then placed a single spirit stone on the table where they were seated. The man looked confused at first, but then he took in a sharp breath. Though he was only a mid-grade master smith, he'd seen one before. "That's a top-grade spirit stone," the man finally said.

"It is," Cha Ming replied. The man would need to forge and sell thousands of lesser-grade weapons to generate that much profit. Even then, it would be difficult to accumulate such wealth, given how many resources normal cultivation required, much less body cultivation.

"I'll still have to say no," the man said, licking his lips. "I like this town. I grew up here. I might not be rich, but I have every comfort I need. If I wanted to stay, I'd need to buy a forge from someone else or convince the administration to reallocate land. It's not worth the trouble."

The man's memories and thoughts ran through Cha Ming's mind. There was truth to his words, but not the full truth. Cha Ming weighed his options and placed a second top-grade spirit stone on the table. "I want this workshop, your attendant's employment contract, your materials, and your forge. You can keep your hammer and all the weapons you've made. You need to leave the city within three days and not return."

The man hesitated. He'd spoken truthfully about his situation, but it was a hard world out there. How often did opportunities like this come by? He winced before pushing the two stones back toward Cha Ming. "Your offer is very generous, but I'll have to pass."

Cha Ming placed a third stone on the table. "In addition to these three stones, I'll give you a smithing inheritance. The inheritance will only be complete to initial master grade, but it should still be useful to your advancement."

These last words struck a chord with the man. His eyes shot up and focused on him. "You'd sell a smithing inheritance? For a workshop?"

"Yes," Cha Ming said. "Do you accept? I don't want to waste any more time."

"Yes, I accept," the man said immediately. He ignored Cha Ming's outstretched hand—perhaps the gesture had no meaning here—and walked over to the back where he found the deed to the property. "I'll need some time to prepare a writ of sale."

"No need," Cha Ming said. He looked through the documents the man presented him and used creation qi and creation essence to make a similar document in an instant. He bit his finger and infused a hint of Pai Xiao's presence onto it, which imbued it onto the page where his name was already written. He then passed the document to the man, whose name he still hadn't bothered to ask.

"There's a mistake here," the man said, pointing to a spot on the page where the date was written. "This is dated ten years ago."

"That's correct," Cha Ming said. "You sold this business to me ten years ago. That shouldn't be a problem, should it? You've owned it for twenty."

The man licked his lips again. He'd begun sweating, despite the absence of the heat from his forge. "That's fine, but there will be discrepancies. I can't retroactively change every transaction I've made, every registration I've filed with the city, and so on."

"You don't need to concern yourself with all this," Cha Ming said. "I'll take care of it, and I'd be liable for this mistake anyhow."

The man nodded. He bit his finger and sent an infused droplet of blood onto the sheet before signing his name, Li Ning. He then took the spirit stones and gave the ownership documents to Cha Ming, who stored them away in the Clear Sky World.

"Will you be needing anything else?" Li Ning asked.

"I'll be all right," Cha Ming said. "Oh, what's the girl's name from downstairs?"

"Guo Xiang," Li Ning replied. "And the blacksmithing inheritance you promised?"

Strangely, the man didn't seem concerned about Cha Ming possibly backing out. People in the South had an unusual faith in contracts, it seemed.

"Right here," Cha Ming said. He shot his finger out with lightning speed. The man couldn't even react before a stream of information poured into his head. His eyes went blank for a moment before he finally regained his wits.

"Thank you," the man said hoarsely. Though what Cha Ming had given him was worth little in the North, the man was almost tearing up. It seemed simple knowledge like this was worth far more than Cha Ming realized.

"Pleasure doing business," Cha Ming said. "Remember, you must leave town within three days."

"I will," the man promised before walking down the steps. As he did, Sun Wukong appeared beside Cha Ming.

"We could have just stolen his things and changed his memories," Sun Wukong muttered. "It would have been easier and less time-consuming. More fun too."

"But that would have made me a thief," Cha Ming said. "It's bad enough that I'll taking on a part of his identity, his memories of this place, and their memories of him as a basis for my identity. Compensating him generously for it was the least I could do."

"Bah, you're too soft-hearted," Sun Wukong said. "Then again, I like a challenge. I refuse to believe you can't be corrupted."

"I heard you were quite the trickster in your days," Cha Ming said.

"If I called myself the second lord of mischief, no one would dare call themselves first," Sun Wukong said, grinning from ear to ear. "It'll take me a few weeks to work my magic on these people. Changing memories and rearranging karma is no easy task. As for the paperwork, you'll need to pay someone to take care of that."

"You just worry about your end of things, and I'll take care of mine," Cha Ming said.

"And what will that be?" Sun Wukong asked.

"Why, forging, of course," Cha Ming said. "I've done so much reading on the subject. If I'm going to pass myself off as a smith with the Wang family, I might as well do a good job of it."

"It's your time, so you can waste it however you like," Sun Wukong said, yawning. He disappeared from the room but didn't reappear in the Clear Sky World. Given his tremendous workload, he wouldn't return for quite some time. So, Cha Ming no longer paid attention to the spirit. Instead, he began studying a small gem he'd summoned from the Clear Sky World. It was a transcendent-grade hammer focus.

Though Cha Ming had seen his disciple Ling Dong working with metal, he'd never personally tried to make anything himself. According to all the books he'd read, casting your own hammer was the first step. He poured his transcendent soul into the clear, unaligned gem. He was surprised to see that the gem was, in fact, a soul-based metal inscribed with a formation and a spatial fragment.

By linking the hammer focus to his soul, he could summon and dismiss it at will. In addition, he could imprint the image of a hammer on it. By infusing his soul force into the gem, it could take on any imprinted shape, like a hammer, a chisel, or knife. Not only would the tool be strong, it would also be highly resistant to heat.

If I want to learn, it's probably not a good idea to start off with a transcendent crafting tool, he thought. Before he could put it away, however, the Clear Sky Brush came rushing out from a gray slit in space and devoured the transcendent hammer focus in a single gulp.

Cha Ming slapped his hand to his face. Of course it wanted to eat it. Unsurprisingly, the Clear Sky Brush had changed forms yet again. It was now a clear smithing hammer with black and white highlights. A faint five-colored light danced inside it, and in the very center, where the gem had once been, was a soft gray mist.

"You'll need to change your appearance if you want me to use you," Cha Ming said. The hammer shook in defiance. "I'm serious. I can't be seen swinging a clear hammer. It'll give me away." It shook again, not giving an inch.

"Fine," Cha Ming said. He banished what he now called the Clear Sky Hammer—that counted as fair use, didn't it?—and summoned a second gem. This time, it was a mid-grade magic focus. He used his strong soul to fight off the Clear Sky Brush, preventing it from darting out and devouring it as he poured his soul into its runic diagram.

The formation drank in a small stream of his transcendent soul, which caused the gem to balloon in size. He wasn't surprised, as transcendent force was much more potent than the incandescent force the hammer focus was meant for. Cha Ming squeezed out whatever transcendent force he could until the ball finally shrank down to a manageable size. He shaped it into a smithing hammer and activated a second formation on the gem, locking it in place. A gem of this level could lock in two forms, so for the other form, he chose a carving knife. Though a chisel was better suited to making large items, a carving knife was better for detail work. The hammer's shape distorted, and he ejected even more transcendent force from it until it became a simple curved blade. Then, locking it into place, he switched back to the hammer.

"A blacksmith needs a flame," Cha Ming muttered. He summoned the Grandmist flame but immediately banished it. If anyone saw the unique flame, his cover would be blown within seconds. No, he needed to do things the hard way here. In the South, he was not Cha Ming but Pai Xiao, a fire-and-metal dual cultivator. He summoned two flames, a gold one and a red one, and forced them together into an orange-gold flame. It would possess superior temperature control while also possessing the ability to mold and shape metal to some extent. It wasn't a common flame, but neither was it rare. It was a perfect fit for Pai Xiao, an undiscovered talent who'd come very far on his own with little formal training.

Nodding in satisfaction, Cha Ming walked downstairs where the worried Guo Xiang was waiting for him as the old smith, Li Ning, was packing as quickly as possible.

"Relax, there's no need to fear for your job," Cha Ming said. "I'll need *someone* to keep people away while I work." She relaxed visibly when he said this, but much of the discomfort remained.

"Now where did Li Ning put the blacksteel?" he muttered.

The attendant jumped at his words and immediately babbled out a string of incomprehensible words.

"Sorry, what did you say?"

"So sorry, Master," Guo Xiang said. "It's in the warehouse, third row from the back. I'll lead you there right away."

"Please," Cha Ming said. The words they exchanged were few but very telling. She wasn't just his employee; she was his servant. Or so he thought, until he spotted a mark on her forearm near her wrist. It contained a number, a pictograph, and many interconnected lines.

He realized he'd seen that mark somewhere before. It had been on one of the documents Li Ning had passed on to him as part of the sale.

Guo Xiang, it seemed, was his slave.

Chapter 6: Reaping

Black rocks melted in a golden cauldron, which hung atop a fire in the back of Cha Ming's workshop. The ore in the cauldron, a dark-gray rock marbled with lighter gray impurities, was eighty percent blacksteel. The dark metal was one he'd grown familiar with over the past two weeks. It was strong, had a low melting point, and was abundant everywhere on the continent. He'd also seen it used in the other smithies in town, which gave him a reference point for his work.

The black liquid that ran off the gray remnants of the ore was the result of the first step in spiritual blacksmithing: extraction. Like alchemy, each step was crucial in the smithing process. Cha Ming stirred as most of the ore was reduced to a thick black liquid speckled with gray solids. Other ores didn't melt so readily; they could only be partially separated, the remaining impurities needing to be hammered out at higher temperatures to complete the purification process.

Melted blacksteel, on the other hand, could be directly cast into a workable metal. The solid black material could be used to make least-grade or lesser-grade magic weapons, depending on the skill of the smith.

After giving the melting pot another half hour, Cha Ming used his soul force to retrieve the grit, which he placed in a second pot.

There, he intensified the temperature. A quarter of the gray flecks melted into a liquid silver puddle in the smaller pot. This metal, true silver, was useless to his current project, so he poured it into a small brick cast, smacking it out with his hammer into a quench barrel upon cooling. He stored the resulting silver brick on a shelf before returning to the golden pot, which contained the melted blacksteel he desired.

A hundred percent black iron is no good for a high-quality blade, he recalled from a book he'd read. *Runes inscribed on the metal are too susceptible to qi erosion.* The quenched metal was also too soft to make higher-grade magic treasures. Unlike mortal swords, runic ones were better off being hard. There were exceptions to the rule, of course. Things like heavy blades and great axes, whose large size allowed for a more spread-out runic diagrams, benefited from a tougher, softer metal. But he'd already fulfilled his childhood fantasy of making a giant sword earlier this week, so for now, he'd make a longsword.

How much more time are you going to waste here? Sun Wukong asked, appearing beside Cha Ming as he worked. *I finished planting the memories two days ago, and your paperwork was finalized a week ago.*

Not much longer, Cha Ming replied. *I just want to finish this blade for the city lord. Consider it my final apology.* He motioned to a shelf on the side and summoned a small dark-gold brick and a larger dark-silver one. The first was an alloying metal called geralsium. He took the brick of metal, which was soft in its pure form, and cut it in half with a single swipe of his soul-alloy knife. He plopped one half of the gold bar into the pot and stirred it quickly. The metal goop within thickened as the bar melted, forcing him to increase the temperature. The two metals would strengthen and harden as they bonded, allowing Cha Ming to forge a much stronger weapon from the base metal.

An hour later, the last of the gold bar finished dissolving. Cha Ming took the dark-silver bar and began whittling away shavings of it into the golden pot. The shavings quickly dissolved into the molten black metal. There was no change in color or texture of the liquid mixture this time—the changes would only materialize on hardening.

Cha Ming rolled up a cast to the side of the hanging pot once the shavings finished melting. He tipped the pot, and the red glowing metal inside poured into the mold, solidifying into a soft but rectangular shape on contact. The cast grew warm from the excess heat but was otherwise unaffected. He nodded in satisfaction.

You needn't go so far for an apology, Sun Wukong said. *You didn't do anything bad to him. You just tampered with a few memories, meaningless ones at that. Plus, who knows what the man is really like? Maybe that façade of his will crumble away the moment he meets anyone strong enough.*

Call it my gut feeling, Cha Ming said, summoning his spiritual hammer, which he used to knock the crude sword out from the cast. He placed it on a soul-alloy anvil with a pair of tongs and began hammering. Sparks flew for the next quarter hour as, little by little, a blade edge took shape. By then, the metal had cooled back down to an oily black color. Cha Ming stuck it back into the furnace and used his golden flame to heat it once more. The blade glowed red within minutes, and he continued the shaping process. *Two days isn't a lot of time. I owe him this much.*

The next city will take longer, Sun Wukong cautioned. *Will you spend two days for every major player you affect there?*

If it lets me sleep at night, Cha Ming said. He summoned his carving knife and began tracing runic patterns into the soft red blade, which now fully resembled a sword. Some of the runes were for strength, while others were for swiftness and sharpness. The city lord cultivated fire, so he added runes that made the blade better at channeling fire techniques. When the last of the lines were finished, Cha Ming reheated the blade. He waved his hand, and three containers filled with elemental dust flew out and opened above it. The elemental dust sprinkled onto the blade and clung to the inscribed runes, lighting them up in a brilliant pattern.

Once the blade had taken in as much dust as it could, Cha Ming stopped sprinkling and took it over to the quenching barrel filled with liquified elemental essence and other alchemical reagents. He plunged the blade in, and the mixture hissed. He used his control over fire to cool the metal as quickly as possible, sending the excess heat into a nearby heat-trap formation.

Cha Ming ran his finger along the blade edge. It cut his skin easily, though the wound healed over almost instantly. He then walked over to the wall where he kept an assortment of hilts. He picked a golden one with no guard and inserted the blade between its two halves. Then, using his blacksmith's flame, he welded the metal together, finishing the sword.

Aside from the golden hilt, the weapon was mostly black. It also contained hints of red that spread out in a billowing pattern. The blade was a half-step core-grade treasure, the best blade he'd ever made. The hilt was weaker, but it was replaceable.

"Guo Xiang!" Cha Ming called out.

The attendant, who usually avoided his forge due to the high temperatures, poked her head inside.

"Yes, Master?" she asked.

"Come to the back," Cha Ming said. She did as she was told. Cha Ming summoned a sheet of white paper that held a picture of her servant mark. "I'm releasing you from your contract. You're free to go."

Previously, he'd thought about the situation long and hard before ultimately deciding to keep her during his stay, if only for appearance's sake. In return for her service, he would now compensate her with her freedom.

Guo Xiang, the servant girl, widened her eyes in surprise. Contrary to the look of exultation he expected, however, a look of horror appeared on her face. "You mean I'm fired?" she said in a disbelieving tone.

"What?" Cha Ming asked, confused. "No, you're not fired. You're free."

"But that's my employment contract," Guo Xiang said, swallowing. "If you cancel the contract and remove my mark, I'll no longer be bound to serve you. You also won't be bound to pay me. I'll need to go searching for other employment in the meantime, and this town isn't as booming as it once was." She started pacing, fidgeting as she spoke to herself. "This is terrible. How will I survive?"

Cha Ming looked at her blankly. He hadn't expected this situation. He'd been so caught up in his smithing, with most of his time spent in the Clear Sky World, that he hadn't bothered to learn more about the situation. Slavery was slavery, was it not? He used his mind-skimming technique, which he tried using as little as possible, and extracted some details about these "employment marks."

What a strange place, Cha Ming thought as he reviewed the information. In the South, rather than dealing with the whims of mortals, employees were bound by strict contracts using marks. These contracts were all issued by clerks of the Spirit Temple. Unlike serf brands, these weren't permanent. If Cha Ming, her owner, dissolved her mark, she would need to go searching for another job.

"Sorry," Cha Ming said, aiming to defuse the situation. "I misspoke. I meant that I would pay out your contract early, as I'll be leaving this city. I've stayed here for too long. It's time for me to go and seek other opportunities."

With Sun Wukong's magic, the entire city now remembered him having lived there for seventy years. Most mortals that had been around back then were long gone.

Guo Xiang was relieved when Cha Ming placed a small pile of mid-grade spirit stones on the table beside her. She swept them up and bowed in thanks. Such a small amount might be meaningless to him, but it was a fortune to a late-stage qi-condensation cultivator like her. Just enough of a fortune to be helpful but not enough for people to try stealing it.

He thought for a moment, then rummaged through the Clear Sky World. He retrieved a short sword and added it to the pile. "A bonus, for your excellent service. Such opportunities are hard to come by, so you should cultivate and break through. No one can take what you don't have. As for the sword, you'll need to protect it yourself."

"Thank you," Guo Xiang said with a bow. Then, with tears in her eyes, she ran out the door. The memories Sun Wukong had given him were happy ones, and soon all she would remember was a distant memory of a generous employer five years ago.

"I really hate inserting myself into people's lives," Cha Ming said softly. "Even if it's the least violent way to do something." The tampering affected their past and undid many of their previous choices. Choice was something very dear to him.

"If you want, we can go about it using Wang Jun's plan," Sun Wukong offered.

"No," Cha Ming said. "The quicker we go about this, the more likely we are to spoil Zhou Li's plans and take them by surprise. We'll get in and out of their lives as quickly as possible."

Cha Ming looked around the forge and retrieved the valuable metals, his anvil, and some molds. He considered storing the larger items like his furnace but decided against it as this might expose him. Then, he traveled to a small shop in an inconspicuous back alley. He dropped an envelope and spirit stones in front of a man, who nodded before putting away his request. This wasn't a pawn shop like most people assumed, but an outpost of the Greenwind Pavilion. They would sell the location to a promising blacksmith using a contract backdated to five years ago. The trail he'd left wasn't perfect, but it would survive a cursory examination.

His property settled, it was time to go see the city lord. Cha Ming, or Pai Xiao, rather, walked back to the main road and continued walking until he arrived at a mansion just north of the central square. The city lord's mansion was well-maintained but not opulent. The guards, accustomed to him both through planted memories and actual visits, immediately allowed him inside. A servant ran ahead of him to alert the city lord, just in case the powerful cultivator hadn't noticed his presence.

"Uncle Pai Xiao," a voice said from beside him. It was the city lord's youngest daughter, Mo Ling. Unlike most people on the continent, her hair was brown instead of black. The young woman's light-brown eyes glimmered with excitement and curiosity.

"How goes your schooling, little one?" Cha Ming asked. He took a seat in the guest room as the city lord prepared himself upstairs.

"I'm hardly little," Mo Ling said, wrinkling her nose. "And school is boring. I understand cultivation, and I'm already a foundation-establishment expert at the young age of twenty-one. But do I really need to learn accounting, of all things? And management?"

"They're both important skills," Cha Ming said. "Whether for your own estate or for your future husband's. I, for one, find myself needing to hire people to do such things. Otherwise my smithy might become insolvent without me realizing."

She looked at him with suspicion. "I just don't want to be contained," she said. "I want to roam the kingdom and be an adventurer. I want to battle fierce demons and clear out bandits like they do in the stories."

"It's not all fun and games," Cha Ming said, leaning back on the sofa and closing his eyes.

"Oh? You've done all these things?" Mo Ling asked, her eyes brightening.

"In my youth," Cha Ming admitted. "But my injuries accumulated. One day, while adventuring, I discovered a basic smithing inheritance. It felt like destiny. So, I sold my sword and dedicated myself to smithing. The rest is history."

Mo Ling nodded and fetched hot water and tea leaves. She poured them tea as they waited for her father, who soon walked into the living room looking flustered. He looked pale and tired, which was odd given his identity as a peak-foundation-establishment cultivator.

"What brings you in today?" the city lord asked, fatigue practically dripping from his words. He took a cup of tea from Mo Ling with trembling hands. The trembling stopped as he took a sip of the soothing hot liquid. A hint of color also returned to his face.

"Is something the matter?" Cha Ming asked, noting his unusual mood. "I can come back at a better time."

"No, that's quite all right," the city lord said. "I have about a quarter hour to spare."

"Then I'll be quick," Cha Ming said. A black longsword appeared in his right hand, golden hilt facing the city lord, Mo Zhen. "This is for you. A gift for all your years of good service during my stay in this city."

The city lord shook his head and pushed Cha Ming's hands away. "This is too great a gift, Master Pai Xiao. And what is this you're saying about a stay in this city? Are you leaving us at last?"

Cha Ming smiled wistfully. "I've reached the peak of what I can achieve in a small city. I can only go so far without gathering more knowledge."

The city lord nodded. Everyone had been discussing the eventual occurrence for quite some time. He hesitated but still firmly pushed the sword back.

"This is too expensive," Mo Zhen said. "Although it's not a core treasure, I can tell it's not a magic treasure either."

"It's a half-step-core treasure," Cha Ming said. "My best work yet. It far exceeds the ten blades I crafted for the city's protectors." He'd crafted those blades as a focus for the web of memories Sun Wukong had created.

"It's too great a gift," Mo Zhen protested again.

"It's what you deserve," Cha Ming said, forcing it back.

Then, seeing that the city lord wouldn't take it, he plunged it into the stone floor. Several servants, who had been listening in on the conversation, gasped in shock. "If you don't like it, I'll leave it here. Perhaps one of your children will claim it, assuming they don't cut themselves on it."

Mo Zhen grinned. "Very well. Perhaps it will come in handy." He grasped it by the hilt, then put it away in his storage ring. Then he leaned forward and whispered a few words. "You should be careful. The reapers are coming."

The term was unfamiliar to Cha Ming, but for some reason, it sent chills down his spine.

"The reapers?" Cha Ming said, wracking his brains for memories or hints of them. He found none.

"It's been a few decades since they've come, but I'm sure you remember the last time," Mo Zhen said.

"Yes," Cha Ming lied. "It was a horrible time." He used his transcendent soul to skim the man's memories, but he only discovered scattered fragments. The man was too strong, and unless Cha Ming was willing to damage Mo Zhen's mind, that was all he would get. Cha Ming closed his eyes and observed the fragments. He saw fear, wailing husbands and wives, and crying parents. Mo Zhen's sister had been taken. The fate Mo Zhen had imagined for her was so terrible he'd surrounded it in a protective cocoon of willful ignorance.

"They can't be avoided, so you should hide instead," Mo Zhen continued. "Run away from this town. Though I doubt they'd pick a fight with you—you have no sponsor. These are uncertain times, so no one can say what will happen."

Cha Ming shook his head. "I'll accompany you. Perhaps with a show of strength, the reapers won't take much."

"If only it were so simple," Mo Zhen said. He was about to continue explaining, but at that moment, horns blazed at the city gates. Mo Zhen's face paled at the sound. "They're here," he whispered. "Spirits above, they're here." He raised his voice and shouted out a command. "Everyone, gather up. Assemble lines. Guard Captain?"

"Sir!" a man said, walking into the living room.

"Have the guards gather all the cultivators in the city within five—no, three minutes," Mo Zhen said. "No exceptions. If anyone tries to hide, even I won't be able to stop the reapers from executing their entire family."

The captain saluted and flew out, shouting orders to the guards. The city buzzed with activity. While mortals hid, cultivators were rustled up from their houses. Even those in closed-door seclusion were interrupted. The city lord's own family was no exception; his wife and four of his children were gathered in the foyer. Seeing that everyone was accounted for, the city lord walked out of the front doors and into Central Square, where all the cultivators in the city had been gathered. Even those with serf brands, who weren't normally allowed into the city, had formed their own group.

The city lord, his family and personal guards in tow, passed the cultivators and serfs and stood before them. He waited patiently as a dozen men in red robes, along with one in a black robe, casually walked down the street toward them. Three of them were peak-bone-forging cultivators, while the rest were late-bone-forging cultivators. Their leader was, impressively, a marrow-refining cultivator. Mortals trembled in fear as they passed merchant stalls, occasionally taking something that interested them. Fortunately, most men knew better than to fight back. They simply cowered behind their stalls, letting the men do as they pleased.

Remind me, please, Cha Ming sent. *What happens now? My memories are a little hazy.*

How lucky for you that they are, Mo Zhen sent back. *The reapers don't come often, but when they do, they usually reap one percent of our cultivators. They take them back to their monastery, where they are never seen again. No one knows what happens to them, but some say they are used to rear terrible blood monsters. Others say blood masters devour men, and the only reason anyone remains in the South is that they only need to eat every year or so.*

Cha Ming's eyes narrowed. *One percent? Out of the ten thousand cultivators here, they'll take and kill one hundred?*

The slave-like employment contracts were one thing, but this? It was effectively institutionalized murder.

Not right away, Mo Zhen said. *I don't know the exact details, but they take them back to the monastery first.*

Why don't we just fight them? Cha Ming asked. *I'm sure that with you and I, we could kill them.*

And what will we do when the monastery sends a punishment squad? Mo Zhen asked gloomily. *We could easily kill them, but the price for our insubordination would be the lives of every man, woman, and child in this city. I've heard tales of those who've crossed them. None have survived.*

Then who tells the stories? Cha Ming said. *Would the king of Ji do nothing if they tried to slaughter us?*

The king is the one who grants them the writ that allows them to cull lives! Mo Zhen said hopelessly. *Anyone who defies the writ has committed treason. Why would he interfere in deserved punishment?* He shook his head. *No, we must endure the loss of the few for the sake of the many. It's just the way things are. All we can do is hope they don't take those we love and console those who remain.*

The red-robed men, who'd taken their time strolling into the city, arrived before the city lord. Ten men, the protectors of the city who'd originally stood with the other cultivators, stepped up beside the city lord in a token show of strength. The lead reaper chuckled as he pulled back his hood, revealing a bald head covered in red tattoos. The others beside him did the same. While most were dark haired and dark eyed, some of their irises were faintly red colored. Two of them had filed teeth. Only one man kept his hood up: the black-robed man from the Spirit Temple who accompanied them.

"I'm glad to see no one sought to escape this time," their leader said. "Though it's exciting to chase down stragglers, we don't have much time today. I take it you recognize this king's writ?" He threw a paper to the city lord, who breathed in sharply when he saw what was written.

"Ten percent?" the city lord said hoarsely. "Are you mad?"

"I hope," the man cut in, "that you're not implying that the king is mad?" He stepped toward the city lord, only stopping once he was a foot away. "The kingdom is preparing for war, my dear city lord. War is expensive, both in money and lives. We cull to strengthen ourselves, to strengthen our kingdom. Everyone must contribute."

The city lord gulped. His sword arm bulged, and his hand clenched and relaxed repeatedly before he finally calmed himself. He closed his eyes. "Just choose and be gone."

"Splendid," the man said. He looked over the cultivators, carefully inspecting them. His eyes lingered on Cha Ming and the many protectors, but ultimately the man looked away. Cha Ming suspected it wasn't worth his effort to pick on the strong.

"For the sake of fairness, we will be picking randomly," the lead blood master said, his voice reaching the entire crowd. "If any of you try to resist, we will find and execute all your relatives, your friends, and anyone who lives within a city block of you. If a hundred resist, we will cull the entire city." He lifted a finger, and a thousand crimson lights appeared. They shuffled around and shot out to those assembled. True to his word, they all struck random targets.

"Everyone hit by a light, step out," the lead blood master said. A quarter of the men and women who had been selected did so, pale and frightened, but many lingered.

"I said STEP OUT!"

Most of the others walked out reluctantly. Those who didn't were glared at by their neighbors until they eventually accepted their fate and moved, if only for the sake of those they knew and loved.

If you're willing to fight with me, Cha Ming sent to the city lord, *we can kill every last one of them. No one will ever never know what happened to them.* The thousand men and women who had stepped out were led into a circle by the blood masters. He recognized a few of the cultivators, but fortunately, none of them were his close acquaintances. Still, that didn't make it an easy pill to swallow. He'd tampered with their memories, after all. He owed them.

You mustn't, the city lord said. *They have ways of knowing. The Spirit Temple will investigate us, and the entire city will suffer.* Though his words urged restraint, his body thought otherwise. His hand clutched his sword, ready to draw it and behead someone at the drop of a pin. Being the city lord in such a situation had to be a difficult burden for anyone to bear.

"That concludes our selection," the blood master said.

The crowd sighed in relief. As he turned toward the group of blood masters, however, a voice cut in. It was the man from the Spirit Temple.

"Wait," the man said. He lifted a bony white finger and pointed toward Cha Ming. As Cha Ming put up a hand to his chest in surprise, the man waved him away impatiently. "Not you, her."

Cha Ming looked back and realized he was pointing at Mo Ling, the city lord's daughter. "She is proper stock for the Spirit Temple. We will take her as well."

Cha Ming's muscles tensed. Potential plans buzzed through his mind, but they were interrupted by the humming and burning of a black sword, a sword he'd just forged.

"You will *not* take my daughter," the city lord said, his voice filled with rage. The air around the man burned brightly as he pushed out toward the man from the Spirit Temple, who simply smirked from beneath his deep hood.

Suddenly, there was a blur of red. The lead blood master, who had only been a few feet away, slashed out with a blade of blood so quickly that Cha Ming couldn't even react. As a marrow-refining cultivator, the man's physical speed was far faster than what even core-formation cultivators were capable of. The city lord's arm dropped to the ground.

The blood master, ignoring the city lord's whimpers, bent down to pick up the black-and-red blade. "Good sword," he said, placing it into his storage ring. He pushed past Cha Ming and grabbed Mo Ling by the shoulder and dragged her toward the crowd in the distance.

You need to relax, Cha Ming told himself. His body was tense, and he wanted nothing more than to bash their skulls in. *If you do something now, the whole city might be destroyed. But if you wait until they leave the city, there could be many reasons for their disappearance.*

Or perhaps he could drag them back to their so-called "monastery." There, he'd kill them all and rescue the captives. As he pondered this, however, his hairs raised on end. He sensed movement from the blood masters. Out of the corner of his eye, he saw the blade of blood rise. Then, faster than he could react, it slashed across the entire crowd, spilling blood onto the stones. Their blood formed a whirlpool that flowed into a bloodred stone the lead blood master held. Out of all those taken, only Mo Ling, who'd been set off to the side, still lived."

"What have you done," Mo Zhen growled. He was kneeling, still holding the bloody stump where his arm used to be.

"There were too many of them to cull at the monastery," the chief blood master said nonchalantly. "Now be a good city lord and raise many more strong cultivators. If the harvest isn't good next time, you and your entire city will be culled."

"You monster," Mo Zhen spat.

"Yes," the chief blood master said. "I suppose I am." He floated up in the air, holding the struggling Mo Ling in his arms. The others all hopped on flying swords and flew out of the city after him.

"It wasn't supposed to be this way," Mo Zhen said, his tears splattering against the stones of Central Square. He ignored the stump of an arm that lay off to his side as he beat the ground repeatedly with his remaining fist. His wife moved in with a piece of torn robe to staunch the bleeding, but he pushed her back. "Pai Xiao, promise me that you won't…" his voice trailed off.

Pai Xiao was already gone. He was an avian demon now, soaring far above the clouds, trailing the blood masters as they returned to their monastery. His eyes glowed red with hatred.

Cha Ming could berate himself all he wanted for not killing them earlier, but he couldn't change what had already happened. Those thousand were dead, as was likely the case in many more cities. All he could do now was follow and save Mo Ling and anyone else they came across. That, and slaughter each and every blood master in the monastery they were taking her to.

He would bury them along with the dead.

Chapter 7: Culling

Cha Ming followed the blood masters as they traveled toward their monastery. He kept a careful eye out on his surroundings as he flew across the skies. To his relief and grief, they didn't stop at many villages like he'd thought they would. Then he realized it was because they'd already been there. Grieving parents lamented the passing of their children, while wives mourned the passing of their husbands and vice versa. Every village, without exception, was holding a mass funeral for their loved ones.

The proceedings were rushed, almost frantic. These smaller villages had been hit even harder than Liaoning. Here, it wasn't just cultivators that had been reaped but serfs as well. A tenth of the mortal serfs had been brutally murdered, leaving only bloody grass behind. Hundreds of thousands of souls had been lost in only a few days. Cha Ming's anger mounted with each passing village.

Two hundred miles later, they arrived. The Blood Master Monastery was a jagged building that jutted out of the lush plain it inhabited. No animals or demons dared approach it, for the place reeked of death and slaughter. It was a small building, enough to house a few thousand men. A large empty practice yard occupied the center of the complex. There, men fought bloody battles that would spell certain death for normal body cultivators. Fortunately for them, they weren't normal; they were blood masters.

The blood masters returned to their training the moment they arrived. Their leader dropped Mo Ling to the ground and took the bloody stone they'd collected to the tall building adjacent to the training grounds. Mo Ling was brought to another, smaller building by the black-robed man from the Spirit Temple. She was placed in a holding cell where she was restrained but otherwise unharmed. She was safe for now, so he waited.

Hours passed as group after group of blood masters returned. At sunset, the skies seemed to weep tears of blood. Cha Ming knew that every team who returned meant hundreds of thousands more had died to the vicious and cruel men and women who lived here. There was only one thought he could take solace in: When he killed them, they'd never be able to harm anyone again.

He waited an entire day before the last of the blood masters returned. Once the last had returned, the head of the monastery distributed small red beads to each of them. They immediately went to work using this concentrated blood vitality to cultivate blood arts and strengthen their cultivation. The strongest among them, the abbot of the monastery and a mid-grade-marrow-refining cultivator, did the same.

An agonizingly slow day passed under Cha Ming's watchful eye. He only moved when the man from the Spirit Temple—a medium, it turned out—entered Mo Ling's holding cell. The man began preparing tools and glyphs he couldn't understand, along with massive piles of sin crystals.

There are ghosts down there, you know, Sun Wukong said. *It's probably best to do something about them.*

Cha Ming nodded. He'd never fought ghosts before, certainly not on such a massive scale.

I only know the few formations I obtained from the Church of Justice back then, Cha Ming said. *I'll need to modify something.*

He took a few precious minutes to rearrange the elementary diagram in his mind, adding to it and expanding it using the many formation principles he'd learned over the years. The result was an early-core-grade grand formation. It was a mile wide and completely circular. From the previous formation he'd set up, he estimated that this new one would be able to detect ghosts below the resplendent realm. *Do you think there are any stronger sprits down there?*

Doubtful, Sun Wukong answered. *It's not a full Spirit Temple, so there's no need for them to spend so many resources spying. What will you do about messages and those trying to physically escape?*

I've learned a few tricks over the past hundred years, Cha Ming said. He took out the Space-Time Camera and held it toward the monastery. He fed a few top-grade spirit stones into the camera, which didn't refuse the abundant offering after so long without. Then, he took careful aim before snapping a picture. A moving picture.

I don't have to take a still shot every time, he explained. *I can simply freeze the boundaries, and the seal's energy will only be depleted when they try to exit. Communication with the outside world will be impossible.*

Satisfied with his barrier, Cha Ming swooped down. He was an eagle now, and the eagle dive-bombed toward the blood monastery. Once it was five hundred meters away, it transformed back into Cha Ming, who threw out 360 formation flags with glowing white runes. There was no need to use top-grade spirit stones to feed it. He drew on Huxian's light-based demonic qi and used it as ink instead. It infused the grand formation with power, which activated and revealed a hundred or so ghosts. The formation hadn't been laid in secret, so the moment it activated, the monks panicked.

"Intruder!" someone yelled. Bells tolled as members assembled in the square. Since time was of the essence, Cha Ming held out his Clear Sky Staff and rapidly extended it toward the building containing Mo Ling. It pierced through the roof, stabbing through the surprised medium's chest with surgical precision. Cha Ming retracted the staff, using the movement to pull himself forward. Mo Ling screamed as he smashed through the roof, slapping the medium's escaping spirit with a wave of creation qi. It screamed as it dissipated to nothingness.

"Stay here," Cha Ming, who was now Pai Xiao, said to Mo Ling. Seeing a familiar face, she let out a sigh of relief. Pai Xiao walked out of the room, large staff slung over his shoulder. The blood masters had all stopped their cultivation and swarmed into the courtyard.

All the better to kill them in one fell swoop.

"Abbot, he's done something to our transmission jades," one of the blood masters said. "We can't send out any messages."

"Abbot," another man said, "we tried to send out a messenger, but he couldn't get past an invisible boundary ten feet outside the monastery."

The grandmaster ignored the men. Instead, he studied Cha Ming, who was calmly approaching them with a staff slung across his shoulder. "Who are you?" he asked calmly. "Why have you come here?"

"Oh, I was just a nobody until recently," Cha Ming said. "But then you decided to cull the countryside. It's too bad you upset the wrong person."

"Oh?" the abbot said. He grinned, revealing a set of sharp, filed teeth. "And you alone will stop us? That's very brave of you. I'll be sure to take my time tasting that strong and delicious body of yours."

"You're welcome to eat me if you can," Cha Ming said. "Now, are you going to fight me one at a time or will you save me the effort and come all at once?"

The abbot took out a black jade slip. He crushed it, and Cha Ming felt the blood in his body boil with excitement. The building behind the abbot blew apart, sending splinters of enchanted wood all around the courtyard. A large pool of blood vitality appeared as a whirlwind of bloody mist. The abbot brought his hands to the front as though praying. Then, he thrust them outward.

The bloody mist split in two. Half of it shot into the majority of the monks, invading their bodies without permission. They didn't rebel against the bloody energy but drank it in greedily. Their eyes glowed red, and large red veins spread out from their hearts, covering their entire bodies in an intricate meshwork of violent energy. Their strength soared, and in only three seconds, they began breaking through one at a time.

Paff. Paff. Paff. The sound of breakthroughs echoed throughout the courtyard. Though they were rushed breakthroughs and would have dire future ramifications, they were still significant increases in strength. Some of the weaker blood masters used the excess energy to shoot for a second breakthrough in the bone-forging realm. More pops filled the air as they closed the gap with their seniors.

The second mass of bloody vitality didn't shoot into these lesser monks. Instead, it shot into the abbot himself. The middle-marrow-refining cultivator channeled the energy into carefully prepared runes on his skin. Unlike the others, this man had clearly been preparing for the increase in power. His energy levels mounted chaotically, and just as the last of the junior monks finished stabilizing their condition, a sharp crack filled the air. The abbot broke through to late marrow refining.

"We might have wasted more than half the blood essence we gathered due to rushing, but we can always get more," the abbot said calmly. "Alas, how else are we to fight one like you, a person I can't even begin to see through?"

"Burn in hell," Cha Ming said. As the men had been transforming, he hadn't been idle. He'd covertly sent 512 combat sigils throughout the entire courtyard and connected them with blazing red qi. He connected the last line and poured most of his fire qi into the sigil network. The entire battlefield erupted in a sea of flames. The blood masters screamed as their skin and blood burned and boiled. They leaped at him with blades, staves, swords, and scythes while simultaneously using their blood arts to restrain his body's movements.

Cha Ming was unfazed by their sudden attack. He shrugged off their feeble attempts and swung out with his staff, striking dozens at a time with the giant pillar. The blow caused the space around the staff to warp and crackle. Despite many of those charging at him being marrow-refining cultivators, with dense reserves of vitality, not a single person survived the dreadful strike from the transcendent artifact.

"Self-detonate!" the abbot ordered coldly. "Our leaders in hell will treat us well for our sacrifices today."

Unlike what Cha Ming had originally expected before coming,

none of the blood masters were devils. It was as though being devilish was at odds with the art they practiced. Instead, every one of them had accumulated a thick ochre glow that rivalled that of the many devils he'd slain.

Bodies exploded around Cha Ming at the abbot's command. Some of them even pierced his qi shields and struck his body, eating deep pits into his skin and muscle. But why would Cha Ming, a peak-marrow-refining cultivator, care about mere flesh wounds? His skin and muscles regrew almost instantly.

As the blood masters self-detonated, avoiding a certain death at the hands of Cha Ming's formation, Cha Ming swung his staff at the abbot, who held up a peak-core treasure to defend. It shattered as soon as the Clear Sky Staff touched it. Crushing chaos burned away at the man's blood vitality as his body stubbornly regenerated around the pillar. At first, the man grinned as he pulled himself forward while his wounds healed. After all, he was a marrow-refining cultivator, and a blood master at that. Killing him was nigh impossible.

His grin soon faded, however, as his pool of blood vitality burned away with no end in sight.

"I am invincible!" the abbot yelled. "I can't be killed by a mere mortal!" He growled, and suddenly, his hands became sharp claws. His figure flickered as he pushed himself along the Clear Sky Staff and appeared before Cha Ming. He dug his claws deep into Cha Ming's chest, and blood vitality began oozing out from the fresh wounds. It funneled into the blood master and began to heal him.

"You think you can handle my power?" Cha Ming asked softly. "Drink it in, then. Drink it all."

He hadn't wanted to waste time with the blood master, but the memories of the slain were fresh in his mind. He wanted the man to suffer, so he emptied his meridians of normal qi and filled them with something most people weren't equipped to handle: destruction qi. His body regenerated as it broke apart bit by bit while delivering the qi to where the man's claws were inserted. The abbot drank it in, and to his horror, the black energy quickly spread throughout his body like a poison. Black lines of destruction traveled into the abbot's body. He pulled out his claws, but it was already too late. His body smoked and hissed as it fell apart, unable to regenerate from the intense destruction it suffered. The square grew silent as the abbot crumbled to ashes and the other blood masters that hadn't self-detonated burned in the formation's flames.

"It's done," Cha Ming muttered. His assailants were dead, so he directed the formation to burn all other buildings and melt the stone in the monastery. The ghosts patrolling the area weren't spared either. By the time he'd finished his work, all that was left of the place was the building containing Mo Ling. She sat down, holding her knees close to her body, crying, trembling, and coughing from all the smoke.

Cha Ming banished the smoke with a wave of his hand and held out his other. "Come. We need to go."

She hesitated, then took it.

"Is that really you, Pai Xiao?" she asked.

The man might be their town's hero, but she'd never heard of him being capable of unleashing such destruction. Where was the kindhearted man she knew, the one who liked helping people and building wonders?

"Yes, it's me," Cha Ming said. "But don't tell a soul what you saw today, all right? The consequences would be catastrophic for you, me, and Liaoning."

Mo Ling nodded.

They walked out of the monastery hand in hand as the flames died down. Then, after setting fire to the last building, Cha Ming picked her up and flew off toward the South with a speed very few in the continent could match. Once he was fifty miles away, he stopped and set up a concealment formation. Then he built them a fire and summoned a shelter using creation qi and creation essence.

"We'll have to stay here for a few days," Cha Ming said, warming his hands over the fire. A powerful presence was heading toward the monastery from not far away. "Someone powerful is out there, and we need to lie low to keep safe."

"Thank you," Mo Ling said. No smile lit her face, and her gaze didn't focus anywhere specific. Cha Ming could practically see the troubled thoughts rampaging through her innocent mind.

Cha Ming, unsure of what to say, poked at the fire, sending sparks into the night sky. It was a starless night, with the moon hidden by a dense carpet of clouds. Minutes passed before finally, the young woman who'd survived when a thousand others had been killed and millions of mortals had been slain, began crying. The emotions she'd bottled up over the past two days emptied out in a few short minutes.

When she was finished, the red-eyed girl looked up to Cha Ming, who'd continued stubbornly poking at the fire. "I can't go back, can I?"

Cha Ming shook his head. "No, you can't. If you do, they'll know you were involved. Not only would your family suffer, but your entire city might be slaughtered." The South was a brutal place, far more brutal than he'd ever imagined until just a couple of days ago. "You'll have to change your name and your identity. It probably wouldn't hurt to dye your hair and change how you dress."

"And what about you?" Mo Ling asked. "Where will you go? You can't go back either."

"I was going to leave anyway," Cha Ming replied. "I'll go to Ashes, the third-largest city in the Ji Kingdom."

"And you'll be safe there?" Mo Ling asked, doing her best to hide her agitation.

"Safe enough," Cha Ming answered. Hearing Mo Ling's stomach rumble, he sighed and summoned rations with creation qi like he'd done in the past. He did the same for water. She ate and drank in silence, but he could tell at a glance what thoughts were running through her mind. "I'll take you with me," he finally said. "For now."

The girl nodded. She ate what she could and fell asleep, leaving Cha Ming to keep watch. He cultivated as they waited, doing his best to ignore the sadness in his heart.

Chapter 8: Icy Heart Pavilion

Within an isolated chamber in the Red Dust Pavilion, Hong Xin sat on a lonely stage. She held a black-and-gold flute in her hands, the same flute she'd trained with at the Red Dust Pavilion. No, trained wasn't the right word; she'd been broken there, and remade. Her passion had been dancing, and they'd taken that away from her, forbidden her from practicing it. Fortunately, all that remained from that painful time was the flute she'd hated with all her heart.

These days, she enjoyed playing the flute. Like any other instrument, it was a tool. It played the music you wanted, but only as well as you could play. And she could play, and well. She wasn't the best, of course—that would take decades of practice—but her songs could move hearts, break barriers, and soothe nerves. Currently, she was doing just that. Her fingers moved as she blew softly over the central mouthpiece, producing a soft whistle of a melody.

What is the Icy Heart Pavilion, really? she thought as she played. *Is it really just like the old Red Dust Pavilion, or have they changed their ways?* Was it a terrible place like she imagined, or was it all in her head? Their members were older members of the Red Dust Pavilion who had undergone the same training as her, but did that mean they taught the same path? Things were different now. For one, they no longer had possession of the Frozen Heart Oath Stone. For another, they weren't ruled by the same person, who'd go to great lengths to extract any bit of value from every young girl who entered their halls. Their current leader was an enigma to Hong Xin, one she hoped to figure out soon enough.

How ironic it was that *they* were the ones who held the stone and used it. But what was she to do? Mistress Shan and the original teachers of the academy had personally broken many of their members. Even more young girls had been driven to their deaths for the sake of results. They had blood on their hands, and she wasn't about to let murderers roam free. Wasn't it a mercy that she spared their lives and put them to good use?

Many similar feelings passed through her mind as she played, wearing away at her resistance toward the Icy Heart Pavilion with music. Today, they would be going on a diplomatic mission in enemy territory.

No, not an enemy territory, Hong Xin thought. *You're doing it again.* She played more furiously, working through her emotions with every note she hit true. She spent a quarter hour easing her raw nerves. A knock on the door came just as she finished.

"Come in," Hong Xin said, flicking a rune beside the door with her resplendent force. The rune turned from green to red, red meaning the room was available. The door opened, allowing Bai Ling to enter.

"Are you ready?" Bai Ling asked. "Our appointment is in a quarter hour."

"And since when has anyone in Gold Leaf City ever been punctual?" Hong Xin asked as she put away her flute. She cleaned it by first extracting the moisture, then heating the entire instrument to evaporate any remainder. There was no wood on the instrument, so the lack of humidity wouldn't hurt it. Corrosion was the main concern.

"In casual or friendly circles, within a quarter hour of the appointed time is fine," Bai Ling said. "But in business circles, within five is preferable. Showing up earlier shows deference. Showing up later signals superiority."

"Then we'll show up precisely on time," Hong Xin said. She

summoned a mirror and briefly adjusted the gold jewelry on her hair. "Let's go."

Bai Ling nodded and led her out of the chamber and down the hallway to where Ji Bingxue and Mistress Huang were waiting. They fell in line behind the two as a few dozen core-formation guards formed ranks around them. The guards, while excessive, were necessary to show off their status. It was also indicative of their group's capabilities.

The procession walked out of the Red Dust Pavilion and headed toward the east exit of Gold Leaf Square. Mortals and cultivators alike gawked at them. Though it was only early afternoon, many parents and grandparents accompanied children, while other people were busy running around for some reason or another, like bees out gathering pollen for the central hive. They traveled for twelve minutes, so by the time the Icy Heart Pavilion was in their sights, only two minutes remained before the appointed time. Bai Ling sped up their pace slightly. They arrived at exactly three o'clock in the afternoon.

Concurrent with their procession's arrival, members of the Icy Heart Pavilion filed out to welcome them. Like them, they'd decided not to wait outside but come out at precisely the same time.

At least we're thinking the same way, Hong Xin thought. Whether it was out of respect for their feelings or arrogance was yet to be seen. The Icy Heart Pavilion was inferior to the Red Dust Pavilion in both membership and finance.

The last member to exit the building was a peak-core-formation cultivator, just like they were. She bowed lightly and gestured toward the open door. "Right this way, Red Dust Mistress," the woman said. "I am one of the three vice heads of the Icy Heart Pavilion, Vice Head Li. You may call me Ling Fei if you wish."

Hong Xin nodded and followed along. "Many thanks for welcoming us to your pavilion, Vice Head Li. We would have to come to see you earlier, but you'd just established yourselves and were expanding at a frightening pace. We were afraid we'd get trampled if we visited earlier."

"Many thanks for your kind words," Ling Fei said. "Though it might seem like we were expanding, we were only securing contracts with existing or past clients. Things are much less busy now that we've stabilized our core relationships."

They walked down a long hallway filled with paintings. While the Red Dust Pavilion featured art filled with life and energy, the Icy Heart Pavilion's paintings featured simplicity and frigid snow. They walked halfway down the corridor before stopping before a black door where a guard stood. "Song Dai, did you have the cooks prepare a meal and wine for the Red Dust Pavilion's honor guard as instructed?"

The guard put his clenched fist to his heart and bowed lightly. "Of course, Vice Head. Everything is ready. I see they've brought a twelve-member guard. Our twelve highest-ranking guards will accompany them shortly."

Hong Xin looked to the head of their own honor guard, a middle-aged middle-core-formation cultivator called Lu Dongjian, who nodded.

"We'll be glad to accept food, but wine might be too strong a drink for us to share so early in the day," Lu Dongjian said.

"I was thinking the same," Song Dai said, ushering him and the other guards into a room filled with tables. "Which is why the wine we prepared isn't the slightest bit intoxicating. We only drink for flavor—after all, we're on duty."

"Then who am I to reject?" Lu Dongjian said. The rest of the guards walked in, and the door closed behind them. There would be no need to bother them, assuming everything went well. If there was a problem, however, he and Hong Xin had already exchanged imprints on their core-transmission jades.

Their procession continued. At the end of the hallway stood a large door made of carved wood. Upon reaching it, Ling Fei walked ahead and grasped a small bronze-colored door knocker. She used it to deliver three soft knocks to the other side. Shortly after, the doors opened, revealing three additional women, matching them member for member.

Unlike the Red Dust Pavilion, the mistresses of the Icy Heart Pavilion wore white and blue. They didn't smile like Hong Xin and her entourage did, preferring to keep a relaxed yet soothing expression. It was impossible to tell their true emotions at a glance, as they were covered in an icy veil that was difficult to penetrate.

That, Hong Xin thought, *or their emotions are completely nonexistent.* In her experience, lack of empathy and shallow feelings came hand in hand with their cultivation method. It wouldn't surprise her if it had been months since any of the four women laughed.

But who is their leader? she wondered as she looked over the four. They were all dressed identically in white-and-blue robes decorated with silver runes. They each wore the same silver jewelry, including a foot-long silver bracelet they wore on their right wrists. Their makeup was pale, and their hairstyles identical. Each of them wore a blue hairpin not unlike the ones Hong Xin and the others wore. Perhaps this was some sort of test?

Hong Xin discarded personal appearance, as it clearly wasn't useful in this situation. It seemed the Icy Heart Pavilion valued appearance much less than they did. So, she looked over each of their expressions. She ignored Ling Fei, for while deceiving Hong Xin might be a biting move, abasing herself and calling herself vice head while also welcoming them personally would be too degrading. Therefore, one of the remaining three would have to be in charge.

The one on the left, while seeming calm as a glacier, had a hint of uncertainty in her eyes. Hong Xin looked over to the next in line, the one in the middle—her eyes seemed lifeless as a puppet's. So she rested her eyes on the woman on the right. Her eyes were bright blue, and when she investigated further, Hong Xin felt a chill run through her body. It was like she'd been plunged into an icy lake. The courage she'd mustered instantly vanished, leaving her heart open to the invasion of countless doubts.

Seeing she'd just been affected by a powerful dousing force, Hong Xin activated her kindling cultivation and melted the frigid anxiety that permeated her. She countered with the sweltering heat of a day in the desert. It invaded her opponent's mind and body, but to

Hong Xin's surprise, the woman showed no outward signs of feeling anything. She simply wore the same impassive expression despite the sweat forming on her forehead. Heated emotions of anger, love, and caring burned inside the woman unnoticed.

"You may call me Headmistress Hong," Hong Xin said to the woman. "Might I have the pleasure of knowing your name?"

"You may call me Headmistress Lan," Headmistress Lan said with the same flat expression. "I told you she wouldn't fooled or affected, Ling Fei. You should stop wasting our time with such foolish games." The headmistress walked away from the two others, and the illusion that had been covering her disappeared. Her clothes were just as ornate as Hong Xin's. She wore much more silver-colored jewelry on her hair than the others, and the silver embroidery on her robes was more intricate. "Introduce yourselves."

"I am Vice Head Xi," the woman with the uncertain expression said.

"I am Vice Head Dong," the puppetlike woman said in a deadpan voice.

"You may call me Bai Ling," Bai Ling said. Ji Bingxue and Mistress Huang introduced themselves as well. Unlike the Icy Heart Pavilion, the Red Dust Pavilion didn't care much for authority titles. Instead, the pecking order was well known, with these three women occupying top positions in Hong Xin's confidence.

Their introductions complete, Headmistress Lan led them to a long tea table where two young girls began serving tea. It was a flower tea made from cherry blossom buds. Though it contained no stimulating agents, it tasted like the freshness of spring.

Are they servants or trainees? Hong Xin wondered as she savored the tea. Their movements were precise, and their expressions, though unpracticed, were just as emotionless as the four other women.

"They're talented, yes?" Headmistress Lan said, catching Hong Xin's glance. "We found these two three years ago. They've gotten the very best training and will soon graduate in the first new batch of full members at the Icy Heart Pavilion."

"I see," Hong Xin said. She took a sip of her tea. "Then you're serious about continuing the Icy Heart tradition in Gold Leaf City." Though she tried her best, it was difficult to hide her displeasure at the notion.

"Of course," Headmistress Lan said, raising an eyebrow. "From what I gather, you're also promoting the same training, along with your new kindling training regimen."

"Hand in hand," Hong Xin said. "And well controlled. Our students don't have to give up their feelings in exchange for power."

"Give up?" Headmistress Lan asked flatly. "I see. So you view getting rid of a weakness as giving it up. Interesting."

"I view washing the color out of a woman's life as heavy-handed, yes," Hong Xin said. "Everyone has hopes and dreams. Would you have your students squash them?"

"Dreams are worthless, and ambition transcends emotion," Headmistress Lan said. "All of our members agree. If they don't, they're free to leave. I won't waste my time on students that have such childish notions on cultivation."

"Childish?" Hong Xin said, her temper rising. She noticed, then calmed herself when she realized she'd spoken a little too loudly. "Excuse my outburst, but I hardly call hopes and dreams childish. The highest achieving cultivators have both of these things."

"My experience has been vastly different," Headmistress Lan said. "And don't worry about your outburst. It's what we expect from the new Red Dust Pavilion, and we aren't so thin-skinned as to take offense."

Hong Xin moved to retort, but Bai Ling cut her off. "I think this conversation might be counterproductive. We've come here to get to know each other better and form a basis for cooperation, isn't that right?"

"Agreed," Ling Fei said, joining Bai Ling in defusing the situation. "While our core philosophies might be different, they are also complementary. After all, most cultivators have these hopes and dreams, and the most efficient way to encourage them is to stoke those same emotions.

"But without tempering these with calmness, they will sprout heart demons that hinder their advancement," Bai Ling said. "Professionals and businesspeople are also better off with calmness as a base. Everything is connected."

"Everything is connected," Ling Fei echoed.

The two women quieted down and waited while Hong Xin and Headmistress Lan simmered on this. They enjoyed their tea along with small snacks that the two ladies served. They weren't overly sweet, but neither were they bland. Nor were they too spongy or too dense. These moon cakes were perfectly balanced creations, much like the relationship they sought.

Though Hong Xin wanted nothing more than to tell them of her grand plans for unification, she held her tongue. Much like a newly lit fire couldn't be used to cook delicious food, relationships needed much nurturing before making significant headway.

"If our discussion thus far has indicated anything," Hong Xin said. "It is the need for further understanding. Perhaps later, we could supervise each other's training. I would be very interested in seeing how the Icy Heart Pavilion raises new members. Seeing these two young ladies serve us tea so calmly, I can't help but think that your training program has diverged from the older, crueler way."

"Likewise," Headmistress Lan said. "I've heard that your new members aren't any slower. This whole business of fostering hopes and dreams might seem like nonsense to me, but yin and yang are complementary parts, after all. Maybe seeing one extreme will help us find parallels or flaws in our own methods."

"How about next week?" Hong Xin asked.

Headmistress Lan paused for a moment, then nodded. "Let's make it an all-day affair. We'll first visit the Red Dust Pavilion during the morning when the sun is rising, then you can visit our Icy Heart Pavilion when the sun is setting."

Both these times coincided with the optimal training times for their disciples.

"Then it's settled," Hong Xin said. Though she had her doubts about the other party's methods, it was important to do as Bai Ling said and keep an open mind. This would not only serve the Red

Dust Pavilion better, it would also put her own mind at ease. The deep scars she bore had been left alone for a long time. Only by confronting past experiences could they be healed.

The sun had already set by the time they returned. Though they disagreed heavily on philosophy, the Icy Heart Pavilion and Red Dust Pavilion shared many commonalities, both in cultivation methods and their reverence for the arts. Their tea had eventually turned into an exchange of talents, a light spar, which led straight into dinner. Their guards hadn't minded, as they'd been properly entertained by the Icy Heart mistresses and the other guards as they'd waited. On the whole, it had been a splendid afternoon.

Hong Xin sighed in relief as she entered her bedchambers but yelped when she saw Wang Jun lying on the lone couch. Fortunately, he didn't seem to notice her reaction and simply lay there, staring at the ceiling.

Since she was back in her private chambers, Hong Xin moved to her vanity mirror and dabbed a white cloth in a pungent-smelling solution. She wiped her face, removing spent runic ink and powders. Within seconds, her appearance was back to normal. She removed a few excess hair ornaments and walked over to the sofa. To her surprise, Wang Jun wasn't staring at the ceiling—he was sleeping.

Sighing, Hong Xin sat beside him and dug into his shoulders with her hands, releasing some of the tension that had built up in his body. His eyes slowly opened, and he smiled when he saw her.

"Silly man, falling asleep while you wait," Hong Xin said. "What if it wasn't me but an enemy that found you?"

"Impossible," Wang Jun said. "Anyone else wouldn't have seen me lying here. Only someone close, like you or my master, would be able to find me."

Hong Xin raised an eyebrow at that. He was good at hiding, but when had he become *that* good?

Wang Jun sat up, and she took another look at him. Though he was still smiling, she could see exhaustion clinging to his face like dampness on a wet shirt.

"What happened?" Hong Xin asked. It wasn't like him to be so tired. Cultivators didn't need sleep. What's more, it had only been two weeks since they'd last seen each other.

"Nothing major," Wang Jun said. "I've been... learning from my master. His teachings are difficult to understand sometimes. They're especially taxing."

She noticed the telltale signs of a lie when he spoke. The slight trembling of his throat, a slight aversion of his eyes. At the same time, she saw the telltale signs of truth. A lack of hesitation and a straightforwardness that was difficult to ignore. It wasn't a lie, but neither was it the complete truth.

"You know that you can tell me anything, don't you?" Hong Xin asked. "I won't share what you say with anyone. Not a soul."

Wang Jun nodded. "I know. How did your meeting go?"

"I don't remember having told you about it," Hong Xin said.

"You remember correctly, but I know many things," Wang Jung said. Though he was weary, she saw pleading in his eyes. He didn't want to focus on his own worries, so he'd shifted to hers.

"It went all right," Hong Xin said. "It was a good start."

"But?" Wang Jun asked.

She took in a deep breath before continuing and let it all out. Wang Jun was usually the reasonable type, and he could probably see her through this logically. "We just have so many differences," Hong Xin said. "They're cautious, and with good reason. They know I have the Frozen Heart Oath Stone, so they're being extra careful. But none of them have done anything overtly wrong, as far as I can tell, so it's not like I'd try to enslave them like I did Mistress Shan and the others."

"I see," Wang Jun said, nodding his head and looking down at his fingers as he pressed them together. "It sounds like you need a good excuse to do what needs to be done."

"Wait, what?" Hong Xin asked, concerned by the sudden turn in the conversation.

"You know what you want to do—you want to control them with the Frozen Heart Oath Stone in case they cause trouble, just like you did the other mistresses," Wang Jun continued. "But you would feel guilty if you did so without them deserving such a fate. I can empathize—I'd feel guilty too."

"It's the other way around, Wang Jun," Hong Xin said, a hint of worry in her voice. "I have the Oath Stone, and I won't use it unless I have to."

"A convenient play on words," Wang Jun said. "One I'm used to. Still, they both mean the same. You haven't considered using the Oath Stone because you don't have a reason, right?"

"I suppose," Hong Xin said, her frown relaxing.

"And you aren't going to use it if you don't get that reason, right?" Wang Jun continued. She nodded. "And if you find that reason, you will use it. It's all the same."

"What are you getting at?" Hong Xin asked. Her initial good mood at seeing him had vanished.

"I'm just trying to get you to confirm what means you're willing to use in which situations," Wang Jun said. "If you don't do that, you'll give yourself a lot of grief when you *do* have to use them. It's best to straighten it out up front." Though he looked calm on the surface, she could see his agitation. His posture was tight, almost competitive, and his breathing slightly quick.

Sighing, Hong Xin sat down beside him and hugged him tightly. She put her head on his chest, and the tension that had crept back into his body melted. She used her dousing abilities to soothe his worries and her kindling abilities to strengthen his resolve. His breathing slowed, and he put his hand on her back and hugged her tighter.

"I've just got a lot of pressure to deal with," Wang Jun said. "Just ignore what I said. Don't mind me. I'll be all right."

"You need to take care of yourself," Hong Xin said, pulling away slightly and looking him in the eyes. "I know things might seem difficult, but you're stronger than this. You'll get past it."

"Thank you," he whispered.

"Don't thank me, silly," Hong Xin said. "Come see me more often. You're not doing anyone any good if you're exhausted."

Wang Jun hesitated but nodded. He glanced at the clock before wincing. "I really need to go. I have a lot to do tonight."

"Are other businesses even open?" Hong Xin asked.

"Most are closed, but not all of them," Wang Jun said. "But what does that have to do with my work?" He opened a portal into the darkness and stepped into it. "I'll be back soon. I promise."

The portal shut, leaving Hong Xin alone in her room.

"Men," Hong Xin muttered. She'd originally been looking to vent her emotions, only to get flooded by his worries. Couldn't he just shut up and listen like he usually did? Sighing, she prepared herself a cup of tea and drank it, allowing the smooth drink to warm her exhausted body. Minutes trickled by.

"Do I really just want to trap them with the Oath Stone?" Hong Xin muttered to herself. She thought she had it figured out—no more oath-binding unless it was absolutely necessary. And from what she could tell so far, it wouldn't be. But was that just because they weren't looking hard enough? "I'll have to bug Bai Ling to investigate even further."

She continued drinking and thinking, and soon, the clock struck eight. Seeing the time reminded her that other businesses might be closed at night, but the Red Dust Pavilion certainly wasn't. The night was young, and she had a lot of work to do.

Chapter 9:
Between Light and Darkness

Huxian felt like an emperor looking over a tiny village as he flew above the Silverwing Mountain Range. He floated above it, his keen eyes easily piercing the light cloud cover above its forested peaks. Natural impediments aside, not even the Pure Jade Defensive Formation covering the mountain range could obscure his demonic sight, which was amplified by both the Devil-Sealing and Demon-Subduing scriptures.

Everything looks much different than I remember, Huxian thought as he inspected the nine mountains and their nine jade plates. Each one was connected to the valley in the center, where a circular jade plate regulated their function. Now that he'd reached the peak of core formation, he could finally see the tender energy lines that crisscrossed each mountain. They seemed incomplete, like an unfinished puzzle. There was a mystery here, just like he'd hoped.

Huxian flew down to the nearest mountain, where the Geomantic Sovereign resided. He could pinpoint the large snake that lay nestled in the very center of the large rock formation. Her lair was protected by layer upon layer of geomantic formations. He pondered trampling on her dignity for a moment before shaking his head and landing in front of the Pure Jade Defensive Formation.

Geomantic Boa, come out and meet me, Huxian said lazily. His voice penetrated stone and soil. The boa stirred, and soon she slithered out through one of the many holes near the base of the mountain. She raised her head and looked down at Huxian, her eyes narrowing.

So, you have returned, the boa said, her tongue flickering. *I suppose you want to enter my mountain, where you'll be able to trample upon me with impunity after you've breached this preliminary line of defense?*

Huxian raised an eyebrow, but she continued.

Don't take me for a fool. I won't let you in no matter what you say.

You foxes are all alike: tricky, and annoying. But out there, you're just another sovereign. You can only stay outside and lament as I stand here and... Her voice trailed off.

Huxian, who'd grown bored with her antics, directly entered the Pure Jade Defensive Formation.

I meant all this only in jest, of course, the Geomantic Sovereign said, recovering quickly. Though he didn't think it was physically possible, he could swear she was sweating. *I wanted you to witness my superior taunting skills, which I unleash each and every time an enemy tries to enter the mountains. I'll kindly accept any constructive feedback. Please follow me. I've kept your cave warm.*

No need, Huxian said, yawning. Rather than beat her up like he normally did, he decided to cut deeply into her honor instead. *It's beneath me to stay on this mountain. A belly-dragger like you would never understand how lofty I am, so I won't waste my time. Is the True Seer Great Owl around?*

The Geomantic Sovereign swallowed the insult and flicked her tail toward the center of her mountain. *He is in the center, as usual. He barely ever sees us, and he only comes out if something important is afoot.* As she spoke, fluttering wings announced the True Seer Great Owl's arrival. *Which your arrival most certainly is, given his timely arrival.*

To Huxian's surprise, the True Seer Great Owl had advanced greatly in strength over the past few years. He was now a middle-core-formation demon beast. As far as demon advancement went, he'd grown by leaps and bounds. He still looked rather daft, but within his eyes, there was a glimmer of something special. Something not of this world.

Hoot! the True Seer Great Owl said. *I knew you would come today. I came as quickly as possible, out of fear that you'd slay the python and impale her corpse on the mountain in a fit of rage.*

Nope, I got over it, Huxian said. *Do I need to slap a fly every time I see one?*

Spoken like a true powerhouse, my lord, the True Seer Great Owl said. *Though to be fair, I eat my fair share of flies, even though I know it won't make a difference in the grand scheme of things. I like the taste. Now come, let us journey to the center of the mountain range.* Huxian nodded and left the Geomantic Boa behind. She'd been deprived of every shred of her dignity, which was what she deserved, given that she'd tried to kill him many times in the past.

How did you know I would come? Huxian asked as they walked down the mountain's rocky slope. The woods thinned as they reached the base of the valley, which was covered in nothing but dust and dead trees.

The same way my ancestor knew you would come, the True Seer Great Owl said. *Fate weaves a tapestry, and while specific details are difficult to define for important characters, it's possible to track the currents they create and predict their behavior. I take it you've come seeking an initiation mark?*

Yeah, Huxian said, looking around the dusty, desolate forest as they approached the central plate and the stone stele. The place really did look a lot different than before. Where he'd previously only seen a single jade plate at the center, he now saw five surrounding it. Each one was nine feet wide and made of a special colored jade. There was one for each of the five elements, and each surface contained a circular depression with various lines coming out from it. *Did you do anything new to the place?*

Nothing, the True Seer Great Owl said with a hoot. *Now that you've reached new heights, you can now see farther than before. Compared to your future vision, you're essentially blind, fumbling around like a newborn child.*

Riiiiight, Huxian said. Despite the wisdom in his words, it was very strange to hear it from a tiny owl that looked like he had more than a few screws loose. *About my initiation. My friends have all found good locations to obtain their marks. One each for swamp, lightning, wind, and mountain. But I'm at a loss. Where can I find a place with both light and darkness? It would be a piece of cake to find one on a transcendent plane, but here in the middle of nowhere? You can see why a lofty being like myself would prefer to die of old age trying to obtain the initiation of time rather than obtain a mediocre initiation.*

Though it might sound silly, many demons had tried this method and failed. It was now jokingly referred to as the kingly way of demonic cultivation. Many demons wasted centuries trying it before a concerned relative broke the news to them that they'd been tricked. A great joke with terrible consequences.

A conundrum, to be sure, the True Seer Great Owl said, his unusually large eyes glittering. *I am guessing you came here because of the stone stele where you obtained your Demon-Subduing Eyes?*

I figured there might be hints? Huxian said uncertainly.

The True Seer Great Owl shook his large head, and Huxian could swear he saw the puff in the little bird's feathers diminish substantially. *The stone stele only contained a hint of true essence of light and darkness. The source of power was left behind by an ancient being. A portion of it was repurposed by my ancestor to craft the stele.*

If it was a portion of the source, the source must be nearby, right? Huxian asked.

In theory, though I can't fathom where, the True Seer Great Owl said. *To make an analogy, what you're asking of me is akin to an estranged relative asking where he can find his long-deceased grandfather's car keys.*

What's a car? Huxian asked, perplexed. Cha Ming occasionally mentioned strange things like this, and he was only too happy to take them in stride. Like coffee. Or these mythical "sandwiches" he occasionally heard of. In fact, he was very curious as to how witches could be made of sand.

Never mind cars, the True Seer Great Owl said. *Wherever the source is, it's beyond me. I can't help you find it.*

Hmm... Huxian said, looking around and sniffing. Like the owl said, he couldn't smell any trace of light and darkness source energy. On a whim, he donned his goggles. All he could see through their violet lenses were extra lines of karma linking the five stone pillars and the central stele. He followed them for a time but came back empty-handed. When he finished, he noticed the owl hopping about.

Would you like to help me with my ceremony? the True Seer Great Owl asked as he hopped toward a small shrine that Huxian hadn't noticed before. Its appearance was sudden, but he'd come to expect such things in this place.

Why not? Huxian said. He followed the owl, who approached the shrine's main door and entered through it. There was a firepit in the center of the shrine. It filled a depression in the black-and-white marble floor. The marble seemed equal parts light and dark on initial observation. When he looked at it, he was surprised to see that the proportions were *exactly equal*, a nigh impossibility in nature.

Would you care to open the other doors? the True Seer Great Owl asked as he hopped toward the back of the shrine. Huxian noticed that aside from the front door—the southern door—there were three other equally large doors leading to the three remaining cardinal directions. He trotted to the east side of the chamber and pushed it open. Beyond the door lay the long shadow of the shrine. It was sunset, and the sun rose in the east. After opening the eastern door, he traveled to the western door and pushed it open. A small amount of sunlight leaked inside, as the sun was still too high to fully illuminate the shrine's floor.

Having opened the two doors, he returned to the center, where the True Seer Great Owl had returned to after opening the northern door. There was a decent amount of light in the temple now, so Huxian could now inspect the marble extending up the walls and onto the covered roof. There, the black and white marks formed a peculiar pattern. Instead of the usual chaotic, disorganized marks marble was known for, the black and white patterns on the ceiling were clumped together like a massive coiling creature with a long body, complete with large claws and large eyes. Its eyes were reptilian slits, though this creature was far greater than any reptile—it was a dragon.

Something tugged at Huxian's ancestral memories when he saw the image, but nothing came of it. So he looked on in amusement as the owl retrieved something demons normally wouldn't use: an oil lamp. He retrieved it from a sealed container, but to Huxian's surprise, it was already lit.

We hold this ceremony two times a year, the owl explained, bringing the lamp closer to the fireplace. *Twice a year, day and night are equal. During these equinoxes, we burn a small bundle of firewood right when the sun is setting. I'm not sure why we do it, but you sure are lucky to come at this exact time. Perhaps this is what they call fate.*

It was too great a coincidence, Huxian agreed. Moreover, how could he not see the connection between what he was looking for and the ceremony? A candle, day and night, black and white. Everything balanced. Something tugged at his memories again, and he remembered bits and pieces of a legend. It was about the origins of sunrise and sunset, but the rest of the story eluded him.

The sun sank a little deeper. By now, the True Seer Great Owl and Huxian had erected a small tent of firewood at the center of the room. After waiting a short while, the True Seer Great Owl lit the bundle with the lamp's small flame. The wood began burning, and as the flame grew, the owl began chanting and hopping on one foot. The sight would have been comedic if not for the hauntingly familiar words he spoke:

> *Black and white, light and darkness.*
> *Forever in balance, forever in harmony.*
> *Who knows whence came these dancing lights?*
> *Who knows whence came their partner shadows?*
>
> *The sun loathes the leering darkness,*
> *Which clings to her like a wet blanket;*

Her soul shudders in ecstasy as she savors his embrace.
Will they ever meet?

Between light and darkness, fate is uncertain.
Between light and darkness, the moon has no eyes.
Between light and darkness, the vision commences.
A beast awakens, while another sleeps.

True Seer Great Owl's words echoed through Huxian's mind as he gazed at the flickering flame. It was a perfect dancing flame that seemed to look back as he peered inside it. The setting sun caused the marble to dance beneath the flickering candle. It was the most surreal thing Huxian had ever seen.

But seeing is believing, and sight is an illusion, Huxian thought. *Wait, what am I babbling about?* He shook himself from his reverie and realized the sun was halfway to setting. In that moment, everything seemed to pause, to freeze. The flickering flame reached some sort of equilibrium, and when light and darkness were equal, it stopped.

Now it resembled a vertical slit. He looked up and realized why it looked so familiar. That slit was the same as the dragon's left eye, which was glowing brightly under the light of the small fire. As Huxian looked at the flame, he felt like he was looking into another world. It was like a slit in time and space, a rift in reality.

And then he felt it. The purest light and darkness energy he'd ever known in his short life. It was coming from the slit, leaking out from the gray light that formed it. It *was* a slit in time and space, he realized. It was a portal to another world. Huxian, who wasn't the type to be intimidated by any situation, acted decisively. He blurred and rushed at the portal with impossible speed. It began to close around him as the brief moment where light and dark were equal passed.

His head managed to sneak through, but he noticed his shoulders getting caught. *Shrink!* he thought. *Shrink!*

He compressed himself like a snake, breaking his bones in the process as he shoved himself through the rift. It seemed like it would clip his tails, so he quickly pulled them back. He lost only a few hairs before the rift finally closed and vanished.

"Well, that was exciting," Huxian thought out loud as his bones healed and he recovered his original size. He looked around and saw an empty land. There was no greenery, nor were there hills. The land was cracked and parched, for no water ran here.

And all around him, the sky glowed with the colors of twilight.

Chapter 10:
Land of Dusk Eternal

Parched earth crumbled under Huxian's mighty paws as he advanced along the desolate plains. Despite his strong demonic eyes, he could see nothing in the distance but the skyline. The twilight sun lit up the entire world with a crimson light. It had done so for days, for the sun never set.

So thirsty, Huxian thought. He panted as he trudged along the desert, or what seemed like one. There was no sand here, only shattered clay. It was evenly spread, like frosting on a delicious cake that had been left out in the sun. Though even the slightest bit of shade would be welcome, the only one he could find was his own. And for some reason, it refused to obey his commands and provide him shelter. It simply sat there like a normal shadow. What nonsense.

How can it be so hot during twilight? Huxian thought as he advanced. He knew the answer, of course, as he'd been walking for quite some time. Despite the sun's moderate intensity, it had likely been this way for centuries. The land never saw darkness, so it never experienced a reprieve from the constant battering of the sun goddess.

Huxian imagined these lands would be fertile plains if the sun were allowed to set. Instead, it kept staring at him, like a half-shut eye gazing over the horizon.

Great, Huxian thought, *just great.* He glared back at the half sun.

While my friends are having the time of their lives, taking over their respective mountains, I'm stuck here in a land where there's neither light or darkness. The aura he'd felt before plunging into the dimensional rift had evidently been fake. He felt none of that strong light and darkness essence now that he was on the other side.

Huxian trudged along, regretting his foolish decision. He thought of Gua in the Evergreen Battlefields, and Silverwing in the Windswept Canyons. He thought of Lei Jiang and the Calamity Cloud Span, and Mr. Mountain picking literally the biggest mountain on the continent. They would soon reach half-step initiation, while he lingered. And he could only blame himself.

Huxian continued for another full day before finally seeing a hill in the distance. Excited, he rushed toward it. It took him a few hours to reach the small protrusion, which ended up being a faraway city. It stood there on the broken plains, its doors wide open yet somehow well-maintained.

Should I go in? Huxian wondered. For some reason, this place gave him the creeps. Still, if he didn't go, he was just wasting his time in what he assumed was a desolate demi plane with no food or water in sight. He built up his courage and walked inside.

A chill breeze washed over him despite the lack of wind as he crossed the city's threshold. The inside of the city, it turned out, was just like the plains outside it. Its streets were empty of all but strange shadows and lights that seemed to move about as he walked. He saw bakeries that could have been baking bread he couldn't quite smell, and tea shops that could have served tea he couldn't quite drink. There were also restaurants, and he could practically smell what they would have sold, were the city not empty.

Since he found nothing in the market, he proceeded to the residential district. There, he saw empty streets that could have been filled with children who played as the last of the sun faded on the horizon. Parents would have been watching them from their homes as they lit candles and lamps in preparation for the approaching night. Yet there was nothing there but a familiar chill, dancing lights, and what he thought might be echoes of possible sounds.

Sighing, Huxian walked to the central square, where unlike most cities, there was a temple. The solitary temple looked familiar. He soon realized why this was so; it was a much larger version of the shrine he'd used to enter this world.

Maybe I can find a way back here? he thought. He looked around carefully as he approached the black-and-white marble temple. The swirling white lines on its steps were an eerie shade of crimson that flickered occasionally, as though the setting sun was obscured by someone who walked past it. He thought he heard echoing footsteps as he scaled the stairs and approached the southernmost door. It was open, leading to the single square room in the temple, where a familiar firepit lay. He knew what needed to be done.

Increasing his size, Huxian trotted up to the eastern door and pushed. Nothing happened. Frowning, he increased his size yet again. Nothing happened. Infuriated that a mere door was stopping him, Huxian grew to a full 330 feet long, the maximum size possible for him until he received his mark. He struggled against the black door covered in white patterns with all his might, refusing to believe there was anything on this demi plane that could possibly resist his mighty demonic body. The door creaked and groaned as he scratched the floor with his sharp claws, but still it refused to budge.

And then he saw it: the large bar blocking the door. Shrinking, he sheepishly approached it and lifted the bar, then pushed the door open with a singular paw without any problems. He proceeded to the northern door, then the western door, allowing the same eerie crimson light to fill the shrine.

I'll have to leave out that embarrassing bit when I retell the story, Huxian thought. *Now, where to find wood?* There was none around him. He thought about going outside to fetch some from town, then remembered who he was bonded to. *Right, creation qi.*

He channeled creation qi and wood qi through his bond with Cha Ming—which still worked for some reason—and began forming wooden log after wooden log. Then, when he'd gathered an appropriate amount of wood, he channeled fire qi. *Heavens, that bond is useful sometimes.* The logs caught fire, and soon there was merry crackling in the temple.

Huxian looked around in expectation. He glanced toward the sun, which ought to move any minute now. He looked to the shadows, which should begin dancing soon. He looked toward the roof, where the dragon lay with half-closed glowing red eyes. Nothing happened. Instead, the eyes glared at him mockingly.

He walked out the southern doors of the temple and looked out at the city, noting that nothing had changed. Everything was still frozen in twilight, not moving or flickering in the slightest. He figured if he captured a dozen images over the course of a day, they'd all be identical. Nothing moved in the ghostly city.

Shaking his head, he was about to leave the temple when he heard a sigh. It was softer than a silken sheet running across marble, softer than a drop of water trickling down a smooth stone. It was softer than a blooming flower, softer than a blinking eye. But he heard it.

There, he thought. He walked back into the temple, and just behind the fire to the north, he saw a flickering image. It was barely visible, but the fire, along with the twilight that now entered the room, caused the light in the room to illuminate it just the right way. It was the transparent figure of a man holding his arms in prayer.

Who are you? Huxian asked, walking up to the man. The man ignored him as he continued to finger prayer beads with his spectral fingers. The prayer beads were odd, given that the man wasn't a Buddhist monk but a Daoist priest, but who was he to argue about convention?

Excuse me, sir? I can see you. With these last words, the man nearly dropped the rosary. He opened his eyes and looked to Huxian in shock. Huxian stared back.

"You can see me?" the man asked, peering into Huxian's eyes. The man's own eyes were crimson, and combined with his transparent body, they gave him an otherworldly appearance.

I can see you, Huxian confirmed. *At least, as long as this fire is burning, I can.*

The man nodded when he saw the fire, then looked to the four cardinal directions. Then, he looked up at the black-and-white picture above the fire and sighed. "This city didn't used to be like this. It was a prosperous city that knew no disease, knew no war, and knew no major suffering. The only ill that plagued it was the ill all mortals suffer: death from old age."

Not even so-called immortals and gods can escape death, Huxian said. Except for Yama, but he was the exception, rather than the rule. The god of death ruled the Underworld with an iron fist, and not even the leaders of Heaven, Hell, and the demon world dared fight him, for fear of destroying the entire universe.

The figure nodded. "We realized this soon after we tried something daring. We tried to cheat death."

How? Huxian asked. History was rife with examples of people doing this same.

"All of us tethered our souls to the sun, locking it in place," the man explained. "For surely, if the sun didn't set, time wouldn't pass. Our lives would be forever blissful, enjoying the final moments before the sun set across the horizon."

You were successful, Huxian said, frowning. That shouldn't have been possible.

"In a way," the man said. "But this was the Candle Dragon's land. By tethering the sun, we restrained the Candle Dragon himself. He was not pleased, and as a punishment for our transgression, he cursed us.

"'If you desire immortality so much, I shall grant it,' the Candle Dragon said. 'You shall remain as ghosts in this unchanging land, forever bound to this city you hold so dear. For all eternity, you shall eat but never be full. You shall play but never know cheer. You shall drink but never be sated, and when you try to sleep, slumber will never take you.'

"We realized our mistake then. We'd tethered the sun, and if the sun did not set, how could there be any fulfillment? We were frozen in cause without consequence. Anything we did had no effect. Thousands of years passed, and by now many of us have lost our minds. We exist in perpetual monotony. We never change our habits, forever roaming this city, which never sleeps."

"You mean there are others?" Huxian asked, frowning. He hadn't seen them on his way to the temple.

"They are invisible to you," the man said. "They, too, are ghosts. Perhaps it is due to the strength of my soul as head priest that you can see me in the first place. With the help of the twilight sun and the light of the candleflame torch, you can barely make me out. Perhaps it is destiny that you can see me." He sighed again.

"Is there anything I can do to help?" Huxian asked. Eating and never being filled and drinking but always being thirsty sounded downright horrible; he could hardly think of a worse fate. Leaving them to suffer such an unreasonable punishment would be immoral.

"Perhaps," the man said. He thought for a moment, then pointed at the ceiling, where a picture of the Candle Dragon was dancing in the firelight. He formed some hand seals, and suddenly a shining golden piece fell from one of its half-red eyes like a tear.

Huxian jumped and caught it in his mouth before placing it on the floor before the head priest. The object was a golden piece of jade. The ghostly man cowered when it landed in front of him. He feared the jade, feared its power. Huxian looked at the object and discovered a single character.

Spirit? Huxian thought, reading it. The moment he did, the jade burst into tiny motes of light and shot into his body. His body tingled as it did, but he didn't notice any other differences. He looked back to the ghost, which was now huddling in the dark room, frightened.

Huxian approached the cowering ghost. "What's that thing supposed to do?" he asked.

"You can still see me?" the ghost asked, trembling.

Huxian frowned. "Yes, of course I can see you. Just like before, the twilight is here, and the torch is lit. And I..."

He looked to the firepit and realized the fire had gone out. Yet despite the missing flame, he could still see the ghostly man.

"Good," the man said in relief. "Very good. It seems my friend the monk wasn't lying."

"The monk?" Huxian asked.

"The monk who warned me not to do this," the ghost said. "He told me that what I was doing was against the laws of the nature. Humans could not live forever, and the consequences of trying to stop time would be disastrous. He gave me that piece of jade and told me it might give hope should the worst come to pass."

Huxian nodded. "Where can I find him?"

The ghost pointed eastward. "Go outside the city. Keep walking until you find him. It will seem impossibly far, and many temptations will arise, but you must keep going. Perhaps he will know what to do about this problem.

"All right," Huxian said. He now had something to do in this place, which was far better than wandering the parched desert without a goal in mind. Perhaps he could solve this mystery, and in turn unlock the dormant powers of light and darkness he'd sensed from the outside. "I'll be back soon. I promise."

"Thank you," the ghostly priest said. To Huxian's surprise, he kowtowed. "We want nothing but to be freed from this wretched fate. If that means death, so be it. We'd gladly rejoin the cycle of reincarnation."

Then the ghost disappeared.

Seeing that there was nothing more he could do, Huxian walked back into the city proper. It was still twilight out, but everything looked different now. In the empty streets, he saw people: merchants, shoppers, cultivators, children, and even guards. The restaurants were serving up transparent dishes—which he tried and found were incredibly flavorless and unsatisfying. The tea houses were serving tea, and the bakers were baking bread that both smelled wonderful and not appealing at the same time.

In the streets, the children played. But these ghostly children could clearly feel no joy. They were trapped in the moment, forever cursed to play the same wretched game over and over, always with the same people and the same outcome. In the houses, the parents watched their children in despair as they tried to light lamps that wouldn't burn to prepare for the night that wouldn't come.

Unable to bear it any longer, Huxian left the city through the open eastern gates. He set out due east as the monk had told him. The land was parched and cracked, just as it had been when he'd traveled here. Still, anything was better than staying a second longer in that cursed city. He wouldn't wish their fate on his worst enemy. Simply imagining it was enough to give him nightmares.

Chapter 11: Life

Sweet potatoes and marinated bamboo shoots sizzled on a makeshift grill on the side of the road. Cha Ming, the one cooking, took care as he applied sauces and seasonings to the thinly sliced vegetables. He waited patiently as the brown concoction hissed and boiled on their surfaces, ready to remove them the moment it began to harden.

"Are they almost done?" asked Mo Ling, who was sitting beside him. Her hair was now short and black, as opposed to the long brown hair she'd worn before. Cha Ming had also alchemically changed her eye color to a light green. Physical characteristics aside, she also dressed much differently than she had in Liaoning. She now wore men's cultivation robes and looked like an amateur swordswoman.

"Patience is a virtue," Cha Ming said, flipping the vegetables over. "You should see waiting not as a chore but as mental training. Don't waste a single moment." Young or old, only diligence and hard work led to progress.

Mo Ling did as she was told and turned her attention to the nearby village. He followed her gaze as she looked from one group of men and women to another. It was nearly dusk, so most of the families had retreated into their wooden houses. They were so weak that even Mo Ling, an initial-foundation-establishment cultivator, could see everyone using her incandescent soul force.

"They're so pitiful," Mo Ling said, looking at their huddled forms. "They work all day from dawn to dusk, never getting any rest and barely getting enough food. Why does the world have to be this way?" As the daughter of Liaoning's city lord, she'd been sheltered from the cruel reality of the countryside. She'd never gone out to see the real world.

Cha Ming sighed. Things were different up north, so it was difficult to explain things in a way Southerners would understand. "It doesn't," he finally said, poking the fire beneath their roasting vegetables. "People can live good lives or bad lives, virtuous lives or sinful lives. For many people, it all comes down to effort and a little bit of luck." He looked toward the village. "Unfortunately, these people have bad luck, and they're weak to boot. They don't get to choose their fate and can only take the life that's dealt them."

"Can't we do something to help them?" Mo Ling asked. "Like you did in the monastery?"

Cha Ming nodded. "I could. Putting aside the fact that I'd need to answer to some of the most powerful people in the Ji Kingdom if I did such a thing, I could. But what then?"

"What do you mean?" she asked, frowning.

Cha Ming shrugged. "Their situation wouldn't change, even if I killed every one of their owners. It all comes down to mentality. They are used to serfdom, so they've grown to rely on someone else to do certain things. They don't know how to distribute resources, sell the goods they produce, or even guard themselves from spirit beasts or bandits." He held out his poker and pointed it to the multi-family housing complex. "In fact, if I got rid of their problem and killed their owners, I doubt they'd last a full month before they either starved to death or ran off to another lord to become serfs once again."

Mo Ling paused for a moment, considering. "Then how can we change these things?"

"Do you think we have the power to change a whole country?" Cha Ming asked.

Mo Ling blushed. "Maybe not a whole country, but a piece of it, maybe?"

Cha Ming nodded. "It's possible. Your father tried to do such a thing. He and the ten protectors tried their best to improve the lot of everyone in Liaoning and in the surrounding lands, serfs included. He fed them more than other city lords would, protected them, and didn't work them as hard. He even tried teaching them basic *literacy*, so they could at least understand their own serf contracts."

This was clearly news to Mo Ling, who wasn't too familiar with her father's work outside of accounting.

"He tried his best," Cha Ming continued. "In the end, he still had to choke back his anger when the reapers came. He only lost his temper when they tried to take you, and for that, they took his arm and his sword.

"Who knows if he will continue to try helping them after such a setback, such a loss in human life? Most men would give up. It's only men like your father who can change things, but perseverance is key. Only with continued effort can things get better. If he can change his small piece of the kingdom, perhaps others can as well. If enough of them succeed, or the kingdom produces a kinder leader, the whole kingdom can change."

By now, the sun had set, and it was possible to make out many shadows through the windows of the housing complex. Despite there being no candles to light the house, they heard music coming from inside it. All the inhabitants were singing a song together. They'd brought out a small fluffy pastry and placed it in front of a thirteen-year-old boy, who was grinning from ear to ear.

"Tell me, Mo Ling," Cha Ming said. "Do they look unhappy to you?" She shook her head. "Everyone is dealt a different hand. Everyone is born in a different situation. They live, and they die. What matters is how everyone plays the hand they're dealt.

"Take that family, for example. Are they wallowing in self-pity after working hard all day for a meager reward? No. Instead, they're happy because one of their children is now thirteen years old. They've even decided to celebrate it. They pooled together their resources to buy enough refined flour to make the pastry he's eating. It's only enough for a single bite, but they're all happy for him. They're even singing and dancing, despite the hunger that gnaws at their bellies."

Mo Ling looked down and pondered what he'd just said. Cha Ming turned his attention back to the barbecue, where everything was now overcooked and slightly burned. Using a smidgen of transcendent force, he pushed down the flames and retrieved their food. He tasted one of the sweet potatoes and was relieved to find that it didn't taste as bad as he'd imagined. They both grabbed what they wanted and began their meal.

Cha Ming was halfway finished with his food when he heard some rustling in the woods beside them. Several dozen men charged out of the woods with weapons in hand and surrounded them. The strongest among them was at the peak of qi condensation, while the weakest was at the fifth level of qi condensation. They surrounded them, pointing their weapons at both Cha Ming and Mo Ling.

"Your spirit stones," the leader said, waving his spear at Cha Ming. "Drop them where I can see them." The man's arms were shaky and his spear unsteady. Both he and his companions looked weak and downright exhausted.

I think I can kill them all by myself, Mo Ling sent to Cha Ming, putting her hand to her sword. While they traveled, he'd spent some time teaching her martial arts. She'd taken to them faster than he'd expected.

Cha Ming shook his head. He motioned for her to stand down and stepped up to the bandit leader. He didn't draw a weapon. "If I'm guessing correctly, you're all escaped serfs from the village," Cha Ming said. "One of you is even an ex-soldier."

They shifted uncomfortably, some of them moving their hands to their foreheads to better cover their brands.

The leader, the only ex-soldier in the lot, thrust his shaking spear closer to Cha Ming's chest. "No need to talk. Just leave your spirit stones, and we'll let you both leave nice and quiet."

"But, boss, that girl—"

He was cut off as the leader slashed at the man with his spear, drawing blood as he cut a shallow line into the side of that man's face. Despite his shaky hands, he was quite skilled in wielding the weapon. "What did I tell you about capturing people? Shut the hell up and let me do the talking." He then moved his spear back to Cha Ming. Despite his previous display, his hands still shook.

"You're not a proper robber," Cha Ming said, pressing up against the spear. He raised the spear tip with a single finger and held it up to his own neck. "You can barely hold your spear in the right position. If you want to kill me and take my things, you ought to slash my throat, where I'm vulnerable."

The man hesitated. He looked toward his comrades and back to Cha Ming. Through his thick beard, Cha Ming could see a gaunt face and sleep-deprived eyes. "Don't think I won't kill you," the man said, forcing the tip of the spear against Cha Ming's neck. A droplet of blood dripped down from where the spear pierced his skin.

"You can take my things if you kill me," Cha Ming said. "Otherwise, it would be best if you left."

The leader's eyes widened at these words. He moved to pull back his spear, but Cha Ming held it firmly in place against his own neck. The man tried pulling it back several times before finally giving up. He dropped his spear and grabbed another man's spear.

"Let's go," the leader said. "We're leaving." He waved his hand for the others to follow him back into the woods. Most of the men followed, but some men stayed behind, not believing what they'd just seen.

"Boss, are we just going to leave your spear and leave them here?" the man said. "What will the other bandit groups think when they hear about this?"

"Am I your leader or not?" the bandit leader snapped. "You'll do as I say, when I say it. Now move, or you're no longer part of the group. If you think those other groups are so great, you can go join one of them. You might even get something to eat, if you manage to survive." Hearing these words, the man reluctantly followed the others. Before long, they'd all returned to the woods.

"Master Pai, is it wise to let bandits off like this?" Mo Ling asked. "What if they try to rob someone else?"

Cha Ming, who'd returned to his plate and was now nibbling on half a bamboo shoot, nodded. "You're right, they probably will. But who am I to stop desperate men trying to feed their families?"

"Desperate men?" Mo Ling asked.

"You might not know this, but not long ago, a group of men fought back when the reapers came," Cha Ming said. He knew this because he'd skimmed the men's recent memories. "The reapers didn't punish them, but to prevent future insubordination, any guards involved were dishonorably discharged. The leader of that group was one of them. Due to the mark on his record, no one would hire him or his fellows. As for the serfs, they were punished with unusually hard labor to be made an example of. Not only were they worked harder than most, they were also underfed. Rather than face certain death from starvation and exhaustion, they ran away from their masters.

"What was originally a single tightly knit bandit group of ex-soldiers took pity on these serfs. They split up to lead several groups to cover more ground. As we speak, they're out hunting spirit beasts that might easily kill one or two of them. They do this to bring food back to their camp, where their wives, children, and the widows of the men who've already died need caring for.

"Now that you know all this, what would you do to those men? Those men, whose guilty conscience made it so they could barely hold up spears while trying to rob someone?"

Mo Ling remained silent. They ate, and when they were done, they smothered the embers and prepared to move again throughout the night.

"I don't know," she finally as they flew away on flying swords. "I don't know what I should do to those men. They might be bandits, but when one of the weaker men had thoughts to do anything to me, their leader cut up his face."

"They haven't done anything too wrong," Cha Ming said. "No yet. I'm not one to kill men for things they might do in the future. Still, if I knew for certain they'd done something that deserved death, I would have killed them myself."

The situation reminded Cha Ming of his own dilemma in a

sense. Helping Mo Ling, though generous on his part, also greatly endangered his plan to infiltrate the Wang family. It was a flaw in his façade that could make his task impossible. It also put Mo Ling at risk—she would suffer greatly if they discovered him and investigated further.

Yet he still took the chance. Mo Ling needed help and companionship. She'd lost everything to the reapers, and Pai Xiao was the only friendly face she knew. Abandoning her at this point would be cold and heartless on Cha Ming's part.

They traveled all night, passing village after village. Soon, roaming guards and merchant caravans became commonplace. The sun rose, and as it did, many more wagons set out from the various villages and inns. Guard patrols grew more frequent, and the number of cultivators they saw flying around increased as well.

Before long, a city appeared in the distance. It was an impressive city with blackened gray walls. Unlike most population centers in the North, but like most in the South, it didn't occupy fertile lands but the most barren ones in the area, completely covering the layer of rock that protruded from the wooded plains nearby. Ashes, City of Fire and Blood, awaited them.

Cha Ming stepped carefully as he made his way through the crowded city streets. His care wasn't due to the large number of blood masters there, nor was it due to the strong cultivators he occasionally sensed. Rather, it was all to avoid the thick soot that covered everyone's clothing. He'd never considered himself an overly clean person, but here, he found something about the soot offensive. The people here were busy, and instead of taking the time to clean off their clothes, they left them dirty between washings, spreading the soot as they brushed against people in the crowded streets.

Mo Ling wasn't with him. He'd left her behind at their temporary accommodations at an inn. Since she didn't have an identity, he'd snuck her into the city. He'd soon have new documents made for her, but for now, it was best if she lay low. The South had paperwork for everything, including identification and travel documents. And unlike most places, they actually checked them.

Cha Ming cringed as yet another dirty kiln worker forced his way past him. *I'll have to take a bath when I get back,* he thought. *And possibly burn my clothes.*

There were three main industries in Ashes, and all of them contributed to the soot problem. The first, most-obvious industry, was smithing. Metal was extracted from nearby Bastion, the capital. While much of the high-grade work was carried out over there for convenience, the dirtier work was done in Ashes. Countless smithies bellowed thick black smoke from large chimneys, covering a good quarter of the city in a black haze that rained dust on the people below.

Where there was demand for metal, there was often demand for buildings and building materials. As such, Ashes had also evolved into the primary manufacturer for various forms of bricks and concrete. Those required clay and high-heat furnaces, which in turn required combustion. The industry, though lucrative for its body-cultivating workers, constantly produced mountains of fine dust that blew into the streets as they waited to be carried away.

Alchemy, ironically, was the worst offender. Most people thought of alchemists as refined masters of chemistry, rarely making mistakes. But that only applied to the upper levels of the profession. The high concentration of body cultivators that fed kilns and worked metal made Ashes a convenient location to learn pill concoction. Most low-grade alchemist exams could only be taken in Ashes, and as a result, exploding furnaces filled the air with toxic chemicals that ate away at everyone's vitality. Fortunately, most mortals stayed out of Ashes.

Cha Ming vowed to impose strict cleanliness standards when he started his own smithy. He'd beat his workers into obedience, regardless of talent. Unfortunately, he still needed to take care of some formalities before he could do this, so he entered a tall green building on a busy commercial street just off Main Street.

The Greenwind Pavilion in Ashes, though simpler in construction than the others he'd been to, was efficient as always. The moment he stepped in, a high-level manager zipped down the stairs and interrupted the normal attendant before she could even speak.

"What can I do for this esteemed guest today?" the manager said. She was a peak-core-formation cultivator who wore the usual green robes. Her black hair was tied back in a bun and fastened with a green-and-gold pin. It was an unusual hairstyle in Ashes, where people kept their hair short, but convenient compared to the flowing hairstyles of the North.

"Perhaps we could speak in a private room?" Cha Ming said.

The woman nodded and led the way up the stairs. They traveled up three floors, stopping just short of the fifth. Cha Ming had only exposed the strength of a middle-core-formation cultivator, so he didn't have the qualifications to access the highest level. After sitting down, the woman served him a black beverage. He took a sip and was surprised to discover that it was coffee. Apparently the beverage had made its way to the South as well.

"You may call me Manager Mu," the manager said. "Please feel free to tell me what you need. As a main branch, we offer our full line of services at this location."

"I require a few things, both tedious and time-consuming," Cha Ming said after putting down his cup. He spoke with a gruff voice and had several strands of gray running through his black hair. Though Pai Xiao was a middle-core-formation cultivator, he'd broken through later on in life at the ripe old age of ninety. This was the equivalent of a forty-five-year-old mortal man. "I need some documents forged, with expedited delivery. I also need to acquire a smithy with twenty workers, including apprentices."

"The smithy shouldn't be a problem," the woman said, nodding. They sometimes took care of troublesome purchases for a fee. "There are many that get bought or sold every month. What documents do you require?"

"I want mid-grade grandmaster spiritual-blacksmith certification," Cha Ming said. "Made out to one year ago. Likewise, I want an early-grade grandmaster certificate made out three years ago and an initial-grade one five years ago. All under my name, Pai Xiao.

"Likewise, I want a paper trail forged. Records of sale, receipts, you name it, of me opening smaller smithies after my arrival in the city five years ago."

"Is that all?" the manager asked. None of these requests seemed out of the ordinary for this premier information agency.

"I also want an identity for a young woman," Cha Ming said. "I want a past for her, nothing too extravagant. No bonded slavery, currently free." He placed a jade on the table. "This contains her details, cultivation, and appearance. Accommodate them as much as possible. Her entire family should be deceased or impossible to find."

"That last one is easy," Manager Mu said. "We can throw it in free of charge, assuming you can afford the rest. Before we agree to anything, however, I'd like to caution you against forging a reputation. It's not that we can't do it, but that your behavior will give you away. When we work, we leave no traces of personal involvement. Therefore, if there are any discrepancies, people will think they are errors. But if enough discrepancies add up, you'll eventually have to answer for them."

"It's nothing I can't take care of," Cha Ming said.

"For you to ask for this service, I'm sure you can handle the consequences," Manager Mu said. "The problem is whether you wish to be exposed or not. A reputation in smithing is nothing with no works to your name. Given enough time, people will realize no one has ever swung a sword you've forged. Even worse, if the kingdom administrators suspect you don't possess the skills your documentation implies, the consequences would be dire."

"I said it's nothing I can't take care of," Cha Ming said. "What's your price?"

As far as he was concerned, the smithy would be the biggest expense. Spiritual blacksmithing followed a different model than alchemy. For one, since the goods were durable, the material costs were much higher, and though failures could be recast as lesser products, it was difficult to bear the cost of these failures. As such, smiths tended to craft low-risk items. A mid-grade grandmaster smith would mostly craft early-grade goods and initial-grade goods. On a terrific month, he might be able to gross 2,000 top-grade spirit stones, but that figure would likely be closer to five hundred depending on business.

Manager Mu licked his lips. "The usual rate for the shop would be around five years of production. Let's call that thirty thousand top-grade stones. Our facilitation fee is usually around ten percent, but you're asking us for something unusual. Adding up all the information tampering. I'd say we're looking at closer to fifty thousand top-grade stones."

Cha Ming winced.

"Too expensive?" the woman asked, disappointed.

"Not too expensive, just complicated," Cha Ming said. "I may need to liquidate certain assets. These assets would need to be kept absolutely secret."

"Define absolutely," Manager Mu said, a light smile on her face.

"By absolutely, I mean that if a transcendent, or even the grand vizier of the Southern Alliance asked, the Greenwind Pavilion wouldn't divulge the secret."

"Ah," Manager Mu said. "That is, unfortunately, above my pay grade. Please follow me." She led Cha Ming outside the room and up the stairs. They arrived at the fifth floor, supposedly the highest one, and to Cha Ming's surprise, a staircase appeared that led to a sixth floor. There shouldn't *be* a sixth floor, at least, not if he judged the building from what he'd seen on the outside.

"We never met, whoever you are," she said, bowing.

Cha Ming looked up the stairs and proceeded up. It seemed that his purchase, along with the request for secrecy, had passed some sort of threshold most weren't qualified to know about.

At the top of the steps, the décor changed drastically. The building no longer conformed to the usual Greenwind Pavilion décor, where wooden construction was preferred over stone. Instead, the walls and the floor were built out of a glowing black rock. They were covered in green runes that emanated a faint trace of light. At the center of the room was a formation that was both familiar and foreign to Cha Ming.

He'd seen such a thing before, he soon realized; it was a teleportation formation, like the one he'd seen on the Bridge of Stars. As he entered the room, the formation glowed, and a white-haired old man in green-and-silver robes appeared.

"I don't often get to meet premium customers in Ashes," the man said. "Don't bother introducing yourself. I hear the same old lies every time. It gets boring."

Cha Ming tried to probe the man with his transcendent force but detected nothing.

"I'd also appreciate if you refrain from any infantile attempts at scanning me, impressive as they are," the man said. "Transcendent souls are rare on this plane. I've narrowed you down to one in a hundred people."

"I'd like for the Greenwind Pavilion to facilitate a purchase and forge some documents," Cha Ming said. "But to do so, I need to liquidate certain sensitive assets."

"Ah," the man said. "Let's see them, then. Regardless of whether we trade, I won't reveal them to anyone."

Cha Ming hesitated, then summoned the only valuable things he had: several bottles of pills, each with Grandmist seals.

"So, you're Brother Cha Ming," the man said. "I'm so pleased to finally make your acquaintance."

Cha Ming winced.

"You were right to ask for secrecy. Fortunately for you, these items are in high demand. They are difficult to import from a transcendent plane. I can offer you two times the list price of standard pills of their grade."

Cha Ming's brow twitched. "They were selling for five times in Haijing."

"But you weren't so desperate back then, and your buyers didn't have access to imported goods," the man said dismissively. "I do. Deal or no deal?"

Cha Ming hesitated. "The purchases I inquired about, and the information tampering. Information on those things is for sale, isn't it?"

The man grinned. "Not the sharpest tool in the shed, but not the dullest either. Yes, complete secrecy will cost you. Double."

"Double?" Cha Ming said, aghast. "Why don't you just rob me?" He'd only ever felt so aggrieved when dealing with the Clear Sky Brush.

"Robbing is unethical," the man said, wagging his finger. "We only deal in legitimate business here."

"Like information tampering," Cha Ming said blankly.

"Like information tampering," the man said enthusiastically.

"Since I'm here, I don't suppose I can order massive quantities of goods while I'm at it?" Cha Ming asked.

"I, Elder Zhong, would teleport them to you personally," the old man said. "Any information you require, I would tell you personally."

"Then do you know the location of a Gold Essence Marrow or Gold Essence Core on the plane?" Cha Ming asked.

The man paused for a second, then nodded. "Our preliminary survey of the plane indicated that if it existed here, it would be in the Shattered Lands. I can import some for you, but the cost would likely be too great for you to bear."

"Try me," Cha Ming said.

"Have you heard of high-grade immortal jades?" Elder Zhong asked.

Cha Ming shook his head.

"Then let's move on to other items."

Since I'm here, I might as well stock up, Cha Ming thought. He listed a large number of medicinal herbs, metals, liquified elemental essence, and elemental essence.

"The total comes to 150,000 high-grade spirit stones," Elder Zhong said.

"Including secrecy?" Cha Ming asked.

"Including secrecy," Elder Zhong said. Conveniently for the older man, this was the exact worth of the fifteen bottles of peak-grade Grandmist pills he'd placed in front of him. Cha Ming had expected this result, which was why he'd added on as many valuable goods as possible. He nodded, and Elder Zhong swiped the pile of bottles away. "Pleasure doing business with someone who appreciates the value of secrecy."

"I don't suppose Zhou Li is one of those who doesn't?" Cha Ming asked.

"Unfortunately for you, he pays a premium for it," Senior Zhong said. "I personally gouge him. The Spirit Temple, on the other hand… I'd be happy to provide you with details on them. For just ten bottles of peak Grandmist pills, I can give you all the juicy details about their dealings in the Ji Kingdom for the past thousand years."

"Not interested," Cha Ming said.

"A pity," Elder Zhong said. "They've always been cheapskates. I could give you a discount. Maybe… eight bottles?"

Seeing that Cha Ming wasn't interested, he sighed and walked over to the side. The formation he'd come through activated, revealing a small ring containing what he'd asked for. Cha Ming inspected the contents and confirmed they were all there.

"Are you sure you're not interested?" Elder Zhong probed. "I'll tell you what. Five pills."

Cha Ming ignored him. It wasn't that he didn't want the information; he simply couldn't afford it anymore. He only had two Grandmist pills left. Fortunately, the rest of his plan didn't involve too much money. Besides, he already had a dossier of information on the Spirit Temple, courtesy of Wang Jun.

"Maybe next time," Elder Zhong muttered. "Is that everything?"

"Yes, that's everything," Cha Ming said.

The man nodded and stepped back into the teleportation formation, traveling to heavens knew where. Cha Ming, goods in tow, exited the Greenwind Pavilion. He made his way back to the hotel, where Mo Ling was waiting.

Chapter 12: Weapon Focus

*A*nother day, another blade, Cha Ming thought, standing up from his cultivation. His room, though small, was well-furnished. It didn't contain a bed—cultivators didn't need beds—but it had a sofa and a tea table, complete with an *Angels and Devils* board. The area where he'd been sitting was inscribed with an energy-gathering formation, which could be used to convert qi from top-grade spirit stones and reinforce his cultivation. It was naturally a cover—the real location where he cultivated was the Clear Sky World, where he could accelerate time by up to five times.

Cha Ming stretched before walking out the door and heading downstairs. He was greeted by a cheerful Mo Ling. At her insistence, she'd become the attendant and bookkeeper in his workshop. Her work, though slow, was impeccable, freeing up much of his time for cultivation and smithing.

"How have the latest negotiations with our material suppliers gone?" Cha Ming asked, stopping in front of the large wooden desk at the entrance. On top of her administrative duties, she also served as a gatekeeper for the workshop, keeping potential customers away as the blacksmiths worked between appointments. Workshops were dangerous places, and it wasn't prudent to let outsiders wander inside.

"They're tough," Mo Ling said, retrieving a pile of papers two stacks over from the one she'd been working on. "I've managed to secure a fifteen-percent discount by playing three of them off each other. I think it might be possible to negotiate a five-percent discount if we guarantee minimum volumes."

Cha Ming thought for moment, then shook his head. "I'd prefer not to lock us in. An open contract is fine with a fifteen-percent discount."

Mo Ling nodded. She'd grown used to his reluctance to commit to anything long term. "I'll shoot for eighteen percent and see what that gets us."

Satisfied with her work, Cha Ming entered the workshop. "Grandmaster," one of the apprentices greeted as he entered.

"At ease," Cha Ming said to the man, who was busy refining lakebed iron. The strong man pounded away at the material, working a fine dusting of amorphous demon shale into it. Lakebed iron didn't need much refining, as much of the sediment had been washed away in underwater currents where it accumulated. The demon shale—at least the amorphous variety—would help mitigate the only downside of the ore: the excess water qi it naturally contained.

Today, Cha Ming was going to make a work of art. It was an important weapon, the first of three that he'd need to create. He walked over to an area at the back, where many important metals were stored. There, he arrived at a heavy black chest that had been delivered yesterday morning. Rather than try to lift the heavy box, Cha Ming opened it using a special key he'd been given; the chest popped open, revealing a dark-red orb.

A bloody aura instantly filled the room. As it did, the apprentice who'd been merrily hammering away at the lakebed iron suddenly yelled in anger and threw the ingot across the room. Cha Ming quickly closed the chest and faced the apprentice, who looked down apologetically.

"I'm sorry, Grandmaster," he said.

"It's my fault," Cha Ming replied. "I've never worked with demon blood steel before. I didn't know its rage-inducing effects would be so potent."

Now, how to mitigate this, he thought. His first instinct was to set up a formation, but Pai Xiao was no formation artist. So he walked to the front, where Mo Ling sat shaking from head to toe. It seemed she, too, had been affected by the malevolent aura.

Cha Ming walked out of the workshop and returned one hour later with an arrogant-looking man. Upon arriving, he looked around the shop and placed many formation discs on the floor. Then, after painting between them with a large brush, he coughed lightly. Cha Ming sighed and placed a pile of high-grade spirit stones on the floor, which were instantly absorbed by the formation that hummed to life. "I'll return once the rental period is over to retrieve the discs," the man said, then left the room.

Once again, Cha Ming opened the small black chest. The bloody aura, though just as potent as before, didn't leak out from the containment. It pooled around Cha Ming, attacking his body with little success. Demon blood steel was an odd metal formed when a dead demon's blood pooled in an area rich with a mutable ore. It took thousands of years to form, and as a result, it was in short supply.

Cha Ming lifted out the orb, which was barely bigger than a fist, straining as he did so with his suppressed body cultivation, and placed it onto his soul-alloy workbench. "Seems about the right weight," he muttered to himself. He flicked his fingers, and an orange-gold flame roared to life in the furnace. Using his qi as fuel, he increased the temperature until it became too difficult to bear. He placed the metal brick on soul-alloy supports and continued heating it for three hours. Not only was the metal heavy, but it also had a very high heat capacity. He continued heating it until it glowed pink, after which he pulled the brick out using soul-alloy tongs and placed it on an anvil just in front of the furnace.

Cha Ming struck while the metal was hot. He summoned his middle-core-grade hammer—he'd replaced his old one long ago—and began pounding away at the metal. As he did, he used his orange-gold flame to make up the heat the metal lost to the open air while using its metal-manipulation properties to aid him as he pounded. Under his direction, the brick became longer and thinner.

He continued until it reached two feet in length, after which he flattened the top and shaped it into a sharp point. It now resembled a very short sword.

Demon blood steel was difficult to work with. Not only was its melting point very high but melting it would destroy the demon blood inside it. So he pounded away at the metal, shaping it slowly but surely. Hours passed as the weapon became not a short sword, but the blade of a long spear. It had two serrated edges and a sharp point. Though such a feature might seem impractical to a normal cultivator, it was actually very useful for its intended recipient: a powerful blood master. Serrated edges drew more blood than their sharper counterparts.

Cha Ming nodded in appreciation as he transformed his spiritual hammer into its chisel hammer form. For most metals, he'd use a carving blade, but demon blood steel was both hard and tough. His heavy strikes barely left a mark in the heated metal. He had to repeat each strike with surgical precision, never straying too far lest his runic marks be ruined. He continued this way for several hours, until finally, the blade's runework was completed.

It was dark outside by the time he finished. The same apprentice from before was done with his work but had remained behind to spectate. Though the pay was terrible for one of his position, the main benefit Cha Ming offered was allowing people to watch him work. The others in his shop either didn't care to see or were off enjoying the few days off Cha Ming had given them. In Cha Ming's opinion, it was their loss.

Instead of directly quenching the blade, Cha Ming placed it back on the anvil and walked over to a rack in the back. There, many long metal rods awaited their companion blades. Cha Ming reached down to the lowest rack and found what he was looking for: a shaft made of nightmare elm wood. The wood was heavy, and Cha Ming's muscles bulged as he lifted it.

"Only a heavy, inflexible wood is suited to such a heavy spear blade," he explained to the apprentice as he hauled it over to the bench. "Any less rigid and the shaft will bend uncontrollably during battle. Any less heavy and the weapon won't be balanced."

The fact that he could barely lift it didn't matter. The weapon wasn't for him, but for a peak-marrow-refining cultivator.

With the runework on the blade completed, Cha Ming moved on to the shaft. Instead of the chisel hammer, he turned his core-grade hammer focus into a carving knife. A core-grade hammer focus could easily accommodate three forms. He carved deft strokes into the wood, demonstrating them one at a time for the young but honest man. The runes were beyond him, but the charm Cha Ming demonstrated as he carved was not. If he could imitate Cha Ming, the boy would make great strides in his profession.

Carving the weapon's shaft took much less time than inscribing the spear blade. Once finished, Cha Ming brought the spear blade back into the orange-gold flame and waited for it to glow pink again. "Spear weapons are often crafted as two parts: the shaft and the spearhead. This is similar to the philosophy behind crafting a sword in two parts, the hilt and the blade."

The apprentice nodded. "The hilt can easily be replaced. The same applies to a spear shaft."

"Yes," Cha Ming said. "And that works great for inferior weapons. I've found that the best spears are crafted as a single piece, however. Strictly speaking, it can't all be done in one piece, as the material requirements are vastly different. But the runic array can be activated as a single entity."

Using tongs, Cha Ming connected the spear haft to the spear blade and twisted. The two parts let out a soft click as runic lines connected. Then, Cha Ming motioned to a shelf at the back. A rainbow of powder poured into the weapon as it absorbed the crystalized elemental essence powder. The apprentice widened his eyes in amazement as the spear grew brighter.

Cha Ming grasped the softly glowing spear when it finished absorbing the powder. He walked further back into the room, where a barrel of liquified elemental essence lay. He poured five vials into it, one for each elemental evanescence. There was more water evanescence compared to the other types. This was to better reflect the properties of the demon blood in the spear. Then he plunged the spear headfirst into the barrel. As the metal quenched, the liquified elemental essence hissed. The runic patterns on the spear lit up with a bloody, malevolent light. This continued for some time before the glow faded, leaving a red spear in Cha Ming's hands.

"Run along now," Cha Ming said to the apprentice. "I'm done smithing for the day."

The man nodded and moved to leave but hesitated on his way out.

"What grade is it?" the man asked. Though Cha Ming thought of him as an apprentice, he was a master smith in his own right.

"Late core grade," Cha Ming grunted. "I lucked out."

The man nodded and left. Only Cha Ming knew how long he'd spent in the Clear Sky World, training his smithing skills to achieve this result. His smithing skills were subpar for his professed middle grandmaster certification, but he more than made up for it with clever runework.

Now to sell it to a man who doesn't deserve it, Cha Ming thought. The weapon, one of the three main focuses required for Sun Wukong's deception array, was to be gifted to the abbot of the Blood Master Monastery in Ashes. The next two weapons would go to the head of the Spirit Temple, and to this city's duke. Each of them was a despicable individual with a terrible history. Unfortunately, he had little choice in the matter if he was going to create an artificial reputation for himself.

"Why are you so grumpy about it?" Sun Wukong asked. "You and I both know what sort of trap you left inside the weapon's runic array."

Cha Ming grinned. "I suppose you're right. Maybe I'm just worried about short-term damage."

"You won't feel bad and chicken out, will you?" Sun Wukong asked mockingly.

Cha Ming shook his head. "Not in the slightest. These men are far from innocent. My debt isn't to them but to the good people in this city."

"And how will you make it up to *them*?" Sun Wukong asked.

"I don't know how much good it'll do," Cha Ming said, "but once my work in Bastion is done, I won't need them to believe my ruse. What's the point in laying a trap if you don't intend to set it off?"

"See? I knew you'd come around," Sun Wukong said.

"Come around?" Cha Ming asked. "You've seen the Blood Master Monastery. You've seen the city lord's information." He shook his head. "I've never needed an excuse to kill evil men. The method doesn't matter."

"You're no fun at all," Sun Wukong said. "Why don't you at least pretend to succumb to corruption? Just this once."

"Why pretend?" Cha Ming asked. "Letting you try again and again without making any headway is satisfying in its own right." He walked out of the workshop and into the reception area where Mo Ling worked. It was past closing time, but the poor girl was at her desk, apparently taking a nap. As quietly as he could, he tiptoed out of the building. He suppressed the sadness in his heart as he heard her mumble the names of the family she'd abandoned and the friends she'd left behind.

As he walked down the crowded streets toward the Blood Master Monastery, he ignored the gawking guardsmen and shivering people that made way for him. Instead, he focused on a very real but pressing problem: Mo Ling had come with him to Ashes, but she could hardly keep following him. He might be able to shield her from the inevitable backlash that ensued when the three most important people in the city died cruel, tragic deaths, but bringing her to Bastion was just asking for trouble. It was only a matter of time before he had to leave her behind.

Chapter 13: Offer

It was a busy day in Pai Xiao's forge. All of Cha Ming's smiths, whether young or old, were busy toiling away to fill the day's orders. The sheer number of weapons and armor requested had increased significantly over the past few days, so no one dared slack off. Anyone forging too slowly would get brow-beaten by their coworkers until they caught up. Mo Ling also worked double-time, frantically pushing papers, paying invoices, and submitting work orders to supply the busy smiths.

Unlike Mo Ling and those men in the forge, however, Cha Ming wasn't particularly busy. He spent most of his free time in the Clear Sky World, perfecting his spiritual blacksmithing as much as he could in as short a time as possible. He didn't need to be the best—that would undermine everything he was hoping to achieve in this city. But he *did* need to be a miracle worker, a smith who, against all odds, forged his way through sheer genius.

The three weapons he'd crafted—a spear for the Blood Master Monastery's abbot, a crook for the Spirit Temple's shepherd, and a saber for the duke of Ashes—were flukes. They were completely different than anything else he'd crafted. His other works were simple, imperfect creations, though in each mid-grade treasure he forged, he left an inconsistency that hinted at what it could be with a little more tweaking.

Since Cha Ming needed to eventually make good on that potential, he studied as much as possible. Pai Xiao was not only a genius smith, but a man of academic talent. He spent most of his time upstairs theorizing, working hard to combine hints of inspiration as the smiths worked the forge's day-to-day operations. Every once in a while, he had an epiphany. When he did, he went downstairs and forged something. He then provided pointers to everyone present before secluding himself once more.

Today, like many other days, Cha Ming stepped out of the Clear Sky World in the middle of the morning. The air in the city, which blew through an open window in his chambers, was unusually good today due to a strong wind from the east. He shut the window and walked down the stone steps that led to the reception area. The smiths gave him rushed greetings as he entered the workshop. Their busy workload was due in large part to his growing reputation. With more work came more practice, and with more practice came increased quality. Now, it was difficult to find anyone who didn't know about Pai Xiao's smithy.

"Ease up on those blows," Cha Ming instructed one of the masters, who nodded and did as he was told. The metal he was working on, golden plum iron, was a soft metal that was typically used to craft defensive jewelry. The man, one of the two jewelers in his smithy, was aware of that fact, but unaware of another. "You'll shape it faster if you pound harder," Cha Ming continued. "But golden plum iron retains its best internal structure from the first casting and quenching. The more force you use, the more you destroy that structure. It's the same reason you didn't heat the metal to more than half its melting point before working with it."

"Thank you for your instruction," the master said, grateful for the advice. His blows softened even more as he adjusted his approach to use the least strength possible in forming the leaflike brooch. It would soon be covered in tiny runes and socketed with many rune-covered gems. He would only realize the benefits of his care during the final assembly, when the runes were integrated into the jewelry. The intact structure of the golden plum iron would lead to better energy conductivity and a slightly faster activation—a crucial metric when assessing the value of the brooch.

Satisfied at the man's progress, Cha Ming continued through the forge. He nodded as he passed some, but to others, he left small pointers. These pointers were all within the bounds of his experience, the epiphanies he'd gained on those three main late-grade weapons and those hundred or so other mid-grade creations.

It seemed like a normal day, but as he walked, he spotted a flash of movement and felt a faint sense of trepidation. "Stop!" he shouted, zipping through the room in a flash, crashing through some workbenches. He arrived just in time to snatch a man's wrist as he was smacking down on a freshly cast sword. The room grew silent, and Cha Ming breathed out a sigh of relief.

"You stupid, stupid man," he scolded.

The smith, confused and uncertain, banished his hammer. Cha Ming motioned to all the other smiths to huddle around the man's workbench. "What do you all see?" he asked the smiths. They looked at each other uncertainly. Was this a test?

"Pyric iron," one of the older, more experienced smiths said. "I've worked with it a few times. Great for forging flame-aligned blades, though it's a little finicky when you try alloying it with anything."

"That's right," another man said. "If you add too much of anything else, it seems to either weaken the metal to the point that it's useless or solidify until it's unworkable and brittle. It'll sometimes crack when you work on it, even when hot."

"Very good," Cha Ming said, nodding. "I've worked with the metal a few times too. You can forge weapons up to peak-magic grade with it. It's best alloyed with fire or metal-based alloys, though earth-based alloys can also be used if you want a little more sturdiness and heft. Limited amounts are fine. If you use water-based alloying metals, any blades you create will crack as you forge, since it hardens so quickly. It's still doable, but anything you make will have to be cast directly without subsequent hammering. Warhammers will work just fine with that method—they'll be hard but a bit brittle."

He tapped on the table near the cast blade, which hadn't even been knocked out of its mold yet. It had been cooling as Cha Ming spoke. "What do you think he alloyed this with?"

One of the men, who'd answered before, shrugged. "I see flecks of red in the metal. I'd guess it's a fire-based alloy."

"I'll have to agree with him there," another man said, nodding. "Look at how those red specks are squirming about in the metal, looking for release. I'd have melted them for longer if I were him, but it's nothing a little hammering won't fix."

The first man nodded.

"And what did you actually use?" Cha Ming asked the man, who'd finally recovered from his initial confusion.

"I was in a mood to experiment," the man said. "Just like you do every day. I decided to see what would happen if I mixed in azure nickel flakes."

He heard a couple of groans from the audience. One of them was the most senior man among them, but another was one of the youngest smiths, the same one who'd seen him crafting the demon blood steel spear.

"It looks like someone's been studying," Cha Ming said with a smile. "Tell me, why is it a bad idea to alloy azure nickel flakes with pyric iron?"

The younger man hesitated, then spoke. "Because pyric metal is mildly pyrophoric."

"Pyro-what?" another smith said. "Use plain words, friend."

"It means," the oldest among them said, "that given enough air, it will catch fire. Burn, as it were."

"But that makes no sense," another man said. "We've got the pyric iron stored in open air in the shed. If it could catch fire, it would have done so."

"In most cases, the concentration of oxygen in the air isn't enough to do anything," the man said, shrugging. "Even at high heat. But if you add in azure nickel... Well, it's a wind-based metal, and the wind-element qi in it doesn't exactly agree with pyric iron. Now tell me, what happens when you put oil and a wick together?"

"Nuthin," the man said. "Nuthin', unless you light the wick."

"Right," the man continued. "Sparks, friction, and the like. Tell me, how many sparks and how much energy do you think a peak-bone-forging cultivator can deliver into a chuck of metal by smacking it? If it was at room temperature, it might not do anything, but this metal is near its melting point, so it's especially easy to set off. There's no telling what would have happened if the grandmaster hadn't caught his hammer." He bowed to Cha Ming. "Many thanks, Grandmaster Pai Xiao."

The smith who'd been about to strike the cast sword paled. "My apologies, Grandmaster. What I've done is inexcusable."

"No harm, no foul," Cha Ming said. "Next time, read up on the metal you're working with. A little reading never killed anyone. You're all free to use my reference library. As for how much damage it could have caused, I know a little about that." He winced and put his hand to his left arm. "I once did something similar when I was an initial-marrow-refining cultivator. Let's just say I didn't recover from the damage until I broke through to early grade."

The implication was clear. If the man had struck it, anyone below core formation would be dead.

Suddenly, as many of them were leaving to return to their workbench, a gleam appeared in Cha Ming's eyes. "Interesting," he thought out loud. "Can I take that from you?" he asked the smith, who wasn't quite sure what to do with his mold. Should he throw the metal out together with the mold or try to separate them once the blade cooled?

"Please," the man said, glad to be rid of it.

Cha Ming lifted the mold and blade, and to everyone's surprise, he took it to the furnace. Then he activated a formation he had engraved in the stone floor. It hummed to life, and a thin shield of force now stood between everyone and Cha Ming's work area.

"The metal is mildly pyrophoric," Cha Ming mumbled. "Does that mean the metal would be different if allowed to react?" He tapped the mold lightly with his finger, and the piece of cast metal fell onto a cushion of transcendent force in the bottom of a large cauldron. Then he activated his orange-gold flame and heated it from below.

The metal had already been near its melting point, so it only took a quarter hour to melt. Soon it was nothing more than a soupy mixture with floating red flakes. Nodding, Cha Ming increased the heat. The reason the flakes hadn't melted was because the smith heating the mixture hadn't been strong enough. So he increased the intensity of his flames and continued until the red flakes dissolved into the mixture, which hissed and crackled as it did.

"This part might be dangerous, so put up your personal shields," Cha Ming instructed the growing audience.

The many smiths did as they were told. They activated smaller shields in front of each of their workbenches, then continued observing from a distance. Once each of the shields were up, Cha Ming separated a small portion of the pyric iron and azure nickel alloy. The molten metal seemed to pulse and sizzle. With just a little more energy, something would happen, so Cha Ming closed the cauldron, which then grew transparent so he and everyone could see inside. He then heated the small block to increasingly high temperatures, until finally, it began to pop and spark.

The small explosion, fortunately, was no match for the cauldron. The blob continued to spit and crackle until finally, it stopped. He continued increasing the temperature, and after a few rounds of subsequent crackling, the metal stopped reacting so violently. After reaching a certain point, a component in the metal evaporated, leaving behind only a translucent red blob.

Encouraged by this result, Cha Ming opened the lid, retrieved the purified blob, and threw in another one. He repeated the process from before, adding the purified product into an increasingly large blob of transparent metal.

"Now what to do with the metal?" Cha Ming muttered after he'd purified everything. The transparent blob was completely different than any metal he'd ever worked with. In fact, its melting point had greatly increased, so its other properties probably had as well.

Shrugging, Cha Ming poured the blob of metal back into the

cauldron and summoned a few other alloying metals. Instead of rejecting the materials like it usually did, this newly refined metal took them all in like long-lost cousins. Once he finished making up for the metal he'd removed in the purification process, Cha Ming poured the mixture into the mold of a sword. The metal cooled, and when it finally solidified, it glowed a light pink color.

Cha Ming proceeded to hammer away at the blade, forging it into a proper sword blade. When he finished, he began carving intricate flame-based runes. They weren't weak runes he'd normally use on such a metal, but the type he'd use on a late-core weapon. He'd personally seen what temperatures the metal it was made of could withstand.

Once he finished carving the weapon, he threw it back into the fire and went over to a rack of premade hilts. He hated crafting them, so he made them in batches. After mulling over his choices for a while, he ultimately picked a hilt made of cold iron essence with blue-gold gilding. A cultivator would want the blade to be hot, so keeping the hilt cool was paramount. Just to be sure, he carved some protecting and insulating runes into the hilt. Then he threw the hilt into the flames as well. After it reached a certain temperature, he joined the hilt with the blade using tongs and heated them even further. The metal sweated together, forming a strong seal that aligned with the runes he'd carved.

Having completed the body of the weapon, Cha Ming didn't summon crystalized elemental essence like he normally did. This time, he took out two blobs of liquified elemental essence from the barrel and dosed one with a high concentration of water evanescence and another with fire evanescence. The essence seeped into the runes of the hilt and blade, and once the last of the potency had disappeared, he shoved the blade into the remaining barrel of liquified elemental essence. The weapon hummed as it drank in heaven and earth energy.

Cha Ming took out the blade and grasped it. He poured fire qi into the blade, and it immediately turned light pink. Even without using any special techniques, such a blade would burn through most things.

"Now who to sell it to?" he wondered out loud as he tested the blade's balance. Like the other three, it was a late-core-grade weapon. Unlike the others, however, he hadn't forged it with a flaw. *Maybe I should keep it and sell it when I head back north,* he thought.

"I'll buy it," a voice suddenly said from the back of the room. Cha Ming and the other smiths in the room looked back to see a middle-aged man in green robes standing there. Mo Ling, who was usually good at repelling unwanted visitors, stood beside him with her head downcast.

"You can't just walk into the smithy while the grandmaster is crafting," one of the smiths said indignantly.

Cha Ming held up his hand to quiet him, however. This newly arrived cultivator wasn't simple. More importantly, his robes were black and his hair was blond. This man was exactly who he'd been waiting for. Cha Ming held the sword with two hands, point down, and bowed. "I'd be happy to discuss selling this blade to Senior Wang."

The men in the room began to murmur. There weren't many people named Wang in Ashes, and none of them were powerful. There was, however, a powerful man with that family name in Bastion, the capital city of the Ji Kingdom. Not only was he rich, but the group he directed owned one of the most profitable forges in the kingdom. Working for them was a dream all Southern smiths aspired to.

"Please, follow me to my office," Cha Ming said. "This lowly smith would be happy to make you tea."

The man smiled lightly at the mention of tea.

"I'm not one to refuse a good cup of tea," the man said. "Lead the way. You may call me Director Wang Yong or Director Yong for short."

"Please enjoy," Cha Ming said, handing a cup of tea to the middle-aged man seated before him. Director Yong smelled the tea appreciatively before taking a sip. He raised his eyebrows in surprise as the hot beverage touched his lips.

"This isn't from the South," Director Yong said. He continued drinking, humming lightly as he did.

"I used to travel in my youth," Cha Ming said. "At some point, I took to tea drinking as a hobby. The one who sold me this called it Meadow Field oolong tea. He claimed it was aged ten years."

Director Yong snorted. "He lied. This is clearly Silver Leaf oolong tea, aged eight. Still, you were right to buy it. It's good tea no matter what name it was sold under."

"It was worth every penny," Cha Ming said. "I can't say I've ever heard of this Silver Leaf oolong tea. And you mentioned the North? Have you been there? I heard it's a very dangerous place to go, especially for Southerners."

"For some, it's difficult," Director Yong said. "But with the right channels, anything is possible. Transporting small expensive things like tea across the border is easiest, though for some reason, tea isn't very popular in the South."

"That's nonsense," Cha Ming said. "I see people drinking tea everywhere I go." They called it tea, at least, but it was very different than what Cha Ming was used to. Instead of pouring hot water over tea leaves for a short period of time, Southerners simmered grains. Richer families didn't stray from this tradition, preferring to simmer spiritually infused grains instead of leaves.

"What they call tea is just a grain's bathwater," Director Yong huffed.

"A fair assessment," Cha Ming said. "I've never liked grain-based teas. They lack flavor and boldness."

"And that, my friend, makes you a man of good taste," Director Yong said. "Now about that blade. I've never seen anything quite like it." The blade was resting on a bench, its translucent pink metal illuminated under the afternoon sun that shone through the open window.

"I got lucky," Cha Ming said. "One of my smiths happened upon an interesting reaction with familiar metals. He didn't have the skill to follow through with it, but I did. By refining the pyric iron, I was able to create a blade far finer than one would think possible for such a metal."

Director Yong nodded in approval. "I'm not a strong smith, as I spend most of my time overlooking finances and managing personnel," he said, "but I know my way around a forge. I also happen to read a lot. I once read something about pyric iron and its refinement in our library. What you did was speculated in those books, but no one ever bothered to look into it."

"Really?" Cha Ming said, feigning surprise. He shook his head. "I should have known. My path isn't an easy one."

"Your path?" Director Yong asked, sipping on his freshly topped-up cup. His eyes twinkled when he asked this.

"To be honest with you, Director Yong," Cha Ming said, "when I was young, I stumbled upon an incomplete spiritual blacksmithing inheritance. Rather than continue as a mercenary or adventurer, I chose to pursue forging. I toiled away for decades until I finally made enough progress to come here."

"Five years ago," Director Yong said, nodding.

Cha Ming raised an eyebrow.

"People talk about you on every street corner these days. What I said was common knowledge. You've made amazing progress for a rogue smith from Liaoning."

"Perhaps," Cha Ming said. "Though it seems my progress has slowed substantially. In a sense, it reminds me of when I started. My smithing knowledge was incomplete, and I didn't yet have the skill to make use of it. I learned by spying on others as they worked, and by rummaging through libraries. More than anything, however,

I relied on trial and error. Occasionally, I'd gain insights, which I'd combine with the knowledge I gained from books to build myself a framework."

"And that all changed twenty years ago," Director Yong said.

Cha Ming, feigning surprise once more, nodded. "Twenty years ago, I finally caught up to the minimum requirements for my inheritance. I advanced by leaps and bounds. When I reached the limit of what I could achieve in Liaoning, I left and came here. I improved steadily, year after year, becoming a grandmaster smith in my first year, an early-grade grandmaster in my second, and a mid-grade grandmaster in my fourth."

"And then you stalled," Director Yong finished.

"And then I stalled," Cha Ming admitted. "My inheritance can take me no further. All I can do is trudge away like I used to, riding mad moments of inspiration until I've accumulated enough knowledge to progress. It's both invigorating and frustrating."

"You know what you're building is unstable," Director Yong said. "Your base isn't as solid as people think, and any basis for advancing to late-grade grandmaster will also be unstable."

Cha Ming shrugged. "What else can I do? I value freedom. Pardon me for being rude, but I rather hate working for others. Wherever I go, I open my own smithy. It might be expensive, but I hate being bound by employment contracts." Absently, he scratched at his forehead, hinting at what could have been there in the past.

Director Yong nodded understandingly.

"About this blade," Director Yong said. "The usual market price for such a weapon is five thousand top-grade spirit stones. Of course, those weapons are made from more expensive materials…"

Cha Ming shrugged. "It's not the material of a weapon that matters but its effect."

"Spoken like a true innovator," Director Yong said. "Therefore, I'm willing to offer you twice its price."

Cha Ming frowned.

"Not for free, of course. I want you to do two things in exchange. I want you to pen your thought process in creating it, write down the exact process you used to smith it, then sell that knowledge to our Blackthorn Conglomerate. I'll also need a copy of the imaging orb you undoubtedly had recording just in case you had a mad moment of inspiration you wanted to review."

"Hmm…" Cha Ming said. "Money is good and all, but knowledge is priceless. Could I instead exchange knowledge for other knowledge?"

"I'm afraid not," Director Yong said. "Our hoarded knowledge is available only to employees, and on a strictly confidential basis. It's not that I want to be black-hearted, but the family rules are strict for a reason. Knowledge is power."

Cha Ming sighed. "Such strict terms. I really can't understand why anyone would want to be bound by them. I don't believe a lifetime of servitude to one company is a fair price for the knowledge to advance."

"It's not like their freedom can't be bought out," Director Yong said. "Some even manage it within fifty years. Besides, you might not know this, but our Blackthorn group has a few types of employment contracts. We have standard contracts, where freedom can be bought out. Assuming a person is of average productivity among those we hire, they'll be free within a hundred years. If they're above average, they can buy out their contract in the minimum of fifty years."

"That's too long," Cha Ming said, shaking his head. "I'd never consider a contract like this." Contractual terms aside, he would also be considered a normal worker. His level would never be high enough to accomplish what he wanted in the Wang family's Southern operations.

"That's a standard contract," Director Yong said. "It's not for creative individuals like you. For one like yourself, who desires knowledge and seeks it at every turn… we have something called a development contract."

"A development contract?" Cha Ming asked, frowning. "I've never heard of such a thing." Another lie.

"For premium producers, we typically set production quotas, with normal rewards and bonuses for extra production," Director

Yong said. "The contract is stable, but the information they have access to is limited. We give them a clear path for success, and many continue to work with us even after they've bought out their employment contract. Rewards are based on production.

"For innovators, however, we have a different path. You see, innovators hate to be bogged down by production quotas; they like access to premium information. As such, it's not fitting to have them on a standard production quota; not only would their time be wasted producing normal things and occasionally producing masterworks, they wouldn't have much time for their research.

"A development contract is therefore more appropriate. We grant full access to knowledge, but normal work doesn't result in any significant reward. Material costs are footed by the company instead of the employee, but there is no corresponding reward, as we expect these employees to waste more material than others."

"Then how do they pay off their employment contracts?" Cha Ming asked, frowning. He served another cup of tea, which Director Yong took eagerly.

"By contributing knowledge to the library," Director Yong said, his eyes twinkling. "Creating something we already know how to make is one thing, but making something new and useful? Much more valuable. Let the other monkeys copy the method. For developing a new method that leads to an increased success rate in production, we offer one hundred times the statistical savings on a piece as a monetary reward. For example, if the failure rate for a piece was thirty percent for the average smith of that grade, and you came up with a method that reduced that to twenty-eight percent, we would offer you two hundred percent of the applicable piece's face value."

"Such knowledge can often apply to more than one piece," Cha Ming pointed out.

"Noted," Director Yong said. "Therefore, the calculation is based on the most valuable increase. For example, if something is worth a thousand high-grade spirit stones, and you reduce failure by five percentage points, that's just as valuable as reducing a five thousand high-grade-spirit-stone item by one percentage point."

"Fair enough," Cha Ming said. "Though failure rate isn't the only way to create beneficial knowledge."

"Right," Director Yong said. "Reducing material costs, like you did with this blade, is also very valuable. Though you've reduced material costs substantially—likely by twenty percent, when everything is said and done—I already know the core of how savings can be accrued. For material savings, we multiply the percentage savings and materials by ten. Normally, a spiritual weapon's materials will amount to roughly half the value of the weapon. You've reduced those costs by twenty percent, so I would offer you double the weapon's value."

"I take it there is a reason for the lower payout?" Cha Ming asked.

"Yes," Director Yong said. "Materials are easier to emulate and copy. We can only maintain a monopoly on such things for so long before our competitors discover it."

"Then that leaves new products," Cha Ming said.

"Indeed," Director Yong said. "For your own innovations, we would award you a percentage of sales. Sometimes, however, clients ask us to make something according to their specifications. In this case, it depends on a few things, like contributions to the project, material wasted, and the like, but all things said and done, it could be as much as ten percent of the project. The final design would go to the client, of course."

"Hmm..." Cha Ming said. "Interesting. That actually doesn't sound so bad. It seems I've misjudged companies."

"I'm afraid you haven't," Director Yong said. "Our company is the only one who would dare do such a thing. The Blackthorn Conglomerate has substantial backing. In addition, our knowledge base is quite large. It's difficult to innovate something that doesn't already exist."

Cha Ming nodded. "About this blade. I'll accept your terms." He took out a jade slip and poured his transcendent force into it, inscribing a full record of the technique he used. Then he took out a small orb, which he'd taken from a stand downstairs after he'd finished forging. He took out another identical-looking orb and touched them together. They glowed softly as he poured qi into them.

Then, when the glowing faded, he handed one to Director Yong, who reviewed it, nodded, and stowed it in his storage ring along with the sword. He then placed a large pile of top-grade spirit stones beside the tea table. Cha Ming swept them up quickly.

"Now that this trivial matter is behind us, Pai Xiao, I was wondering what you thought of my offer," Director Yong said.

"Offer?" Cha Ming replied.

"Don't play coy with me," Director Yong said. "I won't believe for a second if you tell me you thought I'd come to buy a simple sword off of you."

Cha Ming hesitated. "Let me think about it. It's a big decision to make."

"Good," Director Yong said. He flicked his wrist, and a small black scroll appeared in his hand. "The full details of our offer are here on the scroll. If you decide to accept it, simply bind the scroll, and assuming you have no other employment marks we aren't aware of, you'll immediately become one of our employees. The offer is valid for three days, and we expect you in Bastion one week from acceptance."

"I'll think about it," Cha Ming said once again. Pai Xiao was a careful man who had long since grown used to freedom. "Would you like more tea?"

"I'm quite all right," Director Yong said. "I wasn't sure if making you an offer was a good idea at first, but then you served me tea. A man with such good taste couldn't possibly be a mediocre individual, could he?"

"I'd expect the same of an employer," Cha Ming said. "Your offer seems good according to what we've discussed. Still, I like to take my time with things like this."

"Don't take too long," Director Yong said, pulling open the door. "The world is changing. There are great works under way. If you're late, you'll miss them and regret it for the rest of your life." He then headed down the stone steps, shutting the door behind him as he exited the building.

Once he confirmed Director Yong was gone, Cha Ming inspected the contract. As he'd expected, the contract was onerous but not unreasonable. It had clearly been crafted assuming Cha Ming would make a breakthrough to peak-grandmaster rank. Two million top-grade spirit stones might seem like a ridiculous sum to others, but to someone who'd just made ten thousand of them as a mid-grade smith in a single afternoon, it wasn't an unbearable one.

The main restrictions in the contract was that an employee couldn't work for another and couldn't share knowledge obtained during his employment with the Blackthorn Conglomerate. Should he pay off his debt, however, he could use the knowledge gained for his own benefit but couldn't disseminate it for ten years, unless he paid a penalty ten times larger than his initial contract value. Dissemination included inscribing it on any medium or transferring to another individual. Cha Ming was surprised by how thorough it was in eliminating any avenues knowledge might be transferred.

That aside, his work hours would be very flexible, and he would gain full access to their libraries. The only exception, however, was that twenty-five percent of his time, at the minimum, would be allocated to "special projects," for which he would be duly compensated.

One of these special projects must be the one Wang Jun noted in the folio, Cha Ming thought. *Zhou Li's pet project.*

What should have taken him over a decade to accomplish, according to Wang Jun's plan, had only taken him about half a year. Now, all he had to do was wait.

A small hand knocked on Cha Ming's office door. "Master, you wanted to see me?" a feminine voice said from behind it.

"Come in," Cha Ming said.

Mo Ling walked into the dimly lit room.

"Take a seat," he said, gesturing to the chair in front of him. The girl was nervous—as she should be. Over the past few days, Cha Ming had relieved those in his smithy from their duties, severing their contracts with generous compensation for the inconvenience. He'd also put the smithy up for sale, equipment and all, through the Greenwind Pavilion. The smithy would have a new owner, and he'd want to select his own staff. Many of the old staff would likely be snapped up by the new owner.

Cha Ming sighed, put his hands to his face, and pressed them together while looking her straight in the eyes. "I'll need to terminate your employment contract as well," he said. "I'm going to Bastion, and I can't take you with me."

Mo Ling looked down. He saw sadness in her eyes but not the shock he'd expected. Instead, there was disappointment.

"It's not that I don't want to keep you with me," Cha Ming continued. "You're hardworking, and you're very good with books, finances, and administration. You've made this smithy run like clockwork. I'll be honest with you, technically speaking, I'm allowed to hire you under the employment contract I signed just this morning."

"Then why?" Mo Ling said, her eyes tearing up. "I don't *know* anyone here. I had to leave my family back in Liaoning, and now that things are comfortable again, you're leaving me."

Cha Ming knew he was being unreasonable from her point of view. That was what made it all the more difficult.

"But do you know what the worst part is?" Mo Ling said. "The worst part is knowing that you've been up to something this entire time. The people around you change too fast. They're too familiar with you. We've barely been here for six months, but everyone talks to you like they've known you for years.

"I overheard a conversation on the other side of the city. They were talking about how great it was that you came from Liaoning five years ago. They remember *me* from five years ago, even though I wasn't there. No one thinks it's strange, but I remember you, and

I remember being in Liaoning five years ago. Tell me, Pai Xiao, are *those* memories real? Or are theirs the ones that are fake?"

At some point in the conversation, her tone had shifted from an aggrieved little girl to that of an angry, confused woman.

Cha Ming sighed and closed his eyes. He'd ran this risk when he'd asked Sun Wukong to spare her memories. Asking her to just accept that her memories were incongruent with other people's might have been too much for her to handle. Unfortunately, he'd felt guilty for what had happened, guilty for not doing more for the villagers of Liaoning, guilty for the future that was now lost to her. Tampering with her memories a second time had seemed far too cruel.

"They're both fake," Cha Ming said finally. "Pai Xiao isn't even my real name. You haven't known me for long, and I'm no one special to you."

Mo Ling shuddered. She clutched her heart as though she'd been stabbed.

"The monastery?" she asked. "The things that happened there? My family? My hometown? Are they all fake as well?"

"They're real," Cha Ming said. "Unfortunately for you, they're real. Your family still lives in Liaoning. The many deaths at the hands of the blood masters and my rampage through their monastery. Our journey here, and your time here. Those are real."

"But why?" Mo Ling asked. "Why did you bother if you were just going to leave right away anyway?"

"It's difficult to explain," Cha Ming said softly. "Suffice to say that I have a skilled enemy. I have a goal, and to succeed, he can't know I exist. Only Pai Xiao can exist."

"Then why not go all the way?" Mo Ling asked. "Why not just erase yourself from my life?"

Cha Ming sighed. "If that is what you wish, I can do that. If you're willing, it won't take much time at all."

She sniffed, wiping the tears from her eyes. "And is that what you want?" she asked.

"No," Cha Ming said. "However, I won't deny that leaving you this way is a risk. You're a loose end I can't bear to tie up. The more you remember, the easier I'll be to find. You could easily be killed in the crossfire." He shook his head. "I can take care of myself, so there's no need to worry about me. But if you want to forget me… Well, I won't blame you."

Mo Ling sobbed softly when she heard these words. She began crying uncontrollably. Cha Ming could only sit and watch as she wept. Several minutes passed, and when she'd finished crying, her expression turned cold. "I want to forget. Change my memories just like the others."

"Are you sure?" Cha Ming asked, a little bit disappointed inside.

"Yes," Mo Ling said without any hesitation.

"All right," Cha Ming said. He took out a treasure from his Clear Sky World. It was the numerous bound medallions wrapped in metal wires Ling Dong had made for him. An aura of life and death pulsed through them. No, that wasn't accurate. An aura of a lifetime ran through them. He'd discovered its use some time ago—the treasure mollified minds and helped people reconcile their lives and come to terms with their memories. In this case, he was using it to mollify her mind as Sun Wukong drifted out behind her and began working his magic.

Mo Ling's eyes closed. The clock ticked away, and after a few minutes passed, they fluttered open. Cha Ming stowed his treasure, and Sun Wukong disappeared. Mo Ling sighed in disappointment. "But I really enjoyed working with you, Master. Couldn't you take me to Bastion with you?"

"I'm not your master anymore," Cha Ming said, cancelling the contract and placing a pile of spirit stones on the desk. "The bonus is for your inconvenience. I know you've got it harder than others since you don't have any relatives here, so I spoke to one of the many weapons resellers in the city. She said she'd be happy to take you on as an apprentice."

"Really?" Mo Ling asked. He nodded. "If you recommend her, then I'd be happy to work for her."

"She's not the kindest lady, but she's good at what she does," Cha Ming said. "She's also honest. You can trust her to keep her word."

"All right," Mo Ling said. "I'll do as you say."

Cha Ming nodded and wrote down an address on a piece of paper. "Go there this afternoon. She'll have an employment contract waiting for you."

"Thank you for everything," Mo Ling said. She bowed in thanks to the man who'd taken her in shortly after a mysterious man rescued her from bandits years ago. Her family had died there, and she'd been alone and unemployed. Pai Xiao had taken a risk in sheltering her, so she'd worked hard to prove herself and earn her place in his shop.

"No need," Cha Ming said, hiding away his pain. "Go ahead. She's waiting."

Mo Ling nodded and left. As the door closed and the last person left the building, Sun Wukong came out.

"You know she didn't want to forget you," Sun Wukong said. "You didn't have to go through with this so thoroughly."

Cha Ming's eyes reddened, and a single tear fell. "I know that, you fool. But just like she didn't want any harm to come to me because she knew too much, I didn't want her to get caught up either. This way, she's just a meaningless pawn in a game of cat and mouse. Not even worth pursuing."

"Harsh, but true," Sun Wukong said. "Are you sure you trust that woman, though? Will she treat her right?"

"She will," Cha Ming said. Sun Wukong didn't probe any further.

Cha Ming spent the rest of the afternoon tidying up the forge he'd spent six months in. He looked to the various benches filled with smiths that had become a part of his imaginary life. Would they ever meet again? Only time would tell, but he found it unlikely. If everything went according to plan, he'd disappear from the South in less than a year. The contract brand on his forearm was of little consequence.

"So what next?" Sun Wukong asked. They'd finished all the tidying up in the shop. Everything was ready for the smith they'd sold it to.

"Next?" Cha Ming asked. "Next, we make a bit of noise."

They made their way to the commercial district under cover of darkness. There, a young lady had already taken up residence in the medium-sized shop and would start work the next day. Cha Ming ignored the young lady and proceeded to the office, where a middle-aged woman was reviewing sales contracts. He opened the windows with his transcendent force and flew inside.

"Who's there?" the woman said. "Guards!" A few tense moments passed, and no one answered her call.

"Don't worry," Cha Ming said, not moving from the window. "I won't stay long." The woman tried to stand, but Cha Ming pressed her down using raw transcendent force. "You hired a young girl today." It wasn't a question.

The woman nodded but swallowed. "Her circumstances are special," the woman said. "But if your lordship requires her, I'll transfer her contract immediately."

Cha Ming's eyes narrowed. He summoned his qi and every ounce of fleshly body power he could muster. He summoned the might of his transcendent soul and pressed against her. The woman wasn't a strong cultivator, but neither was she weak. But despite being a peak-foundation-establishment cultivator, she could only resist with all her might under the pressure. The slightest lapse would result in her destruction, body and soul.

"You misunderstood me," Cha Ming said. "That girl. You're to make sure she stays safe. Don't coddle her, and don't make things easy for her, but if I ever hear you've tried to give her away or sell her employment contract without her consent, if I ever hear she was mistreated, things won't end well for you. Do you understand?"

The woman swallowed and nodded her head. Her body was drenched in sweat from head to toe. "Might I ask what she is to you, my lord?" she asked.

"No, you may not," Cha Ming said. He then jumped out the window and closed it before flying off. After traveling a short distance, he walked to one of the many city gates and signed out of the city. He wasn't sure how things would go for Mo Ling, but he was certain of two things: First, the woman, unless suicidal, would not dare test him. Second, she would never dare guess that the frightening man who'd threatened her was Pai Xiao, the kind and easygoing smith from Liaoning City.

Interlude
Threat

*B*oom. *Boom.*

Shivers ran down Feng Ming's spine as he heard the dull, almost imperceptible pounding just outside Westvale Fortress.

Boom. Boom.

Such a sound shouldn't be possible. In Feng Ming's mind, anything strong enough to reverberate throughout the fortress ought to make crashing noises or cutting sounds. What he heard now sounded like a bundle of wet noodles crashing against a large gong.

Boom. Boom.

Something about it seemed *wrong*, almost unholy. He grabbed the Magma God's Spear and flew through the corridors, rounding several corners before entering the control room. There, several generals were flipping through screens and assessing the situation. The former Sea God Emperor, Gong Xuandi, was already waiting for him.

It looks like I'm not the only one worried, Feng Ming thought, noticing his crossed arms and serious expression.

Boom. Boom.

"Custodian, what's happening out there?" Feng Ming asked.

"I don't know," a voice answered as a middle-aged hologram of a man appeared before them. "Whatever it is, it's not good for our energy reserves." He pointed to the wall. The runes there had dimmed and grew dimmer with each sound.

Boom. Boom.

"What do you mean you don't know?" Feng Ming asked. "Bring up the battle map."

"As you command," the custodian said. He waved his hand, and two images appeared before Feng Ming and Gong Xuandi. The first image was a map of the wall. Several allied blips could be seen all along the fortress, and many blips representing demons and their enemies, the fiends, were roaming around the mountains. Save for an odd empty area in a valley, everything was as it should be. Except…

"The area right beside the fortress," Feng Ming said. "What is it?"

Boom. Boom.

There was nothing there on the map, not even their own symbols. "Like I said, I don't know," the custodian replied, clearly irritated.

"Strange," Feng Ming said. "What about a three-dimensional view of what's happening?" The image changed into that of a bird's-eye view of the wall. He adjusted the view, then zoomed in. To his surprise, he saw nothing. The image of the wall stopped just before and just after the fortress, leaving a gaping nothingness where he and Gong Xuandi stood. "What in the blazes is happening?"

Boom. Boom.

"Unknown," the custodian said. "This servant suggests you investigate personally." These last words were not heard, as Feng Ming and Gong Xuandi had already left. The black-caped, black-armored Feng Ming held a spear that resembled a piece of molten metal in his right hand. His face, though younger than most of his men, was stony and his eyes hardened with many battles.

Gong Xuandi wore the same black armor he did, though instead of a spear, he wielded a golden trident. Though he'd lost the Sea God's Crown, the white-haired man was still a half-step blood-awakening cultivator. His toned body was covered in blue-gold runes, and the air around him seemed thick and viscous. No one in the Song Kingdom, not even Feng Ming, was stronger than he was. Save the transcendents, of course.

"I reviewed our ancestral teachings but haven't found anything that matches what we're experiencing," Gong Xuandi said. "Whatever it is, it can either obscure or destroy karma, or it can shield itself from the wall's sensors."

Boom. Boom.

"A difficult feat, given that the wall is a transcendent artifact," Feng Ming muttered. "Could it be one of the monarchs on the Ling Nan Demon Ranking?"

"Unlikely," Gong Xuandi said. "Though some of them are stronger than I am, none of them specialize in subterfuge. If one of them acted against the wall, you'd feel more than this constant dull thumping. They'd tear gouges in the rocks that would take at least a few seconds to repair."

Boom. Boom.

"Great," Feng Ming said. "I find that both reassuring and unnerving."

"I, for one," Gong Xuandi said, "prefer a known powerful enemy to an unknown weaker one." Despite his worrisome words, his expression remained stoic and unchanged. The ex-Sea God Emperor had been this way since he'd left with Feng Ming, no matter how much he, the chief marshal, tried to get him to relax.

Boom. Boom.

"Agreed," Feng Ming said. The hallway they were in opened into an outdoor training square, where many confused men were busy putting away training swords and spears and drawing their real weapons. Feng Ming and Gong Xuandi ignored them and flew above the wall. They finally saw the perpetrator: a man-shaped shadow covered in hornlike protrusions. It was busy beating away at the wall with a bare fist while the wall's defenders looked on in confusion. They hadn't even needed to summon the wall's defensive shields, as the creature's blows were unbelievably weak.

"What the hell are you guys doing just looking at it?" Feng Ming yelled. "Kill it!"

The troops, who were originally wondering whether they should use their energy-intensive weapons for such a weak creature, buzzed into action. The wall's formations activated, summoning bladed weapons that slashed at the creature. They cut into its arms, legs, and torso. To everyone's surprise, the blows completely decapitated the creature. It fell into a useless lump at the base of the wall.

"Finally."

"I wouldn't celebrate too quickly," Gong Xuandi said.

Feng Ming nodded. They looked at the pile of severed limbs, which soon began shaking. Then, they shot into the air and reassembled. Within three breaths' time, the creature was back in action.

Boom. Boom.

The men swiped again. This time, however, the severed limbs didn't fall off. Rather, they merged back together, and the creature continued pounding. They tried a few more times, but each time, the creature reassembled even faster.

"It's not working," a red-caped colonel said, floating up beside them. Westvale's soldiers hadn't given up with their initial failure. Like any disciplined army, they continued executing their standing orders without fail.

"Use the energy cannons," Feng Ming said. "If it can't be cut, perhaps it can be blown to pieces."

"As you command," the colonel said. "Prepare the energy cannons!" Several ports opened on the wall, revealing golden metal barrels that concentrated spiritual energy from the wall's energy reserves. "Ready when you are," the colonel said, standing by with spear at the ready.

"Fire!" Feng Ming called out.

The cannons pulsed. Large balls of energy that could annihilate even a middle-core-formation cultivator shot into the creature. Several holes appeared on its massive black body.

Did we injure it? he thought. For several seconds, it only stood there, waiting for heavens knew what.

"Hold," Feng Ming said as the soldiers were preparing to fire a second round. Endless moments passed as they waited for what they knew in their hearts was inevitable. Slowly, at first, the holes began closing. Then, the healing intensified, and the holes grew back. The creature, who'd seemingly suffered a terrible injury, began whaling on the wall once more.

Boom. Boom.

To most of the men on the wall, the sound seemed the same as before. Feng Ming and Gong Xuandi, however, knew better. The sound was different. Somehow, despite having been shot by the cannons, it had grown stronger.

"I think I know what this is," Gong Xuandi whispered. "Though I pray to the Sea God up above that I'm wrong."

Boom. Boom.

"What is it?" Feng Ming asked. Anything that frightened Gong Xuandi was great cause for concern. To him, even the Southern Invasion was just an everyday occurrence not worthy of mention.

"It's a Taotie," Gong Xuandi said, reluctantly. "If I'm not mistaken, it's the same Taotie the North and South allied to suppress ten thousand years ago. The Sea God Emperor ten generations my senior also joined them to seal it away. By his estimates, the seal should have lasted a million years before needing to be renewed."

"Okay," Feng Ming said. "It's been sealed once, so it should be doable. How do we kill it?"

Gong Xuandi looked at him strangely. "We don't. We can't."

Boom. Boom.

"Pardon?" Feng Ming said. If they'd done it before, why couldn't they do it now?

"A Taotie is the power of devouring incarnate," Gong Xuandi said. "Though this one is just an infant, the laws it represents surpasses anything a mortal realm could ever muster. A god could kill it, perhaps, but by doing so, it would destroy the plane. That's why they sealed it off. The idea was to perpetually keep it away from sustenance. Whenever the seal faded, the Sea God Realm would send another seal to replace the old one."

"Great," Feng Ming said. "How do we place an order?" A million years early shouldn't be a big deal, should it?

Boom. Boom.

"I can send a message to the Sea God's Herald," Gong Xuandi said reluctantly. "And I suggest you do the same with your Alabaster Group. Meanwhile, we need to get it away from your wall. We need to punish it, to cost it what it lacks most: time. When it realizes it's wasting its time, it will go away and find another target."

"All right," Feng Ming said. "Colonel, get all men to assume defensive positions. I want everyone to divert energy to healing the wall. I don't want any shields active, and I don't want any weapons used on the creature."

The colonel nodded and moved to carry out his orders. He came back a few moments later. "Sir, how will we repel it without any weapons?" the colonel asked.

Feng Ming grinned. He hefted his spear, which he'd been carrying on his shoulder, and assumed a battle position. "We *are* the weapons." Then, he darted toward the creature. Gong Xuandi, who was carrying a large golden trident, grunted and followed him. They flew at the creature as a pair. Feng Ming's Magma God's Spear glowed red as the Gong Xuandi's trident glowed blue. They stabbed into the creature of darkness, quickly pulling away from the gaping holes they left in the creature's body. Dark devouring force rushed up to grab the weapons, but ultimately, they were too slow.

Slash. Stab. Kick.

"Don't use any energy attacks," Gong Xuandi warned as he hacked away at the monster. "Energy attacks are too easy to absorb. It's better to use physical attacks to cut and disperse the creature. Regeneration costs the Taotie energy."

"What if we just keep hacking away at it?" Feng Ming asked as he lopped off one of its many dark horns. The sharp protrusion wriggled on the floor; it dissociated before rejoining the main body and regrowing near its head. "We could constantly attack it and deplete its energy reserves."

"Regeneration costs it less energy than it absorbs from the air," Gong Xuandi scoffed as he kicked the creature in the chest, forcing it away from the wall. "We're limiting its energy intake by wasting its time, not by expending it."

Heavens, Feng Ming thought. *I hope it's not intelligent.* The two of them were barely keeping it at bay, and if it continued doing what it was doing, it could tie up two of the North's most powerful fighters indefinitely. They could only hope that self-interest drove it away.

Their battle continued, and the Taotie continued bravely advancing, only to be rebuffed every time. Occasionally, the creature launched powerful, energy-consuming attacks on the two men, who rebuffed them with little effort. Only after seven hours did it finally stop.

They looked at the creature. The creature looked back. Time stood still for a few minutes as the creature deliberated its next course of action. Then, finally, it turned. Its slow, lumbering body turned back toward the mountains where it had come. Every step it took withered trees and drained ponds. Its footprints left behind shattered desolation and lifeless dust.

"I sent a message to the Sea God's Herald through my core-transmission jade," Gong Xuandi said.

Feng Ming nodded and did the same to Lu Tianhao in the Quicksilver Kingdom. Then, looking toward the west, he frowned.

"I'm concerned," Feng Ming said, looking toward the demonic mountain.

"About what?" Gong Xuandi asked.

"That it will simply wander through demonic lands and devour everything in its path. Then, once it's strong enough, it will come back to our wall."

"A very real concern," Gong Xuandi admitted. "What do you command?"

Right, Feng Ming thought. *He's basically my indentured servant at this point. He won't do anything unless I tell him to.*

"Let's chase him," Feng Ming said. "Let's harass him when he approaches anything too rich in energy. Then we'll herd him toward the South. Once he gets there, it'll be their problem to deal with."

Gong Xuandi raised an eyebrow. "You want to put the fate of the plane in the hands of devils and evil spirits?"

Feng Ming shrugged. "They want this plane just as much as we do.

They're not about to let it fall. Maybe we'll force their transcendents to act against it too. Or do you have any better ideas?"

Gong Xuandi shook his head. "Colonel, we'll be gone for a while. Call Songjing and tell them to send over one of the new marshals to defend Westvale Fortress."

"Sir," the colonel said. "I'd appreciate it if you were the one to send the message."

Right, Feng Ming realized. Song Guo, Feng Ming's wife, would kill him if she found out he was going on another adventure. Especially just before their anniversary. "Gong Xuandi, you relay the message." The disgraced Sea God Emperor grimaced, but as Feng Ming expected, he flew off toward Songjing.

Someone has to be the messenger, Feng Ming thought. He could hardly think of a better man to take the heat for terrible news than Gong Xuandi.

Feng Ming pursued the beast alone for a few hours before finally being rejoined by the old Sea God Emperor. The man looked worn and beaten down.

"I won't be doing that again," Gong Xuandi said. "Regardless of my requirement to serve you."

"Fair enough," Feng Ming said, sighing. Once was already enough. "Let's keep following it."

It didn't take long for them to find it. Where it passed, death followed.

Chapter 14
Shadow Fate Investiture

Wang Jun walked through the corridors of the Wang family mansion, admiring the impressive décor in the main hallway. Twenty feet wide with a twenty-foot ceiling on the first floor, the spacious home featured many famous art pieces like sculptures, calligraphy, and paintings. It was night out, and the residence was alight with candles and chandeliers. They cast ominous shadows beneath their dim lights.

As he often did during these walks, Wang Jun reminisced about his childhood. The earlier memories were nostalgic: his studies as he learned the basics of investment and trade, the academic competition with his cousins and siblings that decided the resources they were allocated. Most dear to his heart, however, were his adventures with Wang Hua through these special hallways, admiring relics of times past, left behind by their ancestors to instill wisdom and appreciation into their descendants. They were pleasant times, but with happiness came darker memories.

Memories he'd tried to forget. Memories of blood and fear-filled eyes. Memories of betrayal that broke their family apart. It was all caused by one man, the man he'd trusted with his life: Wang Ling. The scars these events left behind were painful to remember and impossible to forget.

"Fancy seeing you here, buzzing around like a money bee."

Wang Jun didn't look away from the painting he'd been admiring as the hateful man walked up beside him. He made a point of staring at the painting even harder, inspecting the details of artistic rendition of his ancestor, who bravely smashed his enemies with mountains of spirit stones.

"Fancy seeing you here, not cooped up or in seclusion," Wang Jun finally said, his voice impassive. "Given how little I see you, I'd thought you were scared to face me like a man."

Over the past few years, he'd only seen Wang Ling a handful of times. Most of these times had been at the annual family meeting, a compulsory event for all those residing in the mansion.

Wang Ling simply smiled at the provocation. He wore his long blond hair in a topknot with a golden pin. His green robes, made of the finest demon silk, were embroidered in golden runes just like Wang Jun's were. "Is it hiding to do what you're good at?" Wang Ling asked. "Like any successful person, I like to play to my strengths." He folded his arms behind his back and silently watched the same painting as Wang Jun.

"And what is it, exactly, that you're good at?" Wang Jun asked with a raised eyebrow. "Your businesses are growing at a snail's pace, and you've missed out on many key opportunities. I've also noticed that your books are in shambles."

"I'm good at winning," Wang Ling said. "You're a very calculating person. That's good. The family needs people that are good with numbers and predicting the success of a venture. I admit, in that sense, I am your inferior."

"Then it seems," Wang Jun said, "that you're admitting to being worse than me at the primary skill required for leading a family of merchants. Honestly, I don't know how you sleep at night."

Wang Ling chuckled lightly. He turned to Wang Jun and faced him. Wang Jun looked to the side, unable to bear the resemblance the man's girlish face bore to his late sister's. "I think you have something wrong, little brother," Wang Ling said. "Winning isn't about making money."

"Our ancestor would disagree," Wang Jun said, tilting his head toward the painting. The ancestor had had it commissioned to convey an important message: With enough money, you could crush any foe.

"I beg to differ," Wang Ling said. He took a small step forward, encroaching on Wang Jun's personal space. Wang Jun could feel the man's breath on his face, and if he wanted to, he could end him here and now with a dagger through the chest. He suppressed that urge. "Winning is more important because you can't take money with you when you die, my dear brother. All the money in the world does no good if you're dead." Seemingly unaware or unconcerned with the threat to his life, he circled around Wang Jun. "Wang Hua is a prime example. She was talented. She could have been our family's second transcendent if she'd survived. But she didn't. She lost."

Wang Jun's arms blurred. A shadowy dagger materialized in his hand and stabbed toward Wang Ling's exposed torso. An invisible shield shattered as the dagger cleaved through it effortlessly, stabbing point first into an unreasonably tough core-grade vestment. The strike was fast, faster than most people could react to. Just a few more inches, and Wang Ling's life would end.

Unfortunately, the dagger stalled. Wang Jun's tense arm was now caught up in Wang Ling's white-knuckled and unusually strong grip. Wang Jun's eyes narrowed as he realized the man was much stronger than he'd been just a short time ago. Had he broken through? Would that explain such a massive increase in strength?

"Watch out, brother dearest," Wang Ling said. "You wouldn't want to do anything *drastic*, would you? Business competition is fair game, but an assault on my life?"

"Some names shouldn't be spoken by those who aren't worthy," Wang Jun said, struggling to push forward. He released the dagger. It puffed into shadow, but as it did, Wang Jun appeared behind Wang Ling. He summoned two daggers this time, their shadowy edges eating away at Wang Ling's qi shield. Dozens more appeared behind the man, but a golden glint cut through them in an instant.

Still, that instant was more than enough for Wang Jun. Wang Ling's qi shield gave way after the fifth strike. As he dove in for a fatal blow, however, Wang Jun's hair stood on end. He disappeared, reappearing a short distance away. A golden blade cut into the floor where he'd just been standing. If he'd reacted just a moment later, he'd have died.

"This shouldn't be possible," Wang Jun said, panting. Just a month ago, Wang Ling had been a peak-core-formation cultivator. He'd minored in body cultivation, but nothing too impressive.

"You're strong, I admit that," Wang Ling said. "But while you were busy making money, I was busy spending it."

It was only now that Wang Jun noticed five powerful treasure auras on Wang Ling. One was the obvious protective garment, which no longer bore a peak-core-grade treasure halo but a transcendent one. The second was the golden sword—it was familiar to Wang Jun. It had been bestowed on Wang Ling by the Patriarch upon being named as a candidate for the head of the family.

The other three treasures, however, reeked a sinister aura. "An honorary blood master bracer," Wang Jun said flatly. "Capable of temporarily boosting body cultivation by burning stored blood essence. Along with a soul-body superposition necklace. Banned by the Church of Justice for using the power of ten thousand souls to greatly enhance sensory capabilities and reaction time. And to top it all off, the Nine-Wrapped Shadow Chain, a gift from my master to the family head to hide all these elicit goods. You've outdone yourself."

"Even money can't buy all these things," Wang Ling said smugly. "With these, along with my half-step-transcendent cultivation, I can end you whenever I choose."

"Assuming you don't need to sleep," Wang Jun said. "Or cultivate further."

"There's no need to cultivate further, my dear brother," Wang Ling said. "Judging by those white hairs on your head, I *will* outlast you."

"And here I was, wondering why you'd come to pay me a visit," Wang Jun said, dismissing his dagger as though he'd never launched a surprise attack. Wang Ling did the same with his sword, dismissing it into his transcendent-grade storage ring. "It seems you came here to gloat."

"Like you, I don't go out of my way to brag," Wang Ling said. "You can blame Father for that good habit. Instead, I came to give you a warning."

"I'm all ears," Wang Jun said.

"You were never going to win this race," Wang Ling said. "You need to realize this and learn your place. You are a business genius, a leader beneath the family head. No one in the family can match you in that regard. Yet it remains that you were never destined for more."

"And why is that?" Wang Jun asked.

"Because of your nature," Wang Ling said. "Because of whom you serve. You can't learn from *that man* and claim you have the family's best interest in mind."

"So you're saying I can't learn from our family's protector, the one who's been keeping us safe all this time?" Wang Jun asked.

"Is that what he told you?" Wang Ling said. He shrugged. "Regardless, it's set in stone. You can't change it no matter what you do. Any further competition will end up causing harm. If you truly want what's best for the family, for your employees, and for the North, you'd best do what you're told and stick to what you're best at: thinking and making money. Let us do the rest."

"You'll have me believe that dealing with the South is in our best interest," Wang Jun said flatly.

"Yes," Wang Ling said. "As terrible as the South is, we must keep dealing with them."

"To line our pockets with souls and suffering?" Wang Jun asked.

"To survive," Wang Ling said, his voice taking on a graver tone. "It's for survival that I've come here and warned you. It's more than you deserve with all the trouble you've caused, but it's what the family needs."

"The family *needed* Wang Hua," Wang Jun hissed.

Wang Ling looked at him for a time and shook his head. "No, it didn't. Perhaps in better times, yes, but not now. She was too kind to do what needed to be done. It was fortunate for us that she suffered that accident."

Calm down, Wang Jun thought, his fists trembling. *You brought her up yourself this time. He's a fiend, but his opinion means nothing.* He breathed in and out, taking the rage and bottling it up inside. His vision dimmed as blood rushed through his head. Despite his agitation, however, he knew that Wang Ling meant what he said. Once could be excused, but one more time, and he'd be better off getting rid of his problems.

In, out, in, out. His breathing slowed. By the time his pounding heart slowed, Wang Ling was gone. "Damn it all," Wang Jun grunted, punching the wall near the painting. The stone, a powerful geomantic structure, still cracked a bit with the impact. In his anger, he'd dismissed the black membrane he'd previously kept covering his skin for protection. Blood dripped onto the floor from the open skin covering his newly fractured knuckles and hand bones.

The pain was sharp but bearable. It pushed the thoughts out of his mind, bringing clarity to his turbulent thoughts. His brother, Wang Ling, was now a half-step-rune-carving cultivator, with a total of five transcendent treasures. Such goods couldn't be purchased easily— most were heirlooms or goods imported through the Greenwind Pavilion for exorbitant sums. Each treasure significantly bolstered Wang Ling's strength. And unfortunately, though Wang Ling wasn't the most gifted in business, he excelled at one thing: swordsmanship. Wang Jun, though good at fleeing, was now outmatched in one-on-one combat.

"One problem at a time," Wang Jun muttered. He looked to the painting of his ancestor, who seemed to be mocking him now. Before, the mountains of spirit stones had seemed like a metaphor for success, but now they seemed to scream a different story: My spirit stones are worthless, so I'm throwing them away. Even with his entire fortune, Wang Jun might only be able to buy a single treasure to close the gap.

Bitter and seething with hatred, Wang Jun stepped into a nearby shadow. He merged with it and traveled ten thousand feet in a single instant, reappearing in a dark alley where no one was watching.

A shadow ran through the streets of Gold Leaf City, unseen beneath the thick lamplight that bathed their carefully cut cobblestones. The shadow was alive, and it was completely unaffected by the watchful lanterns above. Despite its conspicuous appearance, no one seemed to see the dark specter, and neither did they hear its footsteps. Instead, it was the shadow that saw, the shadow that listened. Its steps echoed unheard in an entirely different plane of existence.

Wang Jun, hidden from unwanted eyes and blocked from unwanted ears, took pleasure in the run. There was something refreshing about not flying everywhere, using your own two feet to get to your destination. You could communicate with nature, feel closer to your community, and in his case, take longer to get to your destination. He ran for a full half hour, dancing between the sentries and guards, who ignored him. Eventually he arrived at a rich residential area. He searched, his gaze passing all sorts of ostentatious houses around him.

The houses in this richer area weren't uniform like in many upscale neighborhoods in the city. They were pieces of art, built by well-off families to show off or owned by embassies or lent to important clergymen or government officials. One was made of bricks twice as large as was standard and resembled a fortified castle. Another was built from enchanted wood, its walls twisting the building into what seemed like a grove of giant redwoods. Each house had a theme, a specific message it wanted to convey to those who looked at it.

The house he finally settled on wasn't any different. Instead of odd construction materials that set it apart from the city's décor, this house did the opposite. It blended in with the gray stone streets at the base, which eventually made way for cream-white walls. They were plain and unadorned, with three vertical windows spanning all three floors of the mansion. As it was nighttime, the view through the windows was blocked by golden curtains. They matched the golden borders on each window frame, which in turn matched golden runes that shone at the well-lit entrance.

"May the light bless unworthy men with truth and salvation," Wang Jun muttered as he stood before the doorway. The runes on the frame were runes of detection, specially made to catch those who would sneak onto the premises. He said these words right beside the guards, and the guards, unsurprisingly, didn't hear him. He walked between them and disappeared right before the door, only to reappear behind it. He passed through the welcome room and proceeded up a flight of marble steps. Each dull thud of his feet caused it to vibrate soundlessly.

Wang Jun looked through the hallways, curious as he made his way to the master bedroom. He passed the children's bedchambers, where three young daughters lay snuggled in a single bed, leaving two other beds empty and undisturbed. He passed a sleeping beauty on a larger bed, a contented smile gracing her face. For why wouldn't she be happy? She had a loving family, a loving and honest husband, and a good reputation. She and her husband were both cultivators, and all three of their children had been blessed by providence to follow in their footsteps. One of their children had even been blessed by the goddess with an affinity for light. Their life was wonderful, and their future set. And he? He had come to take that all away. Or at least the purity of it all.

Wang Jun let out a soundless sigh as he walked into the home's study where a bald man, Inquisitor Deng, meditated. His graceful figure was covered in a soft halo of light. That very same light filled the entire room, illuminating everything within it. All save Wang Jun, of course, who took a seat in front of the man, observing him, pondering.

"I never pray," Wang Jun said, "but I was wondering if you might give me some guidance." The man didn't answer. How could he? Wang Jun hadn't permitted him to hear. "I ask you less as a spiritual advisor and more as a sounding board. Perhaps by telling you of my worries instead of keeping them inside, I'll be able to sort out the ethics of the situation." No response again.

"The key question," Wang Jun continued, "is whether it is permissible to do bad things to a good man, and by doing so save many good men from harm, all the while incidentally landing some good people in serious trouble." He held out his palm, and shadows danced within them, forming two large figures and many smaller ones. Characters flew above their heads, the two larger figures bearing the same mark as the smaller figures. Only a few of them, who stood slightly taller than the rest, shared a mark with the pair.

"This is all very confusing, so I'll summarize. You see, Wang Ling definitely deserves to die." He held up the first of the larger figures. "The Patriarch of the Wang Clan, Wang Wuling, is supporting his actions, so he also deserves to die. But should the rest of the family be implicated? Should his employees be implicated? I don't feel any guilt for dragging down those who knowingly did bad things, but what of the innocent? And how much harm is tolerable?"

He paused. "I like to think the harm is outweighed by the benefit of ridding the North of Wang Ling and Wang Wuling. They facilitate the sufferings of many by plundering souls and may even be colluding with the South to destabilize the Golden Kingdom, softening up the North for their inevitable attack. Surely it's worth turning them in, even if a few auditors, inquisitors, and innocent Wang family members get caught up with them?"

He shook his head. "But that's all cover and justification for the real crime. I, Wang Jun, will selfishly bear false witness against you, an upright inquisitor. You have made it your life's duty to root out falsehood and evil, but I will frame you, all to commit fratricide. The rest is just incidental."

Wang Jun looked at the meditating man for a good long while before sighing one final time, tossing a pile of crystal shards on the ground, and forming swift hand seals. Inky black threads burst out from Wang Jun and poured into the man, tainting the halo of light that surrounded him.

The man's shadow grew. Long thin strands extended from it and shot out into his surroundings. They went to the nearby neighborhood, to his workplace, to the commercial districts, and to a dozen odd blurry objects that began taking shape in front of Wang Jun. Endless moments passed as these threads connected Inquisitor Deng to individuals he barely knew, in ways he would have never considered. Some pulsed red with karma of resentment, and others gold with karma of gratitude. These new threads contained intermixed good and bad, specifically implanted to confuse any scrying that might reveal them.

With an inaudible snap of Wang Jun's fingers, they latched into place, and as these threads solidified, the blurry objects he'd placed before him appeared along with them. Some materialized as sheets of paper, others as recording orbs. Some were jade slips containing oral testimony, others accounts and bank records. They hadn't been real moments ago, not in any dimension or timeline. But now that karma had been sown, they were just as real as anything else. They were heresy to truth and light.

Wang Jun panted in exhaustion as his qi, body, and soul were instantly depleted of most of their energy. His soul, in particular, took the brunt of the impact. Shadow Fate Investiture was a frightening ability that bore a frightening cost. Unlike Shadow Fate Redemption, it didn't reclaim what the shadows once knew. Instead, it used shadows to weave a dream, then forced that dream into reality.

When the last of the objects materialized, Wang Jun pulled out an ornate curved black dagger and put it to Inquisitor Deng's throat. The man opened his eyes with a start as the cold steel blade touched his bare skin. His eyes narrowed when he saw Wang Jun's obscured shadowy figure beneath his black cloak. Then he straightened his back and composed himself.

"I see that I, like many others, have caught the attention of the Spectral Assassins," Inquisitor Deng said stiffly. "To what do I owe the pleasure of this visit?"

Wang Jun, surprised by the man's calmness, replied in a hoarse, ghostly voice. "If I wanted to kill you, you would be dead. Fortunately for you, it is not my will that matters, but that of the Shepherd."

"Just get on with it," Inquisitor Deng replied calmly. "Speak plainly. What is it that you want? Why has a powerful specter like you come to this city? Why have you appeared before me of all people? You know full well that, given my character, I'll report you to my superiors."

"Will you?" Wang Jun said. "Is honesty still so prized in the inquisition?"

"I have devoted my life to truth and virtue," Inquisitor Deng said. "As many will attest to."

"But the items before me say differently," Wang Jun said, sweeping his hand out to the dozen objects before Inquisitor Deng. "Feel free to take a look. They are only copies." He took away the dagger from Inquisitor Deng's throat and allowed the man to cautiously reach out to one of the jades. The man frowned as he heard its contents.

"This is clearly false," Inquisitor Deng said, pulling back his hand.

"Humor me," Wang Jun said. The man, clearly outmatched by Wang Jun, reviewed them one at a time. His frown deepened with each viewing.

"What lies and trickery are these?" Inspector Deng asked after reviewing the last one. "How could these items possibly exist?"

"But exist they do," Wang Jun said.

"These mean nothing," Inspector Deng said. "I know that I and my family have done nothing wrong. Karma will prove me innocent. These so-called victims will prove me innocent."

"Will they?" Wang Jun asked. "Are you so sure about that?"

Inquisitor Deng frowned. He looked at the items again, but this time, his eyes turned light gold. They flickered in many different directions—the same directions the black strings had gone before.

"Well done, well done indeed," Inquisitor Deng said. "The Spirit Temple has certainly outdone itself. Forging karma? Well, that's a first. And I suppose you'll say they won't believe me if I speak to the so-called witnesses and have them reverse their testimony."

"Witness intimidation is a serious crime," Wang Jun said. "Besides, think of your beautiful wife and healthy young children.

We wouldn't want anything untoward happening to them, would we?"

The bald man's expression, which had undergone many changes in the past minute, suddenly turned angry. He lunged at Wang Jun, who held up his dagger and placed it to the man's throat as manacles of shadow appeared around his wrists and bound him to the opposite wall.

"Just kill me and be done with it," the man spat. "I loathe you and everything you stand for."

"And your wife and children?" Wang Jun asked.

"Will understand," Inquisitor Deng said. "It is a glory to die in service of the goddess."

"I see," Wang Jun said, taking his blade away. "That's too bad. My request wasn't even so onerous."

"Don't even bother," Inquisitor Deng said. "I know your type. You'll ask me to do something simple at first, but your demands will grow. I've locked up so many of you I have trouble keeping track."

Wang Jun nodded, then placed a piece of paper in front of the man. "It's your call. All I ask is that you do your job and stop ignoring the hidden truths other less innocent men have passed over. The Wang family owes us karma, and we'll have it repaid."

He didn't wait for the man's answer. Instead he stepped backward into a shadow that should not have existed in the room. The shackles around the man's wrists disappeared along with Wang Jun. Then the man, finding himself alone in his study, picked up the piece of paper and frowned.

Will he bite or not bite? Wang Jun wondered, drumming his fingers on the table as Wang Bing spoke. The tapping attracted a rare rebuke from Elder Bai, but the conversation continued regardless. He took a sip of his tea, savoring the harsh mouthful from the foreign leaves.

Bad men and real evidence are easy to anticipate. But righteous, innocent men? It's all a gamble.

Wang Jun didn't place much hope on Inquisitor Deng. What he'd done, he'd done for training more than anything else, a gamble that might pay off. If it didn't, the inspector would reveal this troubling new ability of the Spirit Temple, increasing the Golden Kingdom's vigilance toward them. It would also help frame the relationship between the Spirit Temple and the Wang family as unfriendly.

Then again, I suppose he could do both, Wang Jun thought, taking another sip. *He could share the experience but accede to my suspicious request.* In a way, that would be better than the inspector taking covert action.

"Young master, you seem distracted," Elder Bai said, drawing Wang Jun's attention back to the conversation. "Perhaps a short rest is in order?"

"I'm fine," Wang Jun said. "Continue with your conversation. I'll insert myself where appropriate."

The older man nodded hesitantly and continued their discussion. Apparently, the older man and Wang Bing were cooperating on a project. They were planning something not unlike the Wang family's arrangement: multi-family housing for employees of a large manufacturing company. Those working for the company would be treated like "family," with the company taking an active hand in the family's welfare and culture. The "family" would in turn feel more loyal to the company and better cooperate with their fellow "family members." The concept was intriguing and had Wang Jun's full support.

Wang Jun's mind wandered to Inspector Deng once again. He'd gone through great effort to plant the fake evidence. It didn't point out fraud so much as a breach in another country's tax and accounting laws by trying to abuse certain loopholes. True North Country, the other jurisdiction in question, had an agreement with the Golden Kingdom, which stated that any wrongdoings detected by the Golden Kingdom's authorities would need to be both reported to True North Country and prosecuted by the Golden Kingdom. Extradition, though possible, was hardly practical. This was a healthy middle ground that allowed for the host country to save face by administering justice. It was the grayness of the situation that made it tenable. Assuming, of course, that the documents themselves weren't assumed to be forgeries.

"Then it's settled," Wang Bing said, holding out her hand. Elder Bai took it. They shook firmly, then accepted cups of tea that Wang Jun had already poured. "Seriously, what's wrong with you?" Wang Bing asked. "You're pale and brooding. Are you ill?"

"Don't worry," Wang Jun said, brushing her off. "An illness of the soul is hardly contagious."

She frowned but didn't pursue the matter. As Elder Bai moved to further question Wang Jun, however, a hard knock on the door sounded.

"Come in!" Wang Jun shouted.

A sweaty man opened it and bowed. The short blond man was dressed in standard green robes, though instead of wide cuffs on his sleeves, his shirt was tight and sleeveless. He wore a black silk satchel at his waist, both a useful container and a mark of his identity. The man was a runner, and judging by the three bands of gold on the black wrappings on his wrists, he was of the highest rank. "Young Master Wang, your presence is requested before the elders. Please follow me back."

"What's so urgent?" Wang Jun asked. "I might report to Patriarch Wuling, but I won't dance around at his beck and call for no good reason."

Everyone in the household knew of their intensifying antagonism. What had previously been meek obeisance to the aging patriarch had now been replaced with the competitive arrogance suited to someone successful.

The runner winced, but instead of giving the usual awkward reply, he took out a small scroll from his satchel and handed it to Wang Jun, who took it. He accepted the knife that Elder Bai handed to him and cut through the green seal the Patriarch himself had affixed to the paper.

"Wang Jun," Wang Jun said, reading from it, "as a potential successor of the family, and the family's chief auditor, you are required to report to the elder council before accepting an urgent duty. The Golden Kingdom has dispatched the honorable Inquisitor Deng for a surprise audit on our accounts. Your assistance in this matter, and your unfailing loyalty to the family, is greatly appreciated." Feigning surprise, Wang Jun handed the scroll to Elder Bai for inspection.

"That," Elder Bai said, "is a very politely worded letter. I wonder what they're investigating?"

Wang Jun grinned. "Even the most ruthless of villains become meek as a lamb when they want or need something. I take it you two will get along well without me? Although it's not my first time participating in an audit, we haven't had a surprise one in decades. I'd hate to miss out."

"Don't worry about us, Young Master," Wang Bing said. "We can find someone else to make and serve tea for us while you're gone."

"Though we shall suffer greatly for their incompetence," Elder Bai added.

"Good," Wang Jun said. He stepped outside the room and gestured to the runner. "Lead the way."

The man ran, and Wang Jun ran with him, his steps leaving not a sound behind.

Chapter 15
Bastion

"**B**astion City, fortress of the South," Cha Ming muttered as he flew toward the massive city in the distance. The soil here was different than the soil near Ashes, which was barely suitable for growing crops. Instead of the carpet of communal farms he'd come to expect, the land here was rocky and couldn't be cultivated. Smaller mining camps took the place of farming residences, housing mortals who harvested gravel and sand. Cultivators worked alongside them, picking out more expensive ores from the inexpensive but useful construction materials.

The mining camps became increasingly concentrated the closer he flew to the city. Unlike the other cities and towns he'd seen in the South, Bastion was actually built on a place that was rich in resources. Strong body cultivators dug from deep quarries just outside the city's tall concrete wall. The smooth rune-inscribed structure represented strength and might; it also bore witness to the instability inherent in Southern countries. Many sections of the wall were slightly off color, and anyone with the slightest cultivation talent could clearly see that they'd been built at different times.

Wall aside, Cha Ming could see inside the city due to the shallow but steady incline it was built on. The city snaked through broken mountains, using sheer cliff walls as natural enclosures to the east and west. The buildings in Bastion were as gray as the walls themselves.

Despite the incline, the layout of the city was grid-like, allowing no deviations from the norm no matter what building. This was likely a product of the kingdom's rigid administration, along with its near-religious zeal in following the rules.

What was most surprising about the city, however, was an oddity at the back. A wall stood tall at the end of the city, blocking off the mountain pass toward the North. According to all the maps Cha Ming had seen, the pass didn't lead anywhere—it ended abruptly. Yet this wall was three times taller than the walls protecting the city from human invaders. It also predated the city, which had evidently been built near it out of convenience. True to its name, it was a bastion that protected civilization from the demons infesting the mountains. Without it, the demons of the Shattered Lands would roam as they wish, sowing chaos in the Ji Kingdom and all Southern lands.

"Identification and purpose of visit?" a guard asked gruffly as Cha Ming landed in front of the city's large blacksteel gates. He wore a drab brown uniform complete with tunic and magic-grade mail. He wore a peak-magic-grade sword, above-average gear for a Ji Kingdom soldier.

Cha Ming handed the guard a jade slip listing Pai Xiao's fictional information. Then he handed the man another scroll—his employment contract. "I've come to report for duty with the Blackthorn Conglomerate," he said. The guard eyed the scroll and opened it reverently. He reviewed it, nodding as he did, before bowing.

"My apologies, Grandmaster," the guard said. "You are most welcome in this city. Still, you know as well as I that the spirits watch and remember. Procedures must be adhered to at all times."

"The spirits watch and remember," Cha Ming echoed. He'd met men like these before, devotees of the Spirit Temple. Their members made for the most fervent of administrators and the fiercest lawyers and accountants.

The guard handed his employment contract back and gestured for him to step through a small doorway. The black door was an opening on the larger main gate. It was just wide enough to accommodate two wagons, one passing in each direction. Cha Ming entered it and followed the crush of people into the city. As he passed, he felt a shimmer of light that pushed against his soul ever so slightly. It left as soon as it came, taking note of his arrival.

Like the people lined up to enter the city, the streets were orderly and clean. Common folk walked or rode through the streets at a steady pace, the only exception being core-formation cultivators like Cha Ming. They flew to their destinations instead, though none dared fly higher than twenty feet above the ground. There were rules here, and rules were made to be followed.

The streets in Bastion were clean and free of beggars. For a second, Cha Ming wondered how they'd achieved such a miracle. Then he remembered where he was. They'd likely either been forced into slavery or sacrificed to the blood masters. Either that or society's wretches didn't dare show their face out in the open. There was no pity for those who didn't earn their keep in the South. He'd seen many painful examples during his stay in Ashes.

It took barely any time at all for Cha Ming to traverse the first twenty miles of the crowded streets and reach the inner city. There, he flew past the checkpoint without any questions. As a core-formation cultivator, he belonged there. Other, weaker men were questioned at the entrance. Without exception, all of them were cultivators. The average person walking the streets was a foundation-establishment cultivator, and those who weren't kept their heads bowed low as they milled about to perform their duties.

"Where can I find the Blackthorn Conglomerate's headquarters?" Cha Ming asked as he landed on the gray cobblestone streets.

The man he'd asked, an early-foundation-establishment cultivator in black cultivation robes, bowed hurriedly, then spoke with averted eyes. "This one thanks you for the attention. The Blackthorn Pavilion is located on Twentieth West Street and Tenth Avenue."

"Many thanks," Cha Ming said, flicking the man a mid-grade spirit stone.

The man took it and bowed deeply, then ran off, likely in case Cha Ming changed his mind. Cha Ming ignored him and looked toward the north, where Bastion Wall stood tall. In front of it was a large gray stone castle surrounded by black walls. The center line, he discovered, was named Palace Street. Street numbers increased symmetrically to the east and west, bearing directional designations. Horizontal roads were called avenues. They started from the palace with Castle Avenue, then increased in number with each block southward. There were no named streets in Bastion save these two and Bastion Avenue, the narrow street between the palace and the wall. There was no Central Square, for what could be more important than the residence of the royal family?

Cha Ming eventually found the Blackthorn Conglomerate. A tall gray building, the large complex occupied four city blocks and cut off both an avenue and a street. Its walls were covered in a black thornlike pattern that reminded him of the Jade Bamboo Pavilion's décor.

Not exactly subtle, are they?

Attendants bowed as he landed at the front door. "What can this one help you with, esteemed senior?" the strongest among them said.

"I've come at the invitation of Director Yong," Cha Ming said, holding out his employment contract. The attendant accepted the document reverently, then invited Cha Ming inside the building, where he saw many desks, both buying and selling in the fashion he'd grown used to at the Jade Bamboo Auction Houses in the North.

"Please excuse me while I report to my manager," the man said before leaving Cha Ming at a small table. Servants brought tea, and by the time he drank his first sip, a man in black cultivation robes approached.

"Come on in," the man said, waving him toward the back of the lobby. "No need for decorum. You live and work here now."

"Will I be seeing Director Yong?" Cha Ming asked, following the man to the back. The attendant had returned to the front to welcome other guests, and the deferential attitude he'd seen in the employee before had been replaced by an intense competitive glare that seemed to say: You may be stronger now, but you watch. I'll surpass you, and soon, you'll be the one bowing.

"Director Yong is busy at the moment," the man said. "As you'll find he usually is. My name is Tian Zhi. You can call me Boss Tian, as you now report directly to me."

"Boss Tian," Cha Ming said, bowing his head slightly in greeting. The duo walked out of the lobby and into the open-air complex behind it.

"We'll have your residence ready by tonight," Tian Zhi said. "An attendant will bring your identification badge and introduce the cultivation chambers and other accommodations. For now, you'll follow me to the research and development workshop."

Cha Ming nodded. He followed Tian Zhi through a few smaller winding streets until they arrived at a tall square building in the center of the complex. According to the sign, it was the manufacturing center. They entered the building and proceeded to a metal door at the back. Tian Zhi swiped his identification badge on a rune affixed to the metal door. It opened up into a smaller room. A small panel on the wall was inscribed with simple runes a child could read. Tian Zhi pressed the largest number, and they began moving not up, but down. Cha Ming's eyes widened in surprise, but the surprise ultimately faded.

"Seen a lift before, have you?" Tian Zhi asked. "It's the only way in and out of the research complex."

"Isn't that dangerous?" Cha Ming asked, noticing that the walls hummed with a soft music to pass the time as the dreadfully slow contraption progressed. "What if the lift breaks?"

Tian Zhi shrugged. "It might be a mechanism, but it's a core-level artifice. The whole building is made of stone, and experiments are conducted in explosion-proof rooms. If the lift stops functioning, at least one of us should be able to fix it, and if not, we're all cultivators. We can wait for help."

"Fair enough," Cha Ming said. Safety was so much simpler when cultivators were involved.

Soon enough, the elevator opened into a small room with clear walls. Tian Zhi approached the wall and motioned to a small clear panel on it. He pulled back his sleeve and pointed to a black thorn-covered tattoo on his forearm—his employment mark.

"To enter the facility," Tian Zhi explained, "one must verify their employment contract. It has to be the right kind of employment contract as well. Normal ones will be refused access along with some… unpleasant surprises." Instead of scanning his own arm, he gestured for Cha Ming to do so first. "You're the new one here. Scan your employment mark. If you've been wasting my time and you're a fraud, I'll just kill you and get on with my day."

As a peak-marrow-refining cultivator, the man had reason to be confident in his strength.

Cha Ming gulped, but he did as he was told. He pulled back his sleeve and revealed the employment mark, a tattoo of thorny black patterns complete with a runic identification number. He pressed it against the plate, which hummed. The door opened, and Cha Ming walked inside. It closed immediately afterward, opening once more to allow Tian Zhi inside.

"Welcome to the Blackthorn Conglomerate's Research and Development Center!" Tian Zhi said, holding out his hand.

Cha Ming gaped at what he saw. Instead of the slightly tall ceiling and tight hallways he'd expected of the underground facility, he saw a massive underground structure. It wasn't just a single floor, but several dozen floors in the bottom of the building, all combined in a massive space. The ceiling was illuminated by giant crystalline lights that not only provided light but ambient qi.

Instead of the small laboratories Cha Ming had expected, he saw people walking about, talking happily. Large contraptions were being built out in the open air beside underground herb gardens.

"You can work anywhere you like, really," Tian Zhi said. "But if you kill anyone, we'll kill you, as per Clause 15.3 of your contract. If you're doing anything dangerous, you need to use the research workshops." He pointed to the building closest to them on the left. "Each one is equipped with the best in safety systems, including explosion-proof walls for witnessing tests or shielding during crafting." He then pointed to the back. "That building is our research library, to which you now have full access."

"That," he said, pointing to the building to their right, "is the arboretum." The glass building was mostly transparent and spiraled upward like a beanstalk. "We grow our most exotic plants there for the alchemists. You're not allowed in without permission."

Cha Ming nodded absently. The last plot of land was more an open yard than anything else. It contained a squat but sturdy building. Piles of materials lay within fenced areas on the open ground.

"I take it that's the storehouse?" Cha Ming said.

Tian Zhi nodded. "That's right. If you need any materials, ask them, and they'll fetch them for you. If you need anything special, ask me directly, and I'll get them from the vault upstairs."

"All right," Cha Ming said. "Any orders or assignments?" Pai Xiao would be eager to learn, but he was an employee after all.

Tian Zhi snorted. "Don't bother trying to hide it. You want to shore up what you know and dig into our precious library."

"I wasn't trying to hide it, Boss Tian," Cha Ming said. "I'm just aware that I need to devote a certain amount of time to special projects. You might also have a direction you'd like me to focus my studies on."

Tian Zhi nodded. "Like everyone else, you'll be assigned to reconciliation duty for three months."

"Reconciliation duty?" Cha Ming asked, confused. Was he supposed to apologize to someone on his first day?

"We want productive employees, not distracted ones," Tian Zhi said. "That applies doubly so for research and development staff. If you're distracted by what's out there, you're not doing anyone any good. That's why we have all new employees focus on shoring up their lower-level knowledge. Your assignment is to review the material in the library and propose corrections to it. You can verify anything you like by using a workshop, and the materials will be supplied free of charge. Each of your proposed corrections will be evaluated. Any successful corrections will be rewarded based on your contract rates. Bear in mind that any incorrect corrections proposed, though you won't be punished directly for them, will make me very grumpy. And the last thing you want is a grumpy boss."

"All right, then," Cha Ming said. "I don't suppose I *have* to go back to my residence every night?"

Tian Zhi smirked. "Though you're not supposed to use them for frivolous reasons, people have been known to sleep in the workshops. It's technically against the rules, but who am I to blame a man for working himself to exhaustion and collapsing inside a lab?"

They exchanged a few more pleasantries before Cha Ming went directly to the library. He wouldn't read only to learn, but also to unlearn. If he exposed too much knowledge, the cover he'd spent months carefully crafting would be gone in the blink of an eye.

Chapter 16
Standing Out

Time flowed like a river. In the first month, Cha Ming read every single book on spiritual blacksmithing in the library. Though the contents weren't as thorough as the ones he'd been privy to in Haijing, they provided a solid foundation for anyone who wanted to climb to higher ranks in the South.

While Cha Ming was only a fire-and-gold cultivator on the surface, cultivating two types of qi and using them to refine his body, spiritual blacksmithing wasn't limited to only these elements. In the Blackthorn Conglomerate's library, he "learned" of elemental wood, which could be used to better forge certain metals. This opened up a whole new world of possibilities to Pai Xiao.

At first, Pai Xiao was clumsy—and so was Cha Ming, as he'd grown used to using Grandmist flames for alchemical purposes and an orange flame for smithing—but soon enough, he got the gist of it. Using these new flames as inspiration, he solidified Pai Xiao's base, verifying it through key experiments. By doing so, he left a paper trail of Pai Xiao's incredible rate of learning.

After quickly fixing his mortal-grade fundamentals, Cha Ming skipped correcting any mistakes in their basic knowledge and proceeded directly to magic-grade smithing. There, he found countless holes waiting to be filled. To avoid suspicion, however, he was very selective about which knowledge he supplemented. An inspiration here, noticing a flaw there; the challenge of making himself look outstanding but not overtly suspicious was a refreshing activity.

His amendments to the knowledgebase completed, Cha Ming proceeded to improve some core smithing techniques. Though he was worried about divulging too much knowledge to the South, he needed to demonstrate a drive for profit and innovation. Besides, there wouldn't be much left of the Wang family after he was done here. The competitive scene in the Southern Alliance meant the knowledge was unlikely to spread very far.

Cha Ming's second month was both productive and profitable. Therefore, in his third month, he took a more relaxed approach. He alternated between cultivating in the Clear Sky World and consolidating his demonstrated knowledge with the patchy framework the grandmaster spiritual blacksmiths of the Blackthorn Conglomerate had cobbled together.

With the rest of his time, Cha Ming created and tested dozens of new products. Being a researcher, he had full access to the Blackthorn Conglomerate's catalogue and capabilities. Using his skill as a formation artist, he filled some gaps in their armaments—mostly utility treasures. He hoped it was enough. His target wasn't to become a normal product developer; it was to join the team developing a specific weapon. Only then would he be able to ruin Zhou Li's plan. Incidentally, that would leave the Wang family's reputation in tatters.

"It's an interesting-looking device," Tian Zhi said, unimpressed. He sat at a small desk in Cha Ming's laboratory, fiddling with the metallic emerald fan inscribed with a wind-element runic pattern. "But it's not very lethal, is it?"

"Lethal products aren't the only useful ones," Cha Ming said. He pressed a set of runes, and a few dozen mannequins rose from the floor. Each one was a mobile puppet, something the South excelled in crafting. Not only were they useful cannon fodder, but they were also good test subjects. Live specimens were good and all—cheap too— but their physiques were too variable for standardized tests. So in an ironic twist of fate, the Southern Alliance and all its bureaucracy had the most ethical weapons testing procedures on the continent. The mannequins Cha Ming was currently using were equivalent to early-foundation-establishment body cultivators.

"The formation plate is designed to accommodate any of the five elements, though its preferred element, wind, has a better conversion rate," Cha Ming explained. He poured a predetermined amount of fire qi into the fan, which caused it to glow. "Through a series of conversion matrices, the qi is converted to wind qi."

"Less talking and more doing," Tian Zhi said, waving his hand.

"I would prefer to follow established testing procedures" Cha Ming said. "The spirits watch and remember. As you can see, the fan now contains a standard charge. The strength of the charge depends on the strength of the artifact."

Cha Ming swung the fan, and twenty of the thirty or so mannequins toppled. "The initial burst is enough to topple ten to twenty early-foundation-establishment experts, stunning them for a half second in the process. The middle-grade artifact will do the same for middle-foundation-establishment cultivators, and so on. Naturally, using a larger fan on weaker opponents can do more than knock them over. I'm sure you can see the tactical advantage."

"We'll see," Tian Zhi said uncertainly. "How many charges can it handle before collapsing?"

"Five," Cha Ming said. "Conversion matrix aside, the strain on the artifact is too great."

"Five," Tian Zhi said, nodding. "That's more than I expected. I thought it would be two or three."

"At first, it was," Cha Ming said. "But I had an epiphany and deepened some bottlenecked energy lines, reducing the strain on the fan's material."

"Good enough, I suppose," Tian Zhi said. "I hope that's not all you brought me here to see."

"Of course not," Cha Ming said, pulling out what looked like a small brown pyramid. "This one is much more useful." He tossed it to Tian Zhi, who looked at it in puzzlement before finally realizing what it was.

"It's a gravity well," Tian Zhi said. "I've seen a few—even made some back in my day. They're all right, but nearly useless. Our opponents adapt to them very quickly, so the effect on any battle is limited."

"True," Cha Ming said. "If it was a normal gravity well. I wouldn't waste your time with it."

"And what's special about this one?" Tian Zhi said, manipulating the pyramid in his hands. "I see it's an initial-core-grade item. Those will usually be able to exert a fifty-foot gravity field that will slow down an initial-core-formation cultivator's speed by twenty percent, assuming he gets used to it."

"Why don't you try it?" Cha Ming said, sitting cross-legged on the floor. He also placed his hands on the durable concrete beneath him.

"Why not?" Tian Zhi said. He poured a wisp of qi into the artifact, which suddenly blazed with power. Tian Zhi fell face-first on the floor. He pushed himself up slowly, and for three seconds, all he could do was stand firm. The gravity let up after those three seconds and crumbled to dust.

"What the hell was that?" Tian Zhi said, breathing hard as he picked himself up off the floor. He wiped the dust off the tan apron he always wore atop his black cultivation robes.

Cha Ming grinned, red faced but otherwise fine, as he'd braced himself. "Well, I figured that since a sustained activation gravity well wasn't very useful on the battlefield, at least given its cost, I decided to modify it. I call it an extreme gravity well. I'm not sure exactly how strong the field is, but it's much stronger directly above where the pyramid lands compared to the outer edges. I tested it on myself. Outside the three-foot area near the center, but within fifty feet, it can almost completely immobilize me, a middle-bone-forging and middle-core-formation cultivator during its three-second activation. My techniques might not be outstanding, but that seems much more useful to me than a normal gravity well."

"I think it has potential," Tian Zhi said. "Though it's regrettable that it's single use."

"It was the only way to bring out peak power," Cha Ming said. "Besides, is it a bad thing that it's single use? The user's opponents can't recycle the captured treasure if it's broken."

"I suppose," Tian Zhi said. "I can also see how throwing heavy objects onto incapacitated enemy soldiers would be very effective."

"Indeed," Cha Ming said. "Though, this is only my second-best invention. For this third test, however, I need an unusual test medium. Test puppets or live subjects won't do."

"Oh?" Tian Zhi said. "Is it not an offensive item but a shield? You know full well that shields aren't very popular in our battle arrangements."

In Southern armies, lesser troops formed an expendable vanguard. Well-equipped elite cultivators and blood masters followed. The South pooled defensive items on those few, preferring a war of attrition that sacrificed many lesser lives.

"It isn't a defensive item," Cha Ming said. "It's offensive, but the nature of its target is unusual. Would we happen to have any geomancers around? I need a solid, wall-like object. Preferably the product of an initial-grandmaster geomancer, at least for this iteration."

"Interesting," Tian Zhi said, twiddling with his short beard. "As a matter a fact, I do. We also have a few prototype walls in this building."

"Oh?" Cha Ming said. "That's surprising. I built this on a whim. With any luck, it'll be useful."

"Come with me," Tian Zhi said, nodding. He led Cha Ming to the building's central lift. Cha Ming's workshop was on the third of eight floors. Tian Zhi led him to the top floor. They passed several empty workshops until they arrived at an unoccupied one. When they entered, however, Cha Ming noticed that it wasn't that the other workshops were empty, but that they'd been merged into a single room. Three prototype walls had been erected. The first wall was an initial-core-grade structure, while the other two were early core grade and middle core grade respectively.

"To be honest, I'm not sure how well this will work," Cha Ming said, embarrassed. "In theory, it should work just fine, but in practice? I've only had golems to test with."

"It's worth a try," Tian Zhi said. "Don't worry about the result. You can always work on it if it's ineffective." His words were relaxed, but Cha Ming could see an expectant gleam in his eyes. He nodded and summoned a spear from his storage ring.

The spear was an unusual treasure. For one, it was made of pure metal. Its entire length had been crafted of a single material, making it a sharp but rigid core-grade weapon. The runes were also strange for this type of weapon. Unlike the usual strengthening runes, durability runes, and other things commonly seen, the only runes on the spear's length were energy-gathering and energy-transferring runes. That all changed at the spear's tip, which was covered in all sorts of runes enhancing the sharpness of the weapon. Still, no runes enhancing the weapon's toughness could be seen.

"An interesting weapon," Tian Zhi remarked. "It would last maybe three exchanges before shattering if facing an equivalent treasure."

"Then it's a good thing it only needs to last a single strike," Cha Ming said. He grinned, then poured a predetermined amount of qi into the spear—the entire qi reserve of an initial-core-formation cultivator. The power poured through the spear shaft in less than three seconds, accumulating at the spear's tip, which glowed with an unstable golden light.

Cha Ming wasted no time with a lengthy explanation, for seeing was believing. He didn't worry for Tian Zhi's safety—the man was a peak-marrow-refining expert, a blacksmith among blacksmiths. If he died from a simple demonstration, he'd have no one to blame but himself. So Cha Ming rushed to the wall with the spear, using no techniques to enhance his strike, only raw power. He jammed the spear into the wall. It penetrated a good three feet before stopping.

"Mediocre piercing power," Tian Zhi said in obvious disappointment.

"I'd hide if I were you," Cha Ming said, ducking to the side. Tian Zhi, uncertain of what was happening, didn't heed his advice. He simply waited. Two seconds after the spear had pierced the wall, a sickening crack resounded in the workshop.

"Argh!" Tian Zhi screamed.

Cha Ming looked over and noticed that a foot-long piece of golden shrapnel had pierced the man's thigh. Tian Zhi gritted his teeth and pulled it out. The bones, which had been broken by the strike, instantly mended thanks to the man's fierce regenerative abilities.

"Not bad," he said, stroking his beard as he looked at the spear's handiwork. The wall, which the spear had barely pierced a few seconds ago, had broken in two. Where the spear had once been, there was a nine-foot empty crater filled with smoking metallic dust. Only a few fragments of the spear remained. A crack expanded vertically from the point of impact. The force of the detonation had clearly been aimed in a specific direction.

"And you've never tested this before?" Tian Zhi asked with a raised eyebrow.

"The result is a little embarrassing," Cha Ming said, blushing a little. "I was hoping to channel around half of the energy generated vertically, but it was closer to ten percent. The wall section here is only fifteen feet tall, after all, and most walls are much taller."

"Still, I think you're onto something," Tian Zhi said. "I won't say we'll use it as is, but I'll definitely be filing for a new product bonus for you."

"Thank you," Cha Ming said, bowing.

"No, thank you," Tian Zhi said. "You're wasted on those other things, those gravity wells, those wind fans. I see real potential here with this demolition artifact."

"Sir?" Cha Ming said. "Do you wish for me to continue enhancing it?"

"This?" Tian Zhi said. "No, it's far too primitive compared to what's needed. Instead, I have a special project in mind, if you're interested. The benefit to our empire is astronomical, and the reward for successfully creating it… Well, let's just say that, split amongst the development team, the poorest man could own a mid-sized city if he liked."

Cha Ming licked his lips. "When do we start?" He didn't want to appear too eager, but an entire city? Only a fool or a selfless man would pass up on that. Pai Xiao was neither.

"Tomorrow," Tian Zhi said. "Take the rest of the day off in the meantime. Rest your mind."

"Thank you, sir," Cha Ming said. Seeing that Tian Zhi wanted to be left alone, he left the laboratory. He didn't return to his workshop but followed his senior's advice, ascending to the surface level of the Blackthorn Conglomerate. The first part of his plan had been to craft an identity and infiltrate the Wang family. The second part, getting in on Zhou Li's pet project, had been a balancing act. After all, who wouldn't be suspicious if someone who excelled at said project happened to appear on their front door?

The project's goal was simple: to create a device capable of shattering transcendent walls, allowing Southern forces to pour into Northern lands. Pai Xiao's spear hadn't quite done that, but it had shown potential and destructive innovation that exceeded their knowledge base. The other two artifacts he'd created, though less obvious in their intent, had also shown that he could overcome an artifact's grade limitation, exceeding normal power restrictions with reduced durability as a price.

Chuckling to himself, Cha Ming left the Blackthorn Conglomerate and went south to the entrance of the outer city. He'd been in Bastion for three months and had yet to try out the local cuisine. He was keen on remedying that situation.

Cha Ming walked out of a small but famous restaurant a few hours later. He was completely stuffed, and he had even taken some food to go, something cultivators often did, as they rarely left seclusion.

Who knew the South had curries? he thought. *I'll have to tell Huxian.* Now wasn't the best time to go on vacation, but coming back after the war was over wasn't impossible. That was, if they won.

Despite all this talk of a final confrontation, Cha Ming had seen nothing but strength south of the border. Though he'd never been to any of the battlefields, he'd noticed that the North lacked something in comparison: fighting spirit. Life was a struggle in these inhospitable lands. Getting ahead, and even learning, was a struggle. People here were used to hard work, grueling conditions, and a lot of unfairness. But still, they persisted.

In the North, Cha Ming had only seen relaxed advancement and casual cultivation. There wasn't a lot of pressure for anyone to climb the ranks. For the most part, there was no war in Northern countries, save for the battlefields and occasional border skirmishes. Most cultivators trained for the sake of getting stronger, and many made a living by fighting demons for abundant resources in spirit woods.

The South was different. Kingdoms rose and fell, and people could be killed at the drop of a hat. Spirit woods were few, as were quarries. Kingdoms warred for these scarce resources as fiercely as they fought against the North. They fought with bitterness and unfairness on their lips, wishing they could break apart that arbitrary border and take over those fertile, easy lands that bred people too weak to deserve them.

That's the balance though, isn't it? Cha Ming sent to Sun Wukong, who'd been resting in the Clear Sky Brush. *The balance between good and evil.*

The forces of evil are forged in misfortune and blood, Sun Wukong agreed. *How could they not be stronger for it? A veteran is more lethal than fresh fodder. Even the luckiest of generals would rather have an army of veterans over twice as many new troops.*

Cha Ming nodded. He looked at the people as he walked. Now that he'd wandered off Main Street, he saw what he hadn't seen when he'd entered the city. There were beggars here, but they filled less important streets. They didn't beg for money with no strings attached like those in the North did—they knew the world wasn't kind to them. Instead, they offered themselves up for hard labor, among other things. Other poorer people didn't beg but sold odds and ends on the side of the street. Feeding such a populated city was difficult, especially where mortals were concerned. Small markets sprouted up wherever enough merchants chose to set up their wares. They supplied cheap goods to the underclass, which was the lifeblood of Bastion.

Cha Ming walked for quite some time, taking in the anger and resentment he felt in the general population. He wondered if there was something he could do for them, but he quickly banished that thought. He wasn't here to help them; he was there to hurt them. By hurting their kings, it was inevitable that many weaker lives would be lost. It was the terrible price of war, a price that would be paid regardless of his efforts.

Cha Ming was about to return to his residence, but something caught his eye. He saw a blanket filled with low-grade spirit weapons. To his surprise, the owner of the blanket and the spirit weapons was someone he recognized: Mo Ling. Somehow, she'd traveled to Bastion from Ashes. Moreover, she carried an unexpected burden. Within her weak qi-cultivating body, Cha Ming could hear a quick, pulsing rhythm that beat along with her calm heart. The tiny pulse carried blood from her body and into a small growing fetus. Mo Ling, so cold and alone, was with child.

What happened to her? Cha Ming thought. He saw no employment marks on her arms, but neither did he see a slave brand. She didn't appear unhealthy or beaten, but neither was she thriving. Much of the youthful innocence she'd had before was gone. Conviction and determination had replaced them.

I won't help you on this one, Sun Wukong said. *Not only because of the spirit wards in the city, but because it's something you should do. Just remember one thing: You cut ties with her for a reason. Would you be helping or hurting her if you showed yourself?*

Cha Ming nodded. He walked over to her stall, but instead of stopping there, he passed by. As he did, he reached out with his mind and skimmed her memories. He expected betrayal and anger; instead, he saw a tale of sadness.

When he'd left, Mo Ling had been well-treated by the store owner. She was a hardworking employee and was quickly promoted to a full manager in the store. Her natural gifts for management and financials had impressed many people. Multiple businesses had tried to recruit her, but she'd declined them, saying she was happy where she was.

Then, a man had come into her life. He was an adventurer, and his tales had wooed the naïve Mo Ling almost instantly. After a few passionate nights together, the man had gone to a nearby spirit wood to gather beast cores. A month later, she received terrible news: The man had died, gored by a demonic boar. Roughly around the same time, she discovered that she was pregnant.

In the South, just like the North, it was shameful to have a child out of wedlock. So, unable to face her coworkers and friends, Mo Ling had asked to cancel her employment contract. Then, after selling what little she had, she journeyed to Bastion. Not to find Pai Xiao, but because it was the only other major city she knew of. She'd never tried to find the old smith who had taken her in. Instead, she was determined to make it on her own as a merchant. If she couldn't do it, no one could.

Everyone had to start somewhere. Since she didn't have the necessary capital to start a business, she'd started at the bottom. Instead of a shop, she had a blanket, and instead of premium magic-grade weapons, she had spirit weapons. Fortunately, she was a cultivator. Even with the child growing inside her, she didn't require much in terms of food or sustenance. She saved everything she could, and if everything went as planned, she would soon have enough spirit stones to rent a shop space and fill her inventory.

You're not going to help her? Sun Wukong asked, surprised as Cha Ming walked away.

Cha Ming shook his head. *She doesn't need my help,* he said. *She has everything she needs, and doing more would simply sow more karma between us. That's the last thing she needs.*

So you're just going to leave her there? Sun Wukong said. *All alone in this cruel city?*

If she can't survive this, what will she do after I'm gone? Cha Ming asked. Still, he hesitated. Was he growing harder, or was the cruel environment just rubbing off on him? *I'll check up on her,* he decided. *Once a week, at least. If she's fine, I won't do anything.*

And if not? Sun Wukong asked.

Cha Ming sighed. *Then I'll help her. Karma connecting us might not be the best thing for her, but it's better than dying. Though I somehow doubt it'll come to that.* He looked back to the stand, where a customer was fiercely haggling with Mo Ling, who was fighting for every spirit stone. He watched for a time, then left along with her satisfied customer.

Having toured the outer city, Cha Ming returned to the Blackthorn Conglomerate. He'd succeeded in the first two parts of his plan, but the third and the fourth were still waiting for him. First, he had to figure out a way to sabotage the Wang family. Then, he had to destroy Zhou Li's pet project. More likely than not, he'd need to complete one goal to finish the other.

Chapter 17
Goals

"The past three months were all about evaluating your potential," Tian Zhi said as they walked through the Blackthorn Conglomerate headquarters. "As you may have guessed, your future assignments and research direction will be dictated by the results."

"Aren't we free to research anything we like?" Cha Ming asked, following him as he led the way, not toward the research and development building as he'd expected, but toward a small corner of the outer building.

"Yes, technically speaking," Tian Zhi said. "On your free time. But tell me—do you think your funding is truly unlimited? You need to request it, and if we think it's not worth the expenditure, we would refuse you." He pushed through a small door and entered a mess area where, to Cha Ming's surprise, there were restaurants *inside* the conglomerate.

"I suppose not," Cha Ming said. "The research group must have some focus areas with allocated funding." They stopped at the back end of a line. The line itself was unsurprising, as the South prided itself on lines. Here, even mighty marrow-refining cultivators like him and Tian Zhi had to line up. Though that didn't stop those in front of them from shuffling uncomfortably and letting them pass, if only to breathe easier when they did.

"That's right," Tian Zhi said. "What you showed me yesterday proves you have the skills for one of our most lucrative secret projects." Many ears moved in from the side. Tian Zhi glared at them before shifting to mental communication. *Lately, we've been focusing on demolition weapons.*

Demolition weapons? Cha Ming asked. *What a coincidence.*

Exactly, Tian Zhi said. *You've shown you have a knack for destruction even without knowing about our secret project. So, after discussing with the rest of the team, we've decided to have you spend half your time working on it. You'll use the other half improving your skills however you like. We have deadlines to meet, so the faster you move up the ranks, the more useful you'll be.*

During their short conversation, they'd moved to the end of the line and arrived at a counter that, to Cha Ming's surprise, served coffee in disposable cups. He took a sip of what they called "God's Blessing" that Tian Zhi ordered, and to his surprise, it gave him a slight jolt. He immediately realized why it affected him. Somehow, Jin Huang's runic coffee had made its way to the South as well.

"You don't seem surprised by the taste," Tian Zhi said, taking a sip of his own beverage.

"I've had something similar before," Cha Ming admitted.

"Interesting," Tian Zhi said. "We're one of the few places in the Ji Kingdom that has a chain." He shrugged, ignoring the seemingly inconsequential matter, and led Cha Ming back the way they'd come and into production building. They took the lift down to the research and development area and into the workshop with walls where Cha Ming had tested his spear the day prior. Three other people were present. One, a tall man with sleek brown hair, wore the green robes of an alchemist. He was walking around the debris-laden room, sensing every small residual particle with his peak resplendent force. Another, a woman wearing simple brown robes, was taking measurements and surveying the damage to the wall itself.

The third person was the most conspicuous of the lot. Instead of performing a specific task, he sat cross-legged with his hands in front of him. Tiny threads were connected to the air above his hands from many areas within the room. They poured into a variety of runic symbols that hovered there, glowing with varying intensity. To Cha Ming's surprise, many of the runes were identical to those he'd inscribed into the weapon. Others represented common measures like total energy and energy output over time.

"Attention!" Tian Zhi shouted like a military sergeant. The others immediately stopped what they were doing and formed a line. Cha Ming shuffled uncomfortably but didn't move to join them, as he hadn't been instructed to. "He Yin, report!"

"Yes, sir," He Yin, the alchemist, said. "I've compiled a report on the residual materials detected. I've concluded that though the main impact was caused by a pure single-use treasure, a few metallic combustion reactions further increased the damage to the wall. Approximately seventy percent of the metal actually vaporized in an exothermic reaction, though how this happened, I'm unsure."

"As I suspected," Tian Zhi said. "Pan Su, your results?"

Pan Su, obviously a geomancer, given her preoccupation with the wall itself, replied, "Using basic power-decay assumptions, I've pinned the spear at being able to sever a fifty-foot vertical gash in a longer wall. Too much power is wasted on the central point of impact to go any further. If the weapon's power distribution was further optimized, perhaps it would be possible to travel another thirty feet in each direction. It's difficult to say."

"Good," Tian Zhi said. "Shao Qiang?"

"I would rank the weapon as second class in effectiveness, first class in peak power potential," the black-robed Shao Qiang said. "My auguries show limited potential for this specific line of weapon, however. Perhaps we could optimize something of a similar construction so that it could perform to mid-grade, but nothing further than that." Cha Ming realized at that moment that he wasn't a runic artist but a seer.

Tian Zhi frowned. "That's high for an initial-grade weapon."

Shao Qiang shrugged. "The runes he used are far more advanced than common smithing runes. Either the inheritance he accepted had very high runic requirements, or he's hiding a second profession as a formation master from us. Likely the former, rather than the latter, as formation professions are rather rare around here."

Tian Zhi looked to Cha Ming, who nodded. "It's true that my inheritance focused more on runes than the forging process. Fortunately, the knowledge in the library helped close many gaps in my knowledge."

"And what do you think of their assessment?" Tian Zhi said.

"I can't speak for geomancy, but Grandmaster He Yin is correct," Cha Ming said. "I used an exothermic metallic reaction to fuel the runic activation. Though I don't know about Grandmaster Shao Qiang's view on limitations, I do sense I can improve the design."

"There's no need to improve on it," Tian Zhi said, shaking his head. "We have no time to waste. Shao Qiang, have you found anything that might be useful in our current project?"

"I was about to get to that," Shao Qiang said. He held his right hand out to the side, and the runes he'd summoned earlier followed. Then, he put out his left hand. Other runes tumbled out of his sleeves, forming a complex matrix of information above his left hand. A rune in his right hand glowed, and tiny bright tethers connected them with the complex matrix in his left. "I believe some components of the runic structure are likely to succeed in enhancing the current prototype. The metallic reaction, while pretty, likely won't be of any benefit in our current design. We'd need to approach the project from a different angle for that. I believe we should be able to increase the destructive capabilities of the Breaker by five percent."

"The Breaker?" Cha Ming asked, puzzled.

"It's what we're working on," Tian Zhi said, waving for them to follow. They walked through a smaller door and into an office that only contained a single large table. Tian Zhi pressed on it, and a three-dimensional hologram appeared. It resembled an unusually thick spear with a dull point. He swiped, and the exterior shell faded, revealing a large assortment of interlinking parts. It contained several sharp components wrapped in bundles. "You're thinking of the thorn tips?"

"Yes," Shao Qiang said. He stepped forward and waved, bringing up a three-dimensional model of a thin, sleek instrument. Judging by its runic pattern, it was at least a late-grade-core treasure, a full step above Pai Xiao's level. "I'm thinking of the shaft near the destructive tip more than anything else. The power conveyance." He swiped again, and the three-dimensional projection unfolded, showing the full surface of the object."

"Well?" Tian Zhi said, looking at Cha Ming.

"Forgive me, but this is beyond me," Cha Ming said. "I can work with the runic diagram, but I'm not sure about how it will interact with the materials. I don't think I could craft this."

Tian Zhi chuckled. "You don't need to craft it," he said. "You're part of a team now. What you need to do is narrow down potential options and create prototypes. If you need someone to actually work the metal, I can help with that until you get stronger."

"I suppose I could create less-powerful versions to test the feasibility," Cha Ming said. "Middle core grade, with a similar alloy, hoping it could be scaled up. I'd need to try several iterations to be sure." He pointed to the base of each spike, where several runic lines spread out from the main device. "Judging by the shape of the device, it will be taking power from the bottom-most two thirds of the 'thorn tip' as you called it, am I right? And the power should be delivered swiftly and efficiently to the last third?"

"That's right," Tian Zhi said.

"I think I can work with that," Cha Ming said. "Give me three days, and I'll have a few mid-grade prototypes we can test. Is that acceptable?"

"It is," Tian Zhi said. "If you need anything, go to the third floor, fourth workshop, and talk to Lu Yong. He will get you anything you need."

"I won't disappoint you," Cha Ming said, clasping his hands and bowing.

Tian Zhi chuckled. "Look at him. He's so proper and respectful. Like a child just out of primary school."

"We'll beat it out of him, sir," Pan Su replied. "We'll start by dropping the honorifics. Well?" She glared at Cha Ming, who coughed lightly.

"Pan Su, Shao Qiang, He Yin," he said, nodding to each one. Then he looked hesitantly at Tian Zhi.

"You may still call me Boss Tian," the man grunted. "Now off with you. You have work to do."

"Yes, Boss Tian," Cha Ming said. He nodded and exited the workshop, leaving the other four to their own devices. They likely didn't fully trust his capabilities at this point, and he'd need to make something to earn it.

Now where did he say Lu Yong was again? he thought, pressing the lift's rune to proceed to the third floor.

Two weeks later, Cha Ming sat at a small restaurant in a tiny rundown neighborhood in Bastion. He'd taken the afternoon off after three successful innovations on the project and substantial headway in his smithing abilities. His progress was astounding, if judged by a normal craftsman's standards.

Little did they know that he'd actually spent much more time secluded in his Clear Sky World, frantically working to improve his smithing skills. Fortunately, he was strong with metal despite his weakness with fire, and runes were second nature to him. He was busy, but he still had time to cultivate.

He also found time to watch a young woman who'd just opened a shop across from the restaurant. Mo Ling, an industrious salesperson, had somehow scraped up enough spirit stones and found someone to lend her money. Using these funds, she'd opened up a small weapon shop, similar to what she'd managed for Pai Xiao but of a much lower grade. She'd also convinced two weaker smiths to work for her, despite not knowing anything about smithing.

Maybe I don't need to check up on her so often, Cha Ming thought, thinking about his next steps in the Blackthorn Conglomerate. Although he wanted to foil Zhou Li's pet project, he owed it to

Wang Jun to have the Wang family fall out with the Spirit Temple. If possible, he wanted to drag Bastion's Blood Master Monastery and the Ji Kingdom's royal family into it as well.

But how to do it? Cha Ming thought. He couldn't just show up and break things in those places. Not only would that give him away, his chances of success would probably be minimal as well. Any incriminating interactions he had with them would have to be using his identity as Pai Xiao and the services he provided for the Wang family. He'd need to build something for these groups, and what he built had to have consequences so serious these organizations would turn on the entire Wang family.

The Ji royal family is easy, Cha Ming thought. The Breaker was a project commissioned by them and not directly through Zhou Li as he'd initially suspected. A major failure with the weapon would draw the ire of the Ji Kingdom. The difficult ones to act on would be the Blood Master Monastery and the Spirit Temple.

The Blood Master Monastery regularly deals with the Blackthorn Conglomerate, so there's an opening, Cha Ming thought. *As for the Spirit Temple, it seems they only provide contractual assistance to the Blackthorn Conglomerate in the South. Their soul trade is overt and much less lucrative than in the North.* It was also much less efficient. In the South, countless more deaths were required to produce the same amount of high-quality souls.

Cha Ming sighed. He had much to do and little idea of where to start. He wished he had clearer and more definite goals like Mo Ling did. The young woman, despite being young and pregnant, seemed to know exactly what to do. Two weeks after selling spirit weapons from a blanket, she was already the owner of a store and an employer of two. Her needs drove her to accomplish what most men would think was a foolish fantasy as they toiled away for lords who didn't care for their hopes and dreams.

On his end, Cha Ming had two enmities to instigate, a trap to plan, and a whole lot of guilt to resolve. He wanted to incriminate the Wang family and the Blackthorn Conglomerate, but what of its members? Wouldn't they be implicated in the fallout? And what of his newfound research companions He Yin, Shao Qiang, and Pan Su? What about Boss Tian?

He had many decisions to make, and none of them were easy.

Chapter 18
Opportunity

"Good morning, Grandmaster Pai Xiao," an attendant said with a bow as he entered the Blackthorn Conglomerate's administration office. "How can I help you today?"

It was a fine morning, and the building's peculiar construction allowed light to trickle through the lobby's ceiling windows. The lady at the desk, a wide-eyed foundation-establishment cultivator, practically trembled in excitement as she spoke.

"I'm just here to collect my wages," Cha Ming said, ignoring her fidgety expression. It was common for cultivators, be they male or female, to revere more powerful ones. Some people just weren't very good at hiding it.

The young woman scrambled to a back room and returned with a storage disk. Cha Ming looked inside, confirmed the number of spirit stones was accurate, then transferred all of them to his storage ring in one smooth motion.

"Thank you," Cha Ming said.

"Don't mention it," the attendant said. "Can I help you with anything else?"

"Yes, I was wondering if Boss Tian was in today," Cha Ming answered. As the head of the research and development group, Grandmaster Tian Zhi wasn't always in the workshops. He often had to take care of administrative tasks and meetings. If possible, he liked to lump them all in the span of a few days.

"Yes, he's in today," the attendant said. "He has a fifteen-minute opening in five minutes. Would you like me to book it?"

"Sure," Cha Ming said. "Seventh floor, right?"

"Seventh floor," the woman confirmed.

Cha Ming proceeded up the stairs. The administration building didn't have a lift like the research and development building did. Not only was such a contraption extremely costly, but there simply wasn't a need to shuttle large quantities of heavy materials in a simple office. Here, people only did paperwork and had meetings. Or, heaven forbid, interviews. He shuddered at the thought of Southern interviews. The process was likely thorough and rigid beyond belief.

Though the building didn't house many expensive materials, it *did* house many important people. As such, it was the tallest building in the complex. Cha Ming took in Bastion's city layout as he climbed the steps. Each building sat neatly in its precisely measured position. Citizens lined up for whatever services they required, with higher-ranking members cutting to shorter lines if allowed by the rules of the establishment in question. It all operated like a well-oiled machine.

The Spirit Temple was no exception. In fact, it seemed rules were more strictly followed there than anywhere else. People kept their distance from one another as they waited for a number in the large square before the temple. Inferiors bowed and scraped when required, and everyone there acted extremely politely, especially in the presence of priests; offending the wrong person at the temple could cost you your life, or worse yet, your soul. Despite the risks, however, tens of thousands frequented the temple grounds every day. They had little choice, as the Spirit Temple was the biggest issuer and guarantor of contracts.

Unlike the Spirit Temple, the Blood Master Monastery was chaotic and unruly. No outsiders loafed within its spartan grounds, where its members brutally trained with their lives on the line. Its buildings also let off a hostile aura. Despite the chaos, no beggars could be seen anywhere near the complex. It was said that the monastery occasionally purged the city's undesirables. As a result, most of them left the city voluntarily, even selling themselves into serfdom for fear of getting caught up in a potential sweep.

After much walking, Cha Ming finally arrived on the seventh floor. He passed several wooden doors before arriving at a small waiting area near Tian Zhi's office, where he sat and waited. Five minutes passed, then another five. Whoever Tian Zhi was meeting with, they were running late, an unusual occurrence in Bastion. The door opened after two minutes.

"I'll be sure to get someone working on it," Tian Zhi assured two men, leading them toward the stairwell and passing Cha Ming. The men wore bloodred combat robes, and each one wore a weapon out in the open. There was no need to wonder about their identity; their bald heads, aggressive stares, and bloodred tattoos that crept up from beneath their robes marked them as blood masters.

"Be sure you do," one of the men said before proceeding down the stairs.

"Come," Tian Zhi said, waving Cha Ming inside. "I don't have much time anymore. For all their talk of being disciplined monks, they have no concept of timeliness."

"I think they focus their attention on violence and training," Cha Ming said. "Everything and everyone around them are there to support them and their desires." He took a seat in Tian Zhi's well-furnished office as the man poured them both a quick cup of tea.

"What can I help you with today?" Tian Zhi said. It had been two months since Cha Ming had started working on the Breaker, and he'd made many significant improvements to his design. Slowly but surely, the artifact was pushing itself past the boundaries of a late-grade weapon of structural destruction.

"I'm at a bottleneck in my studies," Cha Ming said, taking a sip of tea. "Unfortunately, focusing on the *project* doesn't seem to be sufficient. I need to work on something else. Something to take my mind off of things."

"Hmm," Tian Zhi said. He tapped his fingers on his desk, thinking. "I have a few projects you could work on. The first one is a request from a coastal kingdom. Something about redesigning certain ship components since a good portion of their naval fleet was wiped out in a storm."

"A storm?" Cha Ming asked, raising an eyebrow. "A single storm wiped out a naval fleet?"

"I didn't say I believed them," Tian Zhi said. "They'll only share what happened if we take on the job. Are you interested?"

"That seems outside my field of expertise," Cha Ming said. "I'm not very good with water-aligned construction methods."

"Fair enough," Tian Zhi said. "The second one is a request to develop larger flight treasures for more efficient transportation. With the war preparations going on across the South, they've finally realized the logistics of the battle are going to be a deciding factor. They need us to think up something—anything—to make transportation cheaper."

"All right," Cha Ming said. It wasn't a bad project for Pai Xiao. Incorporating key weaknesses in the design would be easy, and that could provide the North with significant advantages. "I'll think about it. Anything else?"

Tian Zhi tapped his chin and looked at Cha Ming. "You made a spear for the blood master abbot in Ashes, am I right?"

"Does the abbot here need a weapon as well?" Cha Ming asked.

"Nothing like that," Tian Zhi said. "But we need someone with experience crafting compatible weapons. You know how they are—they focus on offense, offense, offense at all costs. They want a new line of stronger weapons. Their standard-issue weapons—the ones they had designed thirty years ago—are archaic. They want to completely replace the entire lot.

"I'd normally be very agreeable to all this, and so would Director Yong, but our research and development group is already flooded with work. Blood masters are very picky, you see, so we can't just put anyone on the project. It would need to be a core member. But I can't afford to dedicate too much of our time on it. We have a deadline looming for *the project*. If we don't meet it, the most powerful man in the South will have our hides."

"I'm no expert on blood-master weapons, but I'd be willing to give it a try," Cha Ming said. "Do you have designs for the weapons they currently use?"

"I do," Tian Zhi said, taking a bloodred jade from his desk and handing it to him. "Though I don't want you spending too much time on this. A week at most. If you don't have any ideas, we're going to pretend you didn't look at it. Though I don't want to upset the blood masters, I'd rather upset a hundred abbots than a grand vizier of the Southern Alliance."

"All right," Cha Ming said. "I'll see what I can do." He pocketed the red jade and stood up. "I won't stay for another cup. It's time for your next appointment." The long hand on the man's clock had almost reached a quarter after.

"The spirits remember men who respect others' schedules," Tian Zhi said.

"The spirits remember," Cha Ming replied, passing a pair of sinister-looking men on his way to the stairwell.

Who would have thought I'd end up working at an evil research and development company? Cha Ming thought, shaking his head. *Next thing you know, I'll be making extra-scratchy chairs that keep employees uncomfortable as they work to increase their productivity.*

Cha Ming and Tian Zhi were seated on a thick concrete platform, observing red-robed martial artists sparring in the center of Bastion's Blood Master Monastery. Though there were fifty men fighting one-on-one duels, there were only two sides to the fight: the ones using older, outdated weapons and those using test weapons. Both weapons were bloodred—a branding requirement from the monastery. To differentiate between sides, those using new weapons wore black armbands. Thus far, neither side had the advantage.

"You said you had a surprise," the sharp-toothed blood master who had visited the Blackthorn Conglomerate a week earlier said, "but thus far, I'm disappointed."

Xue Xiao was the second-ranking member here. He was a peak-marrow-refining cultivator, and the brimming vitality he let off told Cha Ming he'd survive a fight if all that remained of him was a drop of blood.

"Patience," Cha Ming said. "The previous generation of weapons was the most cost-effective way to arm your forces at the time. We didn't have much to work with given your pricing requirements."

"So you're saying what we asked for was impossible," Xue Xiao said flatly.

"I didn't say that," Cha Ming said. "I just had to look at other ways to improve combat effectiveness. Whether it was the power, sharpness, elemental conductivity, or power-transfer properties of the weapons, all of them were very close to optimal. There was one area, however, where I *could* make some improvements."

"Please enlighten me," Xue Xiao said.

"The blood masters themselves," Cha Ming said solemnly. The battle had started only a half minute ago. At first, it hadn't been obvious, as the fighters were evenly matched. Their weapons, it seemed, were of the same grade. But now, it was growing increasingly clear that the ones with the new weapons were fighting *differently.* They were forsaking their traditional training in favor of more aggression. Moreover, their raw physical strength was increasing. They were surpassing their limits.

It started with a nick here and there. A few drops of blood spilled. A full minute later, these drops of blood accumulated, and the blood masters using the new blades were scoring more and more hits. Everyone regenerated, of course—blood masters were nothing if not durable—but it seemed the ones with the older weapons were weakening, and those using new ones were growing stronger.

"Interesting," Xue Xiao said, taking a goblet of red liquid to his lips and taking a sip. It could have been blood, for all Cha Ming knew, and he tried his best not to probe the goblet. "You've put something into the weapon that digs into their physical potential." He grinned a wolf's grin.

"For most cultivators, this would be a taboo," Cha Ming said. "And most people don't have the know-how to do this. I once had the pleasure of crafting a spear from demon blood steel, however, and happened to discover some runes that aligned with its blood-drinking nature. By combining hypnosis-inducing runes with these blood-drinking properties, the weapon feeds on blood from the blood master—or those he wounds—and intensifies the hypnosis. It removes the body's limits, which exist to avoid damaging it. But since this damage isn't a problem for blood masters, they should be able to use the weapons to great effect. It's only..."

"Only what?" Abbot Xue Xiao asked. "This is a grand idea! Why would we bother with defense when more offense would suffice? Why care about being reckless?"

As he spoke, bodies began hitting the floor. Referees interrupted the battles, though Cha Ming noticed they had to forcefully restrain some of the combatants.

"I'm just concerned about the long-term effects of the hypnosis," Cha Ming said. "As you can see, those blood masters using the blades were a little lacking in self-control. And since blood masters aren't exactly known for their strict discipline—" He heard a crack and realized that the concrete bench Xue Xiao was sitting on had crumbled due to the man's crushing grip.

"I might have misheard," Xue Xiao said. "Surely you didn't just insult our entire organization?"

Cha Ming paled. "I wouldn't dare do such a thing. I'm only being cautious. The results here, though shockingly advantageous, should still be tested by a smaller rollout of such a line of weapons. Anything like this should be done slowly. Cautiously."

Xue Xiao shook his head and pulled his lips into a line. "We don't have time for that. We need something to strengthen our forces, and we need it fast. Armed a month earlier is prepared a month earlier. Fighting could break out at any moment."

"We could arm the entire Bastion Monastery," suggested Tian

Zhi, who'd been sitting beside Cha Ming the entire time. "If all goes well, we could move on with a massive contract for the entire clergy."

Xue Xiao nodded. "You might not know this, but we've approached many weapons manufacturers. We've even had scholars who've studied in Haijing devise new weapons for us. They couldn't do anything worthwhile, not while maintaining the same cost per unit. It just wasn't worth replacing all our existing weapons. This, however, is a substantial improvement. I sensed a thirty-percent increase in battle prowess. Even if the increase can only be sustained a short while, it's still a significant gain."

"Then should I submit a contract to your scribes and begin processing the order?" Tian Zhi asked. He might be a researcher, but he was a businessman first and foremost.

"I'd like them as quickly as you can manage, within budget," Xue Xiao said.

"Great!" Tian Zhi said. "Well, Pai Xiao, let's be off. I'll be sure to apply for the maximum reward for your efforts."

"Thank you, Boss Tian," Cha Ming said. They bowed and left the monastery.

"Blood masters," Tian Zhi said, shuddering once they were out of the premises. "It's so hard to get used to them, even after all this time."

Cha Ming frowned. The man didn't often talk about his past. "You mean there weren't blood masters where you're from?"

"Nope," Tian Zhi said, shaking his head. "But this is the South. You do business with whoever pays you."

"I understand," Cha Ming said. "The Spirit Temple is one thing—it's orderly and organized. But the blood masters… Well, let's just say I don't like the way they look at me. It's like they think I'm food."

Tian Zhi grunted. "They see everyone as food."

A few hundred feet away from the monastery, they started flying back, much to the awe of the pedestrians below.

"Still, I'm concerned about the mental effects," Cha Ming said. "They seemed to recover in the short term, but what about longer-term effects?"

Tian Zhi shrugged. "What can they complain about? They're getting what they want, fast, and you warned them. Plus, I'm going to let our lawyers know to put in all sorts of indemnity language, as well as our recommendation of a pilot test. They'll refuse it, so our rears will be contractually covered."

"If you say so," Cha Ming said begrudgingly. Inwardly, he smiled. After all, the runic diagram he'd supplied, while matching these blades exactly, was a flawed one. It wasn't a matter of *if* they'd suffer mental backlash from using the blades, but *when*. Legal indemnity was one thing, but the loss of goodwill and reputation from such a blunder wasn't insignificant. Likely, they'd come after him, the developer of the weapon, despite his warning.

Everything was going exactly according to plan. Just to be sure, he'd need to make an extra major "breakthrough" in the Breaker, if just to remind the Tian Zhi and Director Yong of his value when things went sideways.

Chapter 19
Progress

For the next three months, Cha Ming spent most of his time holed up in his private laboratory. There, he mostly secluded himself in the Clear Sky World, only making appearances when people visited. No one questioned his work ethic—after all, during this time, he made significant contributions to the Breaker, sometimes in areas outside his expertise with the occasional useful insight. And while he legitimately spent much of his time training his spiritual blacksmithing in the time-accelerated environment, most of his time was spent cultivating.

At least twelve hours a day—which corresponded to two and a half days inside the Clear Sky World—Cha Ming cultivated in seclusion. The gaseous qi in his core grew thick and pure, to the point where many would consider it high time for him to break through. Still, he didn't take that extra step. Not only because of the commotion it would cause when someone broke through to the peak of core formation, but because of his high standards. He'd suffered from the negative effects of an unstable foundation before, and he wasn't going to let it happen again.

Cultivation. Crafting. Researching. Slowly but surely, he was building Zhou Li's dream weapon. It was evident, given the purpose of the weapon, that it would be used to destroy large sections of a wall, allowing the Southern army to blast through the North's fortified defenses and pour into their undefended lands.

Still, he built it. Not only to keep up his disguise, but because with each advancement, he introduced flaws to the project. These flaws wouldn't do much on their own, but when the final product was assembled, they would combine into a much greater one. A catastrophic one. Ironically, sabotaging Zhou Li had become the least of his worries.

"Are you sure these runic components should align that way?" Shao Qiang asked as he traced runic ink on the core.

"I can't say for sure," Cha Ming said, frowning. "But look at the energy conduits here. Surely pushing the energy flow through these soothing runes as they cycle back to the core would lead to a reduced loss of power. Power conserved is power gained, right?"

"I suppose," Shao Qiang said, painting the runes. Not only was Shao Qiang a seer, he was also a runic artist who had studied in Haijing several decades ago. He'd returned to the South with an elder-level mastery of formations. Unfortunately, that was far from enough for him to detect the trap Cha Ming encouraged him to lay one insight or suggestion at a time. At most, some of the changes he suggested would seem superfluous.

It was difficult to argue with results, and as far as Cha Ming knew, a deadline was approaching. He'd heard it in passing several times, but no one was sure about the exact date. All everyone knew was that the deadline kept creeping closer and closer. Everyone scrambled, in case next month was the last month allotted for their very important project.

"It's still not powerful enough," Cha Ming muttered. "We need a purer energy source."

"He Yin is working on it," Shao Qiang said. "All we can do is affect distribution and deployment. Power sources are alchemy based, no matter how you look at it. We can use runes to improve them, sure, but it still all comes down to basic reagents."

Cha Ming didn't correct him. In a month or so, he would slip some sort of inspiration to He Yin. He had a knack for it, something everyone had quickly realized during his time in the group. Everyone would invite him for coffee or tea, and sometimes invite him to restaurants. He often refused, using the latest project he was working on as an excuse. Despite his frequent refusals, they kept coming back. This both pleased and bothered him. On the one hand, it made them easy to manipulate. On the other, he felt increasingly uneasy due to their growing friendship. What he was planning would hurt them greatly, and there was little he could do about it.

"Let's call it a day," Shao Qiang, said, noticing the change in his mood. "You usually go out for dinner around this time, right?"

Cha Ming raised an eyebrow. "Have you been spying on me?"

Shao Qiang shrugged. "It's not like you keep it a secret. Once a week, you always go to that same place in the 64th District. Care for some company? A drink, maybe?"

Cha Ming hesitated. "I guess it wouldn't hurt to introduce him to some customers. He's always hurting for business."

"Great!" Shao Qiang said. They packed up their things, logged their progress on the Breaker, and headed out. On their way out, they saw He Yin racking his brains for a breakthrough. He refused their invitation. Pan Su, on the other hand, accepted. As a pure earth cultivator and the group's only geomancer, she always had time to spare.

A half hour later, they were seated at a table in the small restaurant with a view of the outside. Most of the shops were closed, though one just opposite the restaurant still had its lights on. They could see a few customers haggling with the shop manager—a pretty young girl with a slight bulge on her stomach.

"You weren't kidding when you said he needs customers," Shao Qiang said, shaking his head. He tossed down the menu. "You order."

"So many interesting dishes I've never seen before." Pan Su giggled. "I'll try whatever you're having."

Cha Ming ordered, and soon, a half dozen sizzling hot vegetable plates were served. The restaurant was a vegetarian one, a rarity in Southern lands, though not unheard of.

"Who would have thought that the merchant of death, the one who supplied all those blood masters a new line of weapons, the one who most relishes destruction in our research group, was a vegetarian." Shao Qiang took a bite of a strange blue vegetable. It was a type of spiritually infused bamboo that was very beneficial to cultivators.

"I've just never liked eating meat," Cha Ming said, shrugging. "I don't have to eat it, so why should I?" It wasn't the full truth, but it was a believable and acceptable answer in these lands. That was why, despite the total absence of Buddhism in the South, vegetarian cuisine still persisted.

"Odd people like odd things," Pan Su said, slurping noodles coated in a tangy red sauce. "I'd rather have this than the same old thing little Qiang eats every day."

"Beef stew reminds me of home," Shao Qiang said. "It's not very nutritious—mortals eat it all the time—but who cares about that at our level? Well, maybe Pai Xiao cares, with him being a middle-core cultivator and all. My mother made me beef stew every day when I was young, and I miss it. I miss her."

Silence. Everyone at their level was usually over a hundred years old. No one ever mentioned their age, as it was just a reminder of loved ones lost and cultivation friends who hadn't made it.

Their conversation fell mostly on deaf ears as Cha Ming, who ate mechanically, was spying on Mo Ling. After serving the last of her customers, she went back upstairs to do her business's accounts, draft material orders, and take stock of her inventory. She also went over her smiths' numbers. The smiths, as most high-level cultivators were prone to doing, didn't sleep. Instead, they either cultivated at night or studied. The city's regulations prohibited loud noises in the evening, and their workshop didn't have the necessary soundproofing to do otherwise.

Whatever she could do herself, she did herself. Mo Ling was driven, someone who ignored the unfairness of life and struggled with everything she had. It was clear to Cha Ming from a cursory investigation of her documents that she wasn't planning on staying in that little shop forever. She was planning something bigger, something greater. All the while carrying the growing burden in her bulging abdomen.

He rejoined the conversation, but only half-heartedly. They ordered wine, and he drank with them. Then, well into the night, they returned to the Blackthorn Conglomerate, going straight to their residences instead of their workshop.

Cha Ming slept that night, but it was restless sleep filled with struggle and possibilities. His dreams were haunted by the betrayal he'd soon need to commit and all the people he would hurt in the process. The world was far from perfect, but what could he do about it? He was only one man; he couldn't save everyone.

He woke to a harsh knocking on the door the next morning. Bleary eyed, Cha Ming swiftly cleansed himself with qi and opened his door. He was surprised to see a less-than-impressed Tian Zhi. "Boss Tian? Is something wrong?" he asked uncertainly.

"There is an issue we need to defuse with an angry customer," Tian Zhi said, scratching the back of his head. "Since you are involved, it would be best if you were there."

"Customer?" Cha Ming said. Then it dawned on him. "Don't tell me. I think I already know."

"It's the blood masters," Tian Zhi confirmed. "Come, they're a short-tempered lot, but it's not like we haven't dealt with them before. Don't worry, we've got your back."

Cha Ming nodded and followed the older man. It was about time they realized the damage he'd caused. The blood masters' reaction, and the Blackthorn Conglomerate's response, would dictate the next part of his plan. He only prayed they weren't so upset they'd try to kill him, ruining his carefully crafted disguise.

Xue Xiao's bloody glare was the first thing Cha Ming saw when he entered the room. Tian Zhi cleared his throat uncomfortably, leading

Cha Ming to the back of the room. Director Yong, surprisingly, was seated not at the head of the table, but just off to the side. Another man sat where he usually did. He wore yellow robes—a royal color in the Ji Kingdom—with black trim. His clothes were peak-core treasures, and the weapon at his waist was a half-step-transcendent sword.

"Please take a seat," the man said, motioning to two empty chairs in the boardroom. Cha Ming and Tian Zhi obeyed and took a seat at the large redwood table to await further instructions. "Since I see new faces here, let me introduce myself. I am Prince Shen, crown prince of the Ji Kingdom. I am here to mediate the dispute and ensure that a reasonable resolution is agreed upon." He turned to the blood masters, who were led by Xue Xiao. "Please explain the situation."

"The Blackthorn Conglomerate has crafted a batch of maliciously faulty weapons," Xue Xiao said coldly. "They brought the weapons for testing, and since they were superior to the previous generation of weapons, we placed an order to arm our entire monastery in preparation for the upcoming war.

"At first, all was well. The users of the weapons, though exhausted after they used the weapons for over an hour, recovered within three. This was an acceptable tradeoff for the thirty-percent increase in combat prowess we observed. So, we continued training with them.

"It wasn't until one month later that we realized something was dreadfully wrong. At first, it was only a few reports of insanity. Such reports aren't uncommon in our ranks—blood arts have harsh requirements on the individual, and the weak are culled as food for the strong. But before long, the number of reports exploded. Two weeks ago, we ordered our monks to stop using the weapons and conducted an investigation. The results are recorded on this jade slip, which is accompanied by an affidavit sworn before an official of the Spirit Temple."

Xue Xiao pushed the jade slip to Prince Shen, who touched it and frowned. "Twenty percent of your foundation-establishment members went insane? Another thirty percent had their cultivation stalled? And you didn't notice this earlier? You didn't move to stop it earlier?"

Cha Ming suppressed a gleeful chuckle.

"We may have been overzealous in our training," Xue Xiao said reluctantly. "In the monasteries, it's common for inferior fighters to fall. We thought only a small percentage of our members would succumb to this. Even ten percent would have been acceptable. But twenty percent? That's when we stopped. It was only after we investigated that we found everyone using the weapons was so mentally unstable that they could no longer break through in their cultivations."

Prince Shen did not seem impressed. "Do you have anything to say about this?" he asked Director Yong.

"From a contractual point of view," Director Yong said, pushing a bundle of papers to the prince, "we've received full indemnity against any damage suffered while using the weapons. Which, might I add, specifically includes physical, mental, spiritual, monetary, property, or other damage."

"We also suggested a softer rollout in our proposal," Tian Zhi said. "Though it would have taken longer, the risks would have been mitigated. They refused. Grandmaster Pai Xiao, the designer of the weapon, also cautioned them against such a large purchase. His warnings were repeatedly rebuffed by Senior Xue."

Cha Ming nodded in confirmation.

"Is this true?" Prince Shen said, sighing. He looked to Xue Xiao, who could barely control his anger.

"We've lost a great deal of our fighting force," Xue Xiao said, red faced and red eyed, his sharp teeth practically begging for blood. "This cannot go unpunished." He pointed a thin finger covered in intricate armor to Cha Ming. "*He* is responsible. *He* must pay a price. We will not haggle contractually, but *he* owes us a blood debt."

"Abbot Xue, please calm yourself," Prince Shen said. "I find it highly unlikely that a reputable grandmaster like Pai Xiao would purposefully damage our blood masters at such a sensitive time.

Especially since you were warned by both him and the Blackthorn Conglomerate."

"He must be punished," Xue Xiao said stubbornly.

Prince Shen sighed again. "I'll tell you what," he said to Xue Xiao. "Why don't we send Grandmaster Pai Xiao to the Shattered Lands to mine for a month. He'll know a month of suffering for his mistake, which will deter others from doing similar things."

"At least a year!" Xue Xiao shouted. "If he's going to suffer, it has to be a meaningful amount of time."

"With all due respect," Director Yong said, "this isn't even his fault."

"I'd also like to add that he's a valuable member of my core research group," Tian Zhi said dryly. "Not having him would have a profound impact on a very important project. Which, might I add, the royal family has commissioned."

This seemed to trouble Prince Shen, who tapped his fingers as he thought.

"Three months," Prince Shen said. "And that's final."

Xue Xiao looked like he'd swallowed a lemon, but he could only voice his agreement. "Fine. The prince is wise and fair."

"Please go on ahead," Prince Shen said. "We'll talk later." The three blood masters, Xue Xiao included, stood stiffly and walked out of the meeting room, leaving only Director Yong, Tian Zhi, and the prince with Cha Ming. "I'm sorry. I had to give them something for now. You know how obstinate they can be."

"It really wasn't his fault," Tian Zhi said. "I was there. I saw him tell them we should do a pilot run."

"I know," Prince Shen said. "But war is coming, and we must be united. Morale is important. I understand that this will lead to a slight delay on the project, but it's a price that must be paid. As a middle-marrow-refining cultivator, Pai Xiao won't die like many others do. It will be a boring three months, but what smith doesn't know monotony?"

"I understand," Cha Ming said. "I shouldn't have introduced the product. It was imperfect. Flawed."

"Pride in your work is an admirable trait, but responsibility for results even more so," Prince Shen said. "We must all be united if we are to retake the North from those who stole it from us."

"But Prince Shen," Tian Zhi said, "you might not be aware of this, but around a third of the progress we've made over the past three months on the Breaker project was due to Pai Xiao's contributions, either directly or through insights. Those three months will cost us dearly."

The prince's expression turned grim. "Any delays will not be accepted by the grand vizier." He looked to Cha Ming. "One month. After one month, I'll escalate this to Father and explain the situation. We'll release you prematurely. By then, the blood masters will have calmed down."

"I'll do as instructed," Cha Ming said.

"Good," Prince Shen said. "Grandmaster Pai Xiao, you are dismissed for now. I have further things to discuss with Tian Zhi and Director Yong. Please report to Bastion Wall as soon as possible. You may bring whatever possessions you like, but only one spatial treasure."

Cha Ming bowed and left. He walked down the hallway, down the stairs, and passed a group of gloomy blood masters with his head bowed. He didn't go back to his quarters, for he always carried his important possessions with him. Instead, he went directly to the large wall behind the palace.

Beyond the wall lay the dreaded Shattered Lands, the place where most of the ore in Bastion was harvested. He'd originally wondered how he'd find the time to come here, and in the end, he'd just had to kill a fifth of the Bastion blood monastery. The Shattered Lands were the densest source of gold element energy on the Ling Nan Plane. If Gold Source Marrow existed on this plane, that was where he would find it.

Chapter 20
Impossible

In the Icy Heart Pavilion, thirty or so young women trained in the snow. Hong Xin and Bai Ling watched them from an alcove above the courtyard where they trained, with nothing but cold to keep them company. An icy stream flowed through their training area. Many of the women sat in its frigid waters, cultivating despite the ice that formed around their wet robes. Some of their skins were white, while others were blue. As they risked death with their brutal training regimen, experienced figures watched them secretly from the shadows, ready to dive in if any reached their limits.

"So very different," Hong Xin murmured. "So very painful. I could hardly imagine cultivating in freezing water as a qi-condensation cultivator."

Bai Ling nodded in agreement. When they'd started their training, they were foundation-establishment experts. Even at that level, they wouldn't have dared do such a thing.

A blue-robed woman walked up beside them. It was Ling Fei, vice head of the Icy Heart Pavilion. She looked down at those in the courtyard indifferently. "This is only the most basic training area. The qi harvested from training in this environment gains a frigid quality, we've discovered, which complements the Icy Heart Sutra. There are also side benefits."

"Such as?" Hong Xin asked.

"The process is painful," Ling Fei answered. "And numbing. By shutting out the pain, denying its existence, or at least ignoring it, it is easier to learn the essence of a frozen heart. Our goal is for new trainees to reach the first level of the Icy Heart Sutra within one year. Most make it, if sufficiently talented."

"That's just as fast as in the Red Dust Pavilion," Hong Xin said.

"It's faster, actually," said Headmistress Lan, who was also with them. "Just like you've modified the old training program, we've had to as well. You chose to promote a lax learning atmosphere, and only those driven can succeed. Those who aren't are encouraged to leave.

"It's the same here too. We've chosen a painful method of teaching, and those who do not wish to continue don't have to. They can quit at any time. To succeed, one has to numb the pain and dull the heart. And unlike the Red Dust Pavilion, we don't only want undesirables and naïve women with false hopes, women we entrap into servitude. Here, we just want the best. There are no servants here, just well-treated pavilion members."

This second visit to the Icy Heart Pavilion, just a half day after they'd visited their own headquarters, was an eye-opening experience. They'd expected prisoners and torture. Instead, they saw painful dedication. "What of the members who insist on continuing?" Bai Ling asked.

"Our generosity is limited," Headmistress Lan said. "Those who come from rich families can pay to stay as a visiting member, but only insofar as we have the capacity to accept them. That capacity is dwindling as we speak. Our priority is nurturing productive members.

"That being said, anyone who achieves the first level of the Icy Heart Sutra before foundation establishment becomes an outer member. Anyone who reaches the third level of the Icy Heart Sutra before middle foundation establishment becomes an inner member. Finally, anyone who achieves the fifth level of the Icy Heart Sutra is promoted to a core member. Our core members are supplied with the best resources to form a frozen core and quickly improve their strength, so they can become top-earning members.

"By the end of five years, the training ends. Whatever anyone accomplishes after that is up to their own hard work. They can fund their cultivation with their wages and bonuses; there is work for anyone who has achieved any level of the Icy Heart Sutra, though those who've reached the first level only qualify as attendants. Only the untalented are content to stay in such a role. The others simply aren't suited to our cultivation method. They leave, discard their cultivation, and start on a different path."

"I see," Hong Xin said, shivering slightly from the cold wind that blew out from the courtyard below. It was much colder down there than even the coldest winter on the continent, yet no one wore anything more than a thin cultivation robe. "Why don't we move on?"

Headmistress Lan nodded. Ling Fei led the way down a corridor that led to the east side of the complex. There, they saw several students attending a lecture. They were outer members, and just like those in the courtyard outside, none of them smiled. It was a lesson in emotional dousing, the goal being to calm oneself or others. Off to the side, a senior student played a soothing song to assist the students as they learned.

The system their opposing pavilion had devised was much like their own. At this stage, after kindling their own inner motivation and reaching the first level of the Burning Heart Sutra, they learned to affect others with contagious inspiration. They would first be introduced to different techniques, after which they'd be broken into pairs that would try to influence each other. As though sensing her thoughts, the class did just that. They broke up into pairs and touched hands to transfer dousing energy to each other. At that stage, physical contact was best.

They continued the tour, passing a few classrooms until they found one where inner members were learning. These students used instruments and performing arts in their duels. The elite students in the bunch would often be pitted against several lesser students. It was just like the Red Dust Pavilion. The parallels shouldn't have surprised Hong Xin, since their origins were the same, but it did anyway. Ice and fire were opposites. Her own core, a combined core of dousing and kindling power, was still an amalgamation of forces that were kept separate, lest they fight against each other. It was a miracle she'd succeeded, and anyone who'd succeeded after her had done so because of her direct intervention.

"It seems we're not so different after all," Hong Xin said as they walked into a small room near the main audience chamber. Two attendants poured them tea. Cold tea, but it was still better than no tea. For a moment, she was tempted to warm it with a wisp of fire qi but thought better of it. The Icy Heart Pavilion hadn't chilled their tea when they'd visited, so she would show them the same respect.

"The same seeds sprout different trees, but they'll always share the same origins," Headmistress Lan said, taking a sip of her chilled beverage. Tiny ice crystals floated atop it, refusing to either melt or expand.

"Trees that share the same origins often grow in the same locations," Hong Xin said. "Not only is there safety from the wind in numbers, but both male and female trees are needed to expand a forest."

Headmistress Lan raised an eyebrow. "You're proposing that we mate?"

Bai Ling spat out some of her tea. She tapped her chest as she coughed, expelling some of the liquid that had gone down the wrong way.

"I propose that we work together," Hong Xin said, ignoring Bai Ling. "Merge. Since our training methods are so similar, and our roots are the same, it makes perfect sense to share a household."

"Ah," Headmistress Lan said. She looked to her two attendants, who left in a hurry. Only the four of them remained. "I suppose I should have expected you to say such a thing. The heiress of the household always seeks to take prosperous branch families back into the fold. Forgive me, but I'll have to decline."

"Why so quick to decide?" Hong Xin asked. "There are advantages to sharing a united front. We even have members who dual cultivate kindling and dousing. Your members could gain the same opportunities."

Headmistress Lan shook her head. "Our philosophies are completely different. We are cold and uncaring, and proudly so. Emotions are nothing but a distraction in this cold and ruthless world. To survive, to thrive, we must numb ourselves.

"On the other hand, the Red Dust Pavilion believes that passion is required to grow. Without it, no one can achieve anything. Those who repress their emotions are doomed to mediocrity and failure. Am I right?"

Hong Xin frowned. "With all due respect, I'm living proof that these two don't contradict each other," she said, summoning a ball of ice and a ball of flame in each hand."

"A wonderful point," Ling Fei said. "And it only makes sense that a talented cultivator in both our arts could lead us. Only someone like Headmistress Hong could lead us to greatness."

"Yes, indeed," Headmistress Lan said. "We would be blessed for such an opportunity. Let's fetch the paperwork right now and get ready to move in." Their sarcasm wasn't lost on Hong Xin.

"I said nothing about leadership," Hong Xin said.

"It is implied," Headmistress Lan said sharply. "Which is all the more reason why this is impossible. If we join the Red Dust Pavilion under your leadership, our members will be relegated to the lower ranks." Her eyes widened, and she put her hand to her mouth. "Unless, are you willing to accept *our* leadership? I promise we wouldn't do anything like that. Really."

"You're taking our proposal a little lightly," Bai Ling interjected. "I didn't think jesting was what the Icy Heart Pavilion did."

"Sarcasm is completely consistent with our arts," Headmistress Lan said. "And your lack of understanding on the subject is one more reason why this is bad idea."

"Perhaps we should have this discussion another time," Hong Xin said. "We should continue to get to know one another."

Headmistress Lan shook her head. A rare smile touched her lips. "Any such meetings would be tainted by your intent. They wouldn't be about mutual understanding, but conversion." Before Hong Xin could object, Headmistress Lan continued. "Leadership is only the first of many problems. I'm fully aware of what's in your possession. With the Icy Heart Oath Stone, who would dare move into the same house? You possess our ultimate weakness. We would be mice in a cat's playhouse, free until the cat decides it's hungry. Even if you say that's not your intent, how can a woman like me believe you? Don't you have a few dozen enslaved members in the Red Dust Pavilion?"

"We were forced to do it," Hong Xin said with clenched teeth. "They broke us in that school. They trapped us and killed many of our friends. They deserve every bit of their punishment." Noticing her emotions boiling over, Hong Xin doused her feelings and returned to a calmer state of mind. Headmistress Lan waited for her to finish cooling down before serving her another cup of tea.

"Perhaps," Headmistress Lan said. "I, too, despise them. But what of the other few dozen members in the city? Did they all deserve such a fate? Are you not keeping them for the sake of safety, ignoring their freedom in the process?"

"They are a liability," Bai Ling said. "The result of a necessary action, but one that will likely seek revenge if given freedom."

"And that Oath Stone is a liability," Ling Fei shot back. "We are a business, yes, but we look out for our members. Here, women get to determine their own destiny. We are not like the old Red Dust Pavilion. We are legitimate, and we are free."

"If we release them," Hong Xin said. "Who is to say they won't return to their old ways?"

"Who's to say anyone won't?" Headmistress Lan said. "Is that a reason to keep them under oath? Many of us have dark pasts, but we've turned over a new leaf. We are legitimate businesswomen: advisors, entertainers, and diplomats for hire. Even warriors and bodyguards. We give women futures. Will you take that away?"

Hong Xin pursed her lips. She waited a while before speaking again. "We'll think on what you said. Perhaps we are being unreasonable with those members. We'll have to look into it on a case-by-case basis."

"And if you're willing to do that, we're willing to continue these talks," Headmistress Lan said. "But know this: as long as the Oath Stone is still in play, cooperation simply isn't possible."

"Noted," Hong Xin said. They finished their tea in silence.

The shadow frowned when it saw Hong Xin's disappointed expression. It had heard their conversation, and it wasn't happy about it. While it knew there were valid points on both sides, it couldn't help but be biased in the red lady's favor. She was so passionate, so caring. She just wanted what was best for everyone, while also keeping innocent people out of trouble. Was there anything wrong with that?

The lady in blue, on the other hand, was cold and calculating. Not unlike someone else he knew, who'd sided with much darker powers. Like him, the lady wouldn't see good sense if it stared her in the eye. She would always put herself before the greater good.

The question is, the shadow asked itself, *will the lady in red know what to do? Will she do what needs to be done?* The more it observed her, the more it thought otherwise. She was softening to blue lady's arguments with each conversation. It was only a matter of time before she was eaten up by them.

Should I do something? it wondered. It hesitated. Shadows didn't *do* anything. They just watched and existed. Or did they? The thought intrigued it. It considered a while longer, then moved. The night was young, and much work needed doing.

Chapter 21
Land of Shadows Remembered

Huxian panted as he looked westward, trying his best to expel excess heat from his body. The sun still shone brightly—at least the half that still peeked up over the horizon. It wasn't very strong, but it was relentless. And no matter where he hid, no matter what he tried, he couldn't avoid it. The light was living. The light was ever present. And the heat that built up inside his body seemed to want to stay there. A constant experience without relief, like the ghosts in that wretched city.

His shadow, much taller than he remembered it being, shifted impatiently, as if to urge him to hurry. He gazed at the now rocky ground. It wasn't cracked like the abandoned plains from before, the lands that would have been lush with daily rains. No, this was true rock, not fragile clay. It led to a tiny mountain he'd spotted days ago. Or was it hours? Weeks? He couldn't remember. Time here was an endless blur.

Sighing, Huxian continued toward the mountain, stepping with one paw after another, forcing himself forward with everything he had. It was the longest, most arduous journey he'd ever been on. But what choice did he have? He didn't know the way out. He only had a single hint in the form of an eternal curse on a ghostly city. He'd obtained a piece of a jade tablet and directions to go westward. He'd been journeying ever since.

This leg of the journey was different than the last. To Huxian's surprise, as he neared the mountain, which was growing ever larger in the distance, his shadow grew. And as it did, he picked up speed. There were no foothills like was used to seeing, nor were there any stray rocks that often accompanied mountains. Only flatness. It led to a plateau, which surprisingly cast a shadow toward him. The wrong way.

Huxian stopped just outside that shadow, his own barely brushing against it. It felt wrong, unholy even. Two shadows should *not* face opposite directions; at least, not without demonic or other intervention. Something was here, tampering with the laws of light.

Maybe that's what I'm looking for, Huxian thought. *Maybe the answer is to cover the sun. If the sun is obscured, wouldn't the sun set? Wouldn't those spirits be freed?* He decided to proceed inside the shadows toward the plateau. As he crossed that invisible threshold, his own shadow inverted and merged with the plateau's. And the moment it did, an amazing sight appeared before his eyes.

The plateau wasn't empty like he'd initially imagined. Instead, it was hidden. Within these shadows, there was light. Monks meditated everywhere he looked. Some performed mundane tasks like laundry, cooking, or sweeping. Some even taught children. Moreover, they weren't ghostly figures like the city before, but real individuals made of flesh and blood.

A man in orange robes with a bald head greeted him at the entrance. The man reminded Huxian of Gong Lan, except he was male.

"How can this one help you, benefactor?" he said with a gentle smile, a bow, and a strange hand gesture Huxian figured was part of his religion.

I'm here to find a monk, Huxian said. He looked around uncertainly. There were monks everywhere, but which one was he looking for?"

"I can help you find any monk you desire to meet," the man said. "My name is Ao. Do you wish to learn more about the Buddhist way? A demon joining our ranks would be unusual but not unheard of."

Huxian scoffed inwardly. He wasn't crazy like those Buddhist demons. No, if he ever learned Buddhist arts, he'd probably be like that damned monkey that studied them but didn't really follow their precepts. Following strict rules wasn't his style, and avoiding karma? How could one be as awesome as he was without sowing karma? It was simply impossible.

I'm not sure that I'm suited to the Buddhist way, Huxian said. *But I'm seeking assistance on a matter. I have a friend, no, many friends, who need an exorcism.*

"Ah," Ao said. "That's something that we help with from time to time."

Great! Huxian said. *I don't know if one of you is enough, though. I think I might need everyone's help.*

"Everyone's?" Ao said, looking back to the monastery. "Surely you jest. Even I alone am enough to purge tens of evil spirits."

I wouldn't call them evil spirits, Huxian said. *More like lonely wandering ghosts. None of that evil karma. They're just floating around, unable to leave.*

"A regrettable case," Ao said. "But even so, I alone should be enough."

Huxian suppressed his irritation and thought about how to guide the conversation. He'd never been good at talking to humans. *We're talking about millions of ghosts here. Can you really do that on your own?*

"Benefactor, you mustn't joke like this," Ao said with a frown. He wagged a lecturing finger. "Lies sow negative karma with others. It is better to be truthful, though some exceptions exist, like lying to avoid hurting other."

I'm not lying, Huxian said. *It's really there. An entire city filled with ghosts!* At the mention of the city, Ao's expression darkened.

"I'm afraid I cannot help in this matter," Ao said. "They are suffering the curse they desired. This is karma of the deepest kind."

But—

"Trouble yourself not with those sinners," Ao said, shaking his head. "If there is nothing else, benefactor, I will return to my station." The man walked away and sat cross-legged nearby. There was something odd about the man, but what monk wasn't odd?

Since Huxian had walked all the way here, he couldn't leave empty-handed. He traveled to a monk who was sweeping the flat stone ground. Her every sweep lifted not a trace of dust off the pristine floor. "Greetings, benefactor," she said. "How may this one, Li, help you."

I'm looking for a monk, Huxian said. *A powerful one.*

"There are many powerful monks here," Li said. "I myself am a resplendent monk."

Huxian raised an eyebrow. *And you, a resplendent monk, are sweeping this clean plateau?*

"It is everyone's duty to serve," Li said. "Powerful or weak, big or small, everyone must do their part."

Then you'll help me save that city? The one full of ghosts? Huxian asked.

"Ah, that city," Li said, sighing lightly. "Unfortunately, I can do nothing about their situation. Only they can resolve their own karma. We cannot help, for by doing so, we would anger the guardian of this land."

Huxian frowned. Buddhists, though set in their ways, usually went out of their way to help others. Why weren't they doing so in this case? The woman moved on and continued her sweeping, so Huxian moved on to the next monk.

Like this, Huxian traveled across the entire sunless plateau, questioning every man, woman, or child he saw. All of them were monks and greeted him pleasantly. Each of their expressions darkened when he mentioned the city. It took him an entire day to question everyone on the mountain. Not a single monk volunteered to go help the city, despite all the goodwill they expressed when they greeted him.

Depressed, Huxian lay down. Though there were many buildings on the plateau, most of them made from a wonderful heat-reflecting white stone, he didn't need to take refuge from the sun. The sun didn't shine in these strange shadows that gave off light. The heat within him didn't dissipate, but neither did it increase. It was similar but very different to the outside world, where endless dust reigned.

There must be something here, Huxian thought. *There must be someone who can help.* He'd questioned all the monks he'd seen, but did that mean he'd questioned everyone? Perhaps the one he was looking for was just away for a while. Away from this fully functioning society atop the mountain.

I wonder where the kids come from? Huxian thought. *Or the adults, for that matter.* It was a curious thing to see such life despite the desolation outside. So, as he waited, he decided to observe the people. Small monks, barely more than four years old, and likely abandoned by their parents, learned important lessons on remaining calm and being of service. They were taught by kindly bald men that patiently accepted their antics as they guided them toward monkhood. When they grew older, they would either choose to stay as monks or go back into the world as enlightened participants.

Huxian looked for a while. Then, exhausted from his long journey, he closed his eyes and fell asleep.

"Greetings, benefactor," a voice said, waking Huxian.

Huxian looked up and saw the same bald man who'd greeted him yesterday. He wore the same orange robes as before. Unsurprising, since monk fashion had never been vibrant or prone to change.

Do you need anything? Huxian asked.

"I just wish to know how this one can be of service to you," Ao said. "We monks exist to serve." He smiled lightly.

Huxian, annoyed at the question, snorted. "I already told you want I wanted."

"Oh?" Ao said. "I do not remember meeting you. Perhaps we had this conversation in another life, another time. Perhaps you can repeat your request."

"I only asked you a day ago," Huxian said dryly. "I doubt much has changed. Can you and all these monks go to the nearby city and exorcise a million ghosts for me?"

Ao's face darkened. "I'm afraid I cannot help in this matter. They are suffering the curse they desired. This is karma of the deepest kind. Trouble yourself not with those sinners." He shook his head. "If there is nothing else, Benefactor, I will return to my station." The man walked away and sat cross-legged nearby.

Odd, Huxian thought. *Very odd.* He looked around and noticed everyone was busy. Curious, Huxian walked to the second person he'd spoken to, Li. *Hello, Monk Li,* Huxian said. *How are you doing today?*

"Pardon, Benefactor, but I believe this is the first time we've met," Li said. "Is there something I can help you with?"

A chill ran down Huxian's spine.

Don't you remember me? I asked you about powerful monks, Huxian said.

"I am certain we've never met," Li said. "As for powerful monks, there are many around here. I myself am a resplendent monk."

Huxian, concerned, continued their discussion. *You're a resplendent monk? Why are you sweeping the plateau?*

"It is my duty to serve, just as it is anyone's," Li said. "Powerful or weak, big or small, everyone must do their part." It was almost the same response, but not exactly.

Have you heard of a city full of ghosts? Huxian asked, slightly changing the nature of the question.

"Ah, that city," Li said, sighing lightly. "They are bound by karma to never change."

Can you help me free them from their curse? Huxian asked.

"I cannot," Li said, shaking her head. "If you are needing nothing else, I will continue my duties." She continued sweeping, and Huxian observed as she did so for an entire day, never stopping. He observed the other monks as they worked and meditated, taught children, and learned. Mentors taught their students and junior monks consulted with their masters.

Huxian continued observing, and by the third day, he finally noticed his shadow had gone missing. There was no sun in the sky, despite the light. The monks didn't cast shadows either. Yet unlike the city of ghosts, the monks *did* seem to change. As time passed, they shifted between roles. Ao began sweeping, and Li went to meditate. Teachers finished teaching children and returned to their chambers, where they recited mantras.

As he observed, everything seemed to blur together. One action led to another, and the children began to grow before his very eyes. Older monks went about their daily lives, growing older and older, until finally, some either transcended or died of old age in meditation. This all happened very quickly, almost impossibly so.

Those who'd started as children soon became full monks, but no children came to replace the old. Unperturbed by this, almost expecting it, these full monks continued their meditation, and one by one, they died off or transcended. Finally, no one remained.

What the hell just happened? Huxian thought. He felt as though he'd experienced five hundred years in only a few hours. It was madness, pure madness. He walked around, looking over the buildings the monks had left behind. They were well-maintained and clean, just like the monks had left them. Simple statues of the Buddha could be seen everywhere, and inside each dwelling sat a rosary, abandoned by the monks as they died, their bodies transformed into motes of light as they rejoined the cycle of reincarnation.

All was quiet. And with this quiet came great exhaustion. Huxian's eyes began to droop. He tried to keep them open, to see just a little more of the curious vision, but it proved too much for him, so he closed his eyes and slept.

He woke to familiar words: "Greetings, Benefactor."

Greetings, Benefactor. He let those words wash over him, and the monk eventually lost interest as Huxian ignored him. The monk sat down in meditation, the same as he always did.

Huxian tried avoiding the sweeper, but the sweeper still found him and found a way to introduce herself. He could only sigh and let it wash over him. Was it the hundredth time he'd seen the vision? The hundred and eighth? He didn't feel any older, despite having lived through many of these lifetimes. It wasn't for lack of trying, either. After the second repeat vision, Huxian had decided he'd had enough. He'd tried to walk away from the plateau, but to his surprise, he couldn't leave. When he'd tried walking outside the shadow boundary, he'd found himself reentering it. He'd given up after several dozen tries.

Something was happening, a mystery he needed to solve. Just like the ghostly city, the plateau was home to a large temple, the same temple the monks visited every day. Huxian had gone there many times as well. Unlike the gaudy golden statues of a fat man he saw in his inherited memories, these statues were simple. From what he knew, they were also more accurate renditions of the Buddha.

These Buddhists were different from those ghosts that had clung to eternal life and tried to chain the sun. They spent every waking hour trying to shed their karma, yet here they were, living out their entire lives over and over. What kept them here? Regret? Had they been cursed for failing to avert the disaster? He'd tried asking, but naturally, no one paid attention to the ravings of a mad demon.

So he watched. Huxian watched a half dozen more times, and every time, he saw it less like a real occurrence and more like a memory. A shadow of what had once been.

A shadow? he thought one day. It had been a long time since he'd seen his own shadow. He, like every monk, was also reliving his life. *Does my shadow have anything to do with this?* No one here had shadows. The sun was obscured, despite its presence in the east. The setting sun was invisible here, in the shadow of the mountain. That wrong shadow that gave him chills every time he remembered it.

If this side has a shadow, what of the other side? he suddenly thought. He'd never tried going to the other side of the mountain.

He'd found no need, and the visions passed so quickly, tiring him out. Besides, he'd been preoccupied with escaping the mountain and heading toward the city. Was this the wrong approach to take?

Curious, Huxian trotted west again. He passed the temple with the simple statue of the Buddha and headed behind it. There was no shadow where there should have been, of course. He'd been back here many times. He didn't linger but passed the temple and went to the back of the plateau, where, for the first time, he saw a set of steps leading downward. He trotted down the wide steps, his careful paws feeling dust for the first time.

The steps hadn't been swept.

He continued down them and was surprised to see something he hadn't in a long time: darkness. It clung close to the back of the mountain, like a child holding on to its mother for dear life. Despite its large size, only nine feet of shadow remained at the base. And within those shadows, Huxian saw something he'd missed before. Another monk, one wreathed in darkness.

Huxian went down the steps and entered the shadowy region, and to his surprise, he felt a sense of warmth course through him. He looked down and saw that his shadow, which had been absent for so long, had returned to him. His eyes glowed, and the deeper he went, the more shadows he saw, jumbled and clustered together. He saw Ao's shadow, Li's shadow. He saw the children's shadows and the temple's shadow. Even the broom's shadow rested here, hiding from the half-hidden sun Huxian knew existed beyond the mountain.

"The monks laughed at the city's proposal," an old man's voice said. "Most of them thought tethering the sun was outrageous. It was an impossible feat, they said. What's more, they wanted nothing to do with the enormous karma that would be sown. The city, they said, could do what it wanted, but they would have to live with the result. They didn't try to stop the city, and by the time the curse affected it, it was already too late to save them."

The city? Huxian asked. The voice came not from a shadow, but from a cross-legged body within it. The body was dry, decrepit, and empty of life.

"Not the city," the old man said, chuckling without moving his lips, without breathing. "The monks themselves.

"They erred on two parts. The first part was their obsession resolving personal karma. Instead of taking on the sin of the city and trying to free the sun, they let them do as they pleased.

"Their second mistake was believing the curse wouldn't affect them in the first place. When the city was cursed, their thoughts and beliefs persisted. They'd escaped the city's fate, but many were remorseful about it. Yet how could they free an entire city of ghosts? This initial reluctance, combined with the impossibility of the task, led them to ignore the outside world. They never realized that, just like the city persisted eternally, their minds would as well. They could live out their entire life apart from the city, ignoring it, but the shadows remembered them. They would relive their life endlessly, for all eternity."

And what of you? Huxian asked. *Do you relive your life every day as well?*

"I did, at first," the old man said. "Unlike them, however, I had spoken out against their non-interference. I'd traveled to the city and tried to convince their head priest to abandon this madness. I left something there to give them hope.

"It seemed this difference was enough for me to realize something was wrong. I continued to keep my awareness through repeated lifetimes. Unfortunately, the experience wore on my soul. I knew I didn't have much time left, so I searched for a way out.

"Finally, after much trial and error, I found myself here, among the shadows. My life stopped repeating, but by then, I was too weak to move. I could only wait for someone else to share my experience with."

Huxian gulped. "That thing, to give them hope," he said, "was it the Candle Dragon's tear? Was it that jade character, Spirit?"

The man fell silent for a moment before speaking.

"Yes, I see it now," the man said. "You've acquired the character." He laughed the dry laugh of a dying man. "After all these years, someone has come with the character."

"Then how do I resolve this? How do I free the city?" Huxian asked.

"I once obtained two of three pieces of a tablet when I was wandering in my youth," the monk said. "After obtaining them, I journeyed to the west for many years, preaching the Buddhist way. My followers became numerous, though many evil spirits tried consuming me. Two pieces were not enough to reverse the curse, but perhaps with the third piece, it would be possible to break it."

"What must I do?" Huxian asked.

The man didn't answer. Instead, a small golden light appeared on the speaking corpse. It turned into a soft golden mist that congealed into a single golden character that said *Scripture*. The character shot into Huxian's forehead, and the moment it did, the mountain changed. He no longer saw the pool of writhing shadows as something coincidentally there. It was a prison, with chains extending outward toward the monks, tethering them to their reality. They hadn't stopped the sun from being chained, and thus, the shadow of their regret had chained them to this plane. They would relive their life every day without end.

As he saw these chains, he also saw a boundary, a way out of the shadows. As long as one avoided the chains on the mountain, one could leave this prison. Excited, Huxian tried to break one of the chains binding a shadow to a monk up above. It was Ao's shadow. He bit down on it, but to his surprise, the chain didn't break.

"The karma sown here is too thick," the monk said. "You require greater power than these two characters. To find the third one, you must journey to the land of the setting sun. The remaining piece is there. I was too weak to recover it."

What character was it? Huxian asked out of curiosity.

The corpse's shadow shook its head. "I can't remember. My memory is fading. With the jade piece gone, I will become like the others, forever chained by karma to this mountain, reliving my life like the rest of them."

When he finished these words, the man's shadow drifted out of the corpse and joined the writhing black mass. A thick black chain latched on to it, and the corpse, which had been immune to the shadow's power, disappeared. Huxian had little doubt that it would join the rest of the monks in that repeating reality.

Well, Huxian thought, *it's a start.* He trotted through the shadows, carefully avoiding the chains that lunged at him and approached the membrane that separated light and darkness. Then, his eyes glowing golden, he jumped through the membrane. It tore open and let him through. To his surprise, he wasn't on the west side of the mountain, but the east side. The same place he'd entered it.

What a strange place, he thought, tracing his steps back toward the east. Somehow his steps were quicker as he journeyed toward the half sun on the horizon. His shadow, shivering from its long imprisonment, trotted behind him, safe and sound.

Chapter 22
Shattered Lands

The platform Cha Ming stood on jolted as it started its slow descent down Bastion Wall. He could hear the creaks and groans of powerful cables as they moved through a gearbox at the top. It wasn't a piece of runic equipment; it was a more mundane contraption crafted from enchanted materials. Clever gear arrangements slowed his descent toward a plain building below.

Alongside him stood a few other strong men. Mining was a common occupation in Bastion. They were bone-forging cultivators; using their powerful bodies, they would be able to carry heavy stones mere mortals could only leave behind. Their picks and shovels would be put to good use, and they wouldn't tire like other men did.

Broken cliffs and precariously placed boulders loomed over the canyon they saw from the moving platform. Despite the height of the wall—hundreds of feet tall at the very least—it was tiny compared to the jagged cliffs that loomed above them. Their broken edges weaved in unpredictable patterns, making it so only the nearest four miles were visible to the naked eye. As for soul force, that was just as useless. The dense ores contained in the rock formations blocked out any probing Cha Ming tried. Even a transcendent soul wasn't strong enough to break through this barrier.

"We're almost there," a man with a booming voice said. "Get

off in a neat and orderly fashion. I'll beat whoever shoves his way through."

He was a city guardsman, and his job was to operate the lift. Cha Ming was almost certain the man didn't know his identity or cultivation, for if he did, would he dare utter those words? Still, he nodded in acceptance, and the moment the lift clunked onto the rocks below, he walked out just like the others.

On their way from the platform to the building at the base of the wall, they were greeted by a second guard, who escorted them to their destination. The first guard hooked the elevator to a large bin of ore. The platform heaved as a group of men and demons pushed a large wheel. The men were slaves, body cultivators as well. The black markings on their foreheads caused a spark of rage to ignite in Cha Ming's heart, but he smothered it mercilessly. As much as he cared about their plight, acting on it would likely blow his cover.

The building turned out to be a multi-purpose facility that combined guardhouse, storehouse, and tavern. There were guards aplenty resting at long tables drinking wine or ale, though compared to the ones he'd seen inside the city, they were lax and undisciplined. Their guide ignored those men and took Cha Ming's group past the mess tables to a counter at the back.

"New recruits, I see," a surly, gray-haired woman with half-moon spectacles said in a nasal voice. "Are they aware of the rules?"

"They've each brought one storage treasure," the guard said.

"Very good," the woman said. "Have them place the item on the scale."

He was as confused as the others, but he stepped forward to go first. He placed his storage ring—a much finer device than the bags of holding the others had brought, and the number 500 went up on the device.

"Contents?" the woman asked.

Cha Ming looked at her name tag before replying. "I have a hammer focus and some spirit stones in there, Miss Ge," he said. His other treasures, he'd kept inside the Clear Sky World.

"Please pour them onto the scale and retrieve your ring," Miss

Ge said, just as expressionless as before.

Cha Ming did as he was told. He dropped a small crystal weighing three hundred jin onto the table—hammer focuses didn't weigh nearly as much as the spiritually infused hammers—and another two hundred jin of top-grade spirit stones. That rose eyebrows. "And why, sir, are you here if you possess such a fortune?"

"Punishment," Cha Ming said nonchalantly.

"Ah," Miss Ge said. "One of those. Very well, take your things, and take these." She placed four storage rings onto the table, then thought for a moment before placing a golden storage ring there. It was much more ornate than the others. "Keep the tools inside the ring, but don't lose them. If you do, you'll have to pay a fine or work until you pay off your debt. I expect to get the gold ring back, but the small ones only have to last three ore deliveries."

Cha Ming nodded. He took the five storage rings and was surprised to see that the golden one, though only possessing a small storage space, was exceptionally stable. Inside, he found an initial-core-grade pickaxe. The other rings, on the other hand, contained vast spaces. Unlike the golden ring, however, he could see fissures at the edges of these spaces. These were clearly poor-quality storage rings, meant for only a few trips at maximum weight and volume before breaking.

Having received his equipment, Cha Ming walked out of the guardhouse. He briefly looked over an instruction jade, which contained the rules for mining in the Shattered Lands. The first part listed financial obligations, such as the need to return equipment as well as renumeration rates for ore. They were not permitted to take ore out, and their storage treasures would be weighed and reconciled when they left.

The second part, however, was a warning.

Interesting, Cha Ming thought. He swept his body with his transcendent force and discovered that, as the jade explained, there was a constant drain on his vitality. Apparently, that applied to all the Shattered Lands, and the deeper one went, the greater the drain. Initial-bone-forging cultivators could only maintain one week of activity in the so-called starting zone before replenishing themselves. Qi cultivators wouldn't last even a few hours, as they didn't have the vitality stores or regeneration to fight off the invasive drain. The guardhouse conveniently supplied nourishing meals to replenish the miners. At a cost, of course. It was important to harvest enough ore to recover before the next trip.

Well, at least I won't be bored while I'm out here, Cha Ming thought. *While I'm looking for the Gold Source Marrow, I can find expensive ores to earn some coin.* He wouldn't sell it all, of course. He'd sell just enough to ease suspicion as he stowed away the rest in his Clear Sky World. Rare ores didn't have to be sold like the others but could instead be claimed by the miners after paying a tax, either a portion of the material or an equivalent value in spirit stones.

After familiarizing himself with the rudimentary maps— apparently the landscape changed constantly in the Shattered Lands—he flew down into the canyon. He entered the first zone, causing bone-forging miners to gawk as he flew past.

A few miles later, he entered the second zone, and two miles after that, the third. There was no fixed distance in the zones. As he traveled, the drain on his vitality increased, though he barely noticed it given his current body cultivation. Miners became less and less surprised by his passage, preoccupying themselves either with hammering away at rocky surfaces to expose ores that had worked their way to the surface or fighting demon beasts that occasionally appeared from cracks in the walls or from outcroppings on the cliffs. The highest-level cultivators he saw were peak-bone-forging cultivators. Though strong, their power was barely sufficient to last within the thin miasma that leached away at their vitality.

"No wonder the South is so bitter about their so-called blessed land," Cha Ming muttered. The ore here was rich and easy to pick up, assuming one had the strength to dig just a short distance. But the vitality leaching, combined with the fierce demons that roamed the territory, made that ore unattainable to most. It was like staring at a mountain of gold you couldn't touch or admiring a peerless beauty beyond your reach.

Cha Ming pushed forward. He soon passed the fourth zone and entered the fifth, where he only occasionally saw groups of miners. These early to mid-core-formation cultivators looked up at him warily, despite him being a fellow human. They only relaxed once he plunged even deeper, past a boundary marked off in white and red chalk. It was the entrance to the uncharted zone. Just beyond it, five men were resting. Two were playing cards, and two were sleeping. Another sat in meditation.

"Well, look at what we have here," one of the sleeping men said, opening an eye. "Fresh meat."

The two men playing cards stopped their game and looked up curiously.

"We don't often see new folks around here," one of the men who'd been playing cards said. "Who are you? Where are you from? Which company are you with?"

"Call me Pai Xiao," Cha Ming said. "With the Blackthorn Conglomerate."

"Blackthorn, huh?" the man said. "They don't usually send men out here. They're buyers, not workers." He was a short man, slight of build, and unlike most cultivators, he wore ragged clothing and wore his hair short. He looked weak, if only judging by appearances, but given that he was sitting in such a relaxed manner in this draining area, he was anything but.

Cha Ming shrugged. "Now I'm here. I introduced myself. What's your name?"

The man gave him a considering look, then glanced at the others before answering. "Call me Bear Three." Cha Ming raised an eyebrow. "This big bloke's Bear Five," he continued, gesturing to the large, mountainous man playing cards with him. "We don't share our names out here. Since you're new, you let on more than you should have."

"I'm Bear Four," the lazy man who'd woken up earlier said. His clothes were worn, and he wore a scraggly beard that looked to be in dire need of trimming. "Our napping buddy here is Bear Two. He might not look it, but he's quite strong."

"Especially around the midsection," Bear Three joked. The sleeping Bear Two was a rather fat man, with forearms larger than Cha Ming's legs.

The last member, a bare-chested man with a lean build, bald head, and well-maintained beard, opened his eyes. Unlike most on the continent, his eyes were clear blue. Cha Ming could sense that the man was strong on three fronts. Not only was he a late-body-refining cultivator, but he was also a late-core-formation qi cultivator. His soul force had already reached the peak of the resplendent soul realm.

"I am Bear One," the man said in a strange accent. He clearly wasn't from around Bastion, or the Ji Kingdom for that matter. "Tell me friend, are you looking for some mining companions?"

"What?" Bear Three said. "You're inviting him? But he's from a company, and not too strong at that."

"Not strong?" Bear One said, a bemused expression on his face. "If he is not strong, you're nothing more than a weak babe. I can tell it from the look in his eyes. He is not only strong; he's useful."

Cha Ming hesitated. He hadn't considered joining a group. Then again, he was new to the Shattered Lands. Looking for the Gold Source Marrow would be difficult since he was unfamiliar with the area. "I think I'm better off on my own," he said finally. "I mean no disrespect, but I'd just be a hindrance to your group."

"See, boss?" Bear Three said. "He said it himself. He's useless."

"Oh?" Bear One said, smiling as he looked at Bear Three. "Is a smith useless when digging for metal? Is someone with earth affinity useless when digging through stone? He must have at least three affinities, if my guess is correct. And I sense other useful things about him. Something *bestial* almost." He looked back to Cha Ming. "Perhaps you don't see the benefit of going about with a group."

"Perhaps," Cha Ming said, a little concerned about how much the man could read about him. He'd spent much effort concealing his other elements, yet the man had already exposed his earth affinity. He'd done so without intruding on his soul, of that he was certain. Perhaps it was the man's strange eyes, which seemed to look at something distant even when looking straight at him. "If men wander together, they're more likely to fight over limited ore deposits."

Bear One laughed lightly. "You say this because you are new. You don't know the nature of these lands."

"The nature of these lands?" Cha Ming asked. "Aren't these lands where the Ji Kingdom hunts for ore and has done so for centuries? I find it hard to believe that there's much undiscovered ore."

"This ignorance is why you refuse me," Bear One said. "The ores we seek aren't here yet, but they will come. We wait here not because we are tired or lazy." He looked back toward the wall. "Those behind us will get the dregs, leftovers from each shift. They will fight lesser demons, whose affinities drive them to harvest and consume fresh ore or unwary cultivators."

He put a hand to his chest. "As for us, we will be fighting greater demons, doing our best to gather quickly and efficiently. Each of us has skills that make this easier. Our experience allows us to find better ore deposits faster. Now tell me, is it good to join us? Every member gets an equal share of the total harvest, including myself."

Cha Ming considered for a while. He had no idea how ore appeared, but perhaps by accompanying them, he'd get a better idea. "All right. I'll give it a try. I can't make any promises, but I'll work as hard as I can." If he was going to spend a month out here, he might as well take risks and get rich while he was at it. This, he suspected, was the nature of the punishment. He could either waste his time near the wall with no privacy, no workshop, and no quiet, or he could put his life in danger doing hard labor. His time here could easily kill Pai Xiao if he wasn't careful.

Cha Ming walked over and sat down beside the napping Bear Two and Bear Four. He summoned several flags and began to cultivate, purifying his already mostly clear core. He'd barely started circulating his qi when the land beneath him began to shake, and the men scrambled to their feet. Cha Ming stood up, stowing his flags as he looked around warily at falling boulders the size of buildings that crashed down on the land below, letting out deep, muffled booms as they did.

"Your presence brings us good luck, friend," Bear One said, grinning. "Let us go."

"But the earthquake," Cha Ming protested.

"Now is the best time, or we will be late," Bear One said. "Come, mysterious acquaintance. Let us see what you are capable off."

Bear One ran off, pushing off the land that jutted up beneath his steps to propel himself forward. The others followed in their own way, executing whatever technique they were most familiar with to catch up. Sighing, Cha Ming shot forward into the nightmare of broken earth and falling stone.

Chapter 23
Fissures

Cha Ming dashed forward, propelling himself from a rocky outcropping and into the rain of crashing boulders. He didn't know what he'd find by following the five bear brothers, but he knew one thing for certain: Wherever they went, he could follow. He flew between the rocks with inhuman speed, leaving a trail of rushing wind and rocks behind him. Sun Wukong's training came in handy; the tumbling boulders were easy to sense, and he used his earth qi to repel some and push himself off others.

Bear One, who was closest to him, gave him an approving grin when he saw this. Then, to Cha Ming's surprise, he did the same. No boulders dared strike wherever he passed. At first, Cha Ming thought it might be due to the sphere of earthen influence around the man, but he soon discovered that the way he dodged wasn't simple. Judging by the perfect path the man took through the falling stones, it seemed like he'd mapped out a large area of falling debris and predicted its pathway. He moved not to avoid, but in anticipation of what would come.

Beside them, the other bear brothers used their own respective skills to dodge. Bear Three, like Cha Ming, was a smith. He used fiery movements to jump from stone to stone, summoning a massive blacksmith's hammer to destroy incoming projectiles he couldn't avoid. His wiry frame was disproportionately strong, and the grace in his movements told Cha Ming he used the hammer for fighting more than he did smithing.

The large Bear Five didn't use metal nor fire. Instead, he used his massive, mountainous body to good effect. His raw fists slammed against incoming boulders, crushing them on impact. They didn't leave a single dent on his skin; whether that was due to its toughness or the man's regenerative abilities, Cha Ming was uncertain. A green glow covered Bear Five's skin, and beneath him, the ground was soaked red with blood.

They all have their special abilities, Cha Ming thought. *I should probably show them something to make them trust me.* He thought for a moment before summoning his Clear Sky Hammer, purposefully showing the hammer form before having it morph into a staff. He intentionally suppressed the power of the staff—at least, as much as he could—and used it to crush rocks into tiny pebbles, which he had orbit around him as a loose shield. Whenever he saw larger ones, he had his staff glow white hot and literally melt through the large boulders.

Beside him, Bear Two and Bear Four worked as a team. Bear Four cut through rocks with a rain of thin swords from the safety of a misty bubble, a mass of swirling steam that batted away at the boulders as they fell, redirecting the large ones and simply absorbing the smaller ones in the writhing slurry. The strange mixture of liquid and gas came from Bear Two, who used it as an extension of his body. A total of eight tentacles swatted, crushed, and batted the stones Bear Four couldn't destroy.

They crushed, dodged, cut, and traveled, running through the deep gouges in the Shattered Lands at Bear One's direction. Ten minutes passed before Bear One gave a two-handed signal, causing the others to cluster around him. As they did so, Bear Two changed up his shield of steaming slurry; it expanded above and covered them like a shield. Bear Four moved to the outside, using his swords to cut apart rocks too large for Bear Two to bat away.

"Bear Five, Pai Xiao, with me," Bear One said. The mountainous man joined Bear One near a fissure in the ground. They both placed their hands on the ground, and the land began to heave.

Cha Ming soon realized what they were doing—whatever was happening that caused the lands to shift, they were accelerating it. With his attunement to earth and metal, he could sense a rich ore deposit below. He put his hand on the ground and urged the earth to shift in tandem with the others.

As land poured out, the topmost layer of rock plunged back into the earth. A central pillar roughly six feet in diameter rose up from the ground. Soon enough, large stones that were much heavier than the earth they dug up began appearing. Bear One moved those off to the side and continued his sifting, returning anything not of value into the earth to make room for more valuable ore.

"Bear Three, partial refinement," Bear One said. "Pai Xiao, join him if you can."

Bear Three, who'd been waiting with his spiritual hammer off to the side, began beating the rocks. Tinging sounds filled the air as the hammer struck pieces of ore, knocking aside large amounts of less valuable rock, revealing valuable metal deposits.

Cha Ming joined him. He used the Clear Sky Hammer to strike stones in tandem with Bear Three breaking apart the rocks just as quickly as the experienced refiner. With his help, they finished processing the pile, and from start to finish, their extraction took ten minutes.

"Time to go," Bear One said once the last of the ore rocks were broken apart. The five approached the ore pile with practiced ease, each taking a sixth of the pile and leaving one for Cha Ming, who stored it in one of the lesser storage rings, completely filling the unstable space. They flew off again. By now, the quake had stopped, and they flew easily through the chasm littered with fallen rocks.

"Every few days, this area suffers a large earthquake due to shifting tectonic plates," Bear One explained. "Precious ores are constantly forced to the surface from deep beneath the ground. Every time a seismic event takes place, we must track down exposed ores as quickly as possible." He put his hand to his forehead for a moment, then opened his eyes toward the northwest. "There," he said. "Dig."

They all went to work this time. No matter what their affinity, each of them were body cultivators and had ample strength to move away debris. Small lights appeared on the ground, demarcating the area where the rocky overburden needed to be removed. Bear Two was most efficient at this, using the steaming slurry surrounding his fat body to push aside rocks. Cha Ming summoned the Clear Sky Staff in pillar form and used it to smash aside the lighter debris, forcing it out of the area. Then, joining Bear Five and Bear One again, they began extracting the ore like before.

The ore deposit was deeper this time. Bear Three processed it as it came out, and it took twenty minutes to completely extract the deposit. Though it took twice the time, the value of this deposit greatly exceeded that of the previous one. Due to the weight of the ore, Cha Ming could only fill three of his four cheaper rings before moving to the last, more expensive ring, which held his tools. Then, hesitating, he stored the rest into his Clear Sky World.

They moved again, deeper into the Shattered Lands. As they did, Cha Ming felt an increasing drain on his vitality. Bear Four, the swordsman, began to show the first signs of fatigue. He popped a high-quality vitality-replenishing pill in his mouth, which brought color back to his face.

"We were quick this time," Bear One said to Cha Ming. "With you here, we could avoid fighting by working fast. We might even have time to get a third deposit this time, assuming we don't find strong demons."

The atmosphere in the group changed as they traveled deeper, their members taking vitality-replenishing pills one after another. Only Bear Five seemed to not need them, but only because his body cultivation was special, granting him deeper pools of vitality and faster regeneration.

Soon they arrived at a large crack in the ground. They looked at the fissure solemnly, unsure about how to proceed. There, within the cracked earth, was a chunk of something Cha Ming had only read about: life-leaching gold. The emerald metal glittered brightly for everyone to see; it also increased the strain on everyone's vitality.

Despite the drain, however, they didn't move away. Such a deposit was extremely rare and had a correspondingly high value on the exchange board.

"Do you think we'll have time to take it before the demons come?" Bear Four asked, looking around worriedly. As a combatant with not many auxiliary skills, he was their first line of defense against the denizens of the canyon.

Bear One looked around worriedly. "This is worth more than we've gathered in the past month. We should at least try and take whatever we can."

"All right," Bear Two said, nodding. "Move quickly."

"Pai Xiao, Bear Five," Bear One shouted. He waved them over. "We'll have to approach this one differently. Life-leaching gold is extremely heavy, so we'll need to limit our extraction range and speed. Once we pull it out, we'll need to send it out farther away for processing, so it doesn't wear away at us as we work. Even Bear Five won't last long if he's near it."

Cha Ming nodded. They began shifting the earth, slowly but surely pulling out small golden clumps from the ground. Despite their small size, each fist-sized clump weighed around 10,000 jin. Whenever they managed to work one to the surface, Bear Two was the one to retrieve the ore, using the unusual slurry around his body to surround the ore then pull it way from the tired miners for retrieval later.

Half an hour passed, and the small pile grew substantially in size. They continued digging, but Bear One often had them stop to look over his shoulder. "Stop," Bear One said. They did so and noticed that their surroundings had grown eerily quiet. Each one of them had the distinct impression they were being watched.

Then Cha Ming saw them: black spiders with metallic legs, crawling along the cliffside. They chittered as they walked, and gravity didn't pull them down—they were moving sideways toward the cliff.

"Incoming," Bear Four said, drawing his sword. Bear Two held his tentacles in a defensive pose, and Bear Three joined them.

"We'll finish this final pull and gather what we can before fleeing," Bear One said. "Those are shattered remnant spiders, dangerous demons. They're not uncommon, but even ten of them are a threat to our group."

Cha Ming nodded. There were twenty in total.

As he worked to pull out as many golden chunks as possible, however, he noticed they'd only gathered around a tenth of the deposit. Did they really need to leave it there? Unfortunately, there was little he could do about it, at least, not without exposing his hand.

"Look out!" someone shouted. It was Bear Four, the swordsman.

Cha Ming glanced up and noticed that three spiders had broken through their defensive line. Further, it seemed some others had arrived—small crowlike birds with vicious glowing violet eyes swooped down and pecked at their defenders. They cawed, and as they did, the spiders fought harder and faster.

Seeing their dire situation, Cha Ming mulled over his options. He could easily destroy all these creatures, but he preferred to avoid violence if possible. *They* were the ones intruding on beast territory, after all.

Then he had an idea. There was a way out of this that didn't expose his cultivation. "Keep mining," Cha Ming said, stepping toward the demons.

Bear One began to protest, but his piercing blue eyes seemed to catch a hint of what Cha Ming was planning to do. He looked to Bear Five, who looked at Cha Ming uncertainly. "Well, you heard the man. Keep digging."

They obeyed.

Cha Ming didn't draw his staff, nor did he summon sigils or formation flags; instead, he opened his eyes. Violet rings appeared around his irises. They were accompanied by his Eyes of Pure Jade, and to his surprise, a thin golden ring had also appeared there unknowingly. He glared at the demons, and his eyes burned as he did. The demons, including the ones Bear Four and Bear Two had been fighting with, froze. Then, to everyone's surprise, they shivered. They gave a light bow—at least, it seemed like a bow when given by these creatures—to Cha Ming, whose eyes glowed bright violet. Each bow he received caused the Demon-Subduing Intent in the eyes to grow stronger, and the strain on them to increase. When the last of the demons retreated, he shut them, exhausted. The demons didn't double back, however. They'd admitted his superiority, and they wouldn't dare take that back.

"What are you all gawking at?" Bear One yelled, seeing that the demons were all gone. "Bear Five, keep helping. Bear Two, move that ore out." Then he looked to Cha Ming uncertainly. "Bear Six, are you all right?"

Cha Ming was kneeling down on one knee, massaging his temple. *What the hell just happened?* he thought. *When did using my eye techniques become so taxing?* Did it have to do with the mysterious yellow circle that had appeared around his irises? He reached out to Huxian but got no response. His frown deepened at that—they should be able to talk anywhere on the continent.

"Bear Six?" Bear One said again.

"I'm all right," Cha Ming said. "Give me a moment."

They continued mining, and his headache faded in seconds. Then, grinning, he joined Bear One and Bear Five in extracting the life-leaching gold. Soon they had a small mountain of it sitting prettily off to the side. Bear One walked up to it and retrieved a tenth of the mountain. The others did the same, one by one, until half the mountain remained. Cha Ming raised an eyebrow.

"Do not misunderstand," Bear One said. "We split everything evenly, and that still applies regardless of what you did. Unfortunately, we're all out of storage space."

Cha Ming nodded. He hesitated, then took away a tenth of the remaining pile, half as much as them. "My storage is full too," he lied.

Bear One looked at him for a while, as if to say something. "You are new here. I guess it makes sense you didn't bring enough storage rings." He looked back at Bears Two through Five. "You guys go on ahead. I need to talk to Bear Six here. Alone."

They did as he asked. Once they were out of sight, and due to the nature of their terrain, out of soul sight, Bear One spoke again.

"Look, we are all part of a team. I know you have secrets—we all have them. But…" he said, pointing to the small mountain. "If you've got a way to take that, I don't want you hiding that from us. Large storage treasures are expensive, I know that, but it is a big haul."

"I'm sorry, I don't know what you're talking about," Cha Ming said. He moved to walk away, but Bear One put his strong hand on his shoulder.

"Sure, you don't know what I'm talking about," Bear One said. "Just like I know you only had four of those garbage storage treasures and one good one, much less than we did. Yet you somehow stored three times as much weight as you should have been able to."

Cha Ming's eyes narrowed. He thought for a moment, then released the veil hiding his strength. His body cultivation climbed to the peak of marrow refining, and his qi to late core formation. Since the time for games was over, Cha Ming even released the seal on the Clear Sky Staff, allowing it to radiate the aura of a transcendent treasure. Then he walked up to the pile of life-leaching gold and stored it.

Bear One grinned. "See, that wasn't so bad now, was it?"

"I could end you," Cha Ming said. "End all of them. And no one would know what happened."

"But you won't," Bear One said, still grinning. "It is not your way. I can tell." Then he licked his lips. "That storage treasure. Can you hide it from them?"

Cha Ming hesitated, then nodded again.

"Then I have a business proposal you might want to consider. You see, when we are north of the wall, our storage treasures get inspected by Bastion's city guard, so we have no choice but to sell it to them at a steep discount."

"Your point?" Cha Ming asked.

"My point is that if you can smuggle what we find, we won't have to pay taxes on them," Bear One said.

Cha Ming shook his head. "They'll notice if we don't bring them ore."

"Then it's a good thing we will bring them record amounts," Bear

One said. "As for the rest of the ore, they don't need to know about it. We all keep your secret, and in exchange for bringing the ore past the wall and depositing it in safe storage for us, you will get a forty-percent cut."

"That seems like a losing exchange," Cha Ming said.

"It does," Bear One said, "but a sixth of the original amount is initially yours. In addition, we would need to pay a twenty-percent tax. But that's nothing compared to the need to buy storage treasures. Here, they get very expensive. Those unstable ones they gave you? When they break, they won't give you new ones. You will need to buy them, at many times the market price. Stable ones are even more expensive. They don't let you take more than one storage treasure with you for a reason: They want to gouge you as much as possible while you are here. Hell, those vitality-replenishing potions they supply everyone are way overpriced too. We might not need to buy them, but those weaker miners? Well, let's just say they are not here because mining is their life's pursuit. They are desperate, and this city takes advantage of that."

Cha Ming tapped his fingers on his chin as he thought on it. "We'd need a contract. To make sure no one goes against their word. I want the strictest confidentiality, both on my identity and my abilities."

"Consider it done," Bear One said. He activated his qi, and to Cha Ming's surprise, a golden paper appeared before them. It wasn't formed from the earth or metal qi as Cha Ming had seen him use earlier, but from a different, golden qi. "I'm a prospector. I use earth, metal, and karma to predict where to find the best ores. Contracts are part and parcel with that."

Cha Ming grabbed the sheet of paper and noted all the clauses. He noticed six spots for signatures. Any signatories would be sworn to secrecy.

"All right, then," Cha Ming said, signing with a drop of blood from his finger, his soul infusing the blood drop to authenticate the document with Pai Xiao's presence. Bear One did the same.

"We won't store anything beyond this pile this time," Bear One said. "But next time we go out, we will do what we can to harvest as much as possible. With your strange ability to scare away beasts, and your storage abilities, we will be able to push much deeper than ever before. We'll be set for life in a few months' time."

"I have a month," Cha Ming said. "After that, I need to leave."

"I can work with that," Bear One said. They shook hands, and the two men flew off, chasing after the other four. Though Cha Ming needed to look for the Gold Source Marrow, he could hardly think of a better way to look for it. Besides, cultivation was expensive. He might as well make spirit stones while he had a chance.

Chapter 24
Exploration

No beasts today," Bear One said, grinning as he stored a portion of his ore. "Lucky."

He was right. They'd been harvesting ore for weeks, and despite Cha Ming's exceptional abilities at repelling demons, they usually encountered a wave or two by the fourth ore pocket.

Today, they'd claimed five pockets, with not a single demon to be seen. They'd wandered deeper than ever before, ten miles into the uncharted zone. Would today be the day? Would they find the Gold Source Marrow at long last? The more they gathered, the more convinced he grew that the source of it all—and the likely location of the Gold Source Marrow—was below the ground. He'd soon need to separate from the group in order to find it.

Cha Ming stored the remaining ore after the men took their cut. Their storage treasures were filled to bursting, and he was the only one with enough space. They'd never asked for the details behind his storage space—anything was fine as long as he could smuggle for them and they had a contract in place to ensure delivery. Their faith in contracts bordered on religious, and Cha Ming saw no reason to convince them otherwise.

"Should we go deeper?" Bear One wondered, looking to Cha Ming.

"I don't see why not," Cha Ming said. "If we encounter demons,

I'll scare them off. There's bound to be more ore around here since the demons haven't dared show their faces."

Their strange behavior confused him, but who was he to complain if wealth landed on his lap? The men nodded, and they flew out in their usual positions, protecting Bear One as he surveyed the land.

They traveled another three cautious miles, rounding several jagged and broken cliffs before Bear One stopped them. He looked around, confused, before tapping his foot on the ground. "Here," he said, frowning. "But be careful. There's something strange going on. I can feel it."

The men exchanged worried glances. Bear One's hunches weren't ever wrong.

Cha Ming took his position beside Bear One and Bear Five. This far out, even he felt exhaustion as his vitality left him, like a steady leak in a used faucet. He placed his hands on the ground and churched the earth, which, for some reason, was free of debris. No rocks had fallen down from the tall cliffs behind them, as the quake had been unusually light.

"Would you look at that," Bear One said, shooting Bear Three a grin. "Looks like it's your lucky day."

Bear Three, confused, walked over to them. His eyes widened when he saw a small but heavy chip of translucent black ore in the bald man's hand.

"Nice," Bear Three said. He grabbed the chip, and to Cha Ming's surprise, it melted in his fingers, leaching into his body, starting from his hands and working up his arms through blackening veins.

"Let's keep at it," Bear One said.

Cha Ming, not knowing what was going on, continued to till the earth alongside him. Though the black chips were heavy, they were still much lighter than the life-leaching ore they'd discovered that day. Yet Bear Three seemed more gleeful than ever before.

"You seem surprised," Bear One said, noticing his confusion. "We've been mining for years together, you see, and Bear Three isn't here to collect ores for his smithing, nor is he here to make money."

"Then what is he here for?" Cha Ming asked. Each of the men had their own motives. For example, Bear One had revealed he was here saving up to purchase a Limit Awakening Pill, a rare alchemical product that could provide an impetus to break through his mortal shackles and become a demigod. It was also useful for those in the blood-awakening realm.

"Bear Three is here to hunt for special ores," Bear One explained. "This obsidian glass steel is one of the three ores he's seeking. He practices a rare cultivation method. It is very powerful, and his strength and defenses are already on par with a peak-marrow-refining cultivator."

"You mean he's not one?" Cha Ming asked, surprised. Through soul scanning, he'd analyzed the man's strength. He'd always regarded him as a peak-marrow-refining cultivator, though a weak one compared to others.

"He is a late-marrow-refining cultivator," Bear One said. "Though who knows. Maybe he will break through after this batch."

They continued working, and their pile of black chips grew. At one point, Bear Three stopped absorbing, and his body grew hot. He'd begun refining his body by using his own blacksmith flames. The process seemed excruciatingly painful, and none of them could bear remaining close to him.

Finally, after a half hour of digging and another half hour of painful body refining, the man stopped. He shivered and stood up, shaking himself off and allowing thick carbon coke to break off his body. Then, he clicked his tongue and shook his head in disappointment. He'd not broken through, despite the substantial quantity of ore he absorbed. Cha Ming scooped up the ore, then looked to Bear One, who kneeled down on the ground and frowned.

"Bear Six, help me look down here," Bear One said.

Cha Ming nodded and placed his hand on the ground. The others knew his strength by now, to the point that they respected him almost as much as they did Bear One. He searched through the earth, wandering between grains and residual metal, feeling his way down. His transcendent force inched past Bear One's, then proceeded farther along. A short distance later, he felt emptiness.

"There's a fissure down there," Cha Ming said. "Below the earth."

Bear One nodded. "I thought there might be, but I was not strong enough to find it." He waved the men over. "Let's dig together."

At his direction, everyone took out one of their many picks and shovels and began cutting into the thick broken slate they'd been sifting through prior. They dug and dug, and after a full ninety feet of earth was removed, the ground suddenly caved in, revealing an empty cavern.

"You bring us much luck, Bear Six," Bear One said, his eyes twinkling. "It has been a long time since we've found a vein."

"A vein?" Cha Ming asked.

"This ore that we find around us," Bear One said, "it is forced up from down below. There is a source down there, somewhere at the origin of the shifting plates. Between the plates, there are voids, and these voids are often filled with riches." He shrugged. "Who knows, I might be able to afford my pill. You might be able to do whatever it is you wish to accomplish, and we'll all go back home rich men."

The other four were rubbing their hands expectantly.

They hopped into the cavern, which measured a full thirty feet wide at its narrowest point. Like the earth they'd dug through, the walls were made of shale, though this one was unbroken by the constant digging on the outside.

"Do you think it's safe down here?" Cha Ming said, glancing worriedly at the walls. "The plates might shift again."

Bear One shook his head. "The tremor has already passed. It will be at least two more days until the next one. We have half a day to wander."

Cha Ming accepted the answer and followed the experienced men down the tunnel. The fissure didn't run straight; it went deeper. Soon they discovered ore sticking out of the walls. Cha Ming moved to collect some, but Bear One shook his head.

"If we dig into the walls, we might destabilize the tunnel," Bear One explained. "The risk is great, so we do not dare dig unless the value is high." He shook his head as he looked at the ore, which was of a similar grade to what they'd found earlier. "This is the least of prizes we can find down here."

They walked for hours, refusing to consider even more valuable ores. At one point, they passed a vein of life-leaching iron, a high-grade ore that could be used to forge late-core treasures. Apparently that still wasn't valuable enough. The men didn't pause in the slightest. Cha Ming's heart pounded in anticipation.

Finally, when it seemed like they'd need to turn around and gather that last vein, the fissure opened up into a cave. The cave was a full two hundred feet wide and circular, with many fissures leading out in different directions. At the center of the cave was a crystal that jutted out from the ground below. Cha Ming's heart raced as a thought crossed his mind: Was this the Gold Source Marrow he'd been searching for all this time?

It turned out not to be. Despite the matching aura, whatever was down here wasn't on the same grade of existence. Elemental Source Marrow, he'd realized, was of a transcendent nature.

"Spirits around us, what a wondrous sight," Bear One said, sighing in amazement as he walked up to the crystal column.

"What is it?" Cha Ming asked, walking up beside him.

"It's crystalized gold evanescence," one of the men said.

Cha Ming was surprised to discover that it was Bear Four who said it, and not Bear One. The man had little talent for mining, ores, or smithing.

Seeing the men look at him questioningly, Bear Four shrugged. "I read about it in an old book. They say it's one of the best things to purify one's metal qi. Just holding a piece will make your qi so sharp you can cut peak-core treasures with it.

"How much do you need?" Bear One asked.

"I can only handle a little," Bear Four said awkwardly. "A fist is more than enough, and this? This is a small mountain. A fist weighs a hundred thousand jin, and this mountain is much more than we can carry."

"Its value is great," Bear One said. "I have not heard of this crystal ore, but I can tell its worth from its treasure halo." As a prospector, he had the ability to evaluate metallic materials and treasures. "Tell me, Bear Six, how much can this storage device of yours take?"

The men looked at him expectantly. Thus far, he'd revealed something akin to twenty times the size of peak storage treasure. Normally, physical space was most important, but when the weight in a storage device grew too large, it destabilized.

"Let's find out," Cha Ming muttered.

They approached the mountain, Bear One doing so first. He took out a strange instrument, which looked a bit like a hammer focus, though it was smaller and brighter. It transformed into a tiny hammer with a sharp edge. Bear One tapped the crystal, which let out a sharp hum. He repeated the tapping, until finally, a thumb-sized piece broke off. He picked it up one handed with great difficulty and handed it to Bear Four. The air around the swordsman came to life as his power oozed out from within him and into a thin one-millimeter aura.

Cha Ming whistled. "Pseudo domain. Not bad."

Bear One gave him an appraising look and nodded.

"Yes, this is a very valuable treasure indeed," Bear One said. "Let's hurry up and extract it." He walked up to the crystal and began pounding at its flaws with his little hammer, breaking off tiny pieces with each strike. Cha Ming collected them as they fell. The hammer blows grew louder and louder, and the chamber seemed to tremble.

After breaking off several hundred pieces, Bear One frowned and looked up. The shaking didn't stop. "It shouldn't be so," he muttered. He waited, but instead of abating, the shaking grew even more violent. The ceiling above them began to crack, and to everyone's surprise, jagged rocks started poking out from the ground.

Cha Ming's heart grew cold. "The demons weren't scared of *us*. They were scared of this. The quaking isn't over."

Bear One nodded gravely. "We need to get out of here as soon as possible. It is not safe."

Outside, rocks could only fall from precipices overhead. Remaining underground where the earth shifted unpredictably, however, was suicidal. The slightest shift in the earth would crush them like meaningless bugs.

The six men flew into action, Bear One leading the way. Cha Ming brought up the rear. All around them, the walls and ceiling of the tunnel began to crack, crumble, and fall. Ore, which they'd previously ignored for fear of destabilizing the tunnel, began to drop from the walls and onto their path. They dodged the tiny heavy rocks, ignoring them as they scrambled down the corridor. As they traveled, Bear One took out a small dousing pendant. He held it out toward the exit, and it hummed urgently.

"Run!" Bear One said, but the warning came too late. The tunnels around them exploded with rock and metal spikes. Cha Ming pushed off the walls with fiery steps, summoning his Clear Sky Staff to smash aside obstacles. Bear Five, the mountain of a man, took a spike to his gut. It pierced his thick skin, leaving behind a trail of green blood.

"Leave him!" Bear One shouted.

Cha Ming ignored him. He pushed back against an oncoming boulder and rushed back to the staggering man. He grabbed Bear Five by the arm and dragged him, pulling him off the spike just in time to avoid a large stalactite falling from the ceiling. They ran, and as they did, Bear Five healed. He wasn't as fast as any of them, but his defenses were top notch. Moreover, his regenerative abilities outstripped everyone's in the group but Cha Ming's.

They rushed through the falling debris using everything they had. Cha Ming used his gravity-manipulation abilities to avoid many of the obstacles and his staff to crush the rocks. The heavy Bear Five used his fists to knock them over. Their teamwork allowed them to gain ground on the others, who'd been slowed by a large-scale collapse of the tunnel up ahead.

Just a little more, Cha Ming thought as they approached the team. And then he saw it. A large break up above them. "Look out!" he shouted. A loud crack filled the air as the rocky earth tore apart. The other four, farther down the tunnel, heard his warning and rushed out from beneath it.

I can make it, Cha Ming thought. *But Bear Five can't.* The man was simply too slow and too large to fit through. Not unless he had help.

Time stood still for Cha Ming as he considered his choices. If he rushed forward, he could save himself and join the others as they exited the collapsing tunnel. But if he did so, Bear Five would have to stay behind. Bear Five might be durable, but he wasn't as well rounded as Cha Ming. If he stayed underground, he would likely perish.

Gritting his teeth, he made his decision. Cha Ming grabbed Bear Five's arm and pulled. The man looked outraged for a moment, but then he simply looked resigned. This was the South, where the law of the jungle reigned. Cooperation only lasted as long as there was mutual benefit, and everything was enforced by contracts. It made sense to him that Cha Ming would pull him back to pull himself forward.

Cha Ming rushed ahead past the large man, but then, to the man's surprise, he *pulled*. Then, digging his staff in the ground, the earth cracking around it and his muscles bulging as he did so, he heaved and threw the large man forward beneath the rapidly collapsing ceiling.

The ceiling fell, barely missing him. Cha Ming grabbed his staff, wasting no time to retrieve it, and pushed back. A rush of wind buffeted him from behind as the ceiling hit the ground, blowing whatever tiny rocks were behind him, shoving them into his back like a rain of roughly made arrows. A giant boulder flew down at him; he smashed it with Crushing Chaos, forcing two halves of the impossibly large rock apart and flying through it as the two halves prevented the ceiling from collapsing on him. He let out tiny explosions from his hands, feet, and arms as he blitzed through the air faster than he'd ever confessed to the others. His footsteps like lightning. His footsteps like wind. His footsteps were the storm itself.

He rushed into the empty room where the golden crystal jutted out, and to his surprise, he discovered it wasn't as badly damaged as the others. As the tunnel collapsed behind him, two of the others leading out from the room also collapsed. But this central chamber, the one housing the crystal, remained. Cha Ming let out a single relieved breath as he fell to his knees, exhausted. He'd made it this far; who knew if the others would make it back to Bastion alive?

"Theirs odds are probably better than mine," Cha Ming muttered. He might be safe in this chamber, which seemed to dampen the quakes, but he was alone. Lost. The fissures that led out from the chamber didn't lead back to Bastion. Rather, they ran deeper into the mountain, deeper into the ground. And from these fissures, he felt a presence much stronger than he'd felt before. The leach on his vitality, which had previously been an annoying trickle, turned into a steady flow.

It seemed, he realized, that whatever leached their vitality didn't come from deeper in the Shattered Lands as they'd originally thought. Instead, it was from deep within the earth, where the ore itself came from. That thought both troubled and reassured him. Though he was trapped down here with whatever it was that caused the leaching, there were likely pathways that led to the surface.

He just had to find one of those exits before the last of his life left him.

Chapter 25
Myriad Truths

The darkness of the cavern wasn't as bad as Cha Ming had imagined it would be. The tall golden crystal, or what was left of it, filled the crack-filled chamber with a soft golden light. It suffused every nook and cranny of it, revealing an edge that hadn't been part of the original stone chamber before the quake. This sharpness emanating from the stone was further enhanced by the crystalized gold evanescence. It was also likely what kept the chamber from collapsing atop him.

Isn't this what you wanted? Cha Ming thought, finally taking note of the peaceful emptiness in the chamber. *Didn't you want a place to cultivate? A place to break through?* All this time, he'd been suppressing himself. In part, it was because he'd wanted to polish his foundation, removing any risk of instability when he next advanced. But in truth, that polishing had made no further progress for at least a month. The real reason was much simpler: He didn't want to expose himself during the surge of energy that accompanied a breakthrough.

"Teacher Sun," Cha Ming said, "what would happen if an earthquake caused this chamber to collapse while I'm inside the Clear Sky World?" If he was going to cultivate, he wasn't going to do it in normal time. Time contraction was one of the few advantages he had, and he was going to use it.

The ghostly figure of the Monkey King appeared beside him. His hand on his chin, he walked over to a wall and knocked it with its staff. Surprisingly, a chunk of rock broke off. "It's stable, but who knows how long it will last? If the chamber collapses on your entrance, we would still be able to open it again. Unfortunately, the rock accumulated outside would rush in. You'd need to attack the rocky layer outside the portal with your staff from within the Clear Sky World, but that's a dangerous thing to do, since spatial passageways can be unstable. Causing one to collapse would devastate the Clear Sky World."

Cha Ming nodded. He looked around and threw out hundreds of formation flags, setting a careful perimeter around the crystalized gold evanescence. He didn't reinforce the chamber— that would be foolhardy. He might be a strong cultivator, but fighting against the mighty forces of shifting tectonic plates was an exercise in futility.

Instead, he created a protective bubble. Thousands of top-grade spirit stones crumbled to fine dust, feeding the formation and its protective runic characters. If the room did fall on them, at least the space around the portal would be clear. He doubted loose rocks and gravel would be able to force their way into the spherical shield, which could fend off several blows from even a half-step-rune-carving cultivator.

After inspecting the runic bubble one final time, Cha Ming hopped into the gray portal leading to the world of white. Jade Moon Garden floated where it usually did. A thin, transparent bubble surrounded it, separating the time-accelerated interior from the endless whiteness outside. He floated to the mountaintop where he often trained. There, he found the qi-gathering formation he'd set up months ago.

A pile of top-grade spirit stones—which he'd replenished with the stock he'd obtained from exchanging ore over the past several weeks—would be crushed and converted by the formation into the five basic elements. These pure and concentrated elemental energies would be easy to absorb by his now-healed core.

Cha Ming sat down and breathed deeply, sinking into a trance.

He observed his core, which floated in his Dantian, its runic structure taking up eight tenths of the space within. Then he began to draw in five-element energy and pushed against the confines of the core. The solid structure, completely healed from damage save for five small imperfections, began to creak slightly as it expanded.

He fed it, bit by bit, expanding against the tight restriction of his core. Whenever the bubble gave way, he increased the amount of qi he stored within it, forcing the runic structure outward little by little. This happened several times. The tiny increases pressed up against the invisible but firm barrier. Then, when cracks began to appear all over the exterior shell and showed no signs of healing, Cha Ming finally sucked in sharply, drawing in all the elemental energy he could from the top-grade spirit stones. His core drank greedily. It expanded.

Crystal dust piled up around him as energy surged into the formation. Unsurprisingly, the crystals he'd prepared weren't enough. Cha Ming summoned the rest of his top-grade spirit stones and placed them on the formation. His prolonged "inhalation" sucked a third of the remaining crystals dry as the formation rushed to convert them to the appropriate elemental energies. They hovered around him like a colored mosaic, his body restricting their inflow as his core, which had just broken through, began building upon itself.

The core expanded. The runic structure expanded. As it did, the patches of five colors grew. The black and white lines on his core did as well. They formed larger solid islands on the perfect sphere. Where there were no colors, where there were no black and white islands, there was gray, filling in the gaps where nothing else fit in. The gray was a mixture of all five colors, a mixture of black and white. It was the beginning and the end.

Building this final layer took far longer than it had in the past. It grew by the same diameter as last time, but the increased diameter meant a much greater surface area and volume. Then, when the runic structure was built, and the gaps were filled, the core began to hum in satisfaction. The surface vibrated and began to meld with his Dantian, which was now fully occupied.

The melding was slow and gradual, like a pill that took time to take effect. In a way, it reminded Cha Ming of the process of crafting a runic pill. At first, everything was melted down, like liquid qi. The qi was formed into shapes, like foundational pillars, which he built up into a complex array. Then everything would collapse on itself and form a spherical pill.

Like any pill, it needed an outer shell. No pill seemed to be complete without it. The melding of his Dantian membrane was much like slowly roasting a pill at its melting point, creating a lustrous surface free of imperfections, ideal for inscribing a pill seal. In a sense, rune carving was to his core what pill seals were to pills. And like pills, there were likely grades to these carvings. He wondered what quality of seal he would end up with, if such a thing really did exist for rune carving.

Weeks passed as the melding continued. Then, as quickly as it had started, it ended. He was left with something resembling a multicolored marble floating in a point in space that his qi fed into. There was no Dantian, only a core. But it didn't feel unnatural—rather, it felt like the most natural thing in the world, like this was what the human body was designed to accommodate. Qi cultivation, it seemed, was just an approximation. It was a feeble attempt at recreating what should have been there in the first place.

Cha Ming let a light puff out of his lungs, releasing tiny residual impurities that had broken free during his breakthrough. He didn't immediately get up but continued absorbing energy into his core. It had completely emptied itself out during its rapid growth, so he continued draining away his spirit stones one at a time.

A full week passed before his core was filled to capacity with a thick, fluid qi that felt more like liquid than a gas. It somehow traveled in and out of his core without need for porosity. The solid and fluid overlapped without any issue, just like it always had when his qi was thinner.

"The peak of core formation," Cha Ming said. "At long last."

"The next step is rune carving," Sun Wukong said. "Though I'd imagine you don't want to do that right now. You'd be severely restricted on this plane if you did." He was busy picking his sharp teeth with his staff, as he often did. Despite his strictness as an instructor, he couldn't help but lounge in an undisciplined fashion whenever he was teaching.

"No, the next step isn't rune carving," Cha Ming said, shaking his head. "I still need more power while I'm here. I'll perform a pre-carving first."

The Monkey King stopped picking his teeth.

"Are you sure?" Sun Wukong said, creasing his brow in worry. "If you pre-carve your core, you still need to etch lines. You'll be stuck along this path when you decide to advance."

"Is there really a need to etch?" Cha Ming asked, raising an eyebrow. "I was going to try something different."

"Which is?" Sun Wukong asked, leaning in curiously.

"Why, I have this wonderful brush," Cha Ming said. "I might as well try painting it."

"Painting it," Sun Wukong said flatly. "Painting your core."

Cha Ming shrugged. "If any brush can do it, it's this one."

Sun Wukong thought for a moment, then shrugged as well. Cha Ming ignored him and instead focused on his core, which floated in the void, superimposed with his body. He imagined the Clear Sky Brush, and unsurprisingly, it appeared, floating outside in empty space. It didn't contain any overwhelming presence like it did in the world outside. It behaved like a perfectly normal paintbrush.

Motivated by the stubborn brush's cooperation, Cha Ming urged the liquified elemental essence he kept stored in his brush to the tip. The ink was soft blue, glowing with unaffiliated energy, sterilized from the natural evanescence that normally dosed it. He began painting. He didn't paint runes like he usually did. These were runic fragments like those he'd seen on the Bridge of Stars. He painted them on the lustrous surface one at a time, and to his surprise, they moved about as he did.

The painting was excruciatingly slow. Every character he painted took an hour. While this might not seem like a long time to those outside, it was still around twelve minutes per runic fragment from an outsider's perspective. Every character he painted migrated to its proper place, just like runes did on the Myriad Truths Diagram. Soon he finished painting the 300th character. A full thick circular outline was complete. Only the inside remained.

Since these unaligned runes were finished, Cha Ming changed to colored ink. He first painted the five elements, the core of the thirty. There were thirty elemental runic fragments, one for each of the mixtures. Five creative mixtures of two like water and wood, five destructive mixtures of two like fire and metal. Five allied mixtures of three, such as earth, metal, and water; five opposing mixtures of three such as wood, fire, and metal. Then, five mixtures of four.

The moment the last colored fragment fell into place, the unaligned runic fragments came to life. Color seeped from the inner circle and into the outer circle. It followed the pathways he'd painted in elemental essence, obeying the truth they conveyed. The color bled to each of them, bringing an additional dimension of meaning where uncertain hints had once existed.

When the final colors appeared, Cha Ming's metaphysical hand trembled as he poured white creation essence into the brush. His brush flowed like the wind itself as he painted a perfect circle onto his core. It bit around itself like an ouroboros eating its own tail. He then switched to destruction essence, the riskiest of the bunch. He only dared draw it because the circle of creation essence he'd already painted. The black ink attempted to etch itself into his lustrous core, but fortunately, the white circle kept it from doing so. Instead, it could only wait patiently as Cha Ming painted jagged, lightning-filled lines that threatened to destroy the entire matrix.

He completed the star without a hitch. Then he proceeded to the next step. He concentrated five elemental essences into a gray ink, which, instead of painting normally, he simply dabbed into the center of the diagram in as small a dot as possible.

That small dot brought the diagram to life. The complete Myriad Truths Diagram, which he'd only seen in its full magnificence on Jade Moon Planet, suddenly glowed on his core. Energy from all around him rushed in, completely crushing apart the spirit stones on the outside, and even the flags and ink he'd used to draw the energy-gathering formation so many months ago.

His surroundings screamed, and even Jade Moon Garden trembled as his qi raged. Now his qi was less a fluid and more an embodiment of… something. He wasn't sure. But as he summoned it around his body, he felt its potency had increased threefold and a third. Further, his qi covered every inch of his skin with a multicolored pattern. It was paper thin—no, it was thinner than paper. It was as thin as anything dared be without ceasing to exist.

And it was *his*. That film, so thin, so intangible that it seemed like any blade could easily tear through it, was his and his alone. It seemed like an inviolable part of him, an area that, despite its thinness, he could completely control.

Cha Ming summoned his Clear Sky Staff and willed the film to move. It did so, creeping up the staff at his direction. The air inside the Clear Sky World crackled as he swung his staff casually. He frowned, then stowed it.

"Congratulations," Sun Wukong said. "You've birthed a pseudo domain. It's like a nascent domain but weaker. About a third as weak, though that threefold increase is a greater gap than you can imagine. It is the gap between being powerful in this plane—able to damage it—and being a threat, able to tear it apart with enough effort." He grinned, revealing his sharp, pointed teeth in the process. "You're now a half-step-rune-carving cultivator."

At long last, he had the power to protect himself. He'd fought transcendents before, but he'd found that he was slightly weaker than they were. Of course, the plane's will fought against them every step of the way, but that didn't help the fact that, if he were attacked by enough transcendents, their raw power would overwhelm him despite his regenerative and defensive abilities.

Now, however, he had an additional weapon. This pseudo domain covered him like a thin armor. His qi had evolved beyond being a shield. It would now enable him to defend himself, and even fight back against transcendents. It made his goal in Bastion much more achievable. Now there was only one more thing he could do to strengthen himself—find the Gold Source Marrow and break through to half-step blood awakening.

Chapter 26
Leyline of Gold

Cha Ming summoned a portal and exited the Clear Sky World. The runic shield, which he'd erected before entering the independent space, was still fully functional. Large boulders had fallen onto it, though they hardly posed a threat to the solid, condensed shield that surrounded the crystalized gold evanescence. The earth was trembling faintly, and dust was settling. It seemed a tremor had occurred just before his arrival.

With his return to the outside world, he felt the leaching on his vitality increase again. Even with his superior body cultivation, he would only last around a month within the life-draining miasma.

That's going to be a problem, he thought. Then, wondering, he summoned his qi as a thin membrane like he had before. The membrane only took about a quarter of his qi, but to his surprise, it completely locked out the intrusion of the leaching force. He sighed in relief. Despite whatever was causing the leaching, he now had some confidence in facing it.

Cha Ming turned to the column of crystalized elemental evanesce and placed his hand on it. He transferred the entire thing directly into the Clear Sky World; no sense in leaving it behind if he wasn't staying. The unowned object disappeared, leaving behind a five-foot crater. The crystal had been twelve feet long at its largest.

The chamber trembled slightly as the crystal disappeared. Cha

Ming ignored the trembling and eyed the tunnels, which were more stable than the one he'd come from. They led deeper into the fissure.

"I think it's high time we left, Teacher Sun," Cha Ming said. "We only have so much time to wander about. If we take too long, we might miss out on the show in the city." Things were moving quickly on the surface, and he'd already spent one month mining and one month consolidating his strength and breaking through. He needed to get back as soon as possible.

"My suggestion," Sun Wukong said, "is to find whatever is causing the leaching."

"Oh?" Cha Ming asked. "Why's that?"

"Whatever it is, it's likely alive," Sun Wukong said. "Life-leaching gold is one thing, but this? It's something else entirely."

Cha Ming nodded. Then, cautiously, he entered one of the fissures. The jagged rocks on the walls were cracked, and rubble filled the rocky floor beneath him.

"But even if it's alive, why should we go looking for it?" Cha Ming asked. "Whatever it is, it hardly seems benevolent." He ducked beneath an obstruction, then, seeing the path was clear, he flew forward for a few hundred feet before stopping again. Here, the ceiling had caved in. He summoned his Clear Sky Staff and struck out with an Origin Strike, demolishing and evaporating the stones simultaneously. The strike came easily to him. It seemed his enhanced qi was far better suited to executing the advanced technique.

"I find it very unlikely that it's stronger than you," Sun Wukong said, appearing beside him and peering into the dark tunnel past the remaining rubble. "If it's sentient, it ought to know the area."

Cha Ming raised an eyebrow. "And you're thinking it'll tell us how to get out?"

"Of course," Sun Wukong said, grinning. "If not, I'm sure enough poking and prodding will convince it to let you leave. Wouldn't you agree?"

"Fair enough," Cha Ming said, flying forward once again. "If brute force isn't solving all your problems, you just aren't using enough of it."

They traveled straight for a time, but before long, the tunnel bent. It traveled perpendicular to the previous fissure, continuing until it reached another jagged opening. There, small shivering rocks covered the wall of the fissure. Some were as small as half a fist, while others were larger than a human head. He took a step, and what he'd originally assumed was a rock splashed and cracked beneath his foot. Thick blue blood, cold, not warm, leaked out from it.

"Heavens above," Cha Ming whispered. "What is this place?"

The walls were covered in thousands of tiny pustules, wartlike pieces of flesh that clung to the rocks, refusing to budge. Some shivered, and some heaved as they breathed. Their hard shells crackled as they moved. The larger ones were less smooth. They were covered in soft metallic hairs. This wasn't an underground fissure, it seemed, but a lair. What he'd stepped on wasn't a strange rock—it was a spider egg.

Quick, quick, quick, Cha Ming thought, floating up above the floor and flying forward through the tunnel. A cobweb stuck to his skin as he flew through, torn off the wall. A carcass came with it. It was the small drained carcass of a demon fox. He grimaced and summoned Grandmist flames. They engulfed the web and the corpse, destroying both completely and utterly until not even ash remained.

He flew through the tunnel with uncharacteristic slowness, gazing at the soft but hard-shelled infants that lined it. He didn't hate many things, but spiders were one of the few he did. If it was between spiders and facing Zhou Li again, he'd choose the latter in a heartbeat.

At the end of the tunnel, Cha Ming stopped. He hovered in the hallway and cocked his ear, his eyes widening when he heard skittering sounds. Clenching his teeth, he rounded the corner. He was greeted by the stuff of nightmares.

A giant cave five times larger than the last one appeared before him. The floor, the walls, and even the ceiling of the tunnel was covered in a writhing mass of skeletal spiders. Their metallic exoskeletons gleamed under the illumination of a large golden crystal at the center of the room. Like the last one, it, too, was crystalized gold evanescence. It was ten times larger than the last one.

The spiders scuttled as a unit, squirming when they saw him. Larger ones approached, their dripping fangs biting at him. He wanted nothing more than to smash them all to bits, but with great reluctance, he stowed his staff and held out his hand, summoning a golden shield of combat sigils that repelled them. The spiders clanked off harmlessly. After a few futile attempts, they backed away warily.

Despite his intrusion, the spiders continued their work around the crystal. They didn't chip away at it like Bear One had but covered it in some sort of acidic slime. A pool of gold evanescence lay at its base. Some of the larger spiders took turns sipping at its contents, shuffling away as a golden sheen appeared on their exoskeletons.

To take or not to take? Cha Ming thought, tapping his fingers on his chin. Somehow he felt like a burglar, an intruder who had snuck into their home and was coveting their hard-earned possessions. They'd laid claim to the pillar, and if the soft pustules from before were any indication, this was where they were nurturing their next generation.

He sighed, then called out, "Who is your leader?"

The spiders shuffled as though not understanding. He waited, however, as he knew that demons were intelligent. They could communicate if they chose to do so. A few torturous seconds passed before more skittering filled the cavern. Large legs covered in bristling metallic hair poked out from one of the four entrances to the chamber, revealing the largest spider Cha Ming had ever seen. It eyed him with sixty-four large beady eyes that had a hypnotic quality to them.

Why have you intruded on our lair, human? the spider asked. *Will you take the fight for ore down here to our young? Is your honor so lacking?* It grew slightly as it spoke. Demonic qi rushed into it, causing the metallic hairs on its legs to sharpen and take on a golden hue. *Know this: If we fight here, we fight to the death. I would rather see this cave collapse on you and destroy everyone here rather than risk the rest of our brood.*

Cha Ming shivered as he eyed its mandibles, which dripped

corrosive acid onto the rocky ground. All around him, tiny beady eyes and tiny sets of mandibles prepared to attack him. Even the tiniest of spiders was like a coiled spring, ready to pounce.

"I didn't come here to fight you," Cha Ming said. "I could have easily smashed and stolen this crystal and left before you could even come. Instead, I called you."

The spider clicked its mandibles as if tasting the truth of his words. Cha Ming felt the spider's eyes on his skin, inspecting it for shivers or tells.

"I'm searching for something. Have you seen it?" He held out his hand and summoned a spherical projection. It was a golden orb, and inside it, a liquid floated about, shining in all its natural perfection. "It's called Gold Source Marrow, a precious treasure."

The spider's mandibles clicked again. *And you think we would inform you of this treasure like naïve children? So that you could steal it out from under our very legs? How naïve of* you.

"I wouldn't call it stealing," Cha Ming said. "I have a good friend, a fox. He says demons prize equivalent exchange. I would trade for it." Given that he'd just spent his entire fortune breaking through, he wasn't sure how he'd do that. But he was confident that he could work something out. There were resources aplenty north of Bastion Wall.

The spider considered his words, then shook from side to side, its large legs aiding it in physically showing its disapproval. *Equivalent trade is among equals. You, though strong, are no demon. You are not an equal, only an intruder.*

He's right, lad, Sun Wukong said from the Clear Sky Brush. *You'll have to show him some credentials. Then he'll be willing to talk.*

Cha Ming had been hoping to avoid using his abilities. His Demon-Subduing Eyes, though growing increasingly powerful, had become very strenuous to use. Nothing permanent, of course; his regenerative abilities were on par with those of a half-step-blood-awakening cultivator. But even then, it would take him minutes to recover.

I guess there's no avoiding it, Cha Ming thought. He closed his eyes and opened them again. His irises glowed, the inner jade ring containing his concentrated Devil-Sealing Intent, and the middle violet ring his Demon-Subduing Intent. The soft golden ring on the outside, wherever it came from, did not contain any such intent. Which was fortunate, as he shuddered at what would happen if it did.

The light struck the demons. They quivered in fear at his penetrating gaze. Some of them, the stronger ones, simply brought their skeletal limbs closer. He figured it was the spider equivalent of turning over and revealing its belly or neck. Only the largest spider was unaffected. He soon ended the technique, blinking away tears of blood that appeared there. His vision blurred slightly, but only for a half second before returning to normal.

Perhaps you do have the qualifications to speak with someone, the spider said. *I know not what this thing is, though it seems related to these crystals we harvest. But know this: We do not give away treasures, and some treasures are too precious to trade.*

"Please take me to your leader," Cha Ming said. The spider bowed its large combination of a torso and a head and scuttled away, motioning with one of his legs for Cha Ming to follow. He did so, taking care to avoid crushing the many smaller spiders that skittered all about. The skeletal spiders that had been harvesting the crystals before his interruption continued their arduous task of dissolving the ore one bit at a time.

The spider moved swiftly, using its large legs to pull itself along the walls as the network of fissures expanded the deeper they went. He realized they were also constantly twisting and turning. The fissure network was like a spiral staircase that led to the ground below the massive crystal that jutted out from the ground in the chamber above them.

Thousands of feet turned into miles. The temperature even began to rise, something he found surprising since the Ling Nan Plane wasn't spherical but flat. They passed by groups of larger spiders that lay huddled in other fissures to make way for Cha Ming and his spider escort.

Finally, they entered a massive chamber ten times larger than the one before. Here, large spiders crawled everywhere. The lethality in their movements was smooth and practiced. They'd evidently gone through hundreds of battles, whether amongst humans, demons, or themselves.

At the center of the massive chamber was a large gash in the ground. It resembled a vein, for it pulsed with golden energy that rushed through it on its journey to heavens knew where. Next to the vein, on the ground, many metallic crystals were forming. They spread out in a network that expanded to the walls of the chamber and beyond. With every pulse, the crystals grew, and with their growth, the walls shifted slightly. They were held up by large metallic limbs that resembled spider legs.

No, they *were* spider legs. Strong bones covered in metallic hairs dug into the earth. They were assembled into arches that prevented the chamber's collapse. These legs were each almost as large as those belonging to the massive spider that rested near the vein, its large, bulbous backside heaving as it breathed, its countless eyes glaring at him with contempt, despite the deference its subordinate paid him.

My queen, the spider who'd led Cha Ming down here said. *I've brought the intruder here as you requested.*

Very good, the giant spider said. *Now leave us. All of you.*

Cha Ming's escort and the spiders guarding the queen froze. They blinked in confusion and hesitated.

You cannot fight him, and if we come to blows, you will die a meaningless death. There is no point in you remaining, she said.

We can buy you time if it comes to that, my queen, one of the larger spiders said, scuttling up to her and glaring at Cha Ming.

When did this queen's orders become suggestions? the giant spider asked. *You will leave.*

The spider who'd objected pulled its legs back in in a sign of deference, then one by one, they left, leaving only Cha Ming, the spider, and the golden vein behind.

"Many thanks for meeting with me, Great Monarch," Cha Ming said. "My name is Cha Ming. I'm pleased to make your acquaintance."

Demons were skilled in spotting deception. Keeping up his act as Pai Xiao here would likely backfire.

Monarch Cha Ming, the spider said, *I am known as the Life-Leaching Monarch. Why have you come to these broken lands devoid of life? You are skilled; I can tell as much from your ability to shield yourself from my powers. Why would one such as you, who should care so little for mundane riches, come here of all places?*

"Two reasons," Cha Ming said honestly. "The first reason is I was trapped while journeying above. I entered a fissure with some companions while searching for ore, and the tunnel collapsed."

A common occurrence, the Life-Leaching Monarch said. *It is foolish to journey down here with so little knowledge of the fissure's web.*

"As I now know," Cha Ming said. "The second reason is that I am searching for something: a stone and its contents." He summoned an image of the sphere like he'd done before. The golden image spun above his hand, its fluid core flowing independently of the outer sphere's movement. "This is a Gold Essence Core, and it contains Gold Source Marrow."

The spider, seeing the orb, shivered. Not with excitement, not with fear, but with anger. *You should leave now,* it said. *I do not wish to discuss this treasure.* It motioned with a leg to one of the many exits where the spiders had gone. *That tunnel leads all the way to the surface. You need not return to this place, as I will not change my mind.*

Cha Ming frowned. He didn't want to go back empty-handed. "In the lands up above," Cha Ming said, "I'm considered unsurpassed on the plane in formation arts, alchemical arts, and talisman arts. I'm also all right at spiritual blacksmithing, though less so than my other professions. If it's a matter of price, I'd definitely be able to pay it."

Oh? the spider said, its beady eyes blinking. *Can you make something from nothing? Can you turn back time and reverse cause and effect?*

"I cannot," Cha Ming admitted.

And can you dive into this leyline of gold and coax it to produce another one of these treasures that you want so dearly? the spider continued. It gestured to the pulsing vein in front of it, inviting Cha Ming to come forward. *If so, by all means, go right ahead. While you're at it, my only requisite payment is that you do it again.*

"You don't have it, do you?" Cha Ming said. "Someone already took it from you."

A few months ago, the Life-Leaching Monarch admitted, its mental voice dripping with anger. *I had wanted to use it to gain my mark and enter the initiation realm. It was a once-in-a-lifetime opportunity for treasures like that to appear so rarely. I prepared for many centuries to use it. I coaxed the fissures to form complex formations in the earth to protect me. These preparations were almost complete, but before I could consume the core, thieves came and picked it out from under my very mandibles.* It shivered again. This time, its legs cracked like a man cracking his knuckles before a fight. *Emboldened by this victory, the humans dared intrude ever deeper inside our territory, stealing metallic ore from my younglings and the other demons in the area. They do not fear us as they once did.*

"Do you know who stole it?" Cha Ming asked. "Any distinctive features, like hair color, eye color, or pupils? Does a black-haired man with red pupils ring any bells?" If anyone had done this, it was likely Zhou Li.

Red pupils? A seer? the spider asked. It shook its large body. *No seer came here. As for distinctive features, I'd say the most obvious one was the man's golden hair. He was an older man, a peak-core-formation cultivator. He carried an expensive-looking treasure that shielded me from his aura. He was also accompanied by two strong body-cultivating bodyguards. One cultivated fire and metal, as for the other, I'm not sure. They didn't fight for long and preferred to leave as soon as they retrieved their spoils.*

Golden hair? A fire-and-metal body cultivator? Two such individuals came to mind, and he doubted he'd be able to find another such pair anywhere else in the South.

"I believe I know who you speak of," Cha Ming said. He

summoned a projection of Director Yong and Tian Zhi. "Did they do this?"

The spider shivered in anger.

Yes, the spider said. *The treasure is no longer mine, so I cannot trade what I do not have. You should go now. Do not come back. Life has always been hard for demons, especially when humans are involved.*

Cha Ming thought for a moment. The spider hated humans so much. It was indignant about the cultivators harvesting ore outside. Could he use that? Did he dare use that? A plan began to take shape in his mind. "Would you like to strike back at the humans?" Cha Ming asked. "Not to slay them decisively, but to put fear into them, so that they don't dare come out into the Shattered Lands for a dozen years or more?"

The spider blinked. *That depends on the opportunity and the price that must be paid. We can sacrifice some of our members if the benefits outweigh the costs.*

"I'm not sure if it will work yet," Cha Ming said. "But I'm not from around here. I'm from the North, and I'm here to sabotage their city."

Humans, the spider said. *Always fighting amongst themselves.* It seemed disappointed somehow.

"If you're up for it," Cha Ming continued, "I would consider destroying a very large section of Bastion Wall. What could you do if I gave you that opportunity?"

The spider considered for a moment. *I would send a small force into the city,* the spider said. *Mostly to slaughter powerful cultivators and harvest them for the brood. I would kill the chicken to warn the monkey. I would also make an appearance. Our forces aren't nearly powerful enough to claim the city, but a taste of my life-leaching abilities will give them something to think about for decades. It will remind them that I, the Life-Leaching Monarch, still live, and can come out whenever I so choose.*

Cha Ming closed his eyes. Many lives would be lost if he did this. "It would be difficult to grasp this opportunity," he said. "Unless, of course, you had prior information on the timing of such an event. Then you could rush in almost as soon as the break in the wall occurred."

And what would you like in exchange? the spider asked.

"A small favor," Cha Ming said. "I will leave a sound-transmission mark here so I can give you advanced warning. In exchange, when you charge up, I want you to spare those that bear my mark if you can."

The spider moved its mandibles in agreement. *Very well,* the spider said. *You may leave your marks. I do not guarantee I will go— such an outing is risky. But if I choose to act, I will respect your wishes.*

"I also want you to focus on combatants, if you can. Spare the weak who are running away," Cha Ming said.

"Also acceptable," the spider said. "They provide meager sources of energy."

"Then it's agreed," Cha Ming said. He summoned his Clear Sky Brush and painted white lines in the air. They solidified into a sigil that dropped to the floor in front of the Life-Leaching Monarch. It was a transmission sigil. Then he took out a piece of paper and painted a talisman. It didn't contain a powerful function and was ornamental in nature. "Those who wear these talismans should be avoided and spared if possible."

Very well, the Life-Leaching Monarch said. *If they do not fight us, we will not fight them.* It then turned toward the exit and pointed. *Please leave. You may be a monarch, but you are also human. Humans do not belong beneath the soil. They do not belong near the leylines, which breathe life into this dying world.*

"Leylines?" Cha Ming asked. "Dying world?"

Go, the spider said again.

Cha Ming considered prodding further but decided again it. He flew up to the fissure and flew up it. Within hours, he saw sweet, blissful daylight.

Interlude
Unstoppable

Feng Ming clutched his chest, gasping for breath. Gong Xuandi did the same beside him. He regulated his breathing and sat cross-legged to regenerate his depleted qi. They were exhausted. Many months of chasing the Taotie had taxed both their minds and their bodies. As they rested, they heard screams in the distance. Domesticated animals bleated as the creature advanced, taking advantage of their break to feast on nearby living things. They heard ripping sounds as plants were torn from the earth, and even fertile soil was sucked into the creature's ghastly body.

But what could they do? What alternative did they have? They were mere mortals, and that creature was a god. They fought, rested, fought, rested. The cycle continued, but the creature still grew stronger.

"Has your dearest sister, the Sea God's Herald, heard back from the Sea God Realm?" Feng Ming asked the resting Gong Xuandi.

The large man opened an eye and shook his head. "Not since last time. It seems like it will take much time to manufacture a countermeasure, and even more time to send it over. The process isn't easy, and it only gets worse when you have to transport something across planar boundaries."

Feng Ming groaned. He'd heard similar answers from the Alabaster Group. Both transcendent powers were doing everything they could to contain the creature. And judging from the fact that the South had yet to send anyone remotely powerful enough to intercept or help them, they were also aware of the problem.

"This can't continue," Feng Ming said. "The constant fighting. It's wearing down on us. Even you, a mighty half-step-blood-awakening cultivator, can't keep it up."

The former Sea God Emperor shrugged. "If you sent a force from the North, I'm sure the South would indulge you and let them pass to join the battle. They might even clear a path for you, laying down carpets to mark the way here."

They'd dug deep into Southern territory while chasing the beast. So deep, in fact, that even the peasants knew of their coming. Only stragglers were left behind, those deemed not important enough to warn.

"We need to force them to help us," Feng Ming said. He stood up and stretched. Though his qi had recovered, his body was stiff. He wasn't a body cultivator like Gong Xuandi, as much as he fought like one. His muscles were stressed from overuse, taut in a way that could easily lead to injury. As he stretched, he peered out into the distance, where red lights shone in a darkening sky.

"I'm done," the Sea God Emperor said, summoning his trident. The weapon, though mighty, had evidently seen better days. It was the fifth such weapon he'd used since starting. Feng Ming's Magma God's Spear was no different. Despite his ungodly luck, a weapon could only last so long under constant abuse. It was only a matter of time until the cracks on it widened and the weapon shattered.

"I've heard that blood masters are excellent fighters," Feng Ming said, gazing intently at the red-lit area. "Do you have any experience with them?"

"I don't," the Gong Xuandi said. "Though I've heard they have quite the temper."

"I've heard the same as well," Feng Ming said. "And it seems the South has grown too complacent. They know we guide it toward areas of lower energy density, avoiding demonic mountains, cities, and other important outposts. I think it's high time we change that."

Gong Xuandi nodded. "Do you want to be the carrot or the stick?" He hefted his trident over his shoulder. There was no opposition or complaint. Their months of fighting the beast had made pragmatists of both of them.

"The stick," Feng Ming said, readying his spear. "The beast gets rather frustrated when it keeps missing. It needs a little taste every once in a while to keep it wanting."

"I can't promise to make a good carrot," Gong Xuandi said. "But let's see if it likes seafood." He charged, exchanging a few blows with the frustrated creature before heading off in the monastery's direction. They'd done this many times before and knew the answer to his question: The beast loved seafood, along with anything else they fed it.

Chapter 27
Return

The journey back through the Shattered Lands was swift and unencumbered. Though mentally exhausted from his extended cultivation, as well as the trip through the rocky underground fissures, Cha Ming now knew that Director Yong had taken the Gold Source Marrow. More likely than not, he'd been aided by none other than Tian Zhi.

The theft didn't bother him; that was between them and the spiders. Truth be told, he might have done the same himself if the spider had refused to cooperate. But it *did* make him wonder what had happened to the precious treasure. Wang Jun hadn't alerted him about its discovery, and the Greenwind Pavilion, who he'd commissioned to watch out for the treasure, hadn't told him about it either. That meant it was still in the Blackthorn Conglomerate, likely in their vault. He'd have to get access somehow and retrieve it. Conveniently, he'd also need to raid it to call his plan a success. The pieces were coming together.

The air was free of dust when he finally arrived at the surface. There was no one around the fissure when he exited, which made sense given that he was in the uncharted zones.

"It's deserted but not unexpected," Sun Wukong said, appearing outside the Clear Sky World. Here in the Shattered Lands, he was free to wander about. The Spirit Temple had no wards or spies this far in demon territory.

I hope they made it, Cha Ming thought. *There's a worry in my heart, something I can't shake away.*

"That's something different," Sun Wukong said, shaking his head. "I feel it too."

You? Cha Ming thought. *You're a ghost. You don't have a heart.*

"I have a spiritual one," Sun Wukong said, glaring at him. "Anyway, I feel it more than you do, even in spirit form. This distress isn't something humans should feel, only demons. The plane is in danger, and all of nature is feeling the pressure."

"Is it the South?" Cha Ming asked.

Sun Wukong shook his head. "It's the creature. Huxian warned you before we left for the South. Before, it was only them that felt it because they had local influence. Now, a sense of crisis pervades the entire continent."

"That bad?" Cha Ming muttered. Well, nothing he could do about it down here.

Sun Wukong returned to the Clear Sky Brush, and they flew back toward the wall. The first group of miners he stumbled upon were early-core-formation cultivators trying out their luck in the peripheries.

"Fellow miners," Cha Ming said, landing beside the trio, who frowned when they saw him. Their strong bodies crackled with power as they got into defensive stances. "Have you seen the five Bear brothers?"

A tall but thin man, their leader, scratched his head in confusion. "We're new here," he said. "We've never heard of these 'Bear brothers' of yours. Got a description of them?"

"Bear One is tall but bald, his eyes clear blue," Cha Ming said. "Bear Five is particularly large, and he likes to fight with his fists. Bear Four is a swordsman, and he likes to carry a sword at his waist at all times."

The man shook his head. "Can't say we have, sorry."

"Sorry for troubling you," Cha Ming said. He flew away from

them and back toward the barracks. The fact that they weren't in the danger zone where they usually operated filled his heart with dread. Many heads turned as he flew past. Those who could fly freely in the Shattered Lands were few and far between.

Soon, he reached Bastion Wall. It seemed so tiny now that he'd seen the massive chamber that held the Leyline of Gold. Its walls, made of thick metal, wouldn't last a second under the shifting grounds deep beneath the scurrying miners.

That, he thought, *is likely why they built it here, where there are no quakes.* He now realized it served a dual purpose. For one, it kept the demons out. For another, it kept that dreadful life-leaching aura that the Life-Leaching Monarch emanated at bay.

A few figures walked out of the guard shack when he arrived. He was relieved to see that one of them was a tall bald man with clear-blue eyes. The man broke into a grin when he saw Cha Ming, as did two of those who'd stepped out. It seemed that Bears One, Three, and Four at least had pulled through.

"I am glad that you have made it back," Bear One said, clapping Cha Ming on the shoulder. "I thought you lost in that dreadful tunnel. So did everyone else. There is a betting pool, you see, and we have all lost spirit stones guessing how long it would take for you to come back, if at all." He chuckled heartily. "Though it seems the Iron Lady will be winning a fortune. What a discerning eye she has."

"Miss Ge?" Cha Ming asked, incredulous. She was the last person he'd expect to put money on a bet. Her cold pragmatism and cynicism was well known among the miners. She bent no rules, not for anyone.

"The very same," Bear One said.

"The others?" Cha Ming asked, looking to Bear Three and Bear Four. He noticed that Bear Three had broken through to the peak of marrow refining since their escape. Bear Four had also obtained a new sword. Those were both promising signs.

"Safe," Bear Four said. "Bear Two didn't really need any more money. He was just here to top up his funds before closing himself up again. Something about wanting to increase his qi cultivation.

As for Bear Five..." He shook his head. "That one came too close to death. With his ability, he'd never felt so sure he would die. He decided to go back to his home kingdom after cashing out."

"I see," Cha Ming said. "I don't suppose you still have his contact information? In case I need to send him a message or package?"

Bear One smiled. "I'm sure he would appreciate hearing from you. There is also an agreed-upon gift that you must deliver, if you still possess it." There was no way for them to verify if Cha Ming still had the metal they'd pilfered, but they trusted in their contract. The consequences for breaking it were severe and would hamper his cultivation. Perhaps they even trusted him personally, given their recent life-or-death experience.

"Don't worry, his gift is still here, as is yours," Cha Ming said. "I'll be stopping in town to put it in safekeeping for all of you. Once I leave, that is. I'd imagine that will be shortly." As he spoke, two guards ran over from the lift. "Here, I have something for you." He fished through his storage and took five papers he'd crafted for each of the Bear brothers before arriving. They each bore a copy of the sign Cha Ming had left for the Life-Leaching Monarch.

"What is this thing you have made?" Bear One asked, fingering it curiously. "It looks somewhat like a Northern talisman, though it does not contain their usual power."

"Think of it as a farewell present," Cha Ming said. Then, mentally, he sent a different message. *In the future, there will be trouble north of the wall. Should you see a massive rush of demonic spiders climbing up to the surface, escape as quickly as you can. But before you do so, put on these armbands. They might just save your life.*

Bear One's eyes widened. He took them and immediately placed them in his personal storage treasure. *There is quite the story accompanying your survival, it seems,* he sent back. *One day, when all is peaceful, you will need to share this story.* He didn't press him further.

Up on the wall, a figure suddenly appeared. He didn't use the lift like most people did. Instead, he flew straight down to where Cha Ming and the others were standing. To Cha Ming's surprise, it wasn't

Tian Zhi or Director Yong as he'd expected. It was Prince Shen. His distinctive yellow robes stood out beside the miners, who wore drab colors and didn't bother to clean themselves off. Bear One and the others got down on one knee. Given their prior meeting, Cha Ming didn't feel the need to be overly courteous, so he gave a simple bow.

"Brother Pai Xiao, I was relieved to hear that you were still alive, but seeing is believing," Prince Shen said, his excitement clear from his toothy smile. "We were concerned when we received the news that you'd been trapped underground, as your teammates can no doubt attest."

"The guards questioned us thoroughly," Bear One said, "to eliminate foul play as a cause of death." *We did not divulge anything we shouldn't,* he sent to Cha Ming separately. *As per our contract.*

"I'm happy to hear of your concern," Cha Ming said. "Judging by your presence here, I take it I'm free to return to Bastion?"

"That's exactly what I've come to tell you," Prince Shen said. "In fact, I've been instructed by my royal father to escort you to the Blackthorn Conglomerate personally."

"Then I'll be happy to accompany you," Cha Ming said.

The prince flew up, and Cha Ming moved to follow him but hesitated. For a brief moment, he felt he should return those items he'd borrowed, so he flew toward the guardhouse instead.

"No need to bother yourself with formalities here," Prince Shen said. "As the crown prince of the Ji Kingdom, I have full authority over its assets."

Cha Ming hesitated once again. For some reason, he couldn't help but feel that it would be a bad decision to do as the prince said.

As he stood there, frozen in indecision, the old gray-haired Mrs. Ge walked out the front door. She looked at the prince and sniffed. "You would dare break protocol with me, young man?"

"Na-Nanny Ge?" Prince Shen said, his face paling. He flew back down and clasped his hands, bowing in apology. "I-I wasn't aware that you were stationed here. It's simply been ages, Nanny Ge. How goes your ailing husband?"

"Dead," Mrs. Ge said with her impassive nasal voice. "As you will be if you dare leave without following my rules." Her sharp eyes, hidden behind her half-moon spectacles, bespoke of a strength that Cha Ming hadn't noticed before. He considered testing her and thought better of it.

Let it remain an eternal mystery.

"Of course," Prince Shen said, sweating profusely. "Go on, Brother Pai Xiao, please return her things."

Cha Ming wasn't sure whether to be impressed by the old lady's grasp on the heir to the kingdom or by the hilarity of the situation. Still, he threw up ten storage rings, one of which contained the pick and shovel he'd been loaned as well as some of the heavier, more expensive ores. The other nine had been disposable replacements he'd purchased from them at a usurious price. They were all chock full of ore as well.

Mrs. Ge gave them a quick scan. "Personal storage?" she asked. Cha Ming tossed her the storage ring he'd brought with him the first day. "Still five hundred jin, I see. No need to show me the contents. Whatever ores you could smuggle would be less valuable."

Then she peered at him with a gaze so intense he felt like his body's secrets were bared before her. She could see through his flesh and bone, his marrow, and his qi pathways. Fortunately for him, he'd completely changed his physique and not just the outer shell. The qi in his pathways was of fire and gold, and so was his body-refining technique.

"Congratulations on your breakthrough," she said, noticing he'd advanced the qi cultivation in his disguise to late core formation and late marrow refining.

"Many thanks, Miss Ge," Cha Ming said. He wanted to follow Prince Shen and escape her prying eyes, but he remained standing. Leaving without payment would be out of character. Her eyes continued to search him, even going so far as to probing his soul aura. Then, after finding nothing, amiss, she looked away.

"I take it spirit stones are your preferred payment?" she asked. Cha Ming nodded. She threw a cheap disposable ring over to him. To his surprise, it contained the exact payment he'd expected. It seemed that all the scales, the procedures, and the like, were unnecessary under her inquisitive gaze. The agonizing rules were there for her entertainment and enjoyment.

"Mrs. Ge," Bear One said, "this one accepts his loss."

"Same here," Bear Three said. Bear Four followed closely, and soldiers clamored over, sending their wagers to her. She caught them deftly.

"Let that be a lesson to all of you," Mrs. Ge said. "Be sure to pay attention at all times. Always be watching. Always."

"Madam!" the guards yelled, bowing.

Cha Ming was surprised to see that Prince Shen had joined them.

A short while later, they were trudging up the wall using the lift instead of flying directly. It seemed Prince Shen would rather waste his precious time than further offend the scary lady. They soon arrived atop the wall, which overlooked the Shattered Lands to the north and Bastion to the south.

I'm back, Cha Ming thought, gazing over the pristine and orderly city. Though he'd only been gone for two months, it seemed like ages to him. The city had grown into more than just a place; he had friendly coworkers here, people whom he'd spent substantial amounts of time with. There was also Mo Ling, the industrious girl he'd rescued from Liaoning. Unknowingly, much like Haijing and Quicksilver, Bastion had grown into another home.

A home he'd soon destroy.

The lift locked, and the door opened. Now that the guardhouse down below was out of sight, Prince Shen turned to Cha Ming and handed him a storage ring. Cha Ming inspected its contents and noticed two objects. One was a core-transmission jade, a much smaller one than he was used to seeing. Another one was a golden seal. It radiated a powerful aura of karma. Cha Ming had never seen its like before.

What happened to you was unfortunate, Prince Shen sent silently. *And it happened at an unfortunate time. These two items should ensure that our progress remains unimpeded in the foreseeable future.*

The prince flew off the wall, and Cha Ming followed. Using

Prince Shen's authority, they flew through the streets much higher than anyone else dared, completely bypassing normal traffic as they made their way to the Blackthorn Conglomerate.

What happened? Cha Ming asked as they rounded a street corner. A few lesser-core-formation cultivators who happened to be flying in the streets ducked out of their way.

Our timeline has shifted, Prince Shen said. *We have six months now, and I have a feeling it might shift again. The Breaker must be completed by the time the grand vizier arrives, or all our heads will be served to him on a platter.*

Boss Tian and the others? Cha Ming asked.

Those incompetent fools might be decent craftsmen, but they are terrible innovators, Prince Shen said. *If they were in Haijing, like so many of the professionals in our kingdom were until about a year ago, they would have access to more resources and time essence to mask their incompetence. But here in the South, we do not have such luxuries. This project is much too sensitive in nature to send them there, especially given recent events.*

It all made sense to Cha Ming now, the rush for innovation. In the past, making the Breaker would have been far less challenging. It seemed he'd damaged them far more than he'd realized. Not only had the attack on Beihai been botched, wasting many resources in the process, but he'd personally killed the Obsidian Syndicate's greatest minds. As such, they had to scramble to reinvent the wheel. Furthermore, they had to attack quickly, as the North's advantage would be widening with every passing day. That explained the ever-shifting, ever-dreadful deadline.

What about the blood masters? Cha Ming asked as they entered the Blackthorn Conglomerate headquarters. Staff scrambled out of their way as they flew through the building toward the main office.

Your employer threw money at them, of course, Prince Shen said. *Here in the Ji Kingdom, it's the best form of apology. They reverse engineered many of your improvements, creating a weapon that increased performance by ten percent in short bursts, with no risk of mental instability past one hour of exposure every twenty-four hours.*

This time, they had the good sense to insist on testing.

Cha Ming nodded. He wasn't happy that they'd modified his work, but the results he'd obtained in exchange had been worth it. He'd also gained an understanding on how grudges were settled in the South: with money and blood. If he wanted to set up an irreconcilable grudge, he'd need to cripple the Blackthorn Conglomerate's finances.

They flew up the steps in the corporate office and walked down the hall to the conference room, where Director Yong was holding a meeting. The moment he saw them, however, his body language changed. He stood up and began ushering grumbling cultivators out the door. The grumbling stopped the moment they saw the prince.

"Come in. I've already called for Tian Zhi to come upstairs," Director Yong said. He smiled and turned to Cha Ming. "It's so nice to see that you're safe and sound. We worried about you greatly."

"Thank you for your worries," Cha Ming said. "I'm just happy to be back home and am itching to get back to work. The Shattered Lands are a dreadful place. Very boring, and not a forge to be seen."

"We'll make sure you get an upgrade to your forge," Director Yong said. "I see that your cultivation has increased."

"I had some fortuitous encounters in the Shattered Lands," Cha Ming said. He didn't elaborate. They took a seat in the boardroom, and as Director Yong fiddled with a jade treasure that projected an image on the wall, Tian Zhi ran in. He relaxed visibly when he saw Cha Ming safe and sound.

"Let's get right to it," Prince Shen said. "There's not a moment to waste."

The image on the wall shifted as Director Yong spoke. "As you all know, Project Breaker has been in the works for around ten months. Due to unforeseen events in the North, we've been tasked by Grand Vizier Zhou to construct a device capable of breaking a transcendent-grade wall. Though the hope is to completely destroy the treasure, shattering a portion of it and allowing our troops through is also acceptable."

The image shifted. To Cha Ming's surprise, it showed a replica of

Southhaven Wall, one of the least-important battlefields in the entire North.

"Though the goal is to be able to break through any section of the wall, Southhaven Wall is the true target. This wall is also stronger than most.

"It's difficult to say exactly what the wall can handle. We speculate that it's an initial-grade-transcendent treasure due to its size and length. The plane can only bear so much strain, and sending too great and too large a treasure would be met with fierce resistance from competing transcendent powers."

The image changed again. This time, it showed a broken wall.

"To facilitate our testing, three pieces of ancient wall we obtained in previous wars have been transported to Bastion. Two are here in the Blackthorn Conglomerate, and one is in the royal palace for final testing. We're hoping for the attack to take place a year from now."

"Unfortunately, Grand Vizier Zhou is insistent on his newest deadline," Prince Shen said.

"How long do we have?" Tian Zhi asked.

"Six months," Prince Shen said. "And I have a feeling he'll move it up even further, given some other distracting events occurring in the South. There's a problem in the northeastern provinces he'll be coming to take care of, so I'd imagine he'll want to see results when he comes by. For now, however, he's in seclusion, recovering from his battle up north. From what I gather, he burnt his blood essence to constrain a powerful enemy combatant."

"We'll do our best to speed up the development process," Director Yong said. "Pai Xiao, is there anything we can do for you that would speed up development?"

Cha Ming, surprised by their straightforwardness, tapped his fingers on his chin. He took a sip of tea from a cup that had been poured for him earlier by Tian Zhi, who was nervously fidgeting. Obviously their lack of progress was viewed as completely his fault. "I know it might not be proper," Cha Ming said slowly, "but I currently don't know what materials we have access to. Further, if inspiration hits me, I want to be able to rummage through our stock to try different things."

"You want access to our vault?" Director Yong asked, frowning. "That's a bit much to ask for."

"Not unsupervised, of course," Cha Ming said. "It would be fine if someone else was there with me."

"Hmm…" Director Yong said, fingering his blond beard. "I don't know about this. We have procedures and requisitions for a reason. Only a select few people are allowed inside the vault."

"The timeline for this project is of utmost important," Prince Shen said. "Besides, doesn't he have confidentiality clauses in his contract, as well as enforced punishments for theft?"

"He does," Director Yong said dryly. "But you of all people should know that contracts can sometimes be circumvented."

Prince Shen sighed. "Do what you can. All I know is that, as my father's heir, even I will not be able to escape the grand vizier's fury alive. You should know what to do."

Director Yong hesitated, then nodded. "All right. We'll get him access. Supervised access."

"Good enough," Prince Shen said. "Since that's settled, I won't be keeping you." He looked to Cha Ming. "Work hard. Our fate, the fate of the entire South, rests on your shoulders."

"I'll do my best," Cha Ming said.

The prince left, leaving him with Tian Zhi and Director Yong.

"We'll be off as well," Director Yong said. "Is there anything else you need from us? Anything at all?"

"I don't suppose coffee can be delivered to the research and development area?" Cha Ming asked.

"I'll see what we can do," Tian Zhi muttered. "Spirits know everyone else has been asking the same thing."

Cha Ming smiled. Despite differences in geography and ideology, some things never changed.

Chapter 28
The Vault

"P lease wait here while I retrieve the quartermaster," an attendant said, motioning for Tian Zhi and Cha Ming to sit on a black velvet sofa in a plain waiting room. Tian Zhi grunted and took a seat. He didn't grab any of the refreshments but sipped on his coffee like Cha Ming did. A few minutes trickled by on the clock affixed to the gray wall in an otherwise sterile building.

A tall, thin man soon entered the room. He wore black robes with silver trim, common colors in the Blackthorn Conglomerate's headquarters. His blond hair was tied back in a tight braid, and he wore small circular spectacles. They weren't there for mundane purposes like improving basic eyesight, however. Within their clear glass lenses, Cha Ming saw churning runes and a torrent of information. *They must enhance his observation and analytical skills,* he thought. *He's probably evaluating me as we speak.*

"Are you sure you would like to give this man access to the vault?" the man said to Tian Zhi. He looked at Cha Ming with narrow eyes filled with suspicion. Cha Ming could practically feel the disguise named Pai Xiao peeling off him.

"He has the proper clearances," Tian Zhi said. "And orders from Director Yong. Moreover, he's contractually obligated to sign everything out and will be punished severely via contract should he try to steal anything. Ideally, however, I'll be coming along with him, mostly to reassure you more than anything else. I know how much you prize your precious vault's contents, Wang Bo."

"My precious vault," Wang Bo said stiffly, pushing his glasses up his nose, "is the culmination of our Wang family's work in these parts. I will lay my life down before I let it be pilfered via negligent oversight."

"Don't worry," Tian Zhi said. "If anything happens, it won't be your head that rolls; it will be mine and the director's."

"Both worth a paltry sum," Wang Bo said flatly. He shook his head and waved Cha Ming over. "Come. We'll need to get you registered in the system."

They walked through a rune-covered metal door. It slid open for them with a wave of Wang Bo's hand, letting them into a long corridor. They walked a few doors down before taking the fifth door to the right, which opened in much the same way. They entered an office, complete with a desk, chairs, and a bookshelf.

"We have no custodians guarding the Ji Kingdom's vault," Wang Bo said, "so we need to rely on more mundane means. Give me your hand."

Cha Ming obliged and proffered the arm that bore his contract mark. He'd been surprised by the durability of the mark—it had even regrown when he'd gotten his skin blasted off during an experiment. Wang Bo touched the mark and moved his finger farther down the wrist. He then took out a paintbrush, which glowed with jade ink.

The ink felt cold and tingly as it landed on Cha Ming's skin. It fused with it and the image of Pai Xiao's body in his mind. The mark was that of three jade bamboo branches, thin and hollow, but strong enough to bear much weight if required. "You get tier three clearance. Good enough for any raw materials, but you'll need a requisition for them. Cash equivalents like liquified elemental essence or spirit stones also require special permission."

"Is that really necessary?" Tian Zhi said. "He can technically request unlimited amounts for his experiments already."

"Which you are responsible for controlling and requisitioning,"

Wang Bo said coolly. "In this case, if he makes off with our family fortune, it will be your head on the line."

"I thought you only cared about the vault's safety," Tian Zhi jibed.

"If you thought that also meant I wasn't attached to my own life, you were mistaken," Wang Bo said. "Well? Would you like to stay for tea and snacks? Or would you perhaps like a guided tour of this complex you've frequented so often?"

"We'll pass," Tian Zhi said. He looked at Cha Ming. "Follow me."

They walked further down the hallway they'd come from, with Tian Zhi leading the way. His heavy footsteps echoed against the stone walls and only stopped once they reached a dull gray metal door. There was a hole in the center, barely wider than a fist.

"You'll have to stick your arm in here," Tian Zhi said, demonstrating for Cha Ming. He made a fist and inserted his left arm into the hole. The hole closed lightly around his arm, as though looking for something, then relaxed. Then the door opened. Cha Ming moved to walk in, but Tian Zhi stopped him. "You'll need to do the same. Only one entry per identification. You do *not* want to see what happens to those who try otherwise."

Cha Ming did as he was told. The doorway closed, its two diagonal parts forming a thin vertical line. The metal, he noticed, was several feet thick and made from a mixture of silbium, cold iron, and xanthium. It also bore traces of life-leaching gold. It would be difficult for even Cha Ming to cut through it, assuming he tried to do so wielding only a peak-core treasure.

He stuck his left arm into the hole, which closed around it. To his surprise, he felt a small stab against his skin and a slight numbing sensation. Simultaneously, light traveled the length of his arm until it found his mark. When it did, the prickling faded, and the door released him. He caught a glimpse of the retracting mechanism as the door opened.

There are needles of life-leaching iron worked into the door, he thought. *If unauthorized personnel tried to do what I did, they would die before they knew what hit them.* A body cultivator like him

– 311 –

wouldn't be so easy to dispatch, of course. He was sure he'd last at least ten seconds.

After passing through the first door, he saw a second one. This one opened automatically. It was as strong as the one before, and if the runic patterns running through the walls were any indication, it was linked to the other door. More likely than not, it had a fail-close mechanism. If the door before it was damaged, it would slam shut to buy time for the conglomerate's security forces to arrive. It also served a good second layer of defense against explosions.

"Well?" Tian Zhi said, holding his hands up to the shelves around him. "What do you think?"

Cha Ming looked around the room, his mouth agape. It wasn't the wealth contained within that amazed him but the sheer size of the place. The inside of the storage room was ten times larger than it seemed on the outside.

"A spatial expansion formation," Cha Ming said, tracing the runic lines on the walls and floor of the chamber. "Displays like these make me wish my affinities were different." His proficiency with five elements, though admirable, was still lacking in certain aspects. Illusions were one of those things. They came to him with great difficulty, despite his access to water qi and Huxian's light and shadow qi. Time acceleration and freezing were nearly impossible for him, even with Huxian's preliminary mastery over time essence.

Space was also difficult. Through light and shadow, he could imitate some things like linking points in space or bridging spatial tears. Things like spatial expansion and the crafting of spatial treasures were mostly left to people with a rare affinity to space. It was these people with mastery over spatial qi who could draw those esoteric formations that expanded and contracted reality. They were the ones who crafted storage treasures, big and small, and chambers such as these.

"It's a work of art, that's for certain," Tian Zhi said. "Though I can't say it's the best vault I've seen. There's a vault farther north at our main headquarters that's much more impressive. It even has a custodian—a construct that obeys verbal commands and can even make decisions and keep track of the vault's contents."

"Farther north," Cha Ming said, frowning. "I can't recall any other major cities farther north. Unless you mean…" His eyes widened, and Tian Zhi grinned. "You've been north of the border? You've been to the place we're trying to get to?"

"You were bound to find out sooner or later," Tian Zhi said, picking up a small brick of red metal off one of the heavy metal shelves. It was purified flameweave steel, a great metal for forging thin swords. Though good for physical weapons, it was terrible for conducting flames. "Truth be told, I was born there. So was Director Yong and Wang Bo."

Cha Ming gulped. His surprise was genuine—he'd expected only Wang Yong and Wang Bo to be from Gold Leaf City. "You mean you ran away from paradise? To join the South? Why?"

Tian Zhi shrugged. "What's there to be surprised about? Life is hard, and it's difficult to get ahead. Some things are just more profitable than others. And besides, the South's going to win anyway. I'd rather be down here before the wall falls and even help push it down rather than try to hold it up. It's an unfair world, lad, as I'm sure you know."

"Yes, yes, I do," Cha Ming said, his expression solemn. "And the others? He Yin? Pan Su? Shao Qiang?"

Tian Zhi laughed. "What, you think it's easy to get people South of that dreaded wall? If it was, do you think we'd spend so much time trying to break it down?"

"I suppose not," Cha Ming said. Still, he felt less guilty about his mission as he began looking through the many shelves, the many metals, and the many compounds. If Tian Zhi and Director Yong had betrayed the North, he didn't much care what happened to them as a consequence of his actions. That meant he only had to figure something out for the other three.

"This crystal flower, what's it called?" Cha Ming asked, tapping on a shelf at eye level. It was covered in a clear case, and the flames dancing about its oxygen-deprived confines were entrancing.

"It's called crystal dragon grass," Tian Zhi said. "We've had our eye on it for a while. Can you tell why?"

Cha Ming carefully removed the cover. The heat around him rose instantly, and he was forced to use both his qi and soul force to push the containment back around it. "Explosive power," Cha Ming said. "Even without alchemical processing." His eyes brightened. "I wonder what would happen if we alloyed it with some more combustible metals." He stroked his chin thoughtfully.

"You madman," Tian Zhi muttered. "Well, at least one of us needs to be mad. Take it for your experiments if you wish. I'll mark it down."

Cha Ming stowed it away, protective case and all. He looked past most of the objects on the shelf, as they were either mundane or not high quality enough to be workable. Whenever he saw something interesting, however, he paused to evaluate it. He didn't take everything, of course, as that would arouse suspicion. Instead, he usually said he'd think on it and left it there for another time.

It took several hours for them to survey the entire storage room. Though he wasn't allowed to take weapons, Tian Zhi took him around to where they were stored anyway. Cha Ming obliged him and even spent a good deal of time admiring the craftsmanship he saw.

"A good blade," he said, nicking his finger on one of the swords. The golden blade drank his blood and glowed slightly pink. "Life Drinker. What an accurate name."

"The amount of life-leaching gold that went into it was backbreaking," Tian Zhi said. "Then no one wanted to buy it, because those blood masters are either too broke or too cheap. We bring it out for auction on occasion, in case anyone wants it."

"And that?" Cha Ming asked, pointing to a familiar spear. It was black and covered in powerful white runes. The weapon was completely beyond him to craft. Still, he couldn't help but wonder where he'd seen it before.

"That's a different matter," Tian Zhi said, shaking his head. "It's said to be the spear of the Lucky Marshal, Feng Ming, in the North.

Given the misfortune that accompanies it and its wielders, I'm not sure I believe it. Seems to be more unlucky than anything else."

"Maybe it's unlucky to his enemies," Cha Ming said, nodding. *No wonder it seemed familiar.*

"At first, we were going to give it to Grand Vizier Zhou as a gift," Tian Zhi said. "But then we decided to give him something different. We're giving this one to the Ji royal family to increase the kingdom's morale."

"What could possibly be worth more than an enemy leader's transcendent treasure?" Cha Ming asked. He trembled inwardly. There was only one thing he could think of that fit the bill.

"Hmm..." Tian Zhi said. "Come here, let me show you something."

Cha Ming followed the older researcher to the back of the room. They passed the few materials he hadn't yet seen, each one more expensive than the last. He realized, Tian Zhi had likely kept this place for last. It was better to let him experiment with cheaper materials first and proceed to pricier ones as time progressed.

Tian Zhi didn't give Cha Ming time to inspect those materials. Instead, he led him to a mostly empty shelf in the back. There, on a pedestal and inside a clear case, was a golden globe, its core filled with a viscous liquid that shone brighter than the sun.

There it is, Cha Ming thought. *Gold Essence Core and Gold Source Marrow.* It was the last piece of the puzzle, the one thing he needed to transcend as a body cultivator, assuming the Seventy-Two Transformations Technique didn't let him down.

"It looks impressive, but I don't know what you can use it for," Tian Zhi said. "Perhaps a power core?"

"It might be useful to fuel a sharp weapon," Cha Ming suggested. "Perhaps even the Breaker." If all it took was one failed experiment to cover up the theft, he would happily take the blame.

"Bah," Tian Zhi said. "That'd be a waste. Especially considering Grand Vizier Zhou alerted everyone in the South to keep an eye out for it. He wants it for some reason, and the reward he's posted is higher than what he's paying for the Breaker."

"And you're going to give it to him?" Cha Ming asked incredulously. It seemed like a pretty terrible business move. This was the Wang family headquarters, after all.

"Coal in the winter is worth its weight in gold," Tian Zhi said. "It follows then that the surprise acquisition of a valuable treasure is worth so much more to a man who's recently suffered a devastating loss. This reward was posted two years ago, when Grand Vizier Zhou was at the peak of his power. But recently, I've heard rumors that a ploy involving Haijing and Beihai City has completely collapsed. Grand Vizier Zhou came back heavily wounded and in a terrible mood. He's put a lot of pressure on everyone to succeed."

He tapped on the black case. "This gem here is either for insurance if we screw up, or frosting on the cake if we succeed. If we fail in developing the Breaker, we might be able to assuage his rage by gifting him this gem. And if we succeed, well…" His eyes glittered. "Let's just say we'll be so favored we'll never want for anything ever again."

Cha Ming licked his lips, only partially feigning greed. Though he was deep in enemy territory, should he choose to, he could steal the Gold Source Marrow right here and now. There was little anyone could do to stop him. He could even rob the Wang family's vault while he was at it before fleeing. He thought better of it, however. While doing so would further his own personal goals, they would destroy his chances of incriminating the Wang family. He'd ruin them, of course, but ruining was far from pitting them against the South. Especially since they'd committed so many resources toward ingratiating themselves with the enemy.

"I think I have enough to work with for today," Cha Ming said. "There are a lot of expensive materials here, but there's no point in biting off more than I can chew. At least, not until we bring the Breaker to the peak of core grade."

"You're thinking you might be able to use some of these to boost it to half-step transcendence?" Tian Zhi asked.

"It's the only way," Cha Ming said solemnly. "In my experience, the right treasure, in the right circumstances, overdrawing itself in the process, can destroy a treasure up to two or three grades higher than itself. Any more than that, and it's almost impossible. If we're to stand any chance at breaking Southhaven Wall, a half-step-transcendent treasure is what it'll take. Even then, it might not succeed."

"It had better work," Tian Zhi said, his jaw stiffening. "Otherwise we'll all be held responsible for the result."

"I can build many things, Boss Tian," Cha Ming said. "Many of them even seem impossible. But they were never impossible, only dreams that no one had dared have yet. Miracles are fairy tales for the weak-hearted." He looked to the Gold Source Marrow. "At least you have insurance. That will save some of you, I'm sure." He had little doubt that this protection didn't extend to himself.

Someone had to take the blame, after all.

"Why do you keep coming here?" Shao Qiang asked from across the table. Their tight-knit research group was taking a well-deserved break after a few intense days of progress. The contemplative man picked up a strange piece of purple broccoli and gave it a careful bite. "The food here is nutritious, sure, but it's barely magic grade. It doesn't get rave reviews either. You could always try many of the other vegetarian restaurants if that's what you want."

Cha Ming shrugged. "When it comes to food, I'm a creature of habit. I keep eating at the same place until I'm sick of it." He grabbed one of the purple broccolis and stuffed it into his mouth. It was both crunchy and spicy, a strange flavor for a vegetable. "They've yet to disappoint me so badly."

He would never confess the truth, of course. Coming here was just a pretense for supervising the now-thriving shop across the street. Both the shop and workshop had gained several employees since he'd left. Mo Ling had made excellent use of her skills. She was succeeding.

Her belly was well rounded now, which was no surprise given that she was seven months pregnant. Despite this, however, she'd spurned most outside help. Something in Southern culture, or the Ji Kingdom's culture, he noticed, had wanted her to give up on the child early in the pregnancy. She had refused, which had driven a wedge between her and several of her first friends here.

Now, most people simply spoke behind her back. She ignored them and kept close company with a couple she'd befriended several blocks down the road. They helped her with more difficult things in this late term of her pregnancy. Those in her workshop were also very helpful.

"Well, there's no changing this place, I guess," He Yin said. "Next time, you'd better ask us first. We'll settle on a good place together. And it better have meat."

Cha Ming smiled. "Sure, sure. Though I warn you, I tend to go years without changing places."

He Yin scoffed. "What are years to cultivators like us? I'm two hundred myself. I'll wait."

"Two hundred?" Pan Su scoffed. "Usually it's women who lie about their age. There's no way you're less than two hundred and fifty."

In her defense, He Yin did look middle aged. Then again, he also had a timeless look in his eyes, a youthfulness that couldn't be banished. It was very possible that he just aged quicker than most, despite his cultivation.

"I'm pretty sure I'm the youngest here," Cha Ming said, stretching himself out comfortably.

"But you look old, because you broke through so late," Pan Su said, sniffing.

"You might look young, but you like to coop yourself up while you research," Shao Qiang said with a light chuckle. "You're essentially a curmudgeon, an honorary member of our retirement home."

"To old age, and wonderful company," Cha Ming said, holding

up his cup of wine. The three others cheered and drank. *How am I going to deal with these three?* he thought. *They're not like Tian Zhi or Director Yong. They didn't betray the North. They're just researchers trying to make a living.*

That being said, how was he going to instigate the Spirit Temple and the Wang family in the first place? Sparking a fight between them and the Ji royal family would be easy. All it would take was a disastrously unsuccessful trial with many casualties. But when it came to the Spirit Temple, he couldn't infiltrate them or even see many of their members. If they wanted to run away from him, he'd have no chance at catching them. More to the point, they'd see the truth behind his infiltration in the blink of an eye if he did anything brash.

I suppose I could just kill a bunch of them. Or destroy their temple, he thought. Though they would know who was behind it almost immediately, the Blackthorn Conglomerate would be responsible for at least *some* of the damage.

And then there was the matter of the prince's transmission jade and the golden stamp. The first could be interpreted as a "get out of jail free" card, if it wasn't for the golden stamp. The mystical golden device was something he hadn't known existed. It behaved much like the previous talisman Wang Jun had given him to obscure a great deal of karma. Instead of being generic in its application, however, this Royal Seal of Notwithstanding, as it was called, was specifically crafted to dissolve terms of Spirit Temple contracts. Even high-level employment contracts like Cha Ming's could easily be dissolved by the single-use item.

The combination of the two items was effectively an invitation. Done right, Pai Xiao could take what he knew and take it to the royal family, should the Blackthorn Conglomerate prove a disappointment. This naïve invitation could now be used as one more plot point in the play he was orchestrating.

"Don't you agree?" Pan Su said, yanking Cha Ming from his thoughts. He looked at her blankly. "Even if I'm slightly his senior, at least I'm not as grumpy as he is, right?"

Cha Ming chuckled. "Right you are. And the most amazing part is that, at his age, he hasn't learned the most important lesson of all: that ladies are always right."

Pan Su and Shao Qiang burst out laughing, and even a few customers eavesdropping on their conversation joined in their laughter.

"Youngsters," He Yin muttered under his breath. He lifted his hand to ask for the check and paid for their table. As per their tradition, the one who wanted to leave first had to pay. That had him paying for the bill half the time. It had become a game for them, seeing who could get under whose skin fastest.

If only it wouldn't end. If only he didn't have to leave it all behind. If only there wasn't a war to be fought.

The imperfections of life and the twisted tangle of obligations in this world made everything resemble a tangled knot of gray. He knew which side he was on, but it didn't make him feel better about what needed to be done.

If you don't ruin Zhou Li's plan, Cha Ming thought, *and if you don't sow chaos in the South, they'll hit the North that much harder.*

Telling himself that same story over and over didn't make it any easier.

Chapter 29
Change

I wonder what inspired her to make snacks like these," Hong Xin said, picking up a small white ball from a plate on the table. She bit into the soft but sticky dough of the ball, whose surface was covered in a dusting of something light gold. As she got to the center, a red paste gushed out of the soft dessert, filling her mouth with a gritty but sweet surprise.

In front of her, Ji Bingxue was inspecting her own dessert, spinning it and pinching it as if to test its limitations. The two of them hadn't spent much time together lately, a situation she was looking to remedy. Whereas before, the tall beautiful woman was one of her closest confidants, she now seemed almost uncomfortable sitting beside her.

"She just misses home, I think," Ji Bingxue said, taking a bite. "She's from the Quicksilver Empire, and snacks like these are popular there. She doesn't talk about it, but she must have been the daughter of a baker. I myself was a weaver's daughter. My talents have nothing to do with where I was raised. I just took an interest in singing at an early age. My mother encouraged it while we weaved, as it didn't interfere with our work and helped us pass the time."

"I see," Hong Xin said, taking a sip of tea from the cup beside the desserts. "I didn't discover dance until much later in life."

"But you dance so well," Ji Bingxue said in surprise. "Surely you received lessons in your childhood."

"No," Hong Xin said. "My father was a guard captain. All he wanted for his children was for them to become cultivators, so they could have a good life and help support the family. At least, that's what he wanted for my second brother. My first brother couldn't cultivate, so my father encouraged him to do business.

"It wasn't until I ran away from home that I started dancing. Terrible things happened to me, and I ran until I had nowhere else to run to. I even spent some time farming with an older couple with no children of their own just to hide from trouble." A little redness came to her eyes. "It wasn't till life finally started looking a little bit brighter that I started dancing. It helped keep a fire going in my heart, a small spark that grew slowly but surely."

"And Headmistress Yinyue?" Ji Bingxue asked.

"She found me as I was recovering," Hong Xin said. "She helped me channel those feelings, helped me use them to inspire others. I followed her when she left, and she taught me on the way to the Red Dust Pavilion. The rest is history."

She moved her teacup to her lips and noticed it had grown cold. A wisp of fire qi remedied the situation, and she did so for Ji Bingxue's cup as well.

"My mother wanted me to have a better life than she did," Ji Bingxue said. "I'd spent some time at a local cultivation academy, but all they did was teach us to kill and maim. A lady deserved a peaceful life, she told me.

"Her dying wish was for me to go to the Red Dust Pavilion, where she'd heard women could have a good future. I pray her spirit never discovers the result. I'd wager I have more blood on my hands now, directly or indirectly, than I ever would have as an adventurer or guard."

That was a common feature all of them shared. They came from different backgrounds with different inspirations, but none of them had been prepared for the horror and brutality they'd endured at the hands of their teachers. The process had left them so scarred that even their weekly visits to the Icy Heart Pavilion left them shivering, despite the relative tameness of their training methods.

"Bai Ling seems busy these days," Hong Xin said. "I hardly ever get a chance to talk to her."

"Is that out of necessity or choice?" Ji Bingxue asked. The question was a slap in the face. As headmistress, Hong Xin could make time for anyone.

"Perhaps it's out of choice," Hong Xin admitted. "Every time we talk about things, we argue." She wasn't sure whether the arguments stemmed from the mask of strength she wore or from her own character. The intimidating façade kept many of the others in line.

The nature of their arguments related to their direction now that the matters with the Spirit Temple had been handled. Their business was going well, they were training new members at record speeds, and their relationship with the Icy Heart Pavilion was smoothing out. They were even cooperating on some ventures.

Unfortunately, Bai Ling and Hong Xin disagreed on one key thing: what to do with those initial members of the Red Dust Pavilion they'd enslaved. What was surprising about their discussions was that Hong Xin found herself being the callous and unforgiving one, the block of ice being chipped away little by little by Bai Ling's sharp arguments. The ice had grown so thin that she didn't dare encounter her too often, lest it soften her resolve.

"She's right, you know," Ji Bingxue said softly. Hong Xin looked to her eyes, which were now averted.

"You too?" Hong Xin asked, pained. The last thing she'd expected from the typically demure and agreeable Ji Bingxue was confrontation.

"Tell me, Headmistress," Ji Bingxue said, looking back up and straight in her eyes. "Should a man with a knife, a disagreeable man, be imprisoned and enslaved?"

"I hardly see how that pertains to our situation," Hong Xin said, a trace of irritation appearing in her voice. She suppressed it. A headmistress should be calm and hard as a sheet of ice.

"Then perhaps you'll entertain a story?" Ji Bingxue said. "Since arguments seem to only further reinforce your armor? I've been told I'm quite the storyteller."

"You're going to try to use kindling arts to make your point?" Hong Xin asked, bemused.

"No, I'll just tell you a normal story," Ji Bingxue said. "No kindling arts, no qi. I've found that stories often help us find ourselves, as through them we can ignore our predispositions and slip into a certain mindset we wouldn't otherwise consider."

"All right," Hong Xin said, pursing her lips. "I'm listening."

Ji Bingxue smiled. "Then I'll start with our main character, a man named Li Pin. He was a fortunate man. Though his family was poor, and though he wasn't a cultivator, he managed to get into a prestigious school. He was hardworking, you see, and quite bright. He had a mind for academics, so he got in on a scholarship. There, he learned all sorts of wondrous things. Wondrous but terrible things."

"Terrible?" Hong Xin asked, surprised at her own interruption. Ji Bingxue seemed to have expected it, however.

"Terrible," Ji Bingxue repeated. "For who but terrible men would seek to profit at the expense of others? Who but terrible men would seek to understand history, the weapons of politicians and nobles, who manipulate others on a whim?"

"That makes absolutely no sense," Hong Xin said, her suppressed irritation returning.

"Then wait till you hear what happens next," Ji Bingxue said. "For you will discover what made it so terrible. You see, he went to school with men who grew to be very powerful. Three of them became absolute terrors in the business world. Even mighty cultivators, those with the most right to rule, couldn't help but bow and scrape before them."

"A cultivator hardly has the right to rule," Hong Xin pointed out.

"But according to their culture, this was so," Ji Bingxue said. "For every king who led the country was a cultivator, and every titled nobleman was a cultivator, and most successful businesspeople were cultivators. But those who went to this school were not; the school didn't accept cultivators, you see, for they wouldn't be of the right mindset for generating profit. They wouldn't know the base intricacies of finance and the sufferings of the many."

"What a terrible thing," Hong Xin said. "Knowledge of the lower class, with which one could get along in life. To be honest, I'm surprised this Li Pin's family name isn't Wang. It sounds like a story their family would use."

"Perhaps," Ji Bingxue said. She poured another cup of tea for Hong Xin, heating it as she poured. "It might surprise you then, that as prestigious as the school was, only a few of their members actually became very successful. Most became normal business owners, who still had to bow and scrape to local cultivators. It was their lot in life, and they did the best they could. Li Pin became a restaurant owner. He even took turns cooking in the back, as they were always short-staffed and on a tight budget.

"Unbeknownst to him, however, great powers were waging a war. Those three powerful business owners decided to usurp the throne and depose the cultivators. The war raged on, unbeknownst to the masses. Li Pin knew nothing of it. Many years passed, and finally, through the loss of many lives, the king and his men finally slew those three sly businessmen, and the guards they had hired, at great expense. In their resentment, they passed laws limiting education for non-cultivators. This was to prevent them from ever outgrowing their station."

"A clear overreaction," Hong Xin said. "Though their paranoia is understandable."

"Yes, it is," Ji Bingxue said. "So understandable, in fact, that everyone who went to such schools as Li Pin became an object of public criticism. Li Pin lost his business, and soon he was forced to sell himself into slavery."

"Just like that?" Hong Xin asked, frowning. "This story, it's not treating the main character very well."

"Yes, I suppose it isn't," Ji Bingxue replied. "He eventually worked off his slave debt, but when he finally got the funds to get ahead in life, the government knocked him down. It happened three times before he finally managed to appear in front of a magistrate. In that time and place, magistrates were also cultivators.

"He asked the magistrate: 'Why must I be pushed down so hard every time I try to rise? I'm not even a cultivator. I can barely strangle a chicken, while others as young as sixteen can break walls and dam rivers. Why can I not succeed in life?'

"'Those who succeeded before you caused great suffering,' the magister scoffed. 'Therefore, we must keep you down where you belong, forever obedient and yet forever useful.' Li Pin couldn't help but laugh out loud at the declaration, and for his mockery of the magistrate, he was put in jail. There, he spent his days raving like a madman.

"'Men run around with spears, slaying innocents all around them, while honest cooks with dull knives are condemned as threats to peace. The world is ending. The world is ending.' He died a year later, never stopping his ravings."

"Your story is very strange," Hong Xin said, frowning as she looked at Ji Bingxue. "You've told me an awkward story with a confusing conclusion. It's full of contradictions. Some cultivators might have decided on this course of action, but must all men be silly?"

"Life is strange that way," Ji Bingxue said. "People believe what they want to believe, despite the many contradictions all around them. Men cling to disproved religions, but others refuse to believe miracles before their very eyes. Men spout lies like the truth they believe from the bottom of their hearts. Traditions are sacrosanct, while values are thrown to the wayside. Then, these same traditions are done away with at the slightest inconvenience, traded for something of poorer value than what was tossed away in the first place."

Truth be told, the story made little sense to Hong Xin. Still, if only for her friendship with Ji Bingxue, she relaxed her mind and tried to break down any barriers she had to the story. Knowing how and when to control your emotions, after all, was what she'd learned here. If she could dissect what Ji Bingxue was trying to communicate, she might at least be able to understand what the other woman was trying to convey, even if she didn't agree with it.

Her thoughts were interrupted by a knock on the door. "Come in," Hong Xin yelled a little too loudly. A trainee mistress opened the door looking frightened. "Well? Out with it."

"Mistress Bai Ling asks that both Headmistress Hong and Mistress Ji Bingxue make their way to the first private room," the woman said, looking down as she spoke.

Hong Xin and Ji Bingxue exchanged troubled glances. Usually Bai Ling would come see them personally. Furthermore, the first private room was reserved for their most important guests. Had someone powerful arrived who they needed to greet immediately? She could hardly think of who it could be.

"Thank you for informing us," Hong Xin said. She and Ji Bingxue left their cups and strode out the door, leaving the intimidated junior behind. *Just what are they teaching these girls?* Hong Xin thought. She'd have thought they'd be more mentally resilient than this. They rounded several corridors and entered a room where four of their guards stood at attention. They opened the door for them.

Hong Xin and Ji Bingxue walked in, and to their surprise, they saw no important personage or powerful person. Instead, they saw a woman in blue seated at the table. Bai Ling and Mistress Huang sat beside her. Bai Ling was inspecting the woman with her limited healing abilities with a frown on her face, and Mistress Huang looked pensive.

"Leave us," she told the guards, who nodded and closed the door behind them.

"What might be the problem?" Hong Xin asked, taking a seat.

"She came here asking to join our pavilion," Bai Ling said. "She wishes to break away from the Icy Heart Pavilion. She refused to speak until you came."

"Oh?" Hong Xin asked. "Whatever for?"

They'd never been approached by any of the pavilion's members before. After all, women there kept icy hearts and cool minds. They were cold, calculative. They did nothing without a reason.

"I am known as Mistress Mi," the woman said.

Truth, Hong Xin thought out of habit.

"I've come here because I fear for my life."

Also truth.

"And would you not be safer among your people?" Mistress Huang asked. "Would they not have more incentive to protect you than we, of a different faction, would?"

"I do not know," Mistress Mi said. "All I know is that I am not safe there."

Truth.

"What made you decide to come here?" Bai Ling asked.

"I decided myself," Mistress Mi answered.

Truth.

"Might I take over the questioning?" Hong Xin asked.

Bai Ling nodded. Though Bai Ling was an effective tactician and a bright mind, she didn't have command over others' emotions like Hong Xin did.

"Tell me," she said, looking back to Mistress Mi. "Was there an event that made you decide to come here?"

"Yes," Mistress Mi said.

Truth.

"What happened?" Hong Xin asked. She used her power of kindling to motivate her to speak and used dousing to calm her fears.

"I am hesitant to speak much of it," Mistress Mi said.

Truth. Though Hong Xin could tell she was dancing around in circles.

"Were you threatened?" Hong Xin probed.

"No," Mistress Mi affirmed.

Truth.

"You were attacked?" Hong Xin asked.

Mistress Mi nodded slowly, her impassive mask melting ever so slightly. "It was a spectral assassin," she whispered.

Truth. Fear.

"I and three sisters were able to fight him off, though barely."

Truth.

"I came here because I heard the Red Dust Pavilion is safe from

Spectral Assassins. That you take in women like us."

Truth.

"Spectral Assassins," Mistress Huang muttered. "Why is it always those Spectral Assassins?"

"We were wondering why their activities had quieted down," Bai Ling said, tapping her fingers on the table. "Maybe it had something to do with the Icy Heart Pavilion?"

"Are you aware of any wrongdoing that the Icy Heart Pavilion may have committed that would cause the Spectral Assassins to attack you?" Hong Xin asked, carefully wording her question. She would probe further based on how evasive the answer was.

"I am unaware of any such things," Mistress Mi said, much more clearly than expected. "I have neither participated in such acts, nor have I ever done business with the Spirit Temple. I have never broken a law, though I may have bent some less important rules. I have never slaughtered innocents."

"All of these things are true," Hong Xin said. She looked to Bai Ling. "What do you think?"

Bai Ling shrugged. "I say we take her in. If she's telling the truth, and Spectral Assassins are after her, she won't last a night on her own."

"I am willing to swear your oaths of obedience," Mistress Mi said, bowing her head. She shivered visibly.

Both Ji Bingxue and Bai Ling looked to Hong Xin, awaiting her answer. Mistress Huang simply averted her eyes. She always followed Hong Xin's lead regardless of the situation.

Hong Xin took a deep breath. Perhaps Bai Ling was right. Perhaps she was judging these women too harshly. They just had tools, but that didn't mean they had to use them to inflict suffering on others. The original mistresses they'd captured in their old school had deserved their fate, and the others had been captured out of necessity. But was there a need to do so here? Wouldn't that make her no better than the headmistress before her?

"That won't be necessary," Hong Xin said finally. "I can taste the truth of your words. Though be warned—we will perform a full background check to verify your claims."

Mistress Mi relaxed visibly at these words. "Thank you," she said, bowing deeply."

Hong Xin accepted the bow awkwardly, though she could swear she saw a hint of a smile on Bai Ling's face.

"Mistress Huang, Ji Bingxue, why don't you go see that Mistress Mi is settled in and aware of our rules and regulations?" Hong Xin asked.

The two women nodded and escorted the blue-robed woman out of the room, leaving Hong Xin and Bai Ling alone.

"I thought all those women were cold psychopaths who needed to be locked up?" Bai Ling said. "What changed?"

Hong Xin shook her head. "I don't know. Let's not have this conversation. Not here and now."

"Fair enough," Bai Ling said. She looked distracted, the way she often did when she played *Angels and Devils*. There was also a lot less bite to her than Hong Xin normally saw.

"Well?" Hong Xin asked. "Out with it."

"I'm concerned about this business with Spectral Assassins," Bai Ling said. "It's worth looking into. I've heard whispers lately about such things, but not related to the Icy Heart Pavilion."

"Then I'll be counting on you to look into it," Hong Xin said. "If there's more to the Icy Heart Pavilion than meets the eye, we need to know."

"Yes," Bai Ling said. "I'll do just that."

Hong Xin frowned. "Are you sure there's nothing else that's wrong?"

Bai Ling shook her head and stood up. She walked over to the door, then hesitated and turned back to face Hong Xin. "Tell me you had nothing to do with this," Bai Ling said abruptly.

"Wait, what?" Hong Xin asked. Where was this coming from? "Of course not. How could this have anything to do with me?"

Bai Ling looked at her for a moment that seemed to stretch on endlessly. Then, seeing nothing, she looked away. "I'll be letting Ji

Bingxue take care of some of my duties," Bai Ling said. "She needs to pull more of her weight while I'm looking into this. I'd suggest you make better use of her time as well and teach her a few things."

"All right..." Hong Xin said. "I'll teach her more, but you need to tell me what's going on."

"In time," Bai Ling said. "I need more information for now. When I get it, we'll sit down and talk about it. For now, it's only speculation." She walked out of the room, leaving Hong Xin alone.

Just what is going on? Hong Xin thought. First Ji Bingxue. Then the trainee's fright. And now this? She shook her head and pushed it all to the back of her mind. She'd let Bai Ling worry about that. There was a ton of work on her desk waiting to be done. Maybe she could ask Ji Bingxue to help out, she thought as she walked back to her chambers.

Yes, a little bit of help would go a long way.

"Young master?" Elder Bai said, walking up beside Wang Jun as he stared out the window. "Is everything all right?" The white-haired old man seemed especially weary today; the bags beneath his eyes were a deeper color than normal, and his wrinkles more pronounced than usual. His clothes were also slightly wrinkled, something the prim and proper man would never have allowed in the past.

Wang Jun took in a breath of fresh air and breathed out slowly. "Everything is fine," he lied. They'd been having a meeting, and Wang Jun had felt a twinge of panic. He'd jumped to the window, looking out toward the city with suspicion. He still didn't know what had gotten into him.

These days, he saw things in the shadows he'd never known existed. The more abilities he learned, however, the more he grew suspicious. Were others doing what he was doing as well? Could other people manipulate as he did? And if they could, were they sabotaging him without his knowledge? These days, it certainly seemed that way.

There was a soft knock on the door. Wang Jun closed his eyes and didn't look toward it. "Come in, Patriarch," he said.

The door opened, revealing the green-robed Wang Wuling. No one else accompanied him. "Please continue your meeting elsewhere. It seems the Patriarch would like to have a word with me." Wang Bing and Elder Bai didn't hesitate to pick up their things and scramble out of the room.

Wang Jun didn't bother pouring tea for the man, and the man didn't expect any. He simply continued staring out the window.

The Patriarch joined him. "Is it you who's been doing this?" Patriarch Wuling asked softly. He let the question hang there, without context or setting. Like many things, it was likely a test, or a trap set for Wang Jun to walk into.

"I'm not sure what you're talking about," Wang Jun said, looking to the side.

The Patriarch, despite being several centuries old, didn't seem to have aged in the slightest. His blond hair didn't contain the slightest hint of white, and his face bore no wrinkles.

"The blackmails, the underground dealings," Patriarch Wuling said. "The murders, the turmoil in the underground. I know you were complicit in the Spirit Temple's fight with the Red Dust Pavilion, but for what reason, I am uncertain. Perhaps you exchanged favors? I can understand that. We all fight for benefits in this imperfect world."

"I don't have anything to do with them," Wang Jun said. "Not that you'll believe me. What I do and don't do doesn't seem to matter."

"In this case, it *does* matter," Patriarch Wuling said, almost in a growl. Wang Jun gave him a surprised look. The man rarely lost his temper. "The family is losing significant amounts of money, mostly through lost clients."

"And has it ever occurred to you," Wang Jun said, "that it could be mismanagement? That the man you thought was perfect for the job is nothing more than an incompetent fool?"

"Perhaps," Patriarch Wuling said. "But given that you're a disciple of *that man*, the alternative seems more plausible."

"Ah," Wang Jun said. "Then something else should have occurred to you."

"And what's that?" Patriarch Wuling said.

"If I'd wanted to destroy our family or cripple its finances, I could have done so many times," Wang Jun said. "I could have exposed Wang Ling's dealings to the Church of Justice. Even now, I still could. Or did you think I gave you the actual recording orb?"

Patriarch Wuling's eyes narrowed, but Wang Jun continued. "I could have handed damning information from my audits directly to the king's men. There are many ways I could've implicated this family. And if I did, who would blame me? And if they tried to catch me, would they be able to? No, you need to understand that these things aren't my fault; they are your own fault, and the one you chose. The moment you accept this, everything else will fall into place."

Patriarch Wuling remained silent for a moment, as though mulling over whether or not to say something. "I see," he finally said, walking away from the window.

"Is that all?" Wang Jun asked, surprised at how quickly the discussion had gone. He'd expected anger or bickering, or perhaps some level of defensiveness.

"That's all," Patriarch Wuling said. "I hardened myself to these things many years ago. Nothing comes as much of a surprise to me anymore. But know this: If you're guilty of these things, I'll make sure everyone you hold dear suffers greatly." The door closed behind him, leaving Wang Jun alone in his dimly lit office.

Something about their exchange, short as it was, had been disappointing. It seemed like the Patriarch was close to breaking. All he'd had to do was blackmail, frame, and murder to get there. The finish line was finally in sprinting distance. Further, he was flush with plundered cash and stolen goods, forming a good underground asset base he could use in a pinch.

Victory was near at hand, but something was gnawing at him. He knew that the end justified the means, but the means couldn't help but haunt his nightmares and dreams. In the corner of his eye, he caught a flicker of shadows.

"Come out," Wang Jun said. "What did you see?"

The shadow, his *own* shadow, hopped out into the open room. It landed where his shadow would have been if he had one anymore; shadows didn't cast one of their own.

Images filled his mind. Observations, of course. Useful information the shadow had spied on from its own world of dark light. Wang Jun sifted through the images, looking for something. There was someone out there, doing much the same thing as he'd been doing. It was stealing like he'd been stealing. Killing like he'd been killing.

The strange killings had him worried. They hadn't hurt his goals. In fact, most had even benefited him somehow. Further, his own black market had been the one flooded with pilfered merchandise from the copycat's victims. What bothered him, however, was that these killings were outside of his control. Who knew when the copycat would step out of line, or even commit a crime that implicated him?

"Keep an eye out and let me know if you see anyone else doing the things I've been doing," Wang Jun said after finishing his viewing. "That aside, do as you see fit." The shadow nodded. It gave a mock salute and jumped back into a dark corner of the room.

"What reliable things, these shadow clones," Wang Jun mumbled. It was a pity he couldn't have more than one, for now. It wasn't smart, but it knew how to get things done. He was now better informed than he'd ever been. "If only everyone else was so reliable."

Elder Bai and Wang Bing were all right, of course, but cloning oneself had its advantages. For one, it would think in much the same way as him. For another, it would never betray his interests, unlike those poisonous snakes he called family. Those would have killed him long ago if not for his master's tutelage.

He shook his head. That line of thought was dangerous. As a leader, he had to trust those who reported to him. So he packed his things and made his way toward Elder Bai's office. Some people might slack off, but the old man never would. His tenacity and devotion were one of the few things that kept Wang Jun going. It was a light warding away the darkness that was slowly claiming his soul.

Chapter 30
Land of Time Forgotten

Why does it have to be so hot here? Huxian thought as he ran across the barren plane. The landscape didn't resemble the cracked clay near the city, nor the flat rock near the plateau and the monks. Here, the flat land was covered in dusty earth in much need of rain. Fortunately, there was more than a light dusting of the substance, else his paws would slip due to the greasy and intrusive nature of it; it was packed six feet deep, more than enough to bear his weight.

The dust, though annoying, didn't matter much in the grand scheme of things. What mattered was its source: the blistering sun and its scorching red light. It never seemed to grow closer, but it *did* grow larger. What had started off as big as a large coin was now the size of a mountain. It loomed over him, singeing his fur and evaporating his drool. His eyes were red, both from exhaustion and the lack of humidity.

A few months ago, even a week's worth of walking would have barely increased the sun's size by a sliver. Now he saw its size visibly increase after only an hour of running. He could also feel a soft humming presence from the sun. It wasn't the usual pulsing you'd expect, but rather a burst of heat frozen in time. That same heat that burned his fur and seared his flesh. If not for the ample demonic qi in the air to replenish his stores, he would have become a roast dish weeks ago, a delicacy that even heavenly emperors would fight over.

Thank the heavens I don't have to worry about sun blindness, he thought. Apparently it was a problem for humans and some lesser species of demons. Somehow, demonic evolution had determined that such an immunity was essential to their development. Greater demons like him could stare at the sun all day long, as long as they could bear the pain.

After traveling for a half hour more, Huxian finally noticed something that wasn't a massive sun or a dusty plain. A figure in white appeared along the horizon. Having not seen a living thing in months, he ran toward what ended up being a diminutive man in white robes. The man had black hair tied up in a topknot. He was clearly a scholar, but he was young and had an air of naïve curiosity. Most importantly, he was neither ghost nor buddha. He was a human.

Hello! Huxian called out to the man. To his relief, the man looked back in surprise. He smiled and waved at the fox. Unlike his fur, the man's robes were pristine, untouched by the dust beneath them. He couldn't have been more than twenty years old, and his cultivation realm was at the peak of qi condensation. Huxian wondered how the man could possibly be standing here unharmed where the sun was so hot, but he remembered that many things here didn't make sense. Everything was twisted and mystical, like a deep lesson prepared by a senior for a junior.

"Greetings, fellow traveler," the man said, waving. "I am Yang Mu, a scholar of minor repute. What might I call you, esteemed monarch of the demon realms?"

I am Huxian, Monarch of Light and Darkness, Huxian said, quite pleased at the man's respectful tone. He was, after all, an important demon on the plane he came from. *What are you doing here, so close to the sun? It's dangerous in these parts, especially for one so weak. The heat will burn you burn your body and destroy your soul.*

"Dangerous?" the man asked, perplexed. "Not at all. I've just begun my journey, so how could I possibly be feeling the heat?" Indeed, his robes were still pristine despite all the dust around him. His skin was pale and unblemished. He looked less an adult and more a child, unaccustomed to the hard ways of the world.

And what do you hope to find on this journey? Huxian asked.

"The origin of the sun," the man said proudly. "My master once told me that to grow as a scholar, one must journey thousands of miles and see many things. He cautioned me, however, against focusing on the many. Instead, he said to focus on the one, the origin of all things." He held his hand up to the sun. "To me, his meaning is obvious: I should chase the sun, the origin of everything. If I find the origin, will I not be able to see the many from the one, the multitude from the origin? Will I not see the Dao?"

Huh, Huxian said. *I suppose I never thought about it that way.* Inwardly, he was groaning. The kid would learn a swift lesson in humility. If cultivation was such a simple journey, would there not be heavenly emperors aplenty? As far as Huxian knew, his journey wasn't just foolish; it was dangerous. Immortals, gods, and demons alike pursued the peripheries as they deepened their understanding. The truth of the origin was so powerful, so all-encompassing, that it could shatter the mind and burn the soul. Even the Jade Emperor was only just beginning to comprehend its immensity.

You might want to be careful on your journey, Huxian said. *To my knowledge, this path is dangerous and forbidden. Countless have died walking it, and none have ever succeeded.*

The scholar smiled and bowed. "Many thanks for your advice, Huxian, Monarch of Light and Darkness. My heart is set on the matter, however. There is no deterring me."

He turned toward the sun and began walking. Dust immediately began to stain his immaculate robes, and the heat suddenly came bearing down on the man. He cried out in agony after only a few steps, then crashed down on his knees.

Huxian shook his head. The man's fate was even more pitiful than he'd predicted. He very much wanted to help the man and treat his wounds, but he wasn't the Monarch of Healing and Mercy. Scholar Yang would need to find his own way. It would likely take years for him to recover from the trauma, assuming he survived. And judging by the damage to the man's meridians, he would never be able to cultivate again. He would live a scarred and painful existence, unless he chose the obvious way out and ended it.

Seeing nothing more to do, Huxian continued walking. He walked for a few hours, and in that time, the sun doubled in size. The horizon now seemed like a precipice, an obstacle he could pass before seeing the sun in all its fullness instead of the tease the red half sun had been all this time.

Soon enough, Huxian saw what appeared to be a small black spike in the distance. No, not a spike. It was moving. He ran over toward the object and quickly realized that it wasn't an object but a person. A man. The miniature man grew larger and larger until Huxian could finally make out a set of tattered gray robes that barely hung to his body.

Despite his damaged robes, the man seemed hale and hearty. His skin was a lustrous bronze, and his hair was well kept. It was tied in a familiar scholarly style.

It's him! Huxian realized. He trotted over to the man, who looked over and smiled.

"Huxian, Monarch of Light and Darkness," the man said, bowing deeply. "It is good to see you again. You have my thanks for watching over me all those years ago."

All those years ago? Huxian wondered. It had been nothing more than a few hours. Still, the more he looked at the man, the more he realized that it wasn't just his skin that had changed. The man seemed closer to forty years in age, and his cultivation realm had increased. The meridians that had burned away and the qi pools that had been destroyed had somehow regrown. What's more, they had undergone a revolutionary transformation: The man's qi weaved throughout his body like lines of light. He'd also reached the peak of foundation establishment. His foundation burned hot like the blazing sun up ahead. The burning qi coursed through his body, tempering it with each circulation. He'd somehow reached the peak of bone forging as well.

Scholar Yang, it seems I was mistaken, Huxian said. *Your path has taken you far. You've recovered from your initial trauma, and your cultivation has improved by leaps and bounds. It is good that you ignored my warning.*

The man smiled wistfully but shook his head. "No, I should have heeded your words. That day, I nearly died. I would have died had it not been for divine intervention."

Divine intervention? Huxian asked. *A god came down to bless and heal you?* Such cases weren't exactly common, but they weren't unheard of either.

"Less a god and more a demon," Scholar Yang said. "He told me the path I walked was forbidden, and that I should give up on it."

Which you clearly did not, Huxian pointed out.

"That is correct, I did not," Scholar Yang said. "Therefore, the mighty demon both blessed and cursed me. 'I will grant you the power and the truth you seek,' he said, 'but the journey will be endless and ephemeral. It will be a journey walked for others, and the end will be your demise.' The moment he spoke these words, the power of the sun coursed through my veins. I knew that I could easily take his blessing and leave, but my folly continued." He shook his head. "Though I'm not obligated to keep going, my curiosity will not let me stop."

"Do you wish to have some company?" Huxian asked, curious to see what happened to the man as he walked.

The man shook his head. "My progress is slow, and I dare not hold you back. Perhaps it would be best if you visited again when I've made sufficient progress."

"Very well," Huxian said. "If we're fated, we'll certainly meet again."

The man bowed, and Huxian continued.

The sun grew larger as Huxian ran. Every hour, it doubled in size, straining the limits of his perception. Its scorching powers doubled alongside it, and to Huxian's surprise, it both burned and protected him. The sun was not there to punish, but to teach. It burned a lesson into his flesh as it seared his soul.

Ten times, a hundred times. The more it grew, the more Huxian could make out infinitesimal details in the sun's brightness. Before, it all seemed a uniformly bright spot on the horizon, but now he could see roiling flames and seething, swirling pools of bright plasma. Darker spots appeared on the sun that should have been too blinding to perceive. It resembled less the single light in the sky at day and more the moon in a dimly lit sky, with sunken craters and rigid scars marring its imperfect surface.

And in front of that sun, in front of all this detail, sat a lonely figure. His clothes had finally burned away, as had his bronzed skin. His hair, which had been neatly tied all this time, was ash white. It crumbled to dust, joining the contaminants piled on the ground, still six feet high. They swirled around him, enveloping him, offering to become one with him.

Huxian walked up beside the man. They were now only six feet away from a cliff that finally gave way, revealing the full splendor of the sun. Nigh-invisible chains were wrapped around it, preventing it from moving an inch.

"So, was it worth it?" Huxian asked Scholar Yang, whose face was contorted in pain. His face was crumbling, just like his hair had been, and not a single inch of his skin was unmarred. His eyebrows were gone, as were the small hairs on his arms. Yet to Huxian's surprise, he continued to stare straight ahead. It was as though the burning was a painful yet pleasant agony, like the touch of a lover teasing him ever so slightly, preventing him from ever fully concentrating, frustrating him with every moment.

"I was too close…" the man croaked, his voice barely a whisper. He sputtered dust as he did, making Huxian wonder whether he should continue the conversation or put the man out of his misery.

"Too close to the sun?" Huxian asked.

The man nodded, and more skin crumbled off at his neck. "But you chased the sun all this time. You became stronger for it, discovering more of its beauty. Didn't the sun benefit you?"

The man chuckled painfully. Given his condition, it sounded like nothing more than a death rattle. "Yes, I discovered the sun's beauty. And I found strength in it. But as I unearthed this strength,

I discovered a glimpse of the sun's true nature, and the reason my journey had to end bitterly."

"Which was?" Huxian asked.

Instead of answering, the man blinked a few times, gathering his thoughts. He licked his dusty lips, sputtering out ashes that formed on his tongue in the process. "The sun rises, and the sun sets," the man said finally. "That is the true nature of the sun. One cannot constantly bask in its presence. There is a rise, and there is a fall. There is a summoning, and there is a banishing. Can you not see it, out there in the piercing light?"

Huxian looked out into the sun, and on cue, a slightly brighter spot appeared directly at the center. It grew brighter and brighter but did not grow in size. Then, to Huxian's surprise, it *left* the sun. It darted toward him like a bolt of lightning, and he barely had time to see the piece of broken jade before it smashed into his forehead, rushing straight into his eyes like before. This time, however, he felt searing pain.

His inner iris, filled with Devil-Sealing Intent, was still of a vivid jade coloring. His outer iris, a deep purple ring filled with Demon-Subduing Intent, was slowly but steadily pushed toward the center as the soft golden ring from before finally solidified. It snapped into place, and the moment it did, he knew its name.

The Spirit-Banishing Scripture, Huxian thought. *The sun that rises must fall; the spirit born must leave; offenders to the natural order are banished with unfettered ease.*

With the mnemonic came the knowledge of several new abilities. The first one was the power to see all spirits. It wasn't an all-powerful ability, but it could pierce many cultivation realms, making it so nothing on the mortal plane he normally resided on could evade his detection. The second ability was much like the one shared by his two previous eye techniques: Spirit-Banishing Intent. The more spirits banished or destroyed, the greater the intent. It could, in turn, be used to banish spirits.

The third ability, however, took the cake. Spirits weren't just a problem because of their nigh invisibility but because of their transparency. Only strong yang energies could effectively damage them. The Spirit-Banishing Scripture not only gave the user the ability to see spirits but the ability to interact with them. Their physical and other attacks would be imbued with Spirit-Banishing Intent, which would, in turn, allowed them to touch, hold, and otherwise damage the ethereal beings with ease.

"My mission is complete," Scholar Yang said from beside him. His body began to crumble more rapidly, and chunks of flesh and bones were now falling off in puffs of dust. Even his bones were chipping away. "The sun that rises must fall."

After these last words, the rest of his body gave out as his soul left him. It was forcefully banished by the powerful sun into the Yellow River. As his soul left, Huxian finally saw tiny karmic tethers that had bound him to the sun. It was these tethers that had allowed Huxian to see the man's journey.

The way forward is clear, Huxian thought out loud. *The sun that rises must fall. To do that, it needs to be unchained.* He could now see the writhing mass of karmic threads holding the ball of light in place. They led back both to the city and to the Buddhist temple from before. Energized, he rushed off, away from the sun, its scorching heat increasing his speed. Time blurred around him as he made his way toward the Buddhist temple. After all, the city was his starting point. For any decently poetic ending, its souls would need to be freed last.

His only worry now was the pain. Since gaining the third eye technique, he felt an unreasonable amount of strain in his eyes. The mere thought of even activating the technique to see and banish spirits sent shivers down his spine. Though *he* could probably handle the inevitable backlash from the technique, Cha Ming most certainly could not. He was, after all, only human.

More to the point, Huxian was a decently selfish demon. He could choose not to use these eyes and could lock them away for all eternity. Cha Ming, on the other hand, would never do such a thing. These eyes were a tool with a purpose. Given enough reason, he would use them.

Chapter 31
Justification

Cha Ming let out a bloodcurdling scream as he collapsed to one knee, his project forgotten. He Yin, who'd been working beside him, used his lightning fast reflexes to catch falling reagents with his soul force, preventing the laboratory from erupting in a symphony of destructive energies. This all went unnoticed to Cha Ming, however, as he clutched his forehead. Multiple streaks of blood ran out of each of his eyes from beneath his hands.

Relax, Cha Ming thought to himself. *Accept the pain. Be one with the pain.* As a body cultivator, he'd experienced the destruction and regrowth of his body many times over. He'd had hands blown apart by shards of metal, and the entire surface of his body burned three layers deep. He'd even broken every single bone in his body. But that was nothing compared to the agony was feeling now.

He took deep, ragged breaths as he determined the root of the problem. Spirit-Banishing Scripture? Spirit-Banishing Intent? The ability to see and touch spirits? What in the seven hells had Huxian done? Their link and their ability to communicate had grown thin of late, to the point that they couldn't converse. Only limited access to demonic qi was still available to him, which likely meant the same applied to Huxian.

This isn't a bad thing, Cha Ming thought, using rationality to numb the pain. *This is what I needed. If I can see and interact with spirits, I'll be able to deal with the Spirit Temple. It makes incriminating the Wang family much easier.*

The pain in his eyes finally reduced to a soft, dull pain. He summoned a mirror from a cupboard in their lab and looked into his eyes. Bloody mess aside, there were now three rings in his eyes. One wide jade ring surrounded his pupil. It was in turn surrounded by a violet ring, and finally, a golden ring. Compared to the other times he'd activated the technique, the rings were dull and inactive. Yet when he moved to retract them, or even hide them with his Seventy-Two Transformations Technique, they didn't budge.

What does it mean? Cha Ming thought. He could feel that no Devil-Sealing or Demon-Subduing Intent was leaking out, which meant the technique wasn't technically active. However, as he stared at his hand, he could see a faint jade glow, a mere shadow of what he could usually see with the technique turned on. Looking up at He Yin, he saw that the alchemist had a much thinner glow surrounding his skin, a hint of merit compared to the ocean he himself had harvested.

"Pai Xiao?" He Yin asked again. "Are you all right?" The middle-aged man scratched his short black hair. His laboratory coat, usually immaculate, had gotten stained in whatever Cha Ming had splashed when he'd collapsed. Blood and a mysterious yellow gore, perhaps?

"It seems I've unknowingly broken through in an eye technique I practice," Cha Ming said, standing up. Though he'd wanted to hide his eye techniques, there was no way he could do it now, especially given how much time he had to work with. He summoned flames to burn away the blood on his face and used the power inherent in his laboratory garments to clean them.

"That must be a killer technique if it makes you react like that," He Yin grumbled, wiping the sweat off his brow. Due to the dangerous nature of the alchemical ingredients they'd been working with, half the building could have disappeared if things had gone even a little more wrong. "Is it useful in crafting?"

Seeing an opening for a few more scientific breakthroughs, Cha Ming grinned. "As a matter of fact, it is. It's especially good in detecting energy pathways and runic lines." It was a blatant lie, but it would enable him to reveal a few more of his abilities. If he could blame it on his eye technique, a sudden increase in his already impressive runic knowledge would be acceptable.

"Great," He Yin said. "That's great. With our moved-up deadline, I didn't know what we'd do." Two months had passed since his return, and the half-year deadline they'd been given had been shrunk even further down to four months. Only two months remained.

"I think I have some ideas," Cha Ming said. "Let's try them." He moved up to the bench where the remnants of their experiment lay.

"Are you sure you want to continue?" He Yin said. "Why don't you take a rest?"

"Body cultivators don't need rest," Cha Ming said, focusing on the tiny cauldron of bubbling red metal. Well, not pure metal. Within the strange blend of several metals was the refined essence of the crystal dragon grass he'd discovered in the vault. In front of it lay a sheet of a golden material that didn't melt so much as spontaneously combust once it got hot enough. He'd already cut a runic pattern into it with his spiritual carving knife.

After looking at the metal plate again, which was connected to ten different energy drain points that ran to an energy sink through devices that measured energy output, he took out his knife again.

"These lines aren't deep enough," Cha Ming muttered, cutting deeper into the soft golden metal. He then slashed the metal at other key points, cutting different runes that complemented his original design.

"That's a lot of extra runic lines," He Yin said. "Are you sure they're useful?" For an alchemist, he had a surprising grasp over runic arts. He wasn't a grandmaster, but he had a basic working understanding.

"Let's give it a try," Cha Ming said, cheerfully grasping the small golden cauldron containing the bubbling red mixture. He poured it into the grooves on the plate, letting the red concoction seep into every crack and solidify almost instantly. He didn't spread it evenly, but in a way that the resulting red lines would be flush with the golden plate.

"Now, for the moment of truth," He Yin said, rubbing his hands. "If we succeed, we'll have created a solid-state energy generator."

"A *single-use* solid-state energy generator," Cha Ming noted. "With a limited lifespan." He held his hand out. "Would you like to do the honors?"

"Would I?" He Yin said, his eyes twinkling. Seeing Cha Ming's nod, the man poured a concentrated wisp of core qi into a formation in the center of the plate. As the energy poured in, the red runic pattern began to blaze with energy. The initial qi was a spark, and the red pattern was like a pilot light. Through it, the rest of the fuel would burn.

As the plate heated, Cha Ming and He Yin hid behind a blast shield where they could continue observing safely. The red runes heated up until they reached the temperature dictated by the runic pattern. Then, little by little, a number on a small display beside them began to show ten energy readings, one for each of the outputs on the plate.

"I would never have thought you could use a solid to catalyze a reaction with another solid like that," He Yin said as they watched the rapidly climbing number. The power output was in cultivation equivalents. It had already passed initial core formation and was climbing steadily to early core formation.

"It's not about having them react together but having a pathway for energy transfer," Cha Ming said. "Just like any good weapon doesn't have qi directly react with the weapon, this power source uses the heat from the crystal dragon grass to drive the steady spontaneous combustion of the material beside it. The combustion is regulated by the heat output and the contact area dictated by the runic network. As the sacrificial metal shrinks, the formation will act accordingly."

They waited for a few more seconds before, finally, the power output reached peak-core grade. It struggled there for some time before finally reaching half-step-rune-carving intensity. The golden metal bars were glowing bright white behind the blast shield. The reading struggled there for around thirty seconds before finally dropping down. Then, the glow faded, revealing only ashen remnants of the golden plate.

"We did it," He Yin whispered. "Finally we did it. A half-step-core-formation power source."

"Only for thirty seconds," Cha Ming said, shaking his head. "We'll need longer-lasting sources, and a much larger quantity, not to mention a corresponding accumulation and intensifying diagram."

He Yin blinked in silence.

"What I mean is that we have a long way to go, and no time to rest."

"I'll go report the results to Tian Zhi," He Yin said, nodding.

"And I'll make another trip to the vault," Cha Ming said. "This experience has given me a few more ideas to think about."

Cha Ming remained deep in thought as he made his way to the vault. He'd been there so many times by now that he barely had to think at all as he made his way through winding corridors and security checks. He nodded politely to the secretary at the entrance and paused before the quartermaster's door. The older man waved him through casually. Though he probably should have accompanied him, just as he'd done almost religiously for the first three weeks he was allowed access, Cha Ming's seamless paperwork and his return of unused materials had caused that initial mistrust to fade.

The power source is more or less complete, he thought, sticking his arm into the lock contraption. It assessed his access mark and opened, allowing him inside the fortified structure. *Now all that's left is the distribution network and the primary weapon heads.*

The Breaker, in the end, resembled a thick spear. Its tip could pierce a good way into the wall, by virtue of its materials and construction. That part was easy. What really did the damage, however, was the vast number of smaller spearheads that sprung out at angles with intense piercing force. They needed to do this with minimal distance for acceleration, a difficult task even for Cha Ming.

Sometimes he wondered if he should be worried about what he was teaching them. Then again, it would only take a few years for them to regain the knowledge he'd imparted to them. Instead, he'd decided to railroad the entire project down a specific pathway. At the end of the path was a sure way to achieve the mission's goals. The trick was designing the thing so it would perform a very different purpose by the time it was assembled yet have all the pieces function normally, leading up to the product prior to final assembly.

As for reverse engineering it, he was even less concerned. Step by step, he'd made the project increasingly reliant on himself. The power source was a prime example. No one else would know how much strain it placed even on his transcendent soul to stabilize the crystal dragon grass compound. Since this was a confidential research and development project, only Tian Zhi at most would try to replicate it. He was unlikely to succeed for all but the simplest of portions.

Now for the spearheads, Cha Ming thought. He walked around the vault, examining several shelves of metals he could potentially alloy. He looked over metal after metal, figuring out their potential hardness as well as their resistance to heat. They would need to take a tremendous amount of energy over a short period of time, so heat resistance was paramount. As for hardness, he'd determined some time ago that even transcendent-grade walls were built more with toughness and regeneration in mind as opposed to hardness. With hard enough starting materials, it was possible to pierce through the transcendent wall. It was only a matter of how far the projectile would go before either stopping or breaking.

As Cha Ming picked up piece after piece of metal, he simultaneously probed at several formations he'd discreetly placed in the vault. He first checked the one monitoring the quartermaster. As usual, he was keeping a careful but relaxed eye on Cha Ming through his monitors on the other end. After confirming this, Cha Ming probed the various formation eyes for his concealment formation. *Still intact.*

The third and most important check was on something he'd been monitoring since he'd arrived: the Gold Source Marrow. It was still there, and unsurprisingly, no one had checked on it. It still glowed in its transparent case, its power clear for anyone to see. He'd wanted to take it earlier just in case, but the risk had been too great.

Now, however, things were different. Zhou Li had moved up the deadline yet again, and it was likely that he would do so once more. Cha Ming couldn't wait around any longer. So, using his transcendent force and peak-core qi, he activated the concealing formation he'd taken great care to set, one piece at a time, inside the vault. He then took out something from the Clear Sky World—a golden orb, shining brightly with the power of gold, containing a shimmering liquid in the center. It was an imitation, crafted from the very rare and very expensive crystalized gold essence he'd retrieved from the Shattered Lands.

Cha Ming could barely contain his excitement as he opened the transparent case. He reached out for the Gold Essence Core and grabbed it, allowing its primal energies to course through his fingers and rampage through their sensitive flesh. He took it into his Clear Sky World and placed the replacement onto the pedestal.

Then he went back to where the concealment formation had him currently rummaging, superimposed himself, and banished the formation. He picked up a jade-colored metal and grinned. "This should do nicely."

Five minutes later, Cha Ming trotted out from the vault. He walked over to the quartermaster's office and knocked on the door.

"Come in," Wang Bo said.

Cha Ming entered the room and saw the man hunched over and brooding.

"Is something bothering you?" Cha Ming asked, placing a sheet of paper listing what he'd taken from the vault. He then placed a ring on the desk containing some materials he hadn't needed in the end.

"There's always something bothering me," Wang Bo said gruffly. He took the ring and scanned it. He nodded and placed it on a shelf beside him containing other inbound items. "Not everyone is like you, taking only what they need and bringing back what they don't. We've run another deficit this month, unfortunately, and I think a lot of it has to do with senior managers taking liberties."

"Can't you just suspend their vault access?" Cha Ming asked.

"They don't even enter the vault," Wang Bo said. "It's all over and above board. They justify their expenses, and their superiors approve them. Everyone's so worried about Grand Vizier Zhou's inspection these days, so these managers are fishing in troubled waters. I'm sure they'll think up some reason or another they needed funds, and how they managed to squander them, lining their pockets in the process."

"Don't they have contracts in place?" Cha Ming asked, surprised. He recalled his own contract, which was rather strict with regard to embezzlement.

"There are loopholes everywhere, if you know where to look for them," Wang Bo said, raising his hands up in the air. "But who am I to complain? I'm just a lowly quartermaster. I just guard this vault with my life, and the rest is beyond my pay grade."

"It'll all work out in the end," Cha Ming said. He felt a pang of guilt, given that he'd just done exactly what the man was complaining about. He'd done it using an artifact Wang Jun had given him to hide his contractual obligations. He felt even worse for what he would do just before he left. Traitor to the North or not, Wang Bo had come to the South out of loyalty for his family. He was just doing the best he could for those he cared for.

"I sure hope it does," Wang Bo said. "Regardless, I'll be relieved when this pet project of the vizier's is over and done with. Management will finally get some time to pay attention to the bottom line, and we'll get to coast again for a while."

"I'll work hard to make it happen," Cha Ming said.

Wang Bo nodded and looked back down at his documents, leaving Cha Ming to see himself out. As he walked through the vault's corridor, he heard a soft hum.

A message? he thought. He scanned the orb Prince Shen had left him.

Can you come to the Trueblood Tavern to meet me? Prince Shen had sent. There was no context to the message, no additional details to go by.

Cha Ming didn't think twice before replying. *I'll be there in an hour.*

Did you use the item? Prince Shen sent back. He was, of course, referring to the second item he'd given Cha Ming, the Royal Seal of Notwithstanding. The item, a contract override seal, was a rarity even for the Ji royal family. It was a one-time use item that would allow a cultivator to override any Spirit Temple contract without dissolving it. These seals were an important component of the peace agreement between the Spirit Temple and the Ji Kingdom, for it allowed the crown to keep its advantage in any and all contractual negotiations.

I did, Cha Ming answered. He hadn't, but what Wang Jun had given him had worked just as well. He hadn't wanted to waste the dissolution seal so readily, as the ability to ignore almost any Southern contract, even if only once, was invaluable.

Good, Prince Shen replied. *Meet me at the Trueblood Tavern. Alone.*

See you then, Cha Ming replied. He'd thought he'd need to work his way into the prince's good favor. Now, it seemed it was quite the opposite. Though he itched to use the Gold Source Marrow to break through immediately, that could wait until he heard what the prince had to say. Zhou Li was coming, and no one wanted to be caught unprepared.

The crown prince was no exception.

The Trueblood Tavern was a rowdy place. The customers here, mostly foundation-establishment cultivators, gambled, drank, and fought away their hard-earned spirit stones as attractive ladies and men served them drinks, putting in not-so-subtle efforts to sell their other services. Men and women from all corners of the city drank here. It was a clear sign that, regardless of station, you weren't special in this establishment, and you'd better not cause any trouble.

Not too much trouble, at least. As Cha Ming entered, a brawl erupted at the back of the main room. Blood sprinkled through the air as an arm flew up and landed amongst the cheering crowds of spectators. A few strong men in white, bloodstained shirts watched as two bloodied men fought in the middle of a ring of patrons. They constantly looked at the clock, counting away the minutes before they were forced to intervene.

They didn't, in the end. One of the fighters, too maimed to continue, was left an inch away from death. He was dragged away by his companions, leaving a bitter man who clearly wanted to land the finishing blow.

Cha Ming, hidden beneath a black cloak, pushed through the crowd. No maids or attendants came to ask him if he needed help getting a seat. Instead, he proceeded to the private rooms at the back, where he'd already detected the man he was going to meet. The door slid open as he approached, revealing the usually well-dressed man covered from head to toe in black robes and a black cloak. Cha Ming stepped in and closed the door behind him.

"Thank you for coming on such short notice," Prince Shen said, taking down the hood of his cloak. "I realize it's trying on your loyalties to come meet me. And let me be clear up front about this. I am about to ask you to work against your current employer, the Blackthorn Conglomerate."

This was a test, of course. If Cha Ming hadn't used the seal, as part of the "Protection of Client Interests" clause of his contract, he would be forced to immediately leave or face the consequences of his contract.

Cha Ming sat down calmly, his contract well insulated by the shadows surrounding it. He accepted a cup of wine and took a drink—a sign of trust and acceptance of the man's superiority. "If my priorities are between the Ji Kingdom—my birthplace—and the Blackthorn Conglomerate—my employer—I will, of course, choose the former, assuming the damage I cause isn't too great."

"It seems I didn't misjudge you," Prince Shen said, lifting his glass in a toast. "You're a patriot, but you're also a man who values all his relationships. I'll make sure you're well compensated for the trouble."

Cha Ming smiled and didn't reject the man. They both knew how this game of self-interest and feigned loyalty was played. "What might you be needing this lowly one for?" Cha Ming asked.

"Far from lowly," Prince Shen said. "From what I've been told by Director Yong, you're effectively the linchpin and mastermind of the Breaker Project. The project can't be finished on time without you, and you know every bit of the project as well as the back of your hand, all this despite your lack of knowledge in alchemy and general formation arts."

"I've more than dabbled in many things I find interesting," Cha Ming said. "But yes, you're right. I am currently the best informed. You might also want to know that, in secret, I'm also skilled enough to replicate the entire project, alchemical portions and all."

The crown prince's glass paused midway to his mouth. He looked at Cha Ming intensely and lowered the glass to the table, then put both his hands together. "So you're telling me that, should someone with priority over your contract wish for you to replicate the full Breaker prototype, you could do so? Unaided?"

"Yes," Cha Ming answered simply. This way, he could keep the prince dependent on him and keep the others out of his scheme.

"That definitely changes things," the prince said, tapping his fingers on the desk. "We'd thought we'd need to requisition your *entire* crew, but if it's just you, then we need not introduce potential weak points in our plan."

"And what, might I ask, is your plan?" Cha Ming said. "Clearly it's not taking over the project, as you could have already used your royal authority to do that."

"Taking over the project would demoralize the Blackthorn Conglomerate," Prince Shen said. "Plus, they have the backing of the Spirit Temple, so without enough reason, I can't take them over. Their work is important, however. My royal father and I are both responsible for the project, despite our lack of control. If anything should go wrong or should the Blackthorn Conglomerate grow too greedy and try to extort us, we'd have little recourse but to accept. Even at the end of the project, they will be the ones in sole possession of the blueprints and prototype for the Breaker. The knowledge will be in their hands and their hands only, despite our duty to oversee the project. I'm sure you can see how this puts us at a disadvantage."

"Then do you want me to leave the Blackthorn Conglomerate and join you?" Cha Ming asked.

"Seven hells, no," Prince Shen said. At the mention of hells, Cha Ming took note of the faint yellow aura surrounding him. Sinful, but not overly so. "I want you to remain where you are and not reveal your external loyalties. The timeline is more important than anything else. If you should have time, however, I wish for you to record both the construction method and blueprints pertaining to Project Breaker. I also want you to build me a prototype."

"A full prototype," Cha Ming said flatly. "Amount of time aside, the material cost would be astronomical. You'd need to secretly supply me with the requisite materials without alerting the Blackthorn Conglomerate."

"You can't just have them disappear in some sort of experimental mishap?" Prince Shen said, frowning. "A full prototype is required. With it, and the blueprints, we won't be beholden to the Blackthorn Conglomerate should they choose to double-cross us. Their management is, after all, from the North. They're not patriots like we are."

"My reputation is impeccable," Cha Ming said. "If I suddenly started doing something like stealing materials, they'd suspect me. I understand your need for a prototype, but it will need to be built from materials you supply."

"I see," Prince Shen said. "Very well. You'll need to send me a list of what you need. But before we do anything, I'll need you to sign a contract."

"Naturally." Cha Ming said. No one did business in the South without a contract. Such an act was seen both as stupid and suicidal.

The prince placed a sheaf of golden paper on the table, which

Cha Ming read through in detail. Aside from his deliverables, it stated Prince Shen was responsible for materials and discretion on Cha Ming's situation. No one else in the royal family was responsible, which meant that Prince Shen was the fall man in this operation, should anything go disastrously wrong. More likely than not, that was also the case between them and the Blackthorn Conglomerate.

In the end, however, it was all a smokescreen, as both Cha Ming and Prince Shen knew that with another Royal Seal of Notwithstanding, the other side of the agreement could be made meaningless if push came to shove. Nodding, Cha Ming signed the document. A royal contract mark appeared on his skin the moment he did.

"Here you are, Prince Shen," Cha Ming said, handing him sheet of paper listing all the materials he needed and their approximate value. "I'll be needing these as soon as possible."

The prince winced upon seeing it.

"One more thing before you leave," Prince Shen said. "It would be best if the prototype and blueprints for Project Breaker be completed in thirty days."

"That's an awfully tall order to fill," Cha Ming said, frowning. They'd been told just this morning that they had four months. "Is there something I should be aware of?"

Prince Shen hesitated for a moment, then nodded. "It's carefully guarded knowledge, but a threatening creature has been rampaging across the northeastern Ji Kingdom. Thus far, we've had great difficulty stopping it. From what we can tell, it's heading toward the city."

"Won't you stop it well before it gets here?" Cha Ming asked, surprised.

"We're trying, but the creature is difficult to handle," Prince Shen said. "It's possible that it may even reach Bastion. We've requested assistance, of course, but the war is at a critical point. Every transcendent is accounted for, and two of the three grand viziers are completing preparations for the final push, while Grand Vizier Zhou is currently convalescing from his injuries. We don't know when he'll come, but I assure you, when he does come to resolve this problem we're facing, it would be best if we had the results he's looking for."

Cha Ming nodded. "I'll do what I can." Not only did he not want to face Zhou Li, but this creature, whatever it was, provided the perfect smokescreen for his escape.

"Good," Prince Shen said. "Now please, go on ahead. There's someone else I need to meet with."

Cha Ming got up, clasped his hands, and bowed. On his way out, he stepped over the body of a man who'd just passed out from intoxication. A woman was robbing him in broad daylight. He didn't help the man, as helping would have been out of character. Besides, did the man even deserve his help? Both the Trueblood Tavern and the complex relationship between Prince Shen and the Blackthorn Conglomerate were a stark reminder of what mattered in the South: personal interest. There was little loyalty or shared values. Only the strong prevailed.

The end might never fully justify the means, but to save the way of life he cherished and preserve it for half the people on the continent, he was willing to bloody his own hands. Even if much of that blood came from the innocent pawns manipulated by their country and crown.

Chapter 32
Life

Cha Ming summoned an extra layer of defenses when he returned to his chambers. The stone walls, though enchanted and reinforced, were built only to protect the inside from outside intrusion. Their intricate runes could, to some extent, dampen qi emanations from cultivation. But that was in normal situations, and he was about to do so much more. It was time to complete the first half of the Seventy-Two Transformations.

As the formation hummed to life, he summoned a portal into the Clear Sky World. Not only would this further dampen the inevitable power fluctuations, but he could take advantage of the five-fold time acceleration within it. He proceeded directly to the mountaintop, where Sun Wukong was meditating.

"So, you finally got what you came for, did you?" the Monkey King said, peeking through a single open eye from his cross-legged pose.

"That I did," Cha Ming said, sitting beside him. He summoned the Gold Essence Core, which shone with a golden light. The liquid within it writhed upon sensing his presence, perhaps out of desire to join with him, or perhaps out of fear for its inevitable fate. He took out the Clear Sky Brush and touched its top to the golden orb; the thick liquid flowed out of the core and into the brush, lighting up golden runes all over its surface.

Cha Ming began painting. The runic script this time was 1,080 sigils long, each one containing both power and instructions for the transformation. A longer script was required each time in order to balance the various powers already in his marrow. Further, the transformation sigils needed to force their way into an energy-dense medium, a difficult task given how deep Cha Ming's vitality reserves were.

In all, the script took a day to paint. The moment the last rune was completed, the script broke apart, allowing the sigils to crash into his bones, where they intruded on his marrow.

Pain. Cutting pain. Cha Ming felt like his entire body was being sliced with millions of tiny blades. Though only his marrow transformed, it made his bones reverberate and sent shock waves of power through his nervous system. His marrow, which had previously contained four colors—green, blue, red, and brown—now began to show signs of a fifth color: gold. It sprouted from within the gooey substance like tiny metallic flowers, each one bringing stability to the marrow and connecting everything together.

Metal cut. Wood grew. Water flowed. Fire burned. Earth weighed. All five components began to stabilize, and in that stability, Cha Ming's marrow took on additional but predictable colors: black and white. Creation marrow appeared, raw energy that could be shaped for anything. Meanwhile, tiny black specks of destruction marrow appeared everywhere, and instead of destroying everything around it, it coexisted with the remainder of his bones. Gray flecks also began to appear, and while Cha Ming could sense tremendous power from them, he couldn't sense their purpose. They just stood there, taking up space, just like the unusable gray portion of his core that filled the cracks between colored sections.

The transformation continued for a full day, and at the end, the remainder of the golden energy rushed into the voids within his bones. There, it joined the tiny universe that was taking shape. Metal was birthed deep within the earth of the various planets, and within the meteors floating around space. Golden life forms were born. And with the appearance of gold, wood began to diminish.

Agglomerated runic creatures composed of anywhere between one and five elements began to interact with the world around them.

Cha Ming wondered for a moment if they were sentient. He reached out to the void and discovered that no—such a thing wasn't possible for him. Creating sentient life was the realm of the gods. What he'd made, however, was a pale precursor. The void network in his bones contained an imitation universe. It flowed, thrived, raged, resisted, and refined itself, but it was missing a key element: emotion. Sentient beings felt emotion.

Five elements aside, Cha Ming noticed a pool of energy building up in the center of his makeshift universe. White runes of creation and destruction chased each other in a circle at the center, never making contact but always fighting. And in the center of these, where there were spatial distortions aplenty, a single spot of gray appeared.

Who would have thought that by refining his bones, he could produce Grandmist energy as well? After all, this wasn't the transient, misty qi he generated to use Origin Strike. This was stable Grandmist energy, the type he'd used to feed his Clear Sky Brush on Jade Moon Planet. Try as he might, he'd never been able to find any in the mortal world. It was the reason why his Grandmist seals on alchemical pills were one of a kind.

Three days passed by as his transformation continued. When the final change in his void network was completed, Cha Ming's bones began to crackle. His blood, which had been completely replaced during his transformation, now contained a faint ethereal wisp of something familiar: divinity. It wasn't a full drop of divine blood. If it were, he would already be a blood-awakening cultivator. But he knew that, with the slightest effort on his part, he could condense one.

"So powerful," Cha Ming muttered. He flexed his muscles and discovered that the air around him was different somehow. His relationship with it had changed. From the air, even within his Clear Sky Brush, he felt respect.

"By reaching half-step blood awakening, you've obtained a trace of divinity," Sun Wukong said, waking up and stretching out his arms.

He yawned deeply. "A single step more, and you'll become a demigod. Qi cultivators become transcendents, and each transcendent has a domain. Domains represent control, and qi cultivators will gain control over the elements in their surroundings.

"Demigods, on the other hand, gain the respect of their surroundings. Everything around them will fear damaging them and desecrating their bodies. The universe itself will dampen the damage dealt to demigods and protect them, as their presence is holy. They are personifications of the elements themselves.

"As a half-step blood-awakening cultivator, cultivating the Seventy-Two Transformations Technique, you now possess a third of the strength of a full blood-awakening cultivator—333,000 jin!"

"No more threes?" Cha Ming asked.

"No more threes," Sun Wukong said. "Three threes are the peak of perfection in the mortal realms—pushing past that limit will require you to transcend mortal limitations."

Cha Ming nodded. He looked over his body again and became aware of a third ability granted by the Seventy-Two Transformations Technique. The first twelve transformations had improved his talent and allowed him to change his appearance. The next twelve had given him control over his weight, culminating in giving him control over his shape.

These last twelve allowed him to increase his size as he wished through stored vitality. His regeneration had increased drastically. Now, he could regenerate his body from his vitality stores if even a single drop of blood remained. Furthermore, he could now transform to any size as large as a demon of his level, even in human form. He could shrink his size down to an inch in length. Hiding would be much easier from now on.

"With this," Cha Ming said, "there are very few people I now fear on this plane."

"Even transcendents would have trouble dealing with you," Sun Wukong said in approval. "They might be able to generate the same power as you, but the plane loathes their presence and will fight against them. Anyone who wishes to kill you would need to pay a ghastly price to do so."

Cha Ming nodded. He retracted his power until he reached late marrow refining. He lamented in losing the feeling of being special in the eyes of the world. A portal opened beside him, which he stepped through into the stone room filled with protective formations.

Now that he was powerful enough to achieve his goals without a hitch, he had less than a month to tie up any loose ends in his plan. In addition to incriminating the Wang family, he had important duties to attend to. Finishing the Breaker, or something like it, was at the top of his priority list. The crown prince was counting on him, after all.

Weeks passed by in a blur, and Cha Ming, along with the rest of the research and development group, worked with inhuman speed. Ceaseless trial-and-error runework, as well as various attempts at smelting and combining many ores, took place in a very short amount of time.

Fortunately for everyone, they had Shao Qiang. The normally quiet man wasn't very useful aside from performing calculations, his field of expertise. But as a seer, he made use of his talent to predict relative chances of success or failure. With each prototype piece, their team was able to predict its suitability for its given role, whether it be power generation, distribution, or application.

This was especially challenging for Cha Ming, who not only had to work to improve the project, but also sabotage it. Each individual part needed to function as planned, and every combination, save the final assembly, needed to work well together. It was a puzzle, and despite the many years that had passed since his rebirth, he loved every minute of it.

Two weeks in, they reached a critical point in their research. They tested a prototype, which failed miserably. The reason was something not even Cha Ming had anticipated. While each individual piece was fine and well constructed, when assembled, the earth beneath the Breaker was unable to bear the strain of its activation. They puzzled over it for days until Pan Su, of all people, came to the rescue.

The middle-aged woman, who'd grown increasingly unsatisfied at her inability to contribute to the project due to her major in geomancy, had predicted the problem. She had been experimenting for some time over different base materials in case the increasingly large tremors from the Breaker went out of control. By working with He Yin, and with the help of Cha Ming's superior runework, they were able to manufacture three bases, one for each of their working prototypes. The concrete-like substance was inlaid both with metal and runes that absorbed and diffused vibrations. The prototype breakers were affixed to the platforms with rather expensive clamps that both held the large contraption firmly but allowed for removal when required.

"Well, that was an unexpected development," Shao Qiang said, relieved at their successful deployment this time around. The dust was clearing from the fake wall they'd just destroyed. It was weaker than Southhaven Wall, but only by a half step. Unfortunately, the test pieces they had could only be used for their expected final prototype.

"If Pan Su hadn't been here, we'd all be goners," Cha Ming admitted. Even he, with his many talents and masteries, would not be able to replicate her work. "Though look at how she ignores us now that she's finished her work."

"Only two things excite her," He Yin quipped. "Things that can't be destroyed and destroying things. I think she sees it as a challenge. That's what makes her such a good fit for the project."

"And you?" Cha Ming asked.

"Me?" He Yin thought for a moment. "Nothing in particular. To be honest, I'm not the most skilled alchemist out there. I've heard reports that there are at least ten that are better in the South alone."

"Surely there must be something," Cha Ming pressed.

The man hesitated, then edged a little closer.

"I may have accidentally blown up a large facility and upset many people," He Yin whispered. "I needed somewhere to hide, and Boss Tian happened to be interviewing some people at our lab for this same project. He was so impressed by the devastation I caused, and I was so desperate to find backing, that we almost immediately signed a contract, no questions asked."

"I think you might be underplaying the devastation," Shao Qiang said, walking over to them. "A large facility is hardly the same thing as half a city."

"A *small* city," He Yin said, holding his hands up defensively. "Almost a town. I felt really bad about it. Haven't I spent all my wages trying to make amends to their families?"

Shao Qiang grunted but didn't press the issue.

"I guest that leaves three pieces, then," Cha Ming said. "Power distribution, spear shafts, and ball-bearing projectiles."

"I still don't see why we need those," He Yin said. "Those spear tips can break anything even Boss Tian can make, if used with enough force. Not that I'm complaining, of course. Making the explosive mixture that drives them was refreshing to say the least. I love experimenting with my life on the line."

That last part was the primary reason why he was employed, Cha Ming guessed. Nothing was better for research and development than the willingness to risk your own skin for progress.

"Without them, there's not enough devastation," Shao Qiang said. "One doesn't kill a peak-marrow-refining cultivator with a single spear to the chest. It takes a lot more collateral damage to destroy their vitality stores."

"But that's a living thing, not a wall!" He Yin protested.

"A wall with a very large power network and a reserve to draw on," Cha Ming said. "We need to deplete the local reserves faster than they can be restored. Simple fissures aren't enough damage— they'll be healed over in the blink of an eye. A large gap, however, is far more difficult to fix. If the gap is large enough, it might disrupt the wall's healing mechanism entirely."

He Yin shook his head but walked out of the room and back to his laboratory. The past few weeks had been especially taxing on the man. The explosives he'd just mentioned, the ones to propel the ball bearings, were needed in large quantities. This mixture happened to be very unstable, and even someone with Cha Ming's skill would have trouble mass-producing it. All the man could do was spend what little time he had trying to keep up. They didn't dare leak the mixture to the Blackthorn Conglomerate's remaining alchemists, lest their plans be exposed.

"So, what's next, mighty leader?" Pan Su asked, dusting off her hands. Her tablet was gone, as she'd just finished her inspection. Now that she'd finally contributed to the destruction, she was eager to do more.

"I was thinking that we could work on the ball bearings," Cha Ming said. "I have an idea I might need your help with, if you're willing to try." Her eyes brightened at that. "You know how you built runes and structures within the geomantic support structure to diffuse vibrations?"

"Of course," Pan Su said. "It was the key component."

"Could you do the opposite?" Cha Ming asked. "Could you intensify the vibrations?"

"And make the material easier to shatter?" Pan Su asked with a frown. "I could only do it by etching into the earth."

"Fortunately, we happen to be carving up a lot of wall," Cha Ming said wryly. "If we attacked the wall in a pattern that etches those runes, I'd wager that we'd greatly accelerate the destruction. That way, I'd only need to slightly modify the ball bearings. Unfortunately, I don't know the runic patterns required for such structural weakening."

It was a lie, of course—he did know it, but he wouldn't be revealing that anytime soon.

"I think I might know just the thing," Pan Su said. "Are you free right now?"

"Tomorrow morning, six o'clock sharp," Cha Ming said. "I have something to take care of tonight."

Shao Qiang rolled his eyes. "Here we are, working our hearts out, and you're still taking time off for leisure."

"Relaxing is the key to success," Cha Ming replied. "You should try it sometime. I think you'd like it."

"See you tomorrow, then," Pan Su said, sighing in disappointment. The eager look in her eyes and the slight twitching in her fingers indicated that she'd be playing with some ideas regardless of his absence.

"I'll be back shortly," Cha Ming said, nodding to the remaining two as he left the room.

The streets were busy but orderly when he left the Blackthorn Conglomerate. Despite the sun just having set, many people were just returning home from work. Others had already been home but were now out with friends and family enjoying the evening. Despite being filled to the brim with cultivators, the city still obeyed the social conventions of mortals—work during the day and rest at night. Only powerful cultivators like Cha Ming or businesses that catered to cultivators remained open.

Cha Ming felt restless tonight. He wasn't sure why, but it likely had a lot to do with the closed shop he saw before him. The hardworking Mo Ling, it seemed, had finally taken a day off. Which was understandable, given the size of her belly. The smiths were still busy at their forges, as their work was piecemeal, and their wages were based on production rather than attendance. The storefront, however, was pitch black. Both Mo Ling and her sole attendant had left at the same time. For personal reasons, the sign on the front read.

No time to be distracted by her now, Cha Ming thought, though he wondered if there was more to her absence than mere time off. The play he'd been orchestrating, the sabotage of the Wang family, also added to the burden. The destruction and chaos he'd leave behind was sure to affect her. If not for wanting to avoid further incrimination of the girl, he would have whisked her away and put her in hiding somewhere in the North, where Zhou Li couldn't reach her. It was an impossible task if he wanted to maintain his cover.

Cha Ming pushed these worries out of his mind and made his way to a short but squat building nearby. The building didn't stand out, and not many people went inside. Cha Ming entered it and was waved through by a burly man. The place was a tavern. He'd only been here once before as instructed by Senior Zhong, the mysterious man who managed the Greenwind Pavilion on the Ling Nan Plane.

He passed by many drinking guests unnoticed, walking into a back room that was shielded from any and all scrying. He walked up to a circle inscribed on the floor with gray ink, a simple-looking thing with unbelievable effects. He stepped into it… and reappeared several thousand miles away in an entirely different city. The formation had teleported him, and it was something Cha Ming had no idea how to create.

"So, you've finally come to collect your profits," a man said, appearing in the room beside him. It was Senior Zhong, in the flesh. Only VIP customers like Cha Ming would have the opportunity to secretly travel to this remote pavilion to do business.

"It wasn't convenient before," Cha Ming said. "And I wanted to make sure you had sufficient time to auction off the materials. The rates you offered me for the crystalized elemental essence and the other ores were atrocious."

"We all need to turn a profit," Senior Zhong mumbled.

"Indeed," Cha Ming said. "Which is why I waited."

The man grunted and flicked a ring over to Cha Ming. It contained a small fortune, completely converted into spirit stones, liquified elemental essence, and elemental evanescence. He looked through the list sitting atop the large pile and read it line by line. Then, seeing everything was in order, he put the ring away. "Did you look into the matter I inquired about?"

"I did," Senior Zhong said. "I'm afraid I can't help you."

"Immunity purchase?" Cha Ming asked.

"I'm afraid I can't say," Senior Zhong replied.

His silence was all the confirmation Cha Ming needed. He'd

wanted to confirm Director Wang Yong, Tian Zhi, and Wang Bo had indeed come from the Wang family and betrayed the North. With Tian Zhi's admission and Senior Zhong's omission, however, he didn't need confirmation. There was no other reason those three men would need to hide their history so thoroughly.

"The others?" Cha Ming asked.

"Clean Southern people," Senior Zhong said. "Though I don't see why you care so much. Borders are borders, and people hop between them many times throughout their lives. Good people sometimes do bad things, and bad people often do good things."

"It's the principle of it," Cha Ming said. It was also his justification, one he clung to with a white-knuckled grip. After all, by turning against them, he, too, would be a traitor. That thought of betraying their trust churned his stomach, despite all the lives he could save in the process. The future Southern lives that would be lost also weighed on his conscience, despite not yet having died.

All for a peaceful North, thwarting Zhou Li's evil plan, whatever it was, and for repaying a favor. That last one was just an afterthought at this point. It was a convenient excuse to go ahead with this distasteful mission.

"I must ask," Senior Zhong said. "Are you behind it? I'm not one to believe in coincidence, and the fact that that *creature* is approaching so close to your destination is concerning to say the least."

"Creature?" Cha Ming asked. "The one Prince Shen mentioned?"

Huxian had also mentioned it, and so had Sun Wukong. The older man peered into his eyes, boring into him with a soul force that Cha Ming could barely resist. He didn't breach his soul defenses, but the pressure was difficult to bear. "You asked a question, and it's only fair I ask one back."

"Yes, it's the same creature," Senior Zhong said, relenting. "Though by the look in your eyes, you know about it but aren't involved. I should have known. Someone like you wouldn't dare meddle with such destructive forces. Even immortals and gods dare don't dare take this lightly."

"Is there something I need to know?" Cha Ming asked, frowning.

"Nothing is free," Senior Zhong said, holding out his hand. "A thousand top-grade spirit stones."

"A thousand?" Cha Ming exclaimed. "Come now, surely I get a preferred customer discount."

Senior Zhong rolled his eyes. "Nine hundred."

"Five hundred at most," Cha Ming said.

"Eight hundred," Senior Zhong said. "And I'm not going lower. You'll be needing my information if you want to maintain your sorry life."

The warning gave Cha Ming pause. The man might joke sometimes, but he had never lied to him. Not yet. Cha Ming nodded and handed over the required payment.

"There is an ancient creature heading your way called a Taotie," Senior Zhong said. "It was lured all the way from Eastvale Wall by Marshal Feng Ming and Gong Xuandi, the forcefully retired Sea God Emperor. Their whereabouts are unknown, as they seem to be shielding their presence. The creature has caught the scent of Bastion, however, and it grows restless. It will reach the city in five days, and the South is rushing to amass forces to resist and suppress it."

"So whatever I do, it needs to be within five days," Cha Ming muttered.

"I highly recommend that you be out by the time it arrives," Senior Zhong said. "A Taotie is not to be taken lightly. Even I, as powerful as I am, will leave the plane if it continues to grow."

"That big of a threat, huh?" Cha Ming said. "I'd imagine Zhou Li will come to handle it personally?"

"He and his transcendents," Senior Zhong said. "That's not a secret. There are already a dozen in the city, hidden and waiting. A significant portion of the elite forces in the South are here in this city. The righteous faction is fully aware of it, but they'll not meddle as long as the South is bearing the brunt of its attack and suppressing it. In fact, they might even join hands to deal with it if things get too difficult."

"Do you have an estimated time of arrival?" Cha Ming asked.

"Sunset, a very poetic time," Senior Zhong said. "Now, off you go. I don't have much time to waste with youngsters like you."

"Are there really that many cultivators worthy of your attention on this plane?" Cha Ming asked.

"Whoever said anything about dealing with only one plane?" Senior Zhong mused. "I might be here in person, but dealing with small fries like you is just a wonderful convenience, nothing more. But I do it all in the hopes that I meet a Heavenly Emperor in the making." He gave Cha Ming a meaningful look, then gestured back toward the portal.

Cha Ming sighed and walked back to the simple gray circle, marveling at the formation. He took a step inside it, and the restlessness returned.

The first thing Cha Ming heard was a scream. It was from a voice he recognized, in a place not far away. He scanned the city, looking for where it might be coming from. His transcendent force slipped past the Spirit Temple's wards and spies, searching tens of thousands per minute.

Fifteen minutes later, he found her. His body was a blur, flying through the skies much higher than most cultivators had a right to. Many thought to shout at him but thought better of it when they noticed his speed. He soon arrived before a building, and when he realized what was happening, he concealed his presence and retracted his soul force.

Cha Ming opened the door to the building, shutting it behind him without a sound. He walked up the steps, taking care not to disturb those in the room upstairs. Due to his high cultivation and soul force, he was invisible to them. Their eyes looked over him but found no purchase on his body.

There were two people on the floor, two women, one of them a stranger. The one he knew was gasping in pain. He hadn't known what was happening when he heard her scream, but now he understood the sense of crisis when he'd left the Blackthorn Conglomerate. Mo Ling was lying in a bed, panting. A midwife stood beside her, encouraging her. During his absence, Mo Ling had gone into labor. Her child was coming.

Mo Ling's face, which had gained a bit of weight despite her hardworking nature, was red and contorted. She might be a cultivator, but no woman was immune to such a primal pain. Bringing a new life into this world was a struggle with death itself. Even the strong Mo Ling, who'd persevered despite the odds against her, despite the unlucky hand she'd been dealt, was now at her weakest. It was also the time where she was needed most, for another life depended on her.

She struggled, and as she did, Cha Ming could only watch in both amazement and anticipation. Mo Ling was the one he cared about most in all the South. If things had been a little different, and they were both safe and sound in the North, he'd have acted more like a close uncle than the distant observer he was forced to be now. In his eyes, his nephew was being born; he'd cheated and checked the gender. He was eager to finally see the young boy in person.

Cha Ming had never personally witnessed a childbirth, despite his expansive spiritual sense and the many opportunities to do so. It would have easy to peek in on a stranger, but every time, he'd shied away. There was an indecency to such spying, and delivering a baby was something more personal than spying at someone's unclothed appearance.

She labored, and despite his anticipation, he also felt great anxiety for her. Cha Ming had been through his fair share of struggles. He'd been crippled, enslaved, crippled again, and healed again. He'd fought tooth and nail to fight his way to the top, and his body had been destroyed over a hundred times in the process, assuming you added all the destroyed body parts together. Yet all these struggles at the precipice of life and death seemed like nothing compared to this single act of bravery—the choice to bear a child into this world. It was a selfless decision, a decision that brought great costs and only intangible gains. The baby was the beneficiary, but the woman bore the risk of it all.

Her panting intensified, and the screams as she pushed out the child grew increasingly labored. The midwife encouraged her, and at one point, she called up a third person to come help them. It was Mo Ling's shop assistant, who'd taken the day off to see her through this special day. In Mo Ling's eyes, the shop was all for her son. It was for him that she worked herself to the bone. It was for his future that she clawed her way up from poverty into the middle class, always striving, never satisfied.

As the pushing continued, Cha Ming thought of the many sights he'd seen in the South. He'd seen suffering, yes, but also happiness. There was an entire underclass of serfs, which he'd seen both up close and at a distance. Despite their lot in life, despite the grueling work they put in every day, every group of serfs would still take time to celebrate in their own way.

Many families would share bread for a birthday. They would hold a meager feast of millet porridge for a newborn child. They would even celebrate when those dear to them passed away. It was not a celebration of their death but of the life they'd lived.

Suddenly, a cry rang out in the room. It was a weak, needy cry. A new life suddenly breathed its first breath. The newborn baby was quickly wrapped in a towel and thrust into Mo Ling's outstretched arms. She both smiled and cried as she held her tiny child, and at that moment, Cha Ming smiled and cried with her.

"*This* is life," he thought out loud. Life wasn't about prosperity or growth. It wasn't about opulence or possession. It wasn't about happiness or sadness. It was about struggle. Struggling every day to make things better, to find the happiness in every situation. It was about putting aside your strife for a single moment of peace, about putting down your axe for that moment of rest before continuing your labor.

It was about love. That single moment you'd been waiting for, struggling for, that one person you wanted to dedicate your entire life to. He or she might not even appreciate you for it, but you'd do it anyway, if just for the satisfaction at seeing those happy moments in their lives as they, too, began their personal struggle. Words came to Cha Ming's lips unbidden.

Living life to its fullest potential;
Never questioning his struggle.

Life wasn't about succeeding; it was about doing the best you could with what you had. It was about trudging on despite the odds against you. Some people had it easy; they were born in a life with everything, but in the end, did they truly live? Someone with nothing might be happier than a man with unlimited wealth. It was the struggle, the pain, that gave context to the many wonders in every day life.

Cha Ming was about to walk forward, but he hesitated. *No,* he thought. *I can't involve myself with her. Not after all she's sacrificed.* He shook his head and turned around, leaving the building unnoticed. He was a ghost here, a phantom. A strange intruder in their imperfect life. He was also their protector, but his duty was finished; he wasn't needed any longer.

Cha Ming didn't return to his work once he got back but secluded himself in his chambers. He took out the Clear Sky Brush and began painting out the words he'd spoken earlier. A Living Talisman was completed a short while later, a peak-core-formation talisman with properties he didn't fully understand. Unlike his other poetic talismans, he could go no further than peak-core grade. His understanding of life was too shallow, and he suspected that insight on death would be required to go any further.

Chapter 33
Complications

Tick. Tick. Tick.

The clock on Hong Xin's office wall counted away the seconds as she waited for the inevitable morning visit. The fresh night air that was just now being pushed out by the rising sun clung to low-lying areas with tenacity. One of these areas was conveniently located close to a trapdoor. It was open, allowing the cool air to enter, while hot air escaped out of a similar door near the ceiling. Such a primitive device wasn't necessary, as she had formations controlling the temperature in her room. But something about the freshness of the outdoors appealed to her, so she had kept the device instead of replacing it.

Knuckles rapped softly on the office door. "Enter," Hong Xin said.

To her surprise, it wasn't only Ji Bingxue that entered, but Bai Ling and Mistress Huang as well. "How bad?" she asked, dreading the answer. The question hung in the air while two of them took seats. Bai Ling sat directly in front of Hong Xin, with Ji Bingxue to her side. Mistress Huang stood apart from them, closer to Hong Xin. They'd had another disagreement, it seemed.

"Only one this time," Bai Ling said.

That was a relief, though the potential identity of the victim was troubling.

"Someone important, then?" Hong Xin asked.

"Very," Bai Ling replied. She leaned in closer and looked her in the eyes. "Do you swear that you know nothing about what's going on and who's doing this? Do you swear that Wang Jun isn't behind this?"

"Like I told you," Hong Xin said steadily, "I can't speak directly for him. We aren't joined at the hip. I swear on my mother's name that I know nothing about who is doing this or their reasoning. I also asked Wang Jun, and he swore to me that he isn't behind this, and he knows nothing about it either. I happen to trust him, but that's all I know."

The question from before still hung in the air. The longer it took for Bai Ling to answer it, the more her dread intensified.

"It was the headmistress of the Icy Heart Pavilion, Headmistress Lan," Bai Ling said finally. "It was the straw that broke the camel's back. Before, we only had a trickle of members that wanted to join us. Now, the only remaining vice headmistress, Vice Head Ling Fei, has agreed to your request for a merger. The Icy Heart Pavilion would abandon their current headquarters and move here. We would need to promise to protect them."

Hong Xin frowned. She'd wanted nothing more than their merger, that final check and balance on their dangerous powers. But now, after several months, the opposing faction barely had two thirds of their members left. Their most powerful members had been assassinated, including their headmistress. All that was left were trainees and the less competent.

"One has to wonder how the assassin selected his targets," Bai Ling said, as though reading Hong Xin's mind. "He started with a few normal members, but then he proceeded to assassinate two vice heads, then the headmistress. The only remaining vice head was the one most amenable to a merger. They didn't target randomly—rather, they only targeted individuals with dubious records and stubborn opposition to our proposal."

"It seems orchestrated to unite us," Hong Xin said flatly. "Don't worry, I fully understand how suspicious this seems. I take it there are… other requirements?"

"Yes," Bai Ling admitted. "Two requirements. Ling Fei has made it quite clear that she'd rather die than join without them."

"And without her, their faction will have no leadership," Hong Xin said. "They'll be broken, their spirits in tatters. They'll see themselves as dregs, remnants not worthy of attention or representation."

"Many would likely disperse," Bai Ling agreed. "Rather than join us, they would go their separate ways, hoping they wouldn't be targeted. She is the only one who can get them to join us in one group. And having them under our wing is the only way we can enforce a code of conduct on these women."

Hong Xing closed her eyes. "What conditions?" she asked, already knowing the answer.

"One is acceptable, the other is not," Mistress Huang cut in. "It's preposterous that she demands it."

"We had a discussion earlier," Bai Ling said. "Ji Bingxue agrees that this is necessary. As do I. You disagree, so we can only ask the headmistress for a decision."

"Rightly so," Mistress Huang said. "Though I have half a mind to kill this Ling Fei myself."

"Peace, Mistress Huang," Hong Xin said. "Tell me, Bai Ling. Just get it over with. I can't bear it any longer.

"The first condition is to destroy the Oath Stone," Bai Ling said.

"Done," Hong Xin replied. She summoned the blue orb, which seemed to beat with an icy energy that resonated with their cultivation. Each one of them dual cultivated kindling and dousing, and though they weren't affected by the stone's powers, they still had the same root. She then summoned a second device—a single golden needle.

"I had this commissioned by the Church of Justice. Oath-binding devices are tricky, and destroying them even more so. If not done properly, there could be backlash to every person who has ever sworn upon it."

She swept her hand, and the needle flew up. She poured the entirety of her cultivation into it. Raging fire and calming ice poured out from her core, through her qi pathways, and into the needle, which glowed brighter and brighter. She also infused her soul force into it. The peak resplendent force added a sparkle to the needle. Bright white glyphs lit up on it and resonated with karma-purifying light.

Infusion complete, Hong Xin was overwhelmed with exhaustion. Bai Ling moved to help her, but she held up her hand. "This is my responsibility. I will see it through, regardless of the second condition. We've already made plans to ensure the behavior of the more problematic individuals."

Bai Ling nodded. Hong Xin held the stone firmly in one hand, then stabbed down with the golden needle. It pierced the center of the orb, shattering it completely. In that instant, thousands of tiny threads appeared around it. These blue threads of icy karma were remnants of oaths once sworn. They flickered, then one by one, they unraveled. They disintegrated, starting from the point nearest the Oath Stone. Hong Xin herself felt warmth surge through her as her own oaths, which no longer bound her, dissolved into nothingness.

"All the sisters who were previously bound should have felt its effects by now," Hong Xin said. "You may give her the shattered core as proof." She looked to Bai Ling. "There is no need to mention the second condition. She wishes for me to step down."

Bai Ling nodded slowly. "She feels you are too prejudiced against dousing arts. We all have blood on our hands, but you are ultimately responsible for the deaths of many of the members that were once close to them. Further, they aren't sure who is behind the assassinations. You are their prime suspect."

"All valid points," Hong Xin said. "If I were to choose between the three of you, it would be you, Bai Ling, who should take over."

"You seem to have thought this through already," Bai Ling said, her expression pained. "For the record, I've fought back long and hard. The opportunity just seems too good to pass on this time."

Beside her, Ji Bingxue said nothing. From her, Hong Xin could feel only sadness.

Hong Xin smiled reassuringly. "With this last act, I can ensure that all our sisters are taken care of," she said. "Unfortunately, I will have to leave you."

"You don't have to," Bai Ling cut in. "There's no reason for them to force you out of this very building."

"You know full well why she has to go," Mistress Huang said, her expression stern. "As I warned you, a retired queen will always hold sway. The leadership of the Red Dust Pavilion would be uncertain. She can only leave to grant you all peace of mind." She shook her head. "But you can relax. I will go with her to protect her."

Hong Xin looked up at her. She was both pleased and shocked at her offer. Hong Xin shook her head. "You're needed here, with them."

Mistress Huang sniffed. "I am a dinosaur. A memory of an era best forgotten. I have been heir to your throne twice, and I have far too many skeletons in my closet. Besides, if you don't let me come, I'll just follow you from afar. I have too few hobbies in my old age, so go ahead and try running. I have plenty of spare time."

Hong Xin smiled. Mistress Huang rarely showed it, but she did have an affectionate side within that cold exterior of hers. "Very well," Hong Xin said. She waved her hand, and the simple red robe she wore turned violet. She also changed the glamor on her face. She walked over to a cupboard, where she took out a small bundle. They were her red phoenix dress and her phoenix coronet, the symbols of the Red Dust Headmistress. She'd removed them before they'd come.

She placed them on top of the dresser, feeling the soft fabric of the dress for what would probably be the last time. The peak-core treasure had saved her life many times. She felt for the connection that bound it to her and severed it, freeing it up for Bai Ling's bond.

"No need to see us out," Hong Xin said, walking toward the back of the room. There, a secret door opened into a narrow hallway. Mistress Huang followed behind her, her dress also changing to a purple hue, and her face had changed to an older, plainer appearance.

"Hong Xin," Bai Ling said. By now, she had also teared up. Bai Ling, who never cried, finally shed a tear for her. "Take care."

"I will," Hong Xin said. She closed the door, leaving the only meaningful life she had behind her.

"Well, that was dramatic," Mistress Huang said, eating a dumpling from the soup they'd just purchased at a small shop in Gold Leaf City. "Couldn't have done it better myself. Tears and all."

"It's relieving, in a sense," Hong Xin said. "I thought I'd need to spend the rest of my life in that place. Now I'm free to do whatever I wish."

"I'm sure that won't involve getting closer to a certain someone," Mistress Huang said, rolling her eyes. "Poor old me, retiring from a position of power only to be stuck playing chaperone for two secret lovebirds."

"No one asked you to come," Hong Xin said, sniffing. But yes, that was the plan. Perhaps now, she could truly help Wang Jun in his endeavors. She wouldn't have access to the same resources, but at least now she wouldn't have to distance herself from him on purpose. As for revealing herself to his family, what did she have to worry about? She was stronger than most cultivators. If they refused her, she didn't know what to say. She could take care of herself.

"It won't be all fun and games, you know," Mistress Huang said, fishing out another dumpling from her soup. She bit its corner and dipped it in a bowl of vinegar off to the side, letting the vinegar fill what little space was left within the rubbery shell. Otherwise, the vinegar would simply roll off the smooth dough shell.

"I know," Hong Xin said. "But what's the worst that could happen? They won't like me? They'll call me names? Or will they go all out and—"

"Duck!" Mistress Huang said, throwing the table up. The restaurant they were in exploded, sending bits of wood and metal flying everywhere. Flying swords swung at them, and Mistress Huang threw up dual shields of fire and ice to deflect them, summoning her own sabers in the process.

Hong Xin summoned her fan and swung it. Hundreds of blades were blown away by the raging fire that burst out of it, some cutting into those who'd thrown them. Wherever the flames passed, icy shards came out from the ground, piercing shadowy figures that had appeared all around the restaurant undetected.

"Spectral Assassins!" Hong Xin yelled to Mistress Huang, who nodded as she deflected a few blows and pierced one of them in the heart. Its body collapsed, leaving behind only a cloak and short swords.

Since they'd avoided the initial strike, chains flew out all around them. Hong Xin and Mistress Huang danced around them, slashing at assassins, striking out with ice and flame as they drew closer. They navigated the chain-filled maze with inhuman precision, avoiding the dark chains with everything they had. They wanted nothing to do with those black links that gleamed with a thin violet substance. Likely poison, the kind that could be absorbed through the skin.

"Look out!" Mistress Huang yelled. She grabbed Hong Xin by the cultivation robe and threw her back just in time to avoid a dozen spears. Each of them was a peak-core-formation treasure.

Hong Xin tumbled through the air, and by the time she recovered, she could only look on in shock at the grisly scene of Mistress Huang, who'd been impaled by three of them through the chest. The look in her dying eyes screamed at Hong Xin to run.

And run she did. Rather, she danced. Fire phoenixes and ice phoenixes gathered around her, speeding up her arms, her legs, her entire body as she swerved between swords, sickles, chains, and daggers. Poisonous needles burst out around her, not aiming for anything in particular but trying to cover as much ground as possible. She rushed through all of these, evading them as she made for the only exit in the encirclement, the one Mistress Huang had created in her last burst of power before she'd been killed.

She ran with everything she had. The encirclement tightened as the Spectral Assassins flitted between real and unreal, their ethereal forms fast and unpredictable. She killed one, two, and three as she raced toward the closing gap, finally making it to the final stretch. And then, just as she was about to break out into the open air, something struck her in the chest.

It was a hammer, weighing far more than any hammer had a reason to. Her qi shields, weakened by her activities earlier when she'd destroyed the Oath Stone, barely resisted before finally breaking, allowing the hammer to strike true. She saw stars as she sank toward the ground.

"Tsk, tsk, tsk," a voice said. "We can't have you dying on us. Not after spending all that money to find out just who you were."

Just who I am? Hong Xin thought. *I'm no one.* Then she saw it. Golden hair speckled with white. The hair wasn't Wang Jun's but an older man's. The Spectral Assassins parted for the older figure, who smiled genially as he summoned a pill and forced it into her mouth despite her protests.

No, not this, she thought. *Not this.*

She'd thought she'd be safe by going to Wang Jun. It seemed she'd been terribly wrong. Panicking, she moved to circulate her qi. Not in a cultivating pattern, nor in a combat pattern; she circulated in a self-destructive, life-ending pattern. Anything would be better than getting caught by them and used against him.

Unfortunately, her qi didn't move. It was only then that she noticed a few purple smudges on her arms and legs where she'd been struck by stray chains. The poison didn't kill; it inhibited qi. She glared at the man, who simply smiled as he kneeled beside her, watching her ribs heal up over the next few seconds.

"The venom is very difficult to manufacture," the man said. "It's very expensive, and it uses properties of karma to bind qi. Further, anyone affected by it will quickly build an immunity. It's far less reliable than qi-binding manacles but much easier to apply forcefully."

"Go to hell," Hong Xin spat, twisting to escape the chains binding her.

"But even qi-binding manacles can be escaped," the man

mused, ignoring her struggles. "Therefore, I'll have to use a more… permanent solution." He took out a dagger, its gray blade shining with red runes. Then he stabbed it into the middle of her chest. She gasped as it pierced not flesh, but something she'd thought unreachable—her Dantian. It pierced directly into the independent space and struck her core of ice and fire, shattering it. The space around it collapsed and lost all relation to her.

"What have you done?" she gasped, seeing her qi seep out of her body, her qi pathways drying up as her qi withdrew into the collapsing Dantian.

"Crippling someone's cultivation is tricky," the man explained, still smiling. "And often wasteful. After all, why not just kill someone, when crippling them might cost ten times or a hundred times more?" He answered his own question. "Your life, fortunately, is worth so much more. Your agony as well. The Spectral Assassins were fortunate to have clients willing to pay for both."

He waved his hand, and one of the Spectral Assassins clamped a black-and-red collar around her throat, completely restraining her resplendent force. "Unfortunately, crippling a soul is nigh impossible without killing the victim. Therefore, we can only rely on these crude means."

"You're a monster," Hong Xin said between gritted teeth. "And you work with monsters. Your soul will be damned for all eternity. It's no wonder he hates you so much."

The man pulled the dagger out of her chest. The gray artifact, which had fulfilled its purpose, was now dull and lifeless, its red runes faded.

"Better to live a monster than die a hero," the man said, shrugging. "We all do what we must, both for ourselves and our families."

"Hypocrite," Hong Xin spat.

"No, I think not," he replied. "Trust me, I take no pleasure in this. But my dear junior has forced my hand. He's ruining a plan three hundred years in the making, and I will *not* stand by and do nothing. He needs to be controlled, and you'll serve just fine."

"He'll never give in," Hong Xin said. "He might have once, but no longer."

"We'll see," Wang Wuling said, chuckling lightly.

Darkness took her.

Tick. Tick. Tick.

The clock ticked away the time to Wang Jun's morning meeting. He'd scheduled it for later today, as he'd been busy completing some important paperwork. There was much business to be done, much money to be made. Especially given how cooperative everyone had been lately, even without his interference.

There's something to be said for underhanded means, Wang Jun thought. *They get results, and you don't always have to use them.* Now, just the thought of his threats caused his targets to capitulate on demand. Of course, it helped that a mysterious assassin was aiding his cause, weakening targets he was trying to acquire. He had no idea who was doing it. He had even less of a clue as to who was killing people from the Icy Heart Pavilion, and for what reason. They were connected, he had no doubt about it.

Elder Bai would be coming soon. He moved to brew some tea in advance, partially due to thirst and partially to ease the inexplicable anxiety brewing in his heart. Something was happening, something connected to him. He would divine the cause if he could, but unfortunately, he'd lost the ability to predict anything about himself long ago. He was completely covered in a darkness that shrouded everything related to him in mystery. Or was it that *he* was the mystery, so his predictions were worthless? He supposed it didn't matter.

There's been a development, a voice said just as he was reaching for the teapot. Wang Jun paused, then looked to the floor. His shadow was back.

"What happened?" Wang Jun asked. His shadow was usually silent; he would only alert him if something important happened in the city.

Hong Xin has been abducted. She is gone, and I can't find her.

Pottery shattered.

Wang Jun glared at the shadow. "You'd better not be lying."

I will take you there, the shadow said.

Wang Jun ignored Elder Bai, who'd just walked into the room, and jumped straight into the shadow. It whizzed across the city, teleporting him almost instantly to a place of desolation and ruin. Splintered wood was everywhere, and charred and frozen corpses littered the streets. Despite the carnage, he saw no signs of Hong Xin, no signs of the abductors. He did, however, see the body of Mistress Huang. It was pierced by three bloody holes; the weapons had been removed by guards on the scene.

Wang Jun reached out for threads of karma—surely such a massacre had caused enough of a stir for him to find the perpetrators—but discovered a blurry force keeping the threads away from him. They were frayed, blowing in the wind, unreachable by mere mortals.

Wang Jun's eyes narrowed. "A transcendent?" he whispered. "Why the hell would a transcendent attack Hong Xin?"

Uncertain, the shadow said. *I was out surveilling other targets. I sensed a disturbance. I came, but she was gone.*

"Damn it," Wang Jun said, his face contorted, his lips pulled back into a snarl. "Damn it all."

Such a thing wasn't supposed to happen. He'd seen the writing on the wall, of course. The mysterious killer had been targeting the Icy Heart Pavilion's executive so fiercely, and it was only a matter of time until Hong Xin was forced to leave. He'd planned to welcome her with open arms, working with her to save his family. Perhaps, with luck, they'd live happily ever after. He could take her back to her parents and resolve one of his greatest regrets.

Now, that seemed impossible. Against all odds, a transcendent had acted, despite the backlash from the plane's will. He had a pretty good idea of who had done it—the Spirit Temple. Evil spirits always bore a grudge, and capturing someone alive to exact vengeance was exactly the kind of thing they would do.

But they don't have transcendents, Wang Jun thought. *Was it their Shepherd? Do they have means I don't understand?*

"Shadow," Wang Jun said.

Master, it answered.

"Scour the Spirit Temple," he instructed. "Monitor them with everything you have. Every communication, every going or leaving. I want reports, and I want her found."

It is difficult to evade their mediums, the shadow said.

Is it difficult or impossible? Wang Jun asked.

The shadow hesitated, then answered. *Difficult. I will have to cease all other activities.*

"Do it," Wang Jun said. "I need her found. Don't come back until you find her, or until I call you again."

Affirmative, the shadow said. It jumped into the shade of a half-destroyed building and merged with it. All around Wang Jun, soldiers and patrols were rushing in, trying to make heads or tails of the situation. Healers came and tended to the wounded and dying. Others collected the dead. They passed by Wang Jun, who stood there in silence, unseen, guilt gnawing away at his heart.

Chapter 34
Full Circle

This is it, Cha Ming thought, pressing his finger to a rune. He stepped back and waited for a transparent shield to appear between the test object and their research group. Today, they were testing a smaller prototype. A small wall—Pan Su's best wall to date—was directly in the line of fire of a single spear. The spear was mounted in the device he'd just activated, a much smaller launcher than the Breaker's—which could accommodate hundreds of similar spears and deliver them in a single payload.

This miniature device also contained prototype components. The spears inside it were just like the final product would be. Inside, there were thousands of ball bearings arranged in a precise order. If successful, he would scale up the result to the real Breaker prototype. He wasn't sure if it would work, though initial trials and Shao Qiang's divinations had indicated it was promising.

The small device accumulated power. The power core, which Cha Ming and He Yin had crafted together using the best of their abilities, began to react uncontrollably, feeding power into a storage device that would only last a single launch. This accumulation continued for three long seconds before finally, the spear launched at the wall at a speed that not even a transcendent could avoid.

The main spear pierced the wall with earth-shaking momentum. Large fissures appeared as the spear tip plunged into the concrete. As a result of the sudden loss in momentum, the spear's shaft pressed up against the spear's tip. Together, they compressed a tiny ball of reactive chemicals barely stable enough to launch without worry but unstable enough to detonate mere fractions of a second after impact.

The spearhead exploded in a symphony of molten shrapnel. The ball bearings, which had been carefully packed in a precise pattern, flew outward in a not-so-random fashion. They pressed up against the shattered concrete, etching runic lines upon its surface, causing the wall to weaken. The other ball bearings, not needed for the effect, crashed into the wall and caused massive damage that expanded several feet from the point of impact.

One spear. One launch. Devastation. A half-step-transcendent wall, the best product Southern geomancers could manufacture, was reduced to rubble. The test section had measured twenty feet in each direction. Now, a large portion of it was missing. The point of impact had caused the frontmost three feet of the wall to completely crumble. Beyond that, a long lance of destruction had completely pierced the wall.

Beyond that, a large crack ran vertically throughout the entire piece, which had been forced apart by the collateral damage of the ball bearings. A spherical chunk six feet in diameter was now missing at the center of the rubble.

It was a smashing success. Literally. Tian Zhi sighed in relief, and the others patted Cha Ming on the back. They were about two months away from their official deadline but only two days away from the prince's. Less than half a day remained until the Taotie arrived.

"You did well," Tian Zhi said. "We're within striking distance."

"All that's missing is the power distribution grid," Cha Ming said. "I have some ideas, but I'll likely need to combine everyone's efforts to make it work. I think we'll be able to finish something workable by the end of tomorrow."

"We have time, we have time," Tian Zhi said, waving his hand.

"Let's celebrate!" Pan Su said, clearly cheerful at having broken another record.

Cha Ming shook his head. "I'll keep working all night if I have to, but I'll finish this as soon as I can. You guys go on ahead without me."

He Yin, who'd been looking forward to going out, frowned. "Aren't you the one who's always saying you need to mix rest with relaxation?"

"It's hard to relax when you're so close to the end," Cha Ming said. "Don't worry, I won't stop you from going."

"I'll stay here," Tian Zhi said. "I have work to catch up on." He rarely ever participated in such gatherings.

The three other researchers dispersed. Cha Ming heard them discussing many places they could go since he, the picky one, wasn't coming. He smiled lightly, though inside, he was crying. It was likely the last time he'd see any of them.

"You don't look too happy," Tian Zhi said, making his way toward the door with him.

"I'm just anxious," Cha Ming said. "We're almost there, but I can't help but wonder what's next."

"Something will come up," Tian Zhi said, shrugging. "Worst case, you can take a break."

"Fair enough," Cha Ming said. They walked back to the central R&D room where the Breaker's diagram was displayed. Tian Zhi backed up some data on a jade slip while Cha Ming fidgeted around with the power conversion matrix's diagram. The three prototype Breakers were also in the same room.

Time dragged on, and eventually, Tian Zhi excused himself and headed back to the main office. The laboratory was empty, so Cha Ming could do as he pleased. First, he wandered to a corner of the room where he liked to work. It happened to be outside the surveillance area of the room. There, he took out the Space-Time Camera and poured a large amount of spirit stones into it. *Click.* The image of the room was frozen inside the camera.

Security nullified, Cha Ming walked up to one of the prototype Breakers and summoned a pile of golden bars. He'd cast them before in secret. He lifted a portion of the Breaker, then another, then used his strength as a body cultivator to pull apart the upper shell, revealing an array of copper-colored bars. They formed runic lines that ran across the entire device. He pulled them out, one by one, using qi to break them out as required.

For the next three hours, Cha Ming immersed himself in his work. These bars would allow the Breaker to conduct sufficient amounts of energy to operate at maximum capacity. As he inserted them, he soldered them together. They contained runic lines that would help direct the flow of power. He also connected the bars with smaller pieces of golden metal. These additional pieces were his masterpiece, the thing that would cause the device to perform a different function than originally intended.

Thus far, the prototypes were irreplaceable. He doubted anyone but him could recreate the main components. Aside from that, assembling the device as per the latest design would cause it to short-circuit and self-destruct. That was the second trap. Of course, it was all moot if everything went as planned. He had a very different goal for the device he'd just modified.

Soon enough, he locked the last golden bar into place. He closed the device, then placed the entire prototype, base and all, into the Clear Sky World.

"It's time to end this," he muttered, sighing. He walked up to the next prototype and took it into his Clear Sky World. He did the same for the next one. Then he walked up to the main diagram and activated the Space-Time Camera once more, freezing a bubble in space. He filled that bubble with destructive qi that ravaged the entire diagram and the information within it, and sheared it off where the bubble ended. The spatial lock prevented any alarms from going off.

Nodding to himself, Cha Ming walked out of the room with purpose. He left the laboratory, traveled to the main research and development lift, and exited the underground complex. On his way, he painted some runic lines that burned up, sending a message to the Life-Leaching Monarch north of the wall.

Within a few hours, it said. If all went according to plan, he'd use the Clear Sky Staff to shear a giant gash in the wall and open the city up to the horror of spidery demons. He'd do this just as Southern forces were fighting the Taotie, which would be arriving shortly.

Cha Ming was greeted with nods and bows of respect as he left the basement below the workshop. He returned those nods and proceeded to his next destination: the vault.

"Greetings, Grandmaster Pai," the attendant said.

"Hello there," Cha Ming said, nodding. "Mind if I head into the vault and take a peek?"

"Not at all," the attendant said. "Make sure you stop by the quartermaster's office to check in."

"As always," Cha Ming said with a wave. He entered the corridor leading to the vault and stopped by the quartermaster's locked door, knocking three times.

"Who is it?" the quartermaster, Wang Bo asked from inside.

"It's me," Cha Ming said, peeking in. "Mind if I look around?"

"Knock yourself out," Wang Bo said. The level of trust he now showed Cha Ming made him feel a little guilty. The fact that the man had betrayed the North in the first place helped soothe the ache. He approached the lock and pressed his arm inside. The security tattoo was verified by the door, which opened, allowing him through. He proceeded directly toward a corner he often frequented as he looked over certain metals.

Snap. Another picture, another small mountain of spirit stones gone. He had very little time to act, as Wang Bo would definitely be glancing at the monitoring camera every once in a while. Therefore, Cha Ming began unceremoniously dumping whatever he could into the Clear Sky World.

Piles upon piles of rare ores. Rare medicinal herbs. Pills that hadn't yet been sold. Piles of spirit stones, and even pieces of immortal jade. Not everything was expensive, but he even took cheaper objects, including the nice shelves that held everything for display. After all, if they were able to support the weight of the expensive ores, they had to be worth something.

Only a minute passed, but in that minute, the room had become completely empty. Cha Ming pondered leaving the fake Gold Source Core as a taunt to Zhou Li but ultimately decided against it.

Better safe than sorry, he thought, taking it in as well. The vault was now bare. Having finished his work, he walked out of the vault and proceeded back to Wang Bo's office. On his way there, he sent a message through the jade Prince Shen had left him. *I'll be coming soon. I won't have much time.*

"You're back fast," Wang Bo said as Cha Ming entered.

"There's a problem," Cha Ming said, nodding toward the screen.

Wang Bo glanced at it and nearly fainted from shock. "When was the last time you inspected the vault?"

"The vault?" Wang Bo said, his face pale. "Ju-ju-just this morning. How? How is this possible?"

"I suggest you call Director Yong and Tian Zhi as quickly as possible. Together, we might be able to figure out who did this."

Wang Bo nodded gravely and sent out messages on his core-transmission jade. Then he slumped into his chair, his eyes filled with disbelief as he looked at the monitor once again. "Everything is gone. Even the shelves. Even with a dozen powerful cultivators working together, and several storage devices, it would have taken hours."

Cha Ming's Clear Sky World was a possibility he would never consider. Normally, he wouldn't dare to reveal it, but today was a special day with special circumstances.

"According to what you said, they *had* hours," Cha Ming said. "The only question is, how did they break into the vault without physically damaging it?"

"Yes, you're right," Wang Bo said, peering intensely at the screen. "I don't see the slightest bit of damage to the walls."

"What happened?" a voice suddenly said. The door burst open, revealing Director Yong and Tian Zhi. "You said it was an emergency. You'd better not be lying."

"How could I possibly be lying?" Wang Bo said, pointing to his monitor. "We've been robbed!"

"*Robbed?*" Tian Zhi said, looking to where Wang Bo pointed. His eyes widened. "Impossible. Your monitor must be malfunctioning."

"I saw it with my own eyes," Cha Ming said, shaking his head. "It's best to see it in person."

"Let's go," Director Yong said, leading the way. They walked over to the vault door where, one after another, they authenticated and entered. Cha Ming soon joined the three men, who were staring around the empty vault in disbelief.

"How could this have happened?" the older man muttered.

"I saw something suspicious here," Cha Ming said, flying toward the center. The three men followed him to a message—one that he'd scrawled on the floor and hidden weeks prior—and read it out loud. *"The Wang family sends its regards."*

"What does it mean?" Tian Zhi wondered out loud.

"I don't know," Director Yong said.

Wang Bo was speechless. As they stood there and shook their heads, however, Cha Ming was already activating the formation he'd painstakingly laid within the vault's floor during prior visits. The runes were hidden beneath the floor tiles, but the moment he poured a mountain of spirit stones into the room, they activated. The room came alight with destructive lightning.

"It was you!" Director Yong yelled, drawing a sword and instantly charging at Cha Ming. He might be a director, a non-combatant of the Wang family, but he was still a peak-core-formation cultivator. He'd seen his fair share of death and slaughter. Tian Zhi joined him with a massive blacksmith's hammer trailing crimson flames. They attacked Cha Ming, ignoring the lightning that seared them.

Cha Ming immediately summoned the Clear Sky Staff. Though he'd laid down a formation, it was just insurance. Inside this vault, he was invincible. An aura of half-step rune carving and half-step blood awakening surged out of him. His nascent domain surrounded him in a metallic aura—ideal for cutting. His muscles brimmed with power. He swung out with Crushing Chaos, directly using one of his strongest attacks from the outset.

Director Yong cried out in shock, as did Wang Bo. He sheared through both of them, killing them instantly. Tian Zhi, however, was no slouch. He was a body cultivator, and he'd clearly spent a lot of time fighting. The staff blow caught his leg. It sheared through it, cutting off his foot, which instantly grew back due to his peak-marrow-refining cultivation. He swung his hammer and beat Cha Ming in the chest.

Cha Ming coughed out blood but didn't move an inch. He thrust out his palm, infusing a nascent domain of fire into his palm strike and smashing through the man's ribs. Tian Zhi responded by smashing into Cha Ming's head. His bones, though strong, still cracked on impact. His skull shattered, and his head was reduced to a paste, but it re-formed a fraction of a second later. His strong soul kept him steady. He pushed increasing amounts of fire into Tian Zhi's body.

The spiritual blacksmith, panicking, punched Cha Ming's chest. The blow didn't harm Cha Ming much, but allowed Tian Zhi to push off toward the vault's door. "Who are you? Why did you come here?"

"I'm afraid traitors like you don't need to know," Cha Ming said. His voice was laced with anger, half at the man, but half at himself for repaying kindness with violence.

"Ah," Tian Zhi said. "I see the Alabaster Group finally succeeded in planting a mole. It's too bad you'll never leave the city alive. I've already messaged the prince."

"I'm afraid you haven't," Cha Ming said, shaking his head. "Spatial lock."

Tian Zhi frowned as he took out his core-transmission jade and checked. During their exchange, he'd somehow found time to send a message. It hadn't gone through.

"Any last words?"

Tian Zhi laughed bitterly. "Who would've thought that we'd be caught so close to the end. You toyed with us, lured us into a false sense of security. But tell me, what does it matter? The Breaker prototype still exists. Pan Su, He Yin, Shao Qiang still live. Don't tell me you're so cold-blooded as to kill them too?"

"Without me, the Breaker is just a legend, something that people only wish they had the skill to build," Cha Ming said. "The prototypes are gone, the information destroyed. With your death, and your possessions gone, I doubt there'll be any records left on how to make it."

"The crown prince has moles," Tian Zhi said. "I know it, because he told me. For insurance." His eyes narrowed. "Unless…"

"I *am* the mole," Cha Ming said.

Tian Zhi laughed heartily, then held out his arms. "Fine, I admit defeat. Just give me a painless death. I can't do anything to you anyhow."

"Any last wishes?" Cha Ming said. "You treated me well. You trusted me, and I betrayed you."

"No," Tian Zhi said. "All the family I have is dead. Killed by time and tragedy."

He closed his eyes, and destruction devoured the man as Cha Ming struck down with Crushing Chaos. The destruction qi ravaged the man's body, eating away at his vitality until finally, there was nothing left. Cha Ming took his possessions and crushed his core-transmission jade. He also took Wang Yong and Wang Bo's possessions, then destroyed the remainder of their bodies.

Only the scratches on the floor remained.

"Why in the Sea God's name did we have to come here?" Gong Xuandi complained as they walked through the city streets, their bodies and faces covered in black cloaks. "It gives me the creeps." Their disguise wasn't an uncommon one in the Southern City, where trust only ran so far as a contract dictated. Right now, they resembled acolytes of the Spirit Temple, who wore black robes as a religious prop.

"We're here for opportunity," Feng Ming said, pushing through the busy but orderly streets. Many passersby glared at him. Pushing through lines wasn't something someone did, especially if they had to walk. Anyone with a high-enough station to push would be flying, after all.

"There're so many powerful cultivators here it's not even funny," Gong Xuandi said. "Even I might die if we're discovered."

"Then it's fortunate that they're all distracted by the massive Taotie that's about to knock on their front door," Feng Ming said. "I don't know what they're thinking, waiting till the last moment."

"I heard that it's that gnat Zhou Li," Gong Xuandi said. "He's taking as much time as possible to recover and coming at the last minute. They're all too scared to act without him."

"Selfish bastards," Feng Ming said. "We fought that beast for months. Months!"

"And I'm really strong, and you're lucky as all hell," Gong Xuandi said. "Besides. It's stronger now."

The man did have a point. The creature never stopped eating, and it didn't help that the South's first attempt to halt the beast had failed miserably. Now it was difficult to slow it down as it homed in on the largest reserve of vitality and heaven and earth energy in the area, Bastion City, and the Shattered Lands beyond it.

"I'm sure the royals will help fight it too," Feng Ming said. "When they leave, it'll be our time to shine. We'll swoop in and take their entire treasury."

"You're making it sound like you can actually store all those things," Gong Xuandi said. "Rare treasures are often heavy, their energies too potent. At most, you'll be able to store a few things in a peak-core-grade ring. For anything else, you'll need..." His voice trailed off as Feng Ming pulled out a violet ring from his bag of holding. "You lucky bastard."

"You're right," Feng Ming said. "To think that one of those blood masters had been carrying it, thinking it was a core-grade ring. He'd shake in his grave if he knew it was a transcendent-grade treasure."

Gong Xuandi shook his head in disgust. "I've had it with your luck. It's unnatural. Now tell me, what are we supposed to do while we wait?"

"Hmm..." Feng Ming thought aloud, tapping his fingers on his lips. "I've got it!" Gong Xuandi looked at him expectantly. "Noodles!"

"Sorry?" Gong Xuandi asked.

Feng Ming didn't answer. Instead, he led the man to a high-end restaurant just beside the palace. He rented a room on the top floor facing the open courtyard. A few minutes later, two steaming-hot bowls of noodles arrived. Gong Xuandi grunted but didn't complain as he sipped on a coffee he'd obtained on the main floor. It tasted strikingly similar to the blend they had back in Haijing, with all the same effects. Somehow, he suspected the differently named company was a secret subsidiary of the mighty coffee empire that had started in Gong Xuandi's home city of all places.

Feng Ming hummed in pleasure as he slurped on the broth. "If we're going to wait, we may as well do it in style."

Little did he know that, in a private room just beside them, a half dozen transcendents were also eating noodles. They didn't notice the duo, however, as their full attention was on the creature looming in the distance, as they mentally and physically prepared themselves for the world of pain they'd be in once it arrived.

"Halt!" guards yelled, stopping Cha Ming at the entrance of the palace. It was well past midnight, a suspicious hour for one so powerful to be wandering about.

"At ease," a voice said, causing the guards to immediately retreat. The crown prince, clothed his the usual yellow robes, appeared just inside the gates. "Come inside, Pai Xiao."

Cha Ming nodded and noted the prince's welcoming smile. It was strained, a thin mask he used to veil the fatigue on his face. He'd clearly come at an inconvenient time. Likely it had something to do with the Taotie Elder Zhong spoke of.

"I was growing worried that you wouldn't meet the deadline," Prince Shen said. "My other informants said you were days away. When I saw your message, that you were done a full day before the deadline, I was ecstatic."

"We have a contract, so I did my utmost fulfill it," Cha Ming said, smiling bitterly. "Besides, I discovered something that made me uneasy. It seems the Blackthorn Conglomerate hasn't been honest with me."

"So you finally found out," Prince Shen said, nodding understandably. "Since they're traitors from the North, it only makes sense for us to keep up our guard up against them. If they'll betray their own so easily, what's to stop them from doing the same to us?"

Cha Ming nodded. They walked through a large hallway made of a white stone he'd never seen before. It wasn't marble, but the yellow swirls in the stone reminded him of it. Tall yellow pillars stood to both sides of the main hallway. They seemed to glow in the darkness, providing a dim illumination to the otherwise unlit hallway. It was nighttime, after all, and no one dared buzz about while the king might be sleeping.

"As I said, I don't have much time," Cha Ming said. "If I'm gone for too long, they'll begin to suspect me. For safety reasons, I suggest storing the device in a high-level storage ring, in a protective formation, or as far away from anyone else as possible."

"Will this do?" Prince Shen asked, revealing a golden ring on his pinky.

"No," Cha Ming said. "The device is too large and heavy."

The prince pursed his lips. "The courtyard, then. As far away from prying eyes as possible until I can arrange an alternative."

Cha Ming nodded. They took a right where the main hallway split into three. The hallway continued for quite some time before turning north again. The central palace might be square, but the entire palace complex was a wide rectangle skirting Bastion Wall. They continued as far as they could before exiting the palace into a restricted garden just south of the northernmost wall.

"No one can enter the garden without my or my father's permission," Prince Shen said. "To be sure, I'll be posting some of our elites at the door."

"Good," Cha Ming said. He walked up to a relatively empty area and summoned the Breaker. The entire machine was twenty-five feet wide by fifty feet long, a weapon of mass destruction at its finest. It gleamed in the moonlight, its value apparent for all to see. Cha Ming could see the prince's hands twitching just looking at it, wanting to make it his.

Cha Ming walked away, letting the crown prince inspect it. The man walked around, admiring it from every angle. "At last, the mighty Breaker," Prince Shen whispered. "With this, our kingdom's contribution to the struggle is set in stone." He hesitated, then put his hand on the treasure. The space around it lurched, and the storage ring on Prince Shen's finger cracked. "A pity. I should have listened to your expertise." Such a loss of wealth wasn't irreplaceable, but it definitely stung. "I confess myself impressed. You have a treasure capable of storing such an engine of destruction on your person."

"Alas, it's not for sale," Cha Ming said, smiling. "You and I both know that such treasures would be kept as heirlooms in kingdoms and mighty sects or companies."

"I would never dare offer to buy it," Prince Shen said. "It's only that I must reevaluate you. You are a man of many mysteries, Pai Xiao."

"More than you know," Cha Ming said truthfully. He summoned another item, a blue jade slip. Within it was a modified blueprint for the Breaker. Superficially, the blueprint would seem like a genuine item. It would take a true expert to notice it was riddled with flaws. Correcting them would be an insurmountable task, to the point that it might be better to start from scratch. And though contractually he was required to give him the genuine item, the prince's Royal Seal of Notwithstanding had nulled that requirement. He'd hung up the rope with which to hang himself.

"The hour grows late," Cha Ming said. "I'd suggest testing it as soon as possible. We didn't have time to test it on the ancient wall sections yet, but I'm ninety-nine percent sure it will succeed. If anything goes wrong, anything at all, message me. I'll find a reason to excuse myself and perform any tweaking required."

"Good," Prince Shen said. He flicked a storage ring to Cha Ming, who inspected it to confirm its contents. "Guardian Lin?" A figure appeared beside the prince, a black-cloaked guardian with a gleaming golden saber on his back. "Please see him out safely."

"As you instruct, my prince," Guardian Lin said. The threat of his presence was obvious to Cha Ming, who walked back to the front of the palace. As they walked, he spread out his transcendent force to eavesdrop on the many cultivators there.

Can he really be trusted? Do we dare trust him? a mental voice said.

We will test the device as soon as possible, Prince Shen said. *In the meantime, I suggest we send the imperial tutor to supervise him.*

Agreed, the other voice said. *Though we need the tutor, the Breaker project is equally important. Besides, we have support from the entire South ready to intercept the creature. One imperial tutor won't make a difference.*

Moments later, Cha Ming sensed another presence beside him and Guardian Li. "Take care, Grandmaster Pai," Guardian Li said, seeing him out the palace gates.

"Thank you for the escort," Cha Ming said, giving him a short bow. He flew down the streets, feigning obliviousness to the expert hidden in the shadows.

"I wonder who that was, sneaking in and out in the middle of the night?" Feng Ming muttered, looking at the tall but burly man making his way out of the palace. Another figure followed, a figure he wouldn't have noticed except for a coincidental glint from an exposed piece of jewelry. *People,* he thought, shaking his head. *You'd think they'd be more careful if they were sneaking about.*

"Should I tail him?" the Sea God Emperor asked, slurping loudly. After watching Feng Ming devour three entire bowls, he, too, had decided to try the restaurant's famed noodles. Five bowls later, he'd developed a preference for their fish broth, consuming three entire bowls in quick succession.

"Naw," Feng Ming said. "I have a feeling it's best to leave him alone." He looked at the palace with a concerned frown. "There are so many powerful cultivators there. What we need is something to draw them away."

"You mean like a large creature of the void," Gong Xuandi said, "hellbent on destroying every living and non-living thing on this plane, culminating in a universe-ending calamity that even Yama might have to step in to stop if it gets bad enough?"

Feng Ming coughed lightly. "I was thinking something smaller in scale but inconveniently timed. He looked to the west, and his face brightened. "I know just the thing. Tell me, old friend, how do you like smashing things to bits and causing a ruckus?"

"I'm not your friend," Gong Xuandi said, glaring at Feng Ming and putting his bowl of noodles down. "But yes, I like doing those things. I'm a body cultivator. It's what we do."

"Excellent," Feng Ming said. "I want you to go over to that army barracks, where all the generals and important officers are stationed. Start fighting and killing people, making a lot of noise in the process."

Gong Xuandi winced. "While I'm obligated to aid you, even risking myself to some extent, that's a little too much heat for me to handle."

"It's a good thing you won't have to handle it alone," Feng Ming said. "Most of the powerful cultivators are distracted by the aforementioned world-ending calamity, and I'll be sneaking inside the palace. I'll be sure to cause a ruckus on the way out, and then I'll come help you out. I'm lucky, remember?"

"And I'm not, in case you haven't noticed," Gong Xuandi said. "I lost my crown, and now I'm forced to put up with you."

"But your luck's gotten better," Feng Ming pressed. "I dare you to say otherwise."

The old Sea God Emperor grunted. He picked up his bowl and slurped loudly, downing its entire contents. He then stood up, wiped his mouth, and left the room.

A few tense minutes passed before, finally, a large crashing sound filled the air. He heard many shocked yells from the room just over them. Several dozen flashes of light zoomed out from the palace. One of them was a half-step transcendent, and the rest were peak transcendents. These were most of the palace's reserve, which was a testament to how large a ruckus Gong Xuandi had caused.

"Great," Feng Ming said. He finished his own noodles with a quick slurp, downed his glass of wine, and proceeded down the steps, where all sorts of important people were scrambling about, trying to figure out what was going on. He left a confused waiter a generous tip and walked out the front door, walking over to a convenient shadow he'd spotted earlier. "It should be here somewhere," he murmured, pressing the stones until suddenly, he heard a click. A small door opened in the wall. It led farther down the solid structure.

Feng Ming slipped inside the dark area, using his resplendent force to guide the way. After a few minutes of fumbling about, he eventually found a loose stone, which he pushed in. Another door opened, revealing a small but beautiful courtyard. It was completely empty of people, and a large contraption sat inside it.

What's this? he thought, looking at it. The machine had a dangerous vibe to it. In fact, he had the distinct impression that, should he do something foolish, the device might destroy him, body and soul. "Who just leaves this kind of thing lying around?"

The outer shell of the device was mostly bare, but from the general shape, he could tell that the device behaved much like a spear, if a bit unwieldy. The tip was pointed north toward Bastion Wall, and the entire metallic contraption was mounted on a large stone base.

I wonder how it works? Feng Ming thought. Gong Xuandi's distraction was good and all, but you could never be too careful when looting a palace vault.

First things first, take care of the imperial tutor, Cha Ming thought as he traveled through the city streets. His movements were confusing, but that behavior was well in line with someone who'd just stolen the most expensive prototype on the continent and betrayed his company.

He soon found himself a few blocks away from his destination: the Blood Master Monastery. There, he slipped into an alleyway and concealed his presence, disguising himself as a small mouse hiding in a hole in the wall. Predictably, the imperial tutor followed. He stopped just where Cha Ming had previously been. He looked down at the mouse in disgust and glared down the alleyway.

Just as the imperial tutor was about to leave, Cha Ming suddenly appeared behind him, thrusting out with a green palm that shattered bones and damaged viscera. It pierced through the man's abruptly summoned shields, shattering them. The man cried out, but before he could do anything else, Cha Ming locked down on him with his soul force. At the same time, he sent out hundreds of formation flags, painting with one hand as he held the incapacitated imperial tutor in the other.

Their surroundings merged together as the concealment formation he'd laid activated. He took out a pair of qi-binding manacles and a soul-sealing collar, placing them on the helpless, wide-eyed tutor.

"You qi cultivators should really consider doing weights or something," Cha Ming said. "You're so fragile that you collapse after a single blow."

Of course, his being far stronger than the imperial tutor might also have had something to do with it. The older man could only weep and struggle for breath as Cha Ming confiscated his belongings, which included a core-transmission jade, among other expensive items. To his surprise, it even included a few formation flags. The man was a runic artist.

"You should thank the heavens you're a good man," Cha Ming said, noticing the light merit glow on him. "When this is all through, you might actually survive." That, and the death of the imperial tutor would surely result in an uproar. It was extremely likely that the man was tied to a life slip, a life candle, or some similar device.

For good measure, Cha Ming snapped a picture, sealing the space around the man. Problem taken care of, he flew up above the Blood Master Monastery, holding up the Space-Time Camera as it burned away thousands upon thousands of peak-grade spirit stones. Whereas before, he was economizing, he now had no choice but to put in his all. He couldn't risk letting a single blood master out of his containment.

A few agonizing seconds passed, and his camera flashed. A gray barrier, invisible to most, appeared all around the monastery. Those outside of it would sense nothing as a battle ensued. The barrier would block out all communication, and for the most part, block those trying to escape. Three seconds passed, and the barrier firmed up. Cha Ming nodded and flew through the bubble, not bothering to hide his presence as he smashed down on the main building with his Clear Sky Staff, now in pillar form. Crushing Chaos split the building in two. It crashed down on the blood reservoir of the monastery, evaporating the stored blood vitality in a cloud of red mist.

"Who dares?" a man roared. Dozens of red flashes appeared before Cha Ming. One of them bore an inviolable aura, that of true blood-awakening cultivator. He held a large bloody saber in one hand. It seemed heavy, almost too heavy for him to wield. Beside him stood two half-step transcendents and two dozen peak-marrow-refining cultivators. "You?" the man yelled in surprise, noticing the staff in Cha Ming's hands.

Cha Ming grinned. The time for disguises was over. He banished his disguise and summoned a thousand and eighty combat sigils, which spread out around him and summoned an inferno to burn the weaker blood masters who were gathering or trying to flee. The power of a half-step-rune-carving cultivator was too much for them to handle.

Only a second passed, and most of the blood masters, the buildings they occupied, and even their weapons were already gone. Only those at middle marrow refining or above remained, though those struggled to hold on to their lives under the blistering combat formation. Those at late marrow refining held weapons in unsteady hands, preparing to aid those at peak marrow refining or higher, who were only slightly affected by Cha Ming's flames.

The stone beneath them cracked under the intense heat, which Cha Ming finally released, replacing it with a frigid, slowing cold. It pierced these cultivators to their bones, reducing their reaction speeds and making their bones and muscles more brittle.

"I see you have the capital to invade us," said the head blood master, a transcendent. Lightning crackled around the man and attacked him as his presence mounted and caused space to tremble. "And I see you've mounted a barrier. How wonderful."

"Wonderful?" Cha Ming asked, grasping the Clear Sky Pillar, reducing it to a more manageable form. It contracted until it became an inch thick, just big enough to expand as he fought, but just small enough to be fast and zipping with his movements.

"I haven't gotten to fight to my heart's content in centuries," the head blood master said. "Now that the surroundings are adequately shielded, no one can blame me for going all out." The air around the man shattered, and the lightning intensified, burning at the man's skin, which began peeling off in scorching layers.

Cha Ming's eyes narrowed. "Are you not worried about heavenly retribution?"

The bald man cackled madly as his robes burned away, revealing charred flesh. "I'll survive, but you will not. Blood masters—kill!"

The crowd swarmed around Cha Ming, whose feet became a storm of wind and lightning. He slashed out with multiple iterations of Splitting Heaven and Earth, imbuing different elements for different effects. Some were burning, corporeal blades that seared through skin. Some were heavy blows imbued with vibrations that shattered bones.

One swipe, one kill. Cha Ming started with the small fries, dancing around them using gravity and flow to this advantage. His nascent domain shone around him like a bright protective barrier that also extended to his staff, making it far more lethal than it had a right to be. He destroyed the weaker blood masters with impunity. Unfortunately, they were the least of his worries.

A lethal saber strike suddenly came for Cha Ming's neck. He twisted around, evading it just in time for another one to come at his torso. He banished his Clear Sky Staff, summoning it before him to absorb the shock of the blow. Space shattered at his front, damaging his body, which healed instantly, drawing from his deep vitality stores.

The exchange took mere moments, but in that time, Cha Ming wasn't just on the defensive. He'd retracted his combat formation, and now it formed dozens of blades that struck out and attacked the weaker blood masters. Though each blade felled three, those three stood up almost immediately. These weren't qi cultivators like the imperial tutor, but body cultivators like Cha Ming. They were born for battle.

Cha Ming blocked another saber blow, this one headed toward his chest. At this point, the transcendent didn't bother targeting any specific body parts. He'd guessed that Cha Ming was like him, someone who could be reborn from a single drop of blood. As such, the best way to fight was collateral damage, destroying as much as he could with every blow.

Cha Ming resisted, and despite blocking the saber blows, his bones cracked and shattered, his flesh evaporating to nothingness from the spatial cracks they generated. Lightning surged around the blood master like a storm. Despite being covered in a charcoal-like substance, the insane blood master still grinned evilly. It was like he didn't care that at any moment, his vitality stores could run out, and the storm would end him.

I can't keep going on like this, Cha Ming thought. *Time to change tactics*. He hadn't expected to be fighting a transcendent, which meant that he was likely a new addition, someone from outside their monastery here to deal with the incoming creature. He dodged a few hammer wielders, but this movement was enough to allow the transcendent's blade to strike true, cutting Cha Ming in half. It was a surreal sensation, being in two places at once, but his body instantly formed a connection and came back together. Such was the power of divinity and vitality.

If I can't kill them with swords, I'll grind away at them until they're dead, Cha Ming thought. He recalled his combat formation, which immediately changed shape and became an agonizing ball of fire and blades. It surged toward a late-marrow-refining cultivation and ground into him. As it cut and burned, his body tried to regrow, only to be cut down again. The ball ground away for a second before the blood master finally didn't grow back. Nodding, Cha Ming sent out the ball of fiery spikes to find another target.

"Keep attacking," the now-ebony-skinned man said, still grinning. "If he kills you, you never stood a chance of escaping anyway."

The words egged on the clearly insane blood masters. Many began burning their blood essence, boosting their power and movements until finally, their attacks began to connect with Cha Ming, clipping at his skin and chipping his bones. Though he regenerated with every blow, his vitality stores were limited. In fact, he'd already exhausted a quarter of them.

It finally dawned on Cha Ming that picking off the small fries wouldn't cut it. He simply didn't have enough time, not with the transcendent attacking him with that freakishly huge sword. No, he would need to take the initiative and hope that the plane was doing more damage than it appeared to be doing. Decision made, he flew through the blood masters, withdrawing his combat formation once again and forming a new one.

A giant mountain appeared above Cha Ming and the transcendent blood master, increasing the gravity around them a hundredfold. He then threw out a blue talisman, a half-step-transcendent Flow Talisman. The air around them thickened, slowing down everyone within the immediate area while speeding up Cha Ming's movements. He sent out a second talisman, a half-step-transcendent Matter Talisman. It landed on the surprised blood master's charcoal-covered body, causing it to seize up and crumble. His muscles became stiff, and his bones became brittle.

Then, a third talisman appeared, then a fourth. The third one was golden, and it shone with a sharp light that immediately surrounded the Clear Sky Staff. The half-transcendent Shape Talisman greatly boosted Cha Ming's offense, to the point that even a casual swipe of his staff caused space to crackle, and the heavens to rumble in displeasure. Fortunately, he wasn't a transcendent and was only abusing loopholes. He struck the shocked blood master with staff after staff, breaking down his body before he could even react.

As Cha Ming attacked, a warm light began to glow around him. The Energy Talisman, the fourth talisman he'd activated, wasn't a normal one. It was a transcendent talisman. His body grew faster and faster, his every strike filled with even more energy. It poured into his staff, which began to burn brightly. It didn't just cut into the beleaguered blood master's body, but seared everything around him, burning at the energy stores within his void network.

Three seconds, Cha Ming thought. He only had three seconds at this peak level of power. His attacks intensified, and he unleashed Crushing Chaos, Splitting Heaven and Earth, and even Origin Strike in quick succession. Each hit caused the grin on the blood master to falter, and also caused the lightning's attacks on what barely looked like a man now to intensify.

Two seconds. Frightened by what was occurring, the blood master shouted an order. The dozens of remaining blood masters rushed into the constricted area without concern for their safety. Their movements were slow and sluggish, but Cha Ming had no time to spare for them. They hacked into his skin, their blows glancing off his bones but piercing his flesh, regenerating almost instantly as he redoubled his efforts. One second remained, but his vitality stores were at less than half, their depletion increasing drastically.

The talisman's effects would soon run out, so Cha Ming gathered half of his qi. He gathered his nascent domain, withdrawing it from his body and urging it into the only thing that mattered—his staff. He held on with two hands and unleashed the most powerful Origin Strike he'd ever executed. By now, the Energy Talisman had filled him with an unbelievable burning power that coursed through every inch of his body.

Space all around the transcendent blood master shattered. A swirling vortex appeared around the screaming man, completely enveloping his struggling body. He gritted his teeth and hefted his sword anyway. His aura mounted again as he burned his blood essence, preparing to deliver one last strike at the defenseless Cha Ming. He lifted his arm and swung, but just as the sword was about to connect with Cha Ming, dealing a massive blow to his life force, the sword lost its momentum.

Something seemed to halt, and the man's half-recovered body began to disintegrate into ash. The plane's will, which had been attacking the transcendent constantly, had done its job. The lightning let up, and Cha Ming looked up at the men around him. He activated his combat formation, unleashing a storm of blades as he slashed out with one last staff strike. They couldn't avoid it. Dozens of peak blood masters were instantly reduced to ashes.

Cha Ming collapsed to one knee. He took out a vial from the Clear Sky World and popped three pills into his mouth. The one meant to replenish his vitality stores rushed into the voids in his bones, refilling the void network that had been purged of excess energy. His damaged body healed, while the second and third pills worked to replenish his qi stores. He filled his qi stores up to two-thirds capacity, after which the effects of the pills ended. Unfortunately, it just wasn't possible to instantly restore everything he'd expended. He would need to cultivate to recover any further.

That was too close, Cha Ming thought. His vitality stores had dipped down to ten percent, a razor-thin margin between life and death. The half-transcendent vitality-replenishing pill he'd crafted on his spare time only managed to refill that margin to a third of his full capacity.

Ignoring the pain that came with healing, Cha Ming made his way to an unscorched section on the monastery training grounds. He took out his Clear Sky Brush, willing it to transform into a carving knife, then cut a message into the stone. Satisfied with a job well done, he walked off the platform toward the exit, leaving only blood and ruin behind him. When he left the shield of gray, a loud explosion greeted him, a familiar roar he'd heard months ago.

Feng Ming coughed and gagged as acrid smoke filled the air. He shivered as he pondered what might have happened if he hadn't decided to run just prior to the device's activation. Wasn't it meant to shoot toward Bastion Wall? Fortunately, his instincts had warned him just in time. The device hadn't operated as expected; in fact, he suspected it had been sabotaged. The resulting explosion of fire and magical shrapnel had laid waste to his surroundings.

The entire east wing of the palace he'd taken refuge in was completely demolished. Only a small stub remained of the grand building. The servants and guests that hadn't been disintegrated by the explosion lay dead or dying, most of their corpses missing limbs. The destruction was unlike anything Feng Ming had ever seen in his life. His karma, he'd noticed, had taken a substantial hit from triggering the explosion. Even though they were on the other side, the evil side, killing innocents was *not* acceptable.

His heart hurt as he realized just how many non-cultivators had worked in the palace. They weren't servants—no, cultivators were better suited for such roles in the palace. But those in the palace had families, and not every family member was a cultivator. Wives, children, and even husbands of powerful women had all been obliterated in a fraction of a second.

The place where the weapon had exploded was now an empty crater. It wasn't a perfect circle, but an ellipse that traveled north toward the wall. There, a deep gouge had been torn in the seemingly impenetrable bastion against the Shattered Lands. With the tear came a draining sensation, a miasma that tugged at Feng Ming's vitality. He was no slouch; he'd dabbled in body cultivation when convenient, but lesser mortals wouldn't last very long under the strain. Maybe a day at most, and this was only the beginning. It was no wonder the South had built a massive wall to contain it.

"Who dares trespass in this royal palace!" a voice reverberated all around him.

Not wanting to be caught, Feng Ming ducked behind some rubble and suppressed his strength, shielding himself with powerful resplendent force.

A man flew up from the central palace. Dressed in regal yellow robes and wearing a golden crown that matched them, it was easy to deduce who this man was: the king of the Ji Kingdom, Ji Lingtian. He wore a dreadful gold-and-red sword at his waist, and every garment he wore bore a thick treasure aura. Feng Ming itched to grab just one of them and run off, but his brain wrested control away from his heart before he could act on the impulse.

"You must be out there, little rat," the king said, looking around. He flicked his sleeve, and the sword at his waist disappeared, reappearing just in time to crash into a segment of unbroken wall. "You're close. I can feel it." Another flick, another segment broken.

It's only a matter of time before he finds me, Feng Ming thought. He had to escape, but rushing out of the palace through the entrance was far too obvious. So was escaping into the city, where he'd just learned many powerful individuals were staying. *To the north, then?* Another wall segment shattered, and he took a gamble. Masking his presence, he flew through the crack, leaving an enraged king to pick through the rest of the rubble.

The wall, it turned out, was surprisingly thick. A full hundred feet thick, it should have been impossible to destroy in a single strike. Even a peak demon monarch would have trouble piercing it. Yet the explosion Feng Ming had unwittingly triggered had unleashed devastation on the structure. It seemed, upon initial observation, that the device had been designed specifically to destroy walls. Many tiny holes peppered the structure, which seemed more brittle than intended. Runic patterns were etched deep into the stone.

I should be safe here for now, Feng Ming thought, resting against the wall at the entrance of the mountain canyon. He only had a moment to relax before a chill ran down his spine. He summoned his Magma God's Spear just in time to catch a blow from an unusual weapon, a cane. Cold winds blew past him, filling the air with fog. He could barely make out a short, aged lady with spectacles behind the cane.

"You," the woman said in a nasal voice, "are trespassing on private property. And I suspect that you are the one responsible for this destruction. Prepare to be eliminated." The woman moved fast, so fast that she left behind an afterimage. Feng Ming staggered, swinging out randomly with his spear, hoping to deflect whatever strikes came his way, since he couldn't predict them.

Clank. Clank. Clank. He deflected the first three blows with ease, causing the older woman to frown. Seeing her hesitate, he pressed the attack. The air around him became a blistering sandstorm, the earth beneath him a pool of magma. The woman disappeared, but this time, her afterimage was disrupted by the sand. He *felt* her through the sand, sensing her movements, not toward his side but above him. She struck down with cutting azure runes of wind that blew away the sand, exposing him to the her cane.

Feng Ming did what he did best. He threw his spear up at her, hoping to the heavens above that it struck true. It did just that, crashing against the woman's chest. A shattering sound filled the air as a brooch, which had been fastened to a fashionable overcoat she'd been wearing, fell to the ground.

He held out his hand and caught his spear. He moved to rush in but paused, suddenly looking toward the north. She did the same. The smoke from the explosion, which had filled the mountain valley, was now just clearing.

"Drat," the woman said in a deadpan voice.

A large figured appeared, complete with eight monstrous metallic legs and thousands of eyes. It roared, its mouth opening into row upon row of jagged golden teeth.

The sound hit Feng Ming like a sledgehammer, beating him down, eating into his qi and his vitality. He coughed up blood as he flew into the wall, several ribs breaking in the process. The monstrosity struck out with one of its massive legs, aiming not for Feng Ming but for the wall itself. It pierced into it, taking a large piece out from where the gouge had been. The large piece of rubble fell, and as it did, Feng Ming noticed something else.

Spiders. Spiders everywhere. They crawled upon the ground, the cliffs, and the beast itself. They crawled upon the Shattered Lands and the rock-covered corpses in the canyon. The woman cursed and swept out with her cane, sending blades and gusts of wind at the spiders that blew apart in sprays of silver metal, cutting down their allies, cutting down their *endless* allies, which were so crowded they barely had room to move.

They inched toward the fissure in the wall, and though the lady did her best to try repelling them, the larger spider, who emanated a life-leaching aura that made it difficult for even Feng Ming to breathe, let alone move, attacked her with precise strikes. She deflected the blows, which in turn allowed the spiders to surge forward.

"My king!" the woman bellowed.

Moments later, a figure appeared. It was none other than the angry king, Ji Lingtian. He threw his sword out to the massive spider, who recoiled as though it had met its worst nemesis.

"The Death-Spewing Blade!" the spider hissed, its mandibles chittering angrily.

"My ancestors banished you to the depths of that place, but it seems you've forgotten," the king said, standing tall. "Life-Leaching Monarch, today, I will end you."

"It seems it is you who's forgotten humility," the spider said. "I may not be able to breach this wall, but I can make you feel the consequences of encroachment. The miners you sent are dead, and you cannot stop my children from wreaking havoc in the city."

"It seems you're hellbent on this," the king said solemnly.

"I would be a fool not to take the opportunity, when someone so willingly tore a gap for me," the spider said. "I'll make you wish your ancestors had finished the job all those years ago."

The spider's two front legs shot at the king, who sent out a storm of swords. They fanned out in patterns, deflecting the spider's assault. Despite the creature's massive girth, it wielded its massive, scythe-like limbs with lethal precision.

As the king deflected the limbs, he used the single golden sword he'd held at his side to carve away at the golden metallic shell on the spider's body. He didn't even bother attacking the eyes, as there were thousands, and each one was covered in a transparent membrane that granted them greater protection than the golden shell itself. The sword was extremely effective. In fact, it seemed to have been made to slay this creature. It tore a deep gash into the shell that didn't recover despite the well-known regenerative powers of demons in their homeland.

That wasn't to say the creature couldn't fight back. While the king carved, it focused on spewing miasma. Feng Ming couldn't breathe, but if he didn't move now, he'd be completely paralyzed from exhaustion. Furthermore, the spider was spreading a thick, webby substance on the floor. Wherever it lay, the spiders moved more quickly. Even now, hundreds more of the foundation-establishment spiders swarmed past the desperate older lady as she worked to keep them at bay.

Looks like it's time to bail, Feng Ming thought. He flew toward the crack, but just as he did, he heard a scream.

"It's him!" the older lady yelled. "He's the one who tore open the rift!"

The king growled upon hearing her words. He diverted his attention from the spider for a moment, sending everything, every sword in his arsenal, toward Feng Ming.

Crap! Feng Ming thought, bringing up his Magma God's Spear. He could barely hold the thing, and it took everything he had to mobilize his qi to block the incoming swords. He executed a single technique: Magma God's Thrust. A spray of lava accompanied the spear strike toward the swords, just barely deflecting them away from him. Those that weren't deflected luckily avoided any vitals, cutting him only shallowly in the process. He didn't have time to worry about those small wounds, however. He braced himself, grunting in pain as the king's main sword, clearly a transcendent treasure, struck the Magma God's Spear. The red-hot spear, which had survived months against the Taotie, cracked. Then, the crack widened, and the entire spearhead broke.

"Damn it!" Feng Ming cried out. His spear exploded, and the molten explosion forced back the remaining swords. It also forced him and several spiders through the rift. He used the momentum to accelerate his retreat. The king and the lady didn't follow. They were clearly distracted by the larger spider and the incoming swarm.

The city was a disaster. Nearly a third of the palace was in ruins, with soldiers sifting through the rubble. The northern streets were filling up with deadly miasma and spiders, which the army and the city guard were collaborating to take out. To the west, a fire was burning where Gong Xuandi was fighting. And to the south, there was an unexpected fire. No, not a fire. Smoke was rising from an intact building. Was it a trick of the light?

To the west, an even more terrifying presence was approaching. Dozens of experts were fighting it, slowing it as it crawled desperately toward civilization and the energy it desperately craved. Transcendents stood by, worried about inserting themselves in the conflict, but bitterly acknowledging that if they didn't do anything about it, all would be lost.

Only one word could describe the city's situation: chaotic.

"Chaos is cash," Feng Ming muttered, flying over to the northern section of the palace. Conflicts in four different locations meant that the palace, and therefore, the treasury, was lightly guarded. Now all he needed to do was guess the combination. He was good at guessing.

"Heavens above, I hate spiders," Bear One muttered, hiding in a hastily carved-out hole from the spider swarm that had appeared out of nowhere. He and his group, the new Bears Two through Five, had been preparing to go out with the next quake. Unexpectedly, it hadn't come from the canyon—it had come from the wall itself.

The new Bear Four, a spindly, jovial man, was cut down before they could even react. They were all body cultivators, yes, but how did you deal with a sudden intensification in the life-leaching aura, combined with a dozen fatal wounds to the head? You didn't, it seemed.

Fortunately, Bear One was a fast thinker. He recalled Bear Six's—or whatever his real name was—warning and slapped a protective talisman on his arm and on the remaining three bears. It was a good move, it seemed, as the spiders began avoiding them from then on.

They'd been cowering in their hole ever since. No sense rocking the boat. Lying low was definitely the best course of action, though they'd have a tough time explaining exactly how they'd survived the onslaught.

"Who would have thought there's be so many spiders underground," Bear Two said, shaking his head. "You only see a dozen or so every quake. But here, there are thousands. Tens of thousands."

Bear Three scoffed. "You ever seen a spider's nest?"

Bear Two shook his head.

"Spiders have sacs. They have thousands of little babies, and carnivorous ones are even worse. Why, I've seen mortal spiders the size of my fist dragging goldish out of a pond, then draggin' 'em back to their younglings. Gone in three hours, tops."

Bear Two's eyes widened.

"We can all relax for now," Bear One said. "We are safe, and the spiders are gone. We've got a hole to hide in, and hours to spare until we have to return. Besides…" He sniffed. "The life-leaching isn't so bad right now. We might even have a whole day."

Bear Five, an obese but strong man, trudged up to the wall beside where Bear One was lying. He sat down on the ground, which let out a soft tremor. Bear Five was an odd one. He was dreadfully daft, but results couldn't be ignored. Something about his big bones made it so he could never retract his gravity field, which was many times stronger than normal. While that didn't mean much for everyone else, it meant that his every movement bore his entire strength. He was also much stronger than any marrow-refining cultivator Bear One had ever seen, and he could dig like the devil himself.

"Time to rest," Bear Five said, shutting his eyes.

Bear One flinched and ducked to the side as Bear Five, blissfully unaware of the impact he had on his surroundings, rested on the mountain wall. It collapsed inward. The other bears cursed, but Bear One ignored them.

"Look at what we have here," Bear One said, pleasantly surprised. Bear Five was out cold, since he'd decided to sleep and nothing anyone did could convince him otherwise. The other two bears, however, saw what Bear One saw. A glittering treasure trove, dozens of different colors. Ores, gemstones, and all sorts of goodies lay just beyond the fragile shell he'd managed to collapse.

"Taking that man in was the best decision I have ever made," Bear One muttered, making his way into the treasure trove. He glanced up and noticed the others weren't following. "Heavens above, you damned lazy louts had better get yourselves moving, or so help me god, I am going to give you the beating of a lifetime."

He looked to Bear Five, who was still sleeping, and gave him a good kick. "You too. You're not here to sleep, you are here to work." He'd tried many times now, but replacing the Bear crew wasn't working out like he'd planned. Maybe next time he'd go out on his own. Or back to where he came from. People were sensible on his home plane. They had self-control, they weren't daft, and more importantly, they didn't sleep on the job. And they were stronger. Too strong for his liking.

"I guess that's why I'm here and not there," Bear One muttered. "Best to be a big fish in a little pond than a little fish in a big pond." At least here, he could get more resources. At least here, he could grow without other blood-awakening cultivators trying to stop him.

What in the seven heavens is going on? Cha Ming thought, looking out to the city. He'd just gone into the monastery for a few minutes, but already the city was falling apart. He recognized that roar, or at least recognized its nature if not its ferocity. It was the Life-Leaching Monarch, and it had already launched its attack.

That came as a surprise to Cha Ming. The next step in his plan had been to eliminate the Spirit Temple. After that, he'd planned on smashing a gouge in the wall with his Clear Sky Staff, then using the chaos that ensued from the pincer beast tide and the Taotie to make his escape.

It seemed someone had done that for him. And he had a pretty good idea how. The defective Breaker, which wouldn't operate as planned but would catastrophically self-destruct, hopefully killing the crown prince and a few close associates, had already gone off. He hadn't been counting on it. Rather, that was just one last goodbye present, another nail in the coffin for both the Wang family and for the Ji Kingdom. It seemed that someone had thought it a great idea to activate it where it lay, obliterating a third of the palace and carving a deep gouge in the wall. Cha Ming thanked his lucky stars he'd aimed it northward, or the loss of innocent life would have been even more devastating.

Now, spiders crawled throughout the northern streets. Guards were busy repelling them, and he felt two powerful figures clashing with the Life-Leaching Monarch and fighting it to a standstill. In the west, a strong but familiar aura was busy fighting dozens of cultivators in a brutal clash. Likely, it was a body cultivator causing havoc. In the east, the Taotie was looming ever closer. Unlike the northern beast tide, it made no sound. It simply walked as quickly as it could while dozens of cultivators executed one technique after another to slow it down and buy the city time.

I should have time for one more, Cha Ming thought. He slipped through the streets in Pai Xiao's guise, ignoring shocked gasps as people saw him disappear. He appeared moments later above the Spirit Temple. Unceremoniously, he clicked the Space-Time Camera. It charged up for three seconds, then formed a complete barrier. Cha Ming flew into it. He wasn't welcomed by swords and staves but eerie silence. They were hiding, and with good reason. He saw faint outlines of ghosts taking refuge nearby. Other, more powerful ghosts surrounded him.

"Hiding is futile," Cha Ming said softly. His eyes glowed three colors as he activated his fused Devil-Sealing, Demon-Subduing, Spirit-Banishing Eyes. He glared at his surroundings, his eyes burning with what he now clearly saw as hatred. His eyes hated and wanted nothing more than to sear themselves out, to never see those things that offended them again.

He saw them clearly now, crimson ghosts that monitored Bastion Temple, and acolytes who cowered behind them, along with their companion spirits. Spectral Assassins, half human, half ghosts, swarmed toward him. They thought themselves invisible, but to Cha Ming, finding them was an easy task.

"Die," Cha Ming whispered. His combat sigils flew outward like before, filled with fire, though now they were filled with Spirit-Banishing Intent. They burned through people, buildings, and ghosts alike. Unlike the Blood Master Monastery, the Spirit Temple was a public place. Many hundreds of innocents were here, paying respects or inquiring for services. Clerks were especially prominent here, as producing and enforcing contracts was the Spirit Temple's main duty in the South.

Unfortunately, to destroy the temple, these lives had to be

sacrificed. His heart wept as they died, and with each death, he felt a chain of sin lay down on his soul, tainting it ever so slightly beneath the brilliant jade glow.

Hundreds of thousands of spirits were banished in an instant. And with their deaths, his eyes burned with power unlike any he'd ever experienced. He glanced at oncoming Spectral Assassins that had survived his attack, but the moment he looked at them, they vanished. They couldn't bear his glare, which sent them directly to the Yellow River they'd evaded for so long.

In the main temple, a man howled. An especially large column of souls was oozing out form there and plunging into a yellow river that seemed so vivid and lifelike. He'd banished so many at once that the Underworld and the mortal realm were now intersecting, and they were visible to each other. Above the yellow river, he caught sight of an old man in black robes holding a reaper's scythe. He had a timeless look in his black eyes, and his face bore the hint of a smile. He looked down to the man's hands and was surprised to discover Yama himself giving him a thumbs-up for a job well done. It seemed the keeper of the Underworld had been eyeing this place for quite some time.

"I will *end* you!" the man who'd howled earlier said. A half-step-transcendent soul erupted with power as it began voraciously absorbing the escaping souls. Its pressure mounted until it broke through to transcendence. Clouds above manifested white lightning many times stronger than he'd witnessed with the blood master before. Last time, the heavens had been offended by the blood master's actions. Here, they were utterly enraged.

"Leave now," they said with crackling lightning bolts. "Leave now, or we will *end* you."

But the ghost, who'd broken through by forcefully by consuming so many others, didn't leave. The powerful soul, much stronger than Cha Ming could have ever imagined, bore down on him like a heavy mountain. It pressed on his soul with tangible weight. He was at a complete disadvantage—how could he not be? His transcendent soul was casually cultivated, a secondary path that the universe barely recognized.

But this man was something else entirely. Just like Gong Lan, he was a pure soul cultivator on a powerful path. Gong Lan had cultivated the Buddhist path, and using it, she could fight evenly with apex cultivators like Cha Ming. This man cultivated the evil spirit path. Evil spirits would never let go of a grudge.

The ghost howled as it became thousands of faces that plunged into his spiritual sea. Cha Ming's transcendent soul's eyes opened. He stretched his limbs and summoned an illusory version of the Clear Sky Staff. After all, a transcendent soul was not defenseless. It could move, it could fight. He swung at the invading figures, hacking away at them with Spirit-Banishing Intent while Cha Ming's own glaring eyes wore away at the soul above them. The burning combat formation had shrunk down to only a few hundred meters, and each flame bore the Spirit-Banishing Intent that wore away at the Shepherd faster than he could consume souls.

Then came the lightning. Unable to bear the fact that the Shepherd hadn't obeyed its command, the lightning shot down and encapsulated both Cha Ming and the Shepherd in a sea of light. He roared in agony, and so did Cha Ming. Whereas before they'd been fighting, they could now only shudder as the lightning ate away at their spiritual presence.

But the Shepherd didn't seem to care. In fact, this seemed to have been his goal all along. Cha Ming had destroyed his temple, so he would destroy Cha Ming, whatever the cost. He clung to this plane that hated him so, and Cha Ming could only direct his Spirit-Banishing Intent at the evil spirit. He kept his eyes open, but his eyes bled profusely. Moreover, his vision darkened. He'd activated his eye technique far longer than he'd ever had to since gaining the Demon-Subduing Eyes. Since then, he'd only gained a decent amount of Demon-Subduing Intent.

The Spirit-Banishing Eyes, on the other hand, now had a literal ocean of Spirit-Banishing Intent. The strain these three intents placed on him was great, but unfortunately, it wasn't just his life on the line, but his very soul.

As Cha Ming struggled, a soft white light leaked out from the Clear Sky Staff, shielding him from the onslaught. It was only a small contribution, but every tiny bit mattered in this war of attrition. Even the Monkey King was doing what he could from the Clear Sky World, siphoning a portion of his transcendent force and sending it to Cha Ming's fading soul.

One agonizing second passed after another until finally, the Shepherd let out one last wail. He moved to combust, but the keeper of the Underworld, who'd been watching all this time, scoffed. He swept out his scythe, and the blow reached across entire worlds. It nipped the raging Shepherd's explosion in the bud, dragging him directly into the Yellow River. Cha Ming looked at Yama incredulously, but the man didn't seem to notice. He simply looked up at the sky and whistled, pretending nothing had ever happened. Cha Ming could only shake his head in bemusement.

With the Shepherd's death, the remaining souls could no longer exist. They were forced back into the Underworld, leaving only smoldering buildings and cracked stone where Cha Ming lay kneeling down, his eyes bleeding. He closed them and blinked a few times. He tried to deactivate his eye technique but discovered that he couldn't. But neither could he see. He could open his eyes all he liked, but they were clouded. He was blind.

Sighing, Cha Ming closed his eyes. He didn't know if he could recover, and if he could, he had no idea how long it would take. For now, he could only use his transcendent force. He coaxed his wounded soul back into its place in his spiritual sea and sent out his transcendent force. Looking around this way was like seeing in black and white. He could see no color, no detail. But at least he could function.

Knowing that time was short, he picked up his Clear Sky Staff and walked over to the center of the temple, eyes closed. Then he transformed the staff into a knife and carved a message just like the one before. These messages, along with the destruction of the

Spirit Temple, the Blood Master Monastery, and the defective Breaker, would incriminate the Wang family. The disappearance of their permanent members from the North and their treasury would reinforce that. Even if it was all sabotage, and the karmic trail wasn't quite clear, their resentment toward the Wang family would cause them a falling out in both the North and the South. As for Pai Xiao, who was to say he hadn't gone missing along with them? Furthermore, his karma wasn't traceable like it was for others; Wang Jun had assured him of that.

Cha Ming walked out of the gray shield covering the monastery. He'd barely stepped out when he heard another roar, but this one was a muffled one. It was a roar of triumph, a roar of exultation. He scanned the area to the west and discovered that his transcendent force ended at the city wall. Beyond that was emptiness.

The Taotie had come, and with its arrival, transcendent after transcendent, and hundreds of peak-core-formation cultivators, flew out from important city buildings and began fighting it. To the South, Cha Ming was a pain, a manageable annoyance. The Taotie, however, was a different story entirely. With it, they didn't dare hold back and sent everything they had, transcendents included.

Chapter 35
Leaving

Screaming men, women, and children rushed about as Cha Ming walked away from the smoldering rubble of the Spirit Temple. The shield had faded a short while ago due to his battle with the Shepherd, and its sudden appearance had frightened the local populace. Elsewhere in the city, he felt the Blood Master Monastery's shield shuddering uncontrollably, as though it would break at any minute. Whereas the Spirit Temple's shield had failed due to damage to his soul, the other shield was simply running out of energy. Despite the revelation, however, the Space-Time Camera had done its job. The destruction was obvious, but there were no living witnesses to what had transpired.

Now Cha Ming had to face the cold hard truth. He'd agonized over this moment for a long time and wondered about how he could minimize the massive casualties that would undoubtedly result from his actions. It was only now that he felt the cold reality of it: People were dying, good people. Though most of this was due to the untimely detonation of his sabotaged device, which would ideally have been brought north of the wall prior to its activation, the end result was that a third of the palace had been destroyed, and demonic spiders, metallic legs and all, had broken into the city. He couldn't blame outside interference, either. Regardless of the explosion, he'd planned on doing something similar with the wall prior to leaving.

The demonic tide, coinciding with the Taotie's attack, was simply too much for the city to bear.

Cha Ming was blind now, his normal vision blocked by the Devil-Sealing, Demon-Subduing, and Spirit-Banishing Intent within them. Yet despite this handicap, he could still "see" with his soul. He could feel each wound and each death as it happened. Every bit of suffering he inflicted on the innocent fed a tiny ochre speck of sin that latched onto his soul, tainting it. No amount of merit could get rid of that stain. It could only mask it, outshine it.

What's done is done, Cha Ming thought, continuing his scan as he walked. Right now, his priority was to escape. He had to decide whether he would run opposite the Taotie, avoiding the location where enemy forces were most concentrated, or if he should fly into the chaos, using the fighting as a smokescreen to escape. All around the Taotie, a dozen transcendents were fighting. The emperor was notably absent, but Cha Ming had noticed him fighting the Life-Leaching Monarch along with the surprisingly powerful Miss Ge.

That didn't stop the emperor's sons from fighting, however. They, along with a hundred peak-core-formation cultivators and half-step transcendents, were assisting the transcendents as they could. Prince Shen was especially prominent. He wielded a familiar black spear—Feng Ming's old lucky spear—using it to great effect against the creature's now shrinking body. He fought beside two of his sisters, both powerful cultivators of the Ji royal family. Their bodies were laden with valuable treasures that amplified their strength, defense, and speed.

As Cha Ming pondered over his escape plan, a wall suddenly fell beside him as a shock wave came from the fighting near the barracks. A man with a familiar aura was fighting, long weapon in hand lashing out with sweeping strikes that felled dozens at a time. With every strike, he was wounded by the veritable army that surrounded him. Powerful regeneration healed any injuries he sustained.

Is that a trident he's fighting with? Cha Ming thought. He remembered someone he'd clashed with some time ago. *Gong Xuandi? Is that you?*

No reply. He was confident in his assessment, however—he knew of no other trident-wielding half-step-blood-awakening cultivator who fought with such ferocity. He was surrounded by dozens of peak-core-formation experts, and five half-step transcendents. Despite his power, he was clearly on the losing end.

To help or not to help, he thought. If he helped, he might blow his cover and ruin everything. They weren't very good friends, after all, even if the man did serve under Feng Ming due to Gong Shuren's orders. *To help or not to help. What a troubling question.*

"Stupid, stupid, stupid," Feng Ming chastised himself as he dodged sword, spear, and saber while running through the western wing of the palace. He'd taken about half the treasury before being spotted, a heist he was very proud of. His ring was filled with spirit stones, rare gems, medicinal pills, and weapons. Many rare and unique herbs, which had been carefully stored in jade boxes and preserved for over a decade, were now resting happily in the void space on his finger.

His luck wasn't all good. During his pilfering, he'd triggered an alarm, attracting the remaining few powerhouses in the palace. That included the head of the imperial guard, a half-step-transcendent spear wielder with devastating offensive maneuvers. The man wore black armor instead of the usual golden, and his every attack was filled with destructive lightning.

"Stand still and accept your fate, thief," the head of the guard said angrily. He swept out with his spear, which generated a black lightning dragon that let out a thunderous roar. The roar paralyzed Feng Ming, who'd been weakened by the Life-Leaching Monarch, for a split second. It was enough for the spear to pierce his armor and graze his shoulder, leaving a three-inch gouge that cut down to the bone.

Lightning ran through his body, scorching the flesh where he'd been struck. In response, he kicked out with his boot. He struck one of the two other individuals attacking him, one of the princes of the Ji Kingdom. His boot struck true, and he pushed off, barely avoiding a saber strike that threatened to cut off his foot. The push allowed him to extricate himself from the spear long enough to catch a deep breath, form hand seals, and blow hard.

A raging inferno appeared from his mouth, surrounding the two princes and the head of the guard. They paused to defend, throwing up qi shields to absorb the torrent of fire. Their sudden defense gave him respite, and the force generated by his technique pushed him out even farther.

He flew down the hallway and took a quick right and a left, into an unoccupied room. There, he hefted the spear he'd found—just a late-core treasure—and smashed open the window, which was surprisingly made from core-grade glass. Was it to protect it from kids playing in the yard just outside? Who knew? What he did know was that there was now a clear path to a side entrance to the palace complex, one usually reserved for servants.

He leapt through the window and barreled toward the closed door, not pausing to open it, kicking out with both his feet, flying horizontally as though he was falling. The door burst open, slamming a poor man who'd just knocked on it against the wall. Winded but otherwise unharmed, the man would never know his good fortune as the head of the guard and the two princes whooshed through it, uncaring of the people that stood in their path.

I need to find Gong Xuandi, Feng Ming thought. He was weak, and there was no way he could fight these three off on his own. Not only was his strength insufficient, but his spear was lacking too. It was pink, for heaven's sake! The brilliant pink weapon, according to the description left beside it, was called Cherry Blossom's Dancing Light. It was a light spear, an ornamental one at that, made for graceful dancing. Most of its enchantments relied on illumination and illusion.

That gave him an idea. As he rounded one corner, Feng Ming slashed out with it. Millions of flower petals accompanied the spear light he generated. The pink blossoms filled the air and covered the landscape. These illusory petals also contained charming and calming runes, distracting and slowing down his three pursuers. He used the time it bought to crash into the barracks, where a barebacked fighter covered in blue and gold runes was just about to impale a man with a trident.

Feng Ming flew up beside him, fending off a blow that would otherwise have stabbed the man in the back. He would have survived, of course, but every little bit of vitality mattered. The battle instantly improved for the man, whose opponents began to make careless mistakes, began to slip in blood, whose weapons began to fail. Dodging motions Gong Xuandi made for the chance of escaping were the correct decision, and feints his opponents began making lost their meaning, as he was suddenly able to guess their intention.

With Gong Xuandi's help, Feng Ming's life became a little easier as well. The strong, burly man had his back, giving him enough time to pop a few pills he'd pillaged from the vault. He threw a few to Gong Xuandi and downed the rest. Normally it wasn't wise to take so many at once; if you were unlucky, some negative side effects could crop up.

But Feng Ming had luck in spades. He slashed with Cherry Blossom's Dancing Light, and the air was filled with pink petals that obscured everyone's five senses and spiritual force. The closer one was to the spear the better, as there were fewer petals blocking off the opponent you were targeting.

The head of the guard and the two princes who had been chasing Feng Ming joined the encirclement, but it was meaningless, as only so many people could fight in tandem, even in three dimensions. The two kept the floor beneath their feet, wisely cutting the area in which they could be attacked in half. The rate at which they killed intensified, but luck could only go so far. Spears and swords still snuck in, wounding them. Though they mostly struck the unlucky Gong Xuandi, the old emperor was still gravely wounded from his earlier battle. Neither of them would last long in this encirclement.

"What we need," Feng Ming said, gritting his teeth, "is a miracle.

A lucky coincidence. A helping hand."

He ducked an incoming saber and struck upwards with his spear. The pink spear struck true, catching a man in the throat. He yanked it free, pulling it back just in time to deflect a flying sword that was headed toward his head. It clanked off effortlessly, coincidentally bouncing off the ground and back up into the back of a cultivator who'd stumbled in the fighting.

"If it's a miracle you need," Gong Xuandi said. "An old enemy seems to have reached out to me."

"An old enemy?" Feng Ming asked. "You mean Zhou Li?"

"Cha Ming," Gong Xuandi said. "He's offering us a way out. He's wounded, and he can't fight or reveal himself."

"Tell him we'll take anything we can get, you wonderful, wonderful man," Feng Ming said.

Gong Xuandi winced. "Unfortunately, he said we'd need to get beaten back to make it work. He wants us to take a dive."

"Take a dive," Feng Ming said blankly. He ducked a spear thrust, grabbed the spear from a man, and kicked him back into the crowd of assailants. He then threw his out into a flurry of cherry blossoms, catching a soldier in the face by sheer fluke. "Fine. Let's do it."

"You're serious?" Gong Xuandi said. "You'll take a dive in the middle of a crucial battle and trust this man with your life?"

"With my life," Feng Ming said, nodding. They hadn't interacted much since that time in the woods, only touching base briefly in the Song Kingdom's succession battle, then later near Beihai. "I might be the luckiest man on the plane, but I'm no miracle worker. Cha Ming, on the other hand, is a bit unlucky. Life always throws all sorts of curve balls at him. He keeps falling and picking himself up over and over again, no matter how difficult. But if there's one man who can create a miracle for us, it's him."

"Yes, sir!" Gong Xuandi said, gritting his teeth. Then he did something insane in this situation. He charged into the crowd of surrounding soldiers, flying up in the air. Feng Ming went with him.

Before, they'd been able to protect themselves against a relatively small encirclement. Now, their opponents could attack them in three dimensions. They didn't hesitate to throw one technique after another, sending out flying swords, burning dragons, and icy phoenixes of energy to strike them. They pushed like it was the last push in their life, struggling fiercely to beat their way out of encirclement. Their enemies encouraged their flight, giving way for them but circling around, following them as they escaped.

Then one sword came through, then another, then another. Feng Ming took cuts to the arms and legs while Gong Xuandi began taking entire blades in the torso. He didn't have time to yank them out, so they simply remained there, making him look more like a living pincushion than a human being.

Over here, a voice called out. It came from the floor up ahead.

Feng Ming didn't hesitate. He used everything he had to push himself off toward what called him. He grabbed Gong Xuandi and noticed everything around them sinking into darkness. The darkness obscured both sight and spirit, an absolute blackness more potent than Feng Ming had ever seen.

Where the floor should have been, they found none. They fell through, then something strong appeared above them. Whether it was a formation or a physical piece of wall, he didn't know. The darkness faded, and through their spiritual forces, they could sense their opponents even though their opponents could not sense them. Feng Ming noticed that they were in a refuge completely formed by combat sigils. Thin lines of qi ran around them, shielding them, while others were up above, creating the false ground they hid under, where many others stood.

At that moment, a man crashed down from the air into a house beside them. Half the house was instantly demolished, and the man recovered thirty feet later, pulling himself out of a deep gouge. He struck a heroic pose, his yellow armor in sharp contrast to the familiar black spear Feng Ming had lost so long ago.

No way, Feng Ming thought. He recognized the man from a folio he'd seen at a Northern Alliance meeting. That was Prince Shen, without a doubt. The heir to the Ji Kingdom, the most powerful kingdom in the Southern Alliance.

"Young prince, are you all right?" asked the leader of the royal guard, who'd joined the battle against Gong Xuandi once Feng Ming had jumped in.

"It was just a glancing blow," Prince Shen said, fingering a deep gouge in his chestplate. The gouge didn't seem burnt or bent; it was simply missing. Like it had never been there in the first place. "The enemy is strong. It threw me from all the way across the city. Fortunately, I had this armor. It was able to absorb the blow for me."

"You must take care," the guard leader said. Then he hesitated. "Did you see two strong cultivators, one a spear wielder and one a Haijing royal? They're wreaking havoc in the city. One of them even stole from our treasury."

The crown prince's eyes narrowed. "Are you telling me that while my royal father is fending off the Life-Leaching Monarch to the north, and half the transcendents in the entire South, along with a large contingent of our elites, including myself, my brothers, and two of my sisters, are fighting for the survival of our very city, our very plane, you are here chasing mere *thieves*?"

The guard leader paled. "I was assigned to guard the palace."

"The palace is meaningless!" the crown prince shouted. "It's all meaningless if we don't save this city, don't contain this creature. My father's battle is excusable, because without him, the entire city would fall. But you are all here dealing with petty criminals?" He lifted his spear. "I should cut you down where you stand."

The leader of the imperial guard, so majestic, so heroic before, could only bow his head in shame. He gripped his spear tightly, gulped, then looked up. "What are your orders, my prince?"

"Your orders are to fly to where our elites are and help destroy that creature," Prince Shen said. "Do it now!"

"Yes, sir!" the guard leader said.

Just as they were about to fly off, however, the prince suddenly gasped and fell to one knee. "My prince!" the man said, flying up to him.

"I'll be fine," Prince Shen said, panting heavily. "I just need a little time. The others, they don't have time. Go help them."

"I'll stay and—"

"Go!" Prince Shen yelled.

The head of the royal guard hesitated but saluted. "Let's go, men. We have a duty to fulfill. Not just for our country, but for the South and to everyone who lives here." They rose up in the air and shot out toward the beast, which now towered above the city walls.

Feng Ming pondered attacking the crown prince as the men left. He was a juicy target, someone they had a bounty on in the North. A surprise strike in the back was all it would take, and the spear he'd lost would be his once more. So he jumped out of the hole, concealing his presence as he snuck up behind the man. He gripped his spear, ready to stab down at the man's exposed back, when the man changed before his very eyes. His face, his aura, his armor. Everything. Revealing a familiar figure: Cha Ming.

"Let's go," Cha Ming said. "We don't have much time to waste." Judging by his weary state, he'd also seen his fair share of fighting.

"My friend," Feng Ming said, running up to him and giving strong hug. "You'd vanished."

Cha Ming changed once again, this time into a heavyset middle-aged man with slightly grizzled hair.

"I don't exist," Cha Ming said. "I've never been here." He looked uncertainly toward the Taotie. "We need to move now. Those transcendents are up to something. They've withdrawn from the battle and have taken out a powerful treasure. If we don't leave now, we might not get another chance."

Feng Ming looked toward the battle in the east. He saw the head of the guard and the others joining them, and there was some confusion among their ranks. He saw Prince Shen, the real one, fighting the Taotie with everything he had, yellow chestplate and all. He saw a familiar black spear. His lucky spear.

"Cha Ming?" Feng Ming said, hesitating. "Could you do me a favor?"

Up ahead, the Taotie opened its mouth and roared. Its soundless might reverberated throughout their bodies and souls.

"What happened to your eyes?" Feng Ming asked, curiously glancing at Cha Ming as he led the way toward the last place he wanted to be—right next to the battle, at the base of the Taotie's feet. They were nearing those who fought it at the center of the devastation. There were no civilians, as those who hadn't fled had already been killed by the shock waves of the battle.

All around the beast, wicked tentacles flailed about, latching on to anything it could. And all around it, a strange emptiness presided. The walls that had fallen, the earth that had been churned up by the impact of its heavy feet and claws, the weapons that had fallen to the ground from felled combatants—none of them remained. They'd either been swept clear by the other fighters, who knew full well what would happen if they left tasty morsels for the beast to devour, or had been swept up by the tentacles or their tendrils, which roamed the battlefield in search of prey.

The area around the Taotie was fuzzy, for he couldn't open his eyes. Not only would opening them do nothing productive, but it would also release an intense devil-sealing pressure in a land chock full of devils. There were many of them among the transcendents who fought the Taotie. The creature itself was an outline of darkness so deep that he could almost make out shades from the emptiness.

"We don't have much time," Cha Ming said. He tilted his head toward the chanting transcendents up above. A black grimoire now floated between them, black runic characters floating up from its grisly leather-bound surface. Each rune let off a thick ochre glow that his soul could make out, despite not being able to see. The ochre glow made his spirit shiver in fear; it was clearly not of mortal origins. The transcendent devilish might glowed brightly, and the Taotie, which struggled madly to approach it, also seemed to fear it.

"This way," Feng Ming said, floating over to a collapsed building.

Cha Ming kept up his combat formation, using tricks of light to shield their surroundings. Though not as skillful as Zi Long's illusions, he could still use his transcendent force and formations to effectively mask their group. There, they waited. Feng Ming, Gong Xuandi, and Cha Ming simply stood there, waiting for an opportunity.

"So what's the plan?" Cha Ming asked, taking a moment to recover qi and soul force.

"No plan," Feng Ming said. "We'll wait here for an opportunity. I refuse to believe that my lucky spear actually *wants* to stay with that guy."

Far above them, the crown prince of the Ji Kingdom, Prince Shen, was spearheading the fighters from his kingdom. They were laying down their lives to push back the Taotie, whose power was clearly growing with every passing second.

"Great," Cha Ming said. "You know, if you weren't so damned lucky, I'd abandon you in heartbeat."

"But I *am* lucky," Feng Ming said smugly. "A chance will come. Don't worry."

Cha Ming shook his head, his guts green with regret. "I should have stolen it when I had the chance. It was just sitting there, in the Wang family vault."

"You saw my spear? And you didn't take it?" Feng Ming said, glaring.

"Look, it wasn't at the top of my priority list," Cha Ming said angrily. "I had an organization to infiltrate, deception to plot, a priceless treasure to steal, and a weapon to invent then sabotage."

"So that weapon I set off…" Feng Ming said hesitantly.

"*You're* the one who set it off?" Cha Ming said, slapping his hand against his forehead. "I should have known."

"Stand a little to the right," Feng Ming said suddenly.

Cha Ming frowned but shuffled over.

"A little more."

Cha Ming obliged.

"Sorry, I didn't want you standing there. Bad feeling and all."

"So we're just supposed to stand here and wait for it?" Cha Ming said. "What, will it just fall out of the sky?"

Up above, the battle intensified. The chanting grew louder, and the ochre runes began swirling above the Taotie. The transcendents split up into twelve main groups, and one of them, their leader, shouted at the non-transcendents to keep interfering with the beast.

A massive lightning storm was gathered above the transcendents, attacking their group every so often with calculated bolts of lightning. They were warning strikes, meant to strike fear into them but not kill. Clearly, even the heavens held back as the devilish transcendents chanted to contain the creature. Though the heavens were unthinking and merciless, even they seemed to know fear. They simply stood at the ready, and as the transcendents increased their power with the volume of their chanting, they increased in size as well. The bolts the storm sent grew more powerful, sometimes searing a cloak, sometimes burning an arm.

"Now!" the lead transcendent said. "Pull back!"

"Pull back!" Prince Shen yelled, echoing the command. His men flew away, and he held the rear for a fraction of a second longer. They dived and swerved, avoiding the beast as it tried to catch them with flailing tentacles. Fortunately, it was distracted by the glowing ochre lights above it. It reached out for them, only using a few stray appendages to swat the stragglers.

One of those tentacles, to the prince's misfortune, struck true. It hit him in the back just as he was about to reach safety.

"My prince!" the head of the royal guard yelled, diving to save him. He caught the prince as he fell, Shen's armor disintegrating from the dark energy that siphoned away at it. His face was as pale as a sheet. No one thought to retrieve his spear.

That same spear fell tip first into the ground beside Cha Ming, right where he'd been standing before Feng Ming had instructed him to move over. It disappeared as it entered their concealment. Cha Ming raised an eyebrow as Feng Ming picked it up, inspected it, then nodded. "Good ole lucky spear," Feng Ming said. "Since I lost the Magma God's Spear, I can't well return home unarmed. Though," he said, shaking his head, "it's unfortunate I lost my father-in-law's weapon. He's going to kill me when I get back."

A second spear flew down from the battlefield, this one from an unlucky marshal in the Ji Kingdom's forces. It was a golden spear with red patterns, fire aligned, glowing bright with merit glow.

"Ah," said Feng Ming, picking it up.

"This is too much," Cha Ming said, shaking his head ruefully as Feng Ming stowed the new spear, the replacement for his Magma God's Spear.

Prizes in tow, they flew through the streets away from the carnage. They rushed through the city gates, which were now unguarded due to the chaos, flying past unwitting guards who could only gawk at their passage. They continued flying even when twelve shining pillars of ochre light descended on the creature, locking it in place. Runes glowed on those pillars as they formed chains that bound it, stopping it from moving. They contained its devouring powers, which couldn't quite feed on the transcendent energy they were composed of.

They were safe. They'd accomplished their missions and left the city undetected before Zhou Li arrived. In Cha Ming's eyes, blind as they were, that was the very definition of success. He only wished it didn't taste so bittersweet.

*T*ick. Tick. Tick.

The clock in Wang Jun's office marked each agonizing second as it passed. He sat before Elder Bai and Wang Bing as they went over their morning reports. It was painful to listen, not because of the results—they were doing well—but because of what he'd rather be doing: finding Hong Xin. The fact that he'd finally found her after all this time only to lose her again was both infuriating and depressing. It felt like some god of mischief had a grudge against him, forever filling his life with painful twists and turns.

Elder Bai was reaching the end of his monthly report. At long last, they'd finally surpassed Wang Ling's asset base. "I'm not sure whether it was more due to our aggressive growth lately or his aggressive losses, but results are results," Elder Bai said proudly. His face fell when he saw Wang Jun's distant expression. "Should we schedule this meeting for another time, perhaps? You don't seem as ecstatic as I'd imagined."

"This meeting time is fine," Wang Jun said. "Please, don't worry about me, I'm just tired and overworked. I have many things weighing on my mind."

Elder Bai didn't know about Hong Xin or her identity as Headmistress Hong. Neither did Wang Bing.

"Since it's a day for happy news, I thought I should let you know about my good news," Wang Bing said. She sat there, waiting with her hands folded in front of her cup. He noticed a jade ring on the fourth finger of her left hand.

"Congratulations," Wang Jun said, smiling lightly. "I can't say I caught his name earlier."

"Of course you didn't," Wang Bing said. "I didn't tell you, as I didn't want you sneaking into his house at night threatening his poor little life."

"Surely you can tell me now?" Wang Jun said. "I wouldn't be so cruel as to take away your husband now that you're already married."

She hesitated, then nodded. "He's a designer named Han Shui. He makes the most wonderful clothing out of the finest demon silk."

"Make sure to buy yourself a congratulatory gift from me," Wang Jun said.

"Already have," Wang Bing said. "The shoes are very nice. Thank you."

Elder Bai coughed uncomfortably.

"In any case," Wang Bing continued, "it's clear that you have something on your mind. I just thought I'd give you some extra happy news this morning. You know, aside from the fact that we're winning and all."

"Thank you, both of you, for all your hard work," Wang Jun said. "I know it's meant many long hours, much time away from your families, and extra elbow grease. You're the best team a man could ask for. I'm proud of you."

They both nodded as they packed up their things and shuffled out of the office, leaving Wang Jun to his thoughts.

Tick. Tick. Tick.

The clock's sound, previously a mundane backdrop in his plain office, infuriated him with every passing second. "Shadow?" Wang Jun asked. There was a small delay before the shadow emerged from his own figure, facing the light instead of shying away from it. "What have you discovered?"

Still nothing, the shadow said. *I found the culprits. They are all Spectral Assassins of high rank. But from what I can tell, this wasn't plotted by the Spirit Temple. It was a contract, nothing more. An expensive one.*

"Still nothing…" Wang Jun muttered. A knock came at his door. The shadow, knowing exactly what to do, moved away from the light and imitated Wang Jun's pose. "Come in."

"Young Master Jun?" a quavering voice said.

Wang Jun looked up and saw a younger man with blond hair. A lesser member of the Wang family, so he was relegated to messenger duty. "The Patriarch has requested your presence."

"I'm not interested," Wang Jun said, waving him away.

"He said you'd say that," the messenger said, "so he asked me to tell you he had very special news to share with you, news that would overjoy you."

Wang Jun frowned at that. Just what game *was* the Patriarch playing, today of all days? Would he dangle the leadership in front of him like a carrot, only to snatch it back due to a technicality? He sighed. "Tell him I'll be right there."

The messenger nodded and left. Wang Jun traced the boy's progress back to the elder council room, where he said words and left. Unfortunately, Wang Jun couldn't quite make out who was there. The room was distorted, a powerful presence obscuring everything. His eyes widened. *Could it be?*

The room around Wang Jun melted, merging into shadows. The messenger boy yelped as Wang Jun emerged from the ground beside him. Wang Jun ignored the boy and marched toward the double doors to the elder council, pushing them in. Rage filled his eyes when he saw what was there: the Patriarch sipping tea at a table. A woman in purple sat to his left.

Hong Xin.

A collar had been placed around her neck, and her eyes were red from all the crying she'd done. There were red marks on her wrists where her manacles had dug into her flesh as she'd sought to escape. And her cultivation—no, the lack thereof—stood out especially. He shook as he realized that it had completely vanished. There were many devices that could hide such things, and many qi-restraining devices that could hide the cultivation of a captive. Such tricks had no effect on him, however. She wore no qi-restraining devices, for her cultivation was completely gone.

"What. Have. You. Done?" Wang Jun said, stepping forward. Each step crashed soundlessly, cracking stone and splintering wood. Every shadow in the room danced as they leaned in toward his target, Patriarch Wuling.

"Tut-tut-tut," Patriarch Wuling said, holding up a black dagger.

Wang Jun shook again. This wasn't a normal dagger, but a soul-stealing sacrificial dagger from the Spirit Temple. Anyone killed by it would have their soul bound to the wielder, to do with as he pleased. That included locking it away, never to see the cycle of reincarnation again.

"How *dare* you," Wang Jun said. "First you send me on a wild goose chase. Then you give me an impossible challenge. Now, you kidnap *her*? Where has your humanity gone? Are you still even human?"

"Stop right there where I can see you," Patriarch Wuling said, standing up. "And before we continue, I'll have you know that I've fed her a poison, one that requires a rare antidote every day. I have commissioned the Spirit Temple to curse her three separate ways, all three of which detect tampering. The Ancestor himself, at great expense, has also placed a life-dependency bond on this woman. Should Wang Ling die, she will die with him. Furthermore, this isn't a trigger, but a constant feed. Absence of his presence sending a constant signal to her will result in her death, so cheap hiding tricks before stabbing him in the back won't work."

He walked out from behind the table, leaving Hong Xin on the chair. She seemed absentminded, not quite there. Was she drugged? Was she incapacitated so she couldn't convince him to abandon her? That only made him even more angry, and it took the entirety of his self-control—along with the reminder that if he killed him, Hong Xin would likely die—not to stab the man in the throat.

"You," Patriarch Wuling said, "have been very a bad boy. You've been operating in the shadows, threatening, killing, blackmailing.

You've also been operating a legitimate business, one that brings in so much money that half the elders are willing to back you."

"So you decided to collect a hostage," Wang Jun said bitterly. "To rein me in."

"It wasn't those things I mentioned that forced me to do this," Patriarch Wuling said, gritting his teeth.

Wang Jun could see them now, clear signs of agitation and stress. Something had happened recently, something that was outside of his control. Moreover, he could see several hundreds of bloodred threads connecting the man to another entity. Some were thin, but three were thick, unbearably so. It was a thread of karmic debt, and the debt he owed was massive.

"You've done some things, planned some things. I don't know how you did them, but these things happened, and our entire family is in jeopardy."

"I don't know what you're talking about," Wang Jun said.

"DON'T BOTHER WITH YOUR LIES!" Patriarch Wuling yelled in a rare outburst of emotion. "There was the business with the Spirit Temple in town. Fine. You killed a few Spectral Assassins, and that's something I can compensate with money. You decided to kill a few nobles, blackmail some others. I can live with that. What I *cannot* live with is you messing up three hundred years of careful planning.

"You sent someone. I don't know who, I don't know how. But *someone* snuck into our Southern businesses and somehow managed to destroy a heavens damned Spirit Temple, Shepherd included, an *entire* Blood Master Monastery, traveling transcendent included, destroy half the Ji Kingdom's army garrison, broke Bastion Wall, and provoked a fight between a demon monarch and the king of the Ji Dynasty, who is now mortally wounded.

"And finally, *blew up* half his palace, killing very important political figures from around the South in the process. That doesn't even count the vast resources we invested in the Blackthorn Conglomerate that were raided from the vault. There is no karma leading back to a perpetrator. Our agents are dead. Karma only flows one way, and that's to me and Ling. And you and I both know that there's *no one else* on this continent who can do this except for you and that wretched, freeloading master of yours." After letting it all out, Patriarch Wuling took a deep breath, let it out, and cracked his neck. "From now on, you're on a leash."

"You will free her," Wang Jun said.

"I will not," Patriarch Wuling replied. "I've also identified her family members, dredged up your past history with her. Some of your mutual acquaintances are beyond my reach, but I swear to the seven lords of heaven and the seven lords of hell that if you so much as step a *toe* out of line, I will kill her and everyone she's ever known. Do I make myself clear? You will listen to Ling, help him where he's lacking, and coordinate with him. You are to do as instructed, like the most loyal dog to the most caring master. Do you understand?"

Wang Jun gave no answer.

"I said, do you *understand?*"

Seeing Patriarch Wuling take out his dagger and walk back toward Hong Xin, Wang Jun could only close his eyes and speak the words: "I understand."

The Patriarch paused, then looked up and laughed exultantly. "Heavens above, he sees sense. He finally sees sense."

"I thought I'd grown callous and merciless," Wang Jun said, his voice lacking emotion. "I thought I'd rid myself of my weak heart, all in order to succeed and obtain vengeance. But it seems I was looking in the wrong place. It wasn't my soft heart that was my weakness but my ambition. I wanted to see you all suffer, but because of that, I endangered her. I should have killed the lot of you when I had a chance."

"All past matters," Patriarch Wuling said. "As your first order of business, you are to personally head to the Spirit Temple—sneak in, of course—and apologize. You are to accept responsibility for your actions, but you must swear upon your soul that you'll make things right with them."

"You aren't just playing both sides, are you?" Wang Jun asked. "You're a turncoat, through and through."

"We do what we can to survive, son," Patriarch Wuling said. "And trust me, it was this or the death of our family. The South can't be stopped. Only by joining them can we truly prosper as a family."

"You're beyond redemption," Wang Jun said, stepping back. Despite all the killings, the blackmail, the fabrications, the thought of working for the South to destroy the peaceful North sickened him. He'd done wrong, but this was pure evil.

"*We* are beyond redemption," Patriarch Wuling emphasized, stepping up to him until their noses almost touched. He could smell the man's rancid breath and see the intricate details in the whites of his eyes. "But when you decide you want her dead, that you want to kill her with your own two hands, I'll be waiting." He bared his neck. "Though, I doubt you'll have the courage to take me up on it."

The Patriarch walked back to Hong Xin, who was still struggling to hold her head up. Her eyes seemed to implore him to kill her, to destroy this madman and be done with it. But all the looks in the world could never convince him to do such a thing. He'd lost her once, and he would never do so again. Hong Xin left the room under Patriarch Wuling's escort, and soon, elders began to flow into the room to begin their morning sessions. They gave Wang Jun strange glances but didn't say anything otherwise.

"I have an announcement to make," Wang Jun said, his voice soft carrying throughout the whole room. The elders stopped their shuffling and looked at him. "From now on, I relinquish my claim to the family leadership in favor of Wang Ling. He has my full support, and I look forward to working with him from this day forward."

Half the elders frowned in concern, but the other half smiled. Their mutters masked his silent steps as he left the room, defeated.

Wang Jun made no sounds as he approached the black corridor that no one else could see. He entered its bright confines, barely glancing at the countless doors that led to other locations across the continent. He pushed through the main doors at the back, entering a dark room barely decorated but containing a single dark throne. No one sat there, and no one had been there in quite some time. There was a note on a small table to the side, the one Daoist Obscurus often used to lay fruit on.

Wang Jun picked up the black paper note, reading the even blacker writing intently as he muttered with not a sound. He frowned as he read, and glanced to his shadow, which barely stood out among the black stone floor.

> *To my dearest apprentice,*
>
> *I'm sorry not to be there in your time of need, but I needed to step out to do some field research. It's dreadfully important and can't wait. While I'm gone, you can practice the techniques I taught you and polish them up. When I return, we'll prepare for carving your core, as it's only after you transcend that you'll be able to learn the best of what I have to offer. I know it's difficult, but you need to press on. Your soft heart might be a weakness, but it's also the source of your strength. The best of shadows need light to cast.*
>
> *As a side note, I thought I'd let you know about an ongoing problem you might have missed. It's about your shadow. He's been a bad boy, you see, and I thought I'd let you know about that before he does anything too damaging. Shadow doppelgangers are tricky because they aren't just intelligent— they're exactly as intelligent as you are. That means they need extra discipline, else they'll start doing things on their own.*
>
> *It shouldn't be too big a problem. You should be able to take care of it before I'm back. Be sure to water my plants for me while I'm gone.*
>
> *Cheers,*
>
> *D.O.*

Wang Jun first looked to the plants, which were black, dried up, and didn't require the slightest bit of water. A bit of his master's humor, he supposed. Then he looked to his shadow, dread filling him. "What have you done?"

"Things," the shadow replied.

"What kind of things?" Wang Jun said calmly.

"Things you couldn't do yourself," the shadow replied. "Things that I deemed needed doing, as instructed."

"You hid them from me," Wang Jun accused.

"Yes," the shadow said. "For your own good. For *our* own good."

"Tell me," Wang Jun said. "*Show me.*"

The shadow did just that. Not with words, but with one soft clank after another. Item after item dropped out from the shadows. Treasures, spirit stones, you name it. Occasionally, a limb or a body tumbled out. They were familiar people who had gone missing recently.

The belching continued for some time until finally, it stopped. A large pile of things lay in Daoist Obscurus's audience chamber, and at the top lay some thin blue items. Wang Jun summoned them to his hand. He held them tight and sighed. They were solid blue hairpins, those worn by the Icy Heart Pavilion, taken from their dead bodies. His shadow had killed them, and in turn, Hong Xin had been forced out, only to be captured by the Spirit Temple and his cursed relatives.

He'd told Hong Xin he had nothing to do with the killings, but it seemed her suspicions were well founded. He wasn't just involved; he was completely responsible. He'd caused her predicament. And now he'd gotten what he deserved for it—a collar to tie him to the brother he hated and the family he loathed. A one-way ticket to hell.

Hong Xin blinked, the last of the haze leaving her eyes and revealing a cell. A comfortable cell, mind you, but a cell nonetheless. A dozen guards stood outside, carefully guarding her, lest she escape. Not that she'd make it very far if she tried. The guards, she knew, weren't there to stop her from escaping her prison. They were there to stop her from ending her life.

"Just what went wrong?" Hong Xin thought out loud. "What happened?"

A loud sigh filled the room as a woman appeared there. None of the guards seemed to see her, and their eyes shied away from the dazzling red dust that surrounded her. One by one, their eyelids drooped as they fell asleep.

"Sister Yinyue!" Hong Xin said, so happy she could barely contain herself. She moved to hug the woman but found herself restrained by shackles. She could only sit down ruefully.

"You've suffered, child," Hong Yinyue said. "Much has happened during my absence." She walked up to Hong Xin and stretched out a hand, feeling the spot on her chest where the cultivation-crippling dagger had pierced her Dantian. "I can't heal this. No one short of an immortal or a god can, for it's not a wound of the body, nor is it quite a wound of the soul."

Hong Xin sniffed, wiping tears from her eyes. "It's not so bad. My cultivation wasn't going to be very useful anyway."

"Nonsense," Hong Yinyue said, shaking her head. "If I hadn't had to leave and monitor what was happening in the South, I would have prevented it."

"What happened?" Hong Xin said, noting the worry in her voice. She hadn't seen Hong Yinyue this upset since, well, ever. Hong Yinyue was a composed fairy maiden, a temptress who moved the hearts of others while maintaining her own stable disposition.

"Nothing you need worry about," Hong Yinyue said. "We will see if what we fear truly comes to pass. But it's out of our hands now. What matters now is what *he* chooses. Now, enough of things we can't affect." She looked to the sleeping guards. "The things they have done to you have made it difficult for me to help. I can kill you or save you, but if I save you, you'll die within days no matter what I do. It would be enough time for you to say goodbye to your loved ones."

"Just kill me," Hong Xin said. "End this meaningless life and tell Wang Jun he's free. Let him kill those who did this to me and be done with his awful family once and for all."

"That's an option," Hong Yinyue said. "The coward's option."

"I'm only a burden now," Hong Xin said. "I can't help anyone anymore."

"You're far from a burden," Hong Yinyue said, sighing. She walked up beside Hong Xin and placed a hand on her shoulder. "In fact, as a hostage, you're in a position of great power."

Hong Xin frowned. "I know you're trying to reassure me, but isn't this trying a little too hard?" She shook her head. "I'm a hostage, and a crippled one at that."

"A crippled hostage they don't dare to kill," Hong Yinyue said. "One very close to Wang Jun's heart, the very reason he's playing along with the Wang family in their quest to sabotage the North. You have his ear, child. Not many people can claim the same."

"If I die, he can go ahead and kill them," Hong Xin said. "I'd like to see them collude with the South then." She'd also be done with this miserable life. She'd be free to start a new one after drinking Meng Po's tea.

"Tell me, child," Hong Yinyue said. "To seduce a man, should a woman take off her top and climb on him, mounting him in the middle of a crowd? Or should she play with his heart and tease his mind? Or should she instead talk with him and get to know him and his family? Once she knows him through and through, a simple touch would be all she needs to make him lose his mind. And if she decided to take off her top and mount him in the middle of a crowd, would he be able to resist? There is a time and a place for all things. Here and now is hardly the best time or place for your death. If you're going to die, have it mean something."

Hong Xin closed her eyes as tears fell down her cheeks. "What must I do?"

"The hardest thing you've ever done," Hong Yinyue said softly. "You must teach him to care. For himself, and for others."

"And then?" Hong Xin said.

"And then you'll need to ask him to do the hardest thing he's ever done," Hong Yinyue said. "I don't have to tell you what that is."

Hong Xin opened her eyes. She blinked away the tears and saw that Hong Yinyue, the Red Dust Mistress, had left. Her jailors were awakening from their confused stupor, surprised at the fact that they'd all fallen asleep. They glared at each other, an unspoken agreement forming between them that this embarrassing situation would be best left unmentioned. Amidst their grumbling, she lay back down, closing her eyes once more, hoping she'd never awaken.

At the peak of the world, Gong Lan lay seated beneath the Bodhi Tree. Its long, sinuous branches reached down from the many large stumps that protruded from its main trunk, touching her skin as she breathed in and out, inhaling and exhaling. Everything in the world was connected, and life was but a dream.

Epochs were also like dreams. They continued for as long as those entranced by them allowed them to continue. They puttered on, despite the little bits of corruption that grew in unexpected places, festering as they ate away at wonderful dishes left out to rot.

Like any dream, there must be an awakening. This epoch would soon end, and a new one would begin. Countless souls were leaving this plane for the Yellow River, countless souls released for better places. The World Tree counted each one, carefully blessing them as they left, just as it blessed those who entered. The World Tree was the heart of this epoch, the root of the struggle between good and evil. When everyone awakened, would this tree remain?

Gong Lan opened her eyes and stared ahead. From the mountaintop she could see much farther than most. Down below, fiendish demons clawed away at the barrier protecting the monastery. To the South, a monstrosity was wreaking havoc that even Siddhartha Buddha could never fully heal.

She saw clashing in the mountains to the east. She saw vicious battles in jungles to the west. She saw a flood of ochre soldiers barreling toward large walls, knowing full well that their deaths would provide a solid corpse their comrades could climb on.

The dream was ending. The dreamer was stirring. Only the shadow of a memory would remain in its place.

Ghosts and evil spirits alike evaporated as Huxian trotted through the city, freeing the spirits within from their bondage as promised. They smiled in relief as they broke apart. He hoped that, just before they left, they caught a taste of what they were eating, obtained a modicum of pleasure as they saw their kids play for the last time, or were just a little bit less thirsty from their millionth drink.

Huxian changed his course as the last of the city's ghosts disappeared. Only one figure remained. He could see the Daoist priest clearly, standing beside a fire that was now glowing brightly against the sun, which had almost set on the horizon.

"You've done it," the priest said as Huxian climbed the steps. "You've freed us." He reached out to Huxian, and his touch seemed almost corporeal. But as soon as the hand made contact, it burst into thousands of motes of light. "Thank you," the priest said before vanishing.

The sun, of which barely a sliver remained, finally set on the horizon. With its disappearance, the darkness around him seemed ever stronger, and the flame in the temple ever brighter. He'd gained much on this journey, including those wonderful eyes that could let him both see and taste ghosts—they tasted awful, for the record. All that was missing now was the inheritance he'd been promised. He had a hunch it had something to do with the flame in the temple.

He stared at the flame, so golden and resplendent. It was uncomfortably hot, so he trotted down the temple steps to observe it from afar. *Any minute now,* Huxian muttered, preparing himself from the sudden outflow of light and darkness, which he would use to create his dual initiation mark and a portal home. He salivated just thinking about it. His eyes teared up just watching it. He blinked, and it blinked back. The flame... blinked?

Huxian scrambled backward, claws out and teeth bared at the flame, which now resembled a slit in the darkness. It "blinked" again, and Huxian finally noticed that he was no longer in the city but floating in space. The slit grew larger and larger, and soon he realized what the slit was. It wasn't a fire, but an eye. And not just any eye. Now that he took a good look, he saw that the eye was part of a massive head with reptilian features. It had layers of sharp teeth, a long muzzle, and a forked tongue. The head was attached to a long body that seemed to stretch on endlessly.

He was standing before the Candle Dragon himself.

Sir Candle Dragon, Huxian stammered, barely containing his fear. *Fancy seeing you here.*

"Indeed," the Candle Dragon said. "It's been positively ages since I've deigned to speak to a young pup like yourself." The dragon's voice, physically very loud, also had an edge to it. If the dragon willed it, he could kill Huxian with but a single word. Huxian, who was used to having the upper hand in any conversation, found that especially unnerving.

So, I was thinking, Huxian said. *Since I passed your test and all, I should get a reward. You know, some essence of light and darkness. The good stuff.*

"Test?" the Candle Dragon said in amusement. "What test? You stumbled upon a plane that I had damned for all eternity for their sacrilege to the natural laws. What test? What reward? I should curse you just like I cursed them. Maybe then you'd learn some respect for your elders."

Huxian gulped. This was *not* going as planned. Okay, time for Plan B: groveling. *Oh, esteemed Candle Dragon, Demon Sovereign of Light and Darkness, of dawn and dusk. I had eyes but didn't see Mount Tai, and I dared disrespect you unknowingly. I had thought you'd left behind a test for us mere juniors, but I accidentally disturbed your good deed. I ask that you punish me.*

The Candle Dragon stared at him, unblinking. It snorted, and smoke left its nostrils and encircled Huxian. It looked at him pensively, as though not quite sure what to make of him. "Though it was not designed as a test, let it be such. I will let you choose a boon, though do not choose lightly."

Two spheres appeared in the darkness to Huxian's left. Once was a sphere of deep blackness, the other a sphere of light. They coexisted together, complemented each other. This wasn't just essence of light and darkness. It was the purest form imaginable, and the initiation mark Huxian could generate with it would be unmatched.

"On the one hand, you may choose this boon," the Candle Dragon continued. "Essence of light and darkness, harvested at the birth of the universe itself. I was born beside it and kept it in case I needed a snack. That time never came."

The Candle Dragon looked slightly to Huxian's right. There, a gray portal opened. A force much purer than Huxian had ever experienced oozed out of it. Its presence altered the fabric of reality around the portal, which flickered like it would close at any instant. "Alternatively, you can take my trial. If you do well, you can obtain a Candle Dragon initiation mark, a time-based one, instead of a light and darkness initiation. Light and darkness are only minor elements of space-time. Being initiated with my mark will make you much stronger."

Huxian swallowed. *And if I fail this trial?*

"If you fail, you get nothing," the Candle Dragon said. "No light, no darkness. You will have to settle for something else on the weak mortal plane where you reside. Choose wisely."

Huxian frowned. He sniffed at the light and darkness, sniffed at the portal. This experience was both surreal and confusing. Mighty figures like the Candle Dragon didn't exactly waste their time on lowly beings like him and offer rewards, did they? Just what was going on?

This junior confesses himself confused, Huxian said. *Why this offer for a trial? Why this unforeseen blessing? Did I please you in some way? Did I displease you?* Sometimes, rewards offered by mighty figures were just veiled punishments. It was important to identify them and decide accordingly.

The Candle Dragon looked at him. It blinked once, then, surprisingly, it sighed. "There is a darkness. A deep darkness that surpasses that which I preside over. No light balances it. It consumes endlessly. It devours without limit. It eats away at the fabric of the universe itself. You have seen it."

Huxian nodded slowly. *I have.*

"This blessing is to aid in fighting this calamity. I cannot do much, as direct actions by one like myself would shatter a mortal plane. If you take on my trial, and you prove worthy, you can gain a part of my power. It will aid you in fighting that creature, and perhaps we can save that small speck of a world before it vanishes for all eternity. While we're at it, we'll fix those eyes of yours."

Eyes? Huxian said. *These things?* His eyes weren't bleeding anymore, but they weren't doing very well either. They stung when he blinked, and it was very taxing to keep them open and look around. Yes, his eyes were a problem. He'd forgotten about them in his excitement.

"Your eyes are filled with hatred," the Candle Dragon said. "They seek to see everything and change everything. That's too much strain on a body, Godbeast or otherwise. If you take my trial, I can help you channel that hatred into something more... manageable. It is lucky that you met me when you did."

And my brother? Huxian said. *Can you help him?* Now that he thought about it, Cha Ming wasn't nearly as strong as he was. He was powerful, yes, but a human body didn't quite match up to that of a Godbeast. He only hoped he hadn't done something stupid like kill a few hundred thousand ghosts like he had.

"I cannot," the Candle Dragon said. "He will need to find his own way. Only a Godbeast can merge these eye techniques as I instruct."

Huxian gulped, then looked toward the portal. *I won't die if I hop in there, will I?*

"Only if you're grossly incompetent," the Candle Dragon replied. "And in that case, I can only express my condolences to your father for conceiving such a worthless son." He blinked. "Time runs short. Choose now."

That was a no-brainer. From his inherited memories, Huxian knew exactly how bad fighting a Taotie would be without serious firepower. He needed an edge, and he wouldn't say no to a Candle Dragon inheritance. Besides, taking on another Godbeast initiation would really stick it to his old man, who had basically disowned him. He could already taste the vengeance.

With that thought, Huxian leaped into the gray portal and didn't look back.

Cha Ming blinked as he looked at Southhaven Wall and the army stationed before it. The army was waiting, its cooking fires burning strong as the men prepared for battle. Here and there, Cha Ming could sense men sharpening weapons. Others sparred and practiced, while a few professionals crafted a few extra items for the upcoming conflict.

He sensed everything but saw nothing. His eyes could no longer see. "Why did it come to this?" Cha Ming asked Feng Ming, who flew up beside him. "They're not all bad. So many died in Bastion, but very few deserved to." The sin he'd obtained from his actions was a testament to that fact. Many innocent men had been blown away by the storm he'd created.

"Men live and men die," Feng Ming said. "Who truly deserves death is difficult to decide." He pointed. "Even this army. They're all here to invade the North, but are they really to blame? Most of them probably signed up for the army when they heard about good pay and good treatment. Their governments told them it was their right and their obligation to serve their country, to serve the South in obtaining a better future.

"To them, the Northerners are nothing but spoiled brats. They have ample resources compared to the South, but they squander the luck they've been given. Northerners deserve to die, and Southerners deserve what they have. It's the North's fault for building a wall to stop them from migrating there in the first place."

"Then what is right?" Cha Ming asked.

"Right is acting virtuously," Feng Ming said without hesitation. "Conduct yourself with honesty and integrity. Be kind. Be courageous. Work hard. Don't take more than what you should have. Be tolerant."

"And wrong?" Cha Ming asked.

"The opposite," Feng Ming replied. "Everyone needs to do the best with the hand they're dealt. Playing well is harder with a bad hand, but the rewards are so much richer when you win."

"We should go back," Cha Ming said, nodding. "Do we just fly over the wall? Will our men just let us through?"

"It's a little more complicated than that," Feng Ming said. "We'll have to go through a checkpoint." He frowned suddenly, then summoned a jade orb. "Unfortunately, it seems like we'll need to hold that thought. The war's started, and not where we thought it would." He looked toward the east. "We need to head to the Eastern Desert as quickly as possible."

"Through Southern lands?" Cha Ming asked. "Dangerous."

"Dangerous, but faster than the alternative," Feng Ming said. "Do you have any flight treasures?"

"Something better, I think," Cha Ming said. He began to grow. His neck grew longer, as did his body. His boots melted away as claws formed where they'd been. Feathers erupted from his skin, and in seconds, Cha Ming was a 333-foot-long falcon, an imitation of Silverwing. Unlike Silverwing, however, his body was riddled with qi pathways that led to his Dantian. Qi poured out from his massive body and into 1,080 gray sigils, which joined together with white light, summoning winds and clouds upon activating.

You going to hop on? Cha Ming asked, looking down at Feng Ming and Gong Xuandi, who were gaping in shock. Feng Ming was the first to recover. He took it in stride and hopped on Cha Ming's back.

"So you can transform into a demon, can you?" Feng Ming said. "What else can you change into?"

"I'm not sure," Cha Ming said as Gong Xuandi hopped on. "Let's find out." He flapped his massive wings, taking them up a mile high in an instant. He flapped once more, speeding off toward the east, wind and clouds trailing behind them.

Zhou Li knew something was wrong the moment he landed. The smoldering wreckage of a city aside, it was a feeling deep within his gut. He saw angry blood masters arguing over what was left of their monastery, and three shepherds had come from other cities. They had dousing needles out and were trying to divine the true culprit behind things.

He closed his eyes, and images appeared. Three messages, all scrawled by the same hand. *The Wang family sends its regards,* they read, but that was too obvious. The Wang family had been their agents for many of his lifetimes. Why would they suddenly turn against them?

The blood masters were incensed, and rightly so. The Spirit Temple had already sent an ultimatum to the Wang family. To Zhou Li's surprise, however, Wang Jun had capitulated. That relieved him more than the destroyed temple and monastery bothered him.

The wall to the North was a complete wreck. Though the Ji Kingdom's ruler lay mortally wounded in bed, he had fortunately chosen a successor. A wounded successor, but a successor nonetheless. That was far better than what the Northern kingdoms would get once the war was over. The beast that had devastated the Northern tenth of the city was gone, leaving tens of thousands of metallic corpses behind. The cost in lives was devastating, but those valuable corpses were a good consolation prize. Their smiths would forge them into weapons for the upcoming battle.

As for the Breaker… he'd known about its fate before even landing. No messages had been required to inform him of the fate of his pet project. He'd discarded the weapon the moment it had detonated. It had clearly been tampered with, so anything to do with it was suspect. Likely, that had been the mole's goal in the first place. The skillful mole who'd infiltrated the Wang family. Heavens knew who it was or how he'd done it.

Soldiers avoided Zhou Li as he flew toward the caged beast in the distance. The Taotie, the vicious creature that had effectively destroyed half a city and a good portion of their experts, sat in its cage, patiently waiting. It had been down this road before, so it knew the drill. It fully expected to be sealed for another few thousand years.

Transcendents bowed as Zhou Li landed in front of the ochre cage, a black-and-ochre seal in hand. Last time, it had been the North who'd sealed it. This time, they were the ones to bear the brunt of its onslaught. And just like last time, they couldn't kill the damned thing. They could only trap it and hope the seal held for as long as possible.

"Such a pity," Zhou Li mumbled, fingering the disc.

"A true pity," a man said, walking up beside him. It was Yao Xifeng, chief warlord and one of the grand viziers of the Southern Alliance. He was a tall, regal man who wore jet-black armor. He wore a large silver blade at his back that he never parted with. A wicked scar ran across his face, a burn he'd suffered in his childhood. And like Zhou Li, he, too, was a reincarnator.

"We had just ordered the first strikes against the North to take advantage of their distracted transcendents," Yao Xifeng said. "Unfortunately, some powerful intruders wreaked havoc in the city as we fought the beast. They even killed one of our transcendents. Our losses were much greater than anticipated, and it will affect my calculations for the upcoming struggle."

"It's fortunate we didn't commit so many forces to Haijing," Zhou Li said. "Your suggestions on that front were wise."

"A general never commits too much on a long shot," Yao Xifeng said, nodding. He looked up at the creature pensively. "Such a beautiful creature. Destruction incarnate."

"Exactly the pity I was referring to," Zhou Li said. "Such a beautiful creature, perfectly suited for what we wish to achieve. Rather than seal it, shouldn't we... guide it?"

"That is... madness," Yao Xifeng said flatly. "It can't be done. The creature is intelligent, yes, but barely so. Moreover, its goal is to destroy us all."

"We're losing," Zhou Li whispered. "I can feel it. So can you. If we don't do something, we'll lose this war."

"We can try again," Yao Xifeng said stiffly. "As many times as it takes."

"But can your soul bear it?" Zhou Li asked. "Can you last a dozen more cycles of reincarnation? A hundred more? Every man has their limit, and most of us have reached ours. We need to do something extreme if we are to win."

The general sighed. "I agree, to some extent. But how will you communicate with the beast? Is it even possible to make a deal with it?"

Zhou Li shrugged. "Let's find out." He flew up a few hundred feet, staying just ten feet away from the solid orange bars that now restrained the Taotie. Its hollow black eyes stared at Zhou Li, and its mouth opened expectantly. *Food?* It seemed to say.

"Food," Zhou Li said. "You want food. I give food. You want?"

The beast cocked its head.

"I take you to food. You eat. Good?"

It lifted one of its large claws and scratched its head. Small hairs of darkness splashed down on the ground, annihilating whatever they touched.

"How is it going?" Yao Xifeng asked.

"Better than I expected," Zhou Li replied. "Now all I need is a cup of coffee, the best contract specialists we have—preferably with a background in educating three-year-olds—and time."

"You have three days," the general said, shrugging.

"What's the worst that could happen?" Zhou Li said. He'd had it with being on the losing end of things. He'd had it with fighting against pampered, self-righteous brats as they hid behind their wall, enjoying their riches. If he couldn't change these lands, he would shatter them, using the rubble to bury their dead.

– End Book 8 –

A Note to Readers

If you've enjoyed this book, I would greatly appreciate it if you left a rating and/or review on the site where you purchased it. Ratings lead to credibility in this competitive marketplace, and by leaving one, you signal to the world that this book is worth reading.

Cha Ming's disciples grew a great deal between Book 6 and Book 7. That's because, during their master's absence, they had their own adventures. It's difficult to do them justice as part of the main series. If you're interested, you can find out more about them in *Violet Heart* (Book 1 of 2 in the Violet Fate Duology).

I send out updates to readers from time to time, such as writing progress, release announcements, and the like. If you're interested in receiving these updates, subscribe to the Painting the Mists newsletter at:

http://eepurl.com/dymvO1

You can also find a link to the newsletter at www.paintingthemists. com. As a bonus for subscribing, you'll receive exclusive biography sketches for each of the key characters, starting with Huxian!

Here are other ways to keep up to date on the latest news:

Facebook: https://www.facebook.com/PatrickGLaplante/
Twitter: @PatGLaplante

The Cultivation Systems

This record is a summary of the cultivation systems on the Ling Nan Plane. Note that cultivation systems can change depending on the type of plane or the stability of the plane.

Qi Cultivation (Human)

Some humans are talented in harvesting the ambient energies of heaven and earth. They cultivate qi, enabling them to perform fierce magics by bending the elements themselves. Angelic cultivators gravitate toward this powerful but complex path.

Qi Condensation – Cultivators start their cultivation journey by condensing qi from their surroundings into their Dantian. They can circulate this qi in their qi pathways, executing qi techniques by expending it. A cultivator's qi pool expands and deepens as they cultivate. Many schools separate each step of the process into grades.

Foundation Establishment – After forming a sufficiently large qi pool, cultivators solidify it into solid pillars known as a foundation. Their foundation grows from the bottom of their Dantian and eventually grows tall enough to reach the top. Their qi thickens, and the amount of thickened qi they control depends on the height of their foundation. Foundation-establishment cultivators can fly a short distance from the ground using treasures like flying swords or special boots.

Core Formation – When their pillars reach their maximum height, cultivators melt them into a core, the most efficient way to store qi. Qi now takes the form of a fluid that travels in and out of their core. The core grows until it reaches its maximum size. At this point, cultivators are able to use their potent qi to fly unaided.

Rune Carving – By carving runes onto their core, mortal humans can transcend. Not much is known about this realm, but legends say rune carving cultivators can generate a "domain."

Body Cultivation (Human)

Let's face it, some people aren't as smart as they are strong. For those people, body cultivation is the preferred way to get ahead. Devilish cultivators and descendants of deities are drawn toward this brutal, straightforward path. Body cultivation makes one physically stronger, tougher, and nearly unkillable at higher cultivation levels.

Body Strengthening – Body cultivators start off by performing a basic strengthening of their body, purifying it in the process. Typically, the body is nourished with qi and then refined with an opposing qi, removing any impurities.

Bone Forging – After sufficiently strengthening their body, body cultivators must forge their bones to further support their growth. Bones are the basis of strength and durability. They traditionally subject their bones to intense quantities of qi, strengthening and tempering them in the process. They become akin to magic treasures, making it extremely difficult to shatter them using strength of an equivalent realm. Bone-forging cultivators gain the ability to manipulate their weight by using voids that are formed in their bones, making it easier to wield heavy weapons and use their immense strength to their advantage.

Marrow Refining – Once the bones are strong enough, it is necessary for cultivators to refine their marrow. Marrow is the basis of their blood, which feeds the remainder of their body in turn. Marrow-refining cultivators gain powerful regeneration abilities stemming from the deep pool of vitality hidden within their marrow and the voids in their bones.

Blood Awakening – To transcend, body cultivators must awaken the divinity within their blood. How this is done is uncertain, though descendants of a god have a much easier time in doing so.

Soul Cultivation (Human)

The foundation of a cultivator is their soul. Sufficient soul force is necessary to become a professional, such as an alchemist or spiritual blacksmith. In some cases, a sufficiently strong soul is required to advance in cultivation. Buddhists and evil spirits often lean toward soul cultivation.

Innate Soul – Cultivators are born with an innate soul, and it grows as the cultivator advances in qi condensation. Eventually, with sufficient cultivation, the soul will make a rapid breakthrough into incandescence.

Incandescent Soul – In the incandescent realm, the soul begins to shine with incandescent light. Advanced soul manipulation of objects and mental communication is then possible.

Resplendent Soul – Once the soul is sufficiently incandescent, it becomes resplendent. A wrapping appears around the soul, which is called a resplendent vestment. It embellishes the soul and prepares it to transcend. Long-range scanning is possible at this realm.

Transcendent Soul – A transcendent soul grows sufficiently large and gains the ability to move. Since it has broken free from its shackles, it can then leave the mortal body and operate independently from it.

Demonic Cultivation

Humans aren't the only ones who can cultivate. Demons, manifestations of natural forces in the material world, take a different path. They are incapable of cultivating their qi, body, and soul separately. For demons, these three components are part of a complete cultivation system. Demon bodies can grow to massive sizes.

Demonification – Spirit beasts are products of nature. By gaining demonic qi from their natural surroundings, they grow in power. If their bloodline is sufficiently potent, they can break through and become demon beasts.

Purification – Bloodline purity is essential for a demon's advancement. Demons in the purification realm continuously purify their bloodline with demonic energy they gain by either consuming other demons, humans, or natural treasures. They can also do this by living on a demonic mountain, but the process is much slower. Demons who possess sufficiently pure and potent bloodlines can awaken ancestral memories.

Core Formation – When a demon's bloodline is sufficiently pure, it can be crystalized into a demonic core. By feeding this core with demonic energy, a demon grows stronger. Core-formation demons can fly.

Initiation – To reach the initiation realm, demons must first gain approval of the land. They condense demonic energy into an initiation mark that anoints them as initiates.

About the Author

Patrick Georges Laplante was born in a small town in the Canadian prairies in 1987. He began publishing Painting the Mists online under the pseudonym RedMirage in January 2018.

An engineer by trade, he graduated from the University of Alberta in 2009 and completed his master's degree in 2011. While writing and engineering have little in common, he actively utilizes his experiences and attention to detail in fleshing out a vivid world and answering the "whys," which are often left unanswered in xianxia fiction.

As an avid vegan, he aims to prompt internal reflection in his readers through various themes like non-violence, choice, and begging the question: Is personhood restricted to humanity? And what is proper conduct, morality, and love?

His work is inspired by a combination of Western fiction, *Dungeons and Dragons*, Chinese web novels, and various Japanese, Korean, and Chinese comics and illustrated novels.

www.ingramcontent.com/pod-product-compliance
Lightning Source LLC
Chambersburg PA
CBHW051533250626
47157CB00001B/30